The Plight of Others

Rachel Welland

ACKNOWLEDGEMENTS

To my incredible family and friends, for your endless love, support, and encouragement, thank you from the depths of my soul. I love you forever and always.

To anyone who helped shape this novel in any capacity, I am forever grateful.

~ Rachel

ETIENNE

Avignon, August 1910

Even for an August evening, it was uncomfortably hot. Yet the city remained lively with crowds flocking to the outdoor seats of cafés and restaurants, to drink in the refreshing breeze that drifted along the river. From his vantage point peering over the crumbling wall running along the river Rhône, Etienne could see Avignon's stunning summer scene in all its glory. He spotted large gatherings of people along the riverfront sipping cold glasses of white wine, the cold beads of sweat forming on the rim bringing them sweet relief.

There was a buzz to the city on this summer's evening, Etienne could feel it in his fingertips. The citizens were animated, their loud conversations breaking the stillness of the humid air. He smiled towards the businessmen sauntering out of the offices, mopping their furrowed brows with their handkerchiefs before they too meandered their way over to the tables overlooking the river. Cigarettes alight, and slumped into their chairs, Etienne could hear their collective sighs of relief tinged with exhaustion as he watched them all loosen their shirts and ties in unison.

Further downstream, choruses of laughter wafted up towards Etienne's position, the unmistakable sound of joyous titters of mischievous unchaperoned ladies was complemented by the giggles of children splashing around in the shallow of the river. A sound that Etienne had heard many times this summer, and never failed to put a smile on his face.

As the church bell chimes serenaded the descent of the sun over the river, Etienne continued to watch in awe as the trees, boats, and city walls became silhouettes. The surface of the river burst into a glorious dancing kaleidoscope of purples, oranges, and pinks, which all shimmered in the gentle motion of the waters swaying in the heat haze, Etienne traced the intermingling of the colours with his finger.

Unlike many six-year-olds, Etienne observed the world with deep fascination. He was well accustomed to the overlooked beauties of the city. From the smoothness of the cobbled stones to the intimidating magnificence of the Palais des Papes, Etienne absorbed every small detail, his moment of bliss interrupted by the gentle touch of his mother's hand slipping into his.

Leaning down to him, she whispered,

'Ma pêche, you are a million miles away,' smiling at him with a warmth that made Etienne's heart sing.

She smelt of lavender, not the cheap smell that perfumes tried to replicate, but fresh and authentic; her due reward for working for hours in its fragrant delight, but she was far from a rugged gardener's look. This evening, Camille Touelle was breathtaking, an image that Etienne knew there and then that he would never forget. She was graceful, poised, elegant; looking as if she could mingle effortlessly in the most elite circles of the province. A life that she could have had. Her waves of thin mousy brown hair, that were usually seen cascading beyond her tiny waist, were pinned back into a neat bun at the nape of her neck, secured by a jewel-encrusted silver hairpin, a family heirloom, the only one she had kept, and by far the most expensive object that she owned. She wore her best cream-coloured cotton dress with intricate lace details on the sleeves which extended across the neckline, the skirt flowed down just before her ankles, revealing a small, smart pair of black boots with a short-court heel. Her cheeks were delicately brushed with powder and rouge, maintaining all of the youth of her twenty-six years.

With a firm grasp on his hand, Camille led them down the cobbled back streets, each twist and turn forcing Etienne's concentration.

'Careful, Etienne!' She warned as Etienne tripped over a large stone, thankfully falling against his mother's leg.

He was trying desperately to focus on his steps, which was taxing on his little legs, taking all his strength to navigate through the groups of people that were beginning to accumulate and shuffle towards the Opera d'Avignon. Small glimpses of pillars and the balcony began to appear in Etienne's eye line, and he could not help but stare open-mouthed at the place that he loved the most in all of Avignon.

He and his mother pushed their way through the growing crowds, hurried up the stairs, paced through the foyer, and through a side door. People were pinned tightly against them as they began to climb a carpeted staircase that circled ever higher. Etienne stretched his neck to catch a glimpse of the gleaming walls and pillars, pausing briefly in his steps to glance up at the beautiful ornate, mosaic-like pattern on the ceiling high above.

'I'm sorry Etienne, but we need to keep moving,' his mother whispered, squeezing his hand to urge him on.

They were both breathing hard by the time Camille stopped at a large balcony that circled the Opera.

'Here we are,' Camille gasped as she ushered Etienne into his seat, promptly taking hers next to him, two plush-covered seats on the next to last row.

It didn't matter to him that his mother had not been able to get tickets in front of the orchestra. It did not matter that he could only just make out the stage from behind the brass railings. He was there for one thing, and one thing only, to hear the violins. Etienne chose to sit back in his chair and allow himself a precious moment to dwell on his earliest recollection.

***

Avignon, June 1907

He was a chubby toddler sitting in his father's workshop staring up at the dark etched words *'Charpentier Touelle'* which proudly stood out against the cedar wood background. The sign always swung at a strange angle in the breeze, which Etienne found odd, but his father insisted that its familiar squeak was the shop's first greeting to prospective customers.

Pierre Touelle was truly a genius when it came to selecting, shaping, detailing, and preserving wood. His skills were renowned throughout the city, and he offered his expertise to wider areas of the province.

He was a practical man through and through, he valued the importance of a warm welcome, but then he was straight to business. He was commonly seen huddled over in deep conversation with customers, piecing together every minute detail of their artistic visions, no matter how simple or complicated. His long black hair would sweep around the sides of his chiselled jawline, which only added to his private and rather mysterious aura.

On this particular day, Etienne was seated near the front of the shop, watching and listening to the door sign sing its high-pitched greetings, whilst pushing sanded pieces of wood around on the floor. He hurriedly crawled after each piece as soon as it got too far away from him. It was during mid-chase of a piece that had scurried off underneath his father's desk when a strengthened gust blew the door open, and in the entrance stood a tall woman dressed all in black, brandishing her cigarette in one of those fancy holders that Etienne had only seen rich women holding in the most exclusive restaurants.

Her perfectly styled short brown bob framed the most piercing green eyes that Etienne had ever seen. Instead of fear, however, a strong feeling of fascination overcame him, and all he could do was fixate on every movement, gesture, and sound of this strange individual who had walked into his world. She swept into the shop, her strapped high-heeled shoes clicking on the wooden floor. Every movement she made swayed with elegance, and she carried her head proudly to complete the image. Her black dress wrapped in a criss-cross over her chest and ran smoothly over her thin frame, skirting over and creasing in the right flattering places.

4

As she continued to stride in with silent but forceful authority, a breathless, sweaty middle-aged man with thinning hair, burst into the shop, the commotion of which finally stirred Pierre from his work to glance up.

The accompanying gentleman furiously mopped his face with a silk handkerchief with an embroidered crest in the corner. He was clearly a man of importance, and he looked agitated, Etienne thought. The man took a deep breath before starting,

'Monsieur Touelle,' another gasping breath, 'you remember our business meeting of course.'

Pierre solemnly nodded in agreement. Usually, his father's customers were so happy to see him and what he had created, and Pierre took great joy in showcasing it. But this meeting was more serious, Etienne sensed, as he shuffled back slightly.

'Our commission is ready, yes?' The man asked, rather indignantly.

'Oui, Monsieur,' Pierre replied, standing to attention as he spoke. Etienne only ever saw his father do this in esteemed company.

Tired of being ignored despite the drama she was silently stirring, the lady thrust her hand forward, now revealing rings and a bracelet, all dazzling in diamonds.

'Madame Lavigne,' she declared.

Delicately taking her hand in greeting, Etienne saw a small blush creep across his father's cheeks at this interaction.

'I know who you are Madame,' he smiled shyly, 'it is an honour to meet you.'

Madame Lavigne flashed a wide smile, highlighting her prominent high cheekbones and tiny creases formed beside those incredible green eyes.

'My violin, Monsieur Touelle, Claude here tells me that you are the best in the province. I trust that you have restored her perfection entirely?'

'No corners cut Madame,' Pierre reassured her, 'I shall bring it out for your inspection.'

As Pierre hurried out of the workshop to the storeroom located at the back of the building, Madame Lavigne's eyes finally found Etienne's, still fixated on her.

'Bonjour petit,' she cooed, crouching down close to him, not even breaking eye contact when gesturing to Claude to take her cigarette. She lightly brushed Etienne's cheeks with her immaculately manicured hands, smiling sweetly at him.

'Je suis vraiment désolé Madame!' Pierre exclaimed as he placed a beautiful mahogany case on the desk. He rushed over, sweeping Etienne up into his arms.

'This is my son, Etienne,' he said, somewhat sheepishly, but catching his son's eye behind the backs of Madame Lavigne and Claude, gave him a reassuring smile and wink.

'Oh, but Monsieur, he is precious!' trilled Madame Lavigne.

Unsure of what to make of all of the fuss, Etienne shyly nuzzled closer into his father's shoulder. Dissatisfied with the spectacle, Claude cleared his throat loudly.

'To business, if we may,' he growled.

Peering at the side of his father's chest, Etienne saw Pierre release the locks on the sleek, brown mahogany box, revealing the most exquisite royal purple velvet lining, Etienne had to fight the urge not to touch it.

'The damaged back plate has been completely replaced with the finest maple,' Pierre explained.

Claude and Madame Lavigne both nodded and smiled close-lipped in approval.

'However…' Pierre began.

Claude jerked up and stared viciously. Etienne felt his father swallow hard.

'I noticed that the tailpiece was also not sitting quite right. So, this has been replaced with the finest ebony I could source. It has been measured meticulously, and the stringing has been done with the utmost care…'

'That was not what you were ordered to do, Monsieur Touelle!' Claude thundered. Etienne winced at the tone and Pierre held him tighter.

'Please Monsieur, not in front of my son,' Pierre pleaded gently.

'We agreed on a price, and now you will be wanting far more!'

'I could not leave the job half done Monsieur,' Pierre said defiantly, 'when I am asked to fix an item, and certainly one as special and as famous as this one, I will do my best to bring it back to its full glory.'

Now almost puce in the face with rage, Claude raised a threatening finger at Pierre, before being slapped away by Madame Lavigne, who had stood in stone-cold silence the entire time. Knowing his place, Claude begrudgingly stepped back.

Madame Lavigne had not stopped looking at her beloved violin since Pierre had opened the box. She remained in a motionless gaze, which felt like an eternity before she opened her mouth and uttered, as quiet as a whisper,

'Claude. My bow.'

Claude turned hastily on his feet to the case he had placed on the side table. He carefully lifted the bow out and placed it softly in Madame Lavigne's hand. As she approached, both Pierre and Claude parted ways to open a path for her, her magnetism palpable. Carefully prising the instrument from its regal slumber, she swiftly placed the rest to her chin. She shifted slightly to the side, and Etienne saw her eyebrows rise. She lowered the bow onto the strings and gracefully glided it over, creating the most stunning yet melancholy melody that Etienne had ever heard. He moved completely out of his father's embrace to watch and listen in awe, silent tears running down his cheeks.

Madame Lavigne was grinning from ear to ear.

'It is truly perfect Monsieur Touelle!' She gasped. 'I have known that the tailpiece has not been right for years. But everyone who assessed it has said otherwise and there cannot be anything wrong with a violin of this pedigree. How did you know?'

'I… it… was only fractional, b…but it felt unbalanced in its hold Madame.' Pierre said fumbling for the right words.

'Do you play Monsieur Touelle?' She grinned.

'Oh, no Madame! My grandmother did, years ago. She always said that the balance had to be just right,' Pierre replied.

'A wise woman indeed,' Madame Lavigne purred, 'it is what is required for a perfect performance, and I have not been perfect for some time.'

'Madame! Your performances are sublime!' Claude protested.

'See? They only tell you what you want to hear,' Madame Lavigne sighed, causing Claude to retreat into a resigned silence.

'You and I feel things differently Monsieur Touelle,' she said.

Startled and slightly embarrassed, Pierre just smiled politely in recognition of her compliment.

'You must have taken the entire thing to pieces to do this?' She continued.

'Yes Madame, but I promise that every piece was handled with meticulous care. I have even held onto the original damaged parts if you so wish to keep the original materials?' Pierre offered.

'That is most kind of you Monsieur, but how did she look inside?' She asked with the eagerness of a small child waiting to open a gift.

'Magnificent Madame, it is truly one of the most wonderful instruments I have ever had the honour to observe, let alone work with,' Pierre beamed.

'They were right about you Monsieur Touelle,' smiled Madame

Lavigne.

Before Pierre could thank her, Etienne's stuttered sob startled the room.

'Oh, but I did not mean to scare you sweet one!' Exclaimed Madame Lavigne.

Pierre turned his son to face him, wiping away Etienne's tears with a confused look on his face.

'That's strange?' He stated. 'Etienne's a funny child, he never cries, never fusses, he just watches the world… I don't think he is scared, look at the way he watches you with the violin. I have never seen him like this.'

Looking directly at Etienne now, he asked affectionately,

'How did it make you feel my boy?'

Madame Lavigne's jaw dropped, and her dramatic eyes widened in wonder.

'That was exactly what happened when I first heard the violin too,' she breathed.

She moved right in front of Etienne's eyeline, and their eyes met once again. The silent tears continued to stream down Etienne's face. Addressing Etienne, as if they were the only two people who understood everything.

'It moves your very soul. You are no longer in reality, but in a place where all you can do is feel everything, and everything all at once.'

Breaking away, she curtly turned towards Claude.

'Pay the man the extra money and double your agreed price.'

'Madame!' Claude and Pierre unanimously protested. But Madame Lavigne silenced them with a wave of her bejewelled hand.

'No less!' She barked.

Placing the bow and beautiful violin back in their cases, she grasped her cigarette from Claude and gestured for him to retrieve the precious cargo.

'Good day Monsieur Touelle, Etienne, and thank you for believing in her.'

'Good day Madame,' Pierre beamed breathlessly. And with that, they were gone.

Pierre held Etienne close to him, kissing the crown of his head. Not a word was uttered between them. There was just a feeling, an acknowledgement of what was truly precious in the world.

It was not until years later that Etienne found out that Madame Lavigne was in fact Madeleine Lavigne, married to prominent theatre owner Julien Lavigne, but more importantly, a world-renowned violinist. She never failed to sell out a venue, such was her gifting, and Etienne treasured that intimate moment where he got to bask in her magic, and on his own doorstep, nonetheless.

Furthermore, the instrument in question that his father had painstakingly, yet delicately restored to perfection, was the world-famous Belle Rose, the final violin that had been created by the infamous luthier, Benedict Laurent before his untimely death aged only thirty-seven in 1847. The instrument had sold at auction to the Dubois family for one million francs and eventually was handed down as an heirloom until it fell into the hands of their standout musical prodigy, Madeleine Lavigne, née Dubois.

***

Avignon, August 1910

The scene looked rather different now as Etienne resumed his gazing around the opera. As more people filed in it became almost unbearably stuffy, yet Etienne did not care, he just knew that tonight would be perfect. He was dressed in his Sunday best; he had insisted on it. Even though sweat ran uncomfortably down the back of his neck, he pushed the physical discomfort to the back of his mind and fixated on the stage in front of him.

More people started filling the seats, Etienne fidgeted in his chair and mumbled his displeasure at the amount of people squeezing in around him.

'Pardon Madame.'

'Pardon Monsieur.'

It must have been at least twenty times that Etienne had heard this hastily whispered apology, the sincerity of which had worn off after the fifth time. After stout old Jacques Guilbert got his seating position wrong and nearly sat on him, that was the final straw.

'Faites attention Monsieur!' Etienne's mother hissed, tight lines drawing in close around her mouth. Despite his ever-increasing deafness, even Jacques Guilbert, a high-flying businessman in his heyday, could not help but cower at the threatening tone of Camille Touelle's commands.

Etienne could see how tense his mother was. Up to this point she had carried herself with such authority. She was not going to let this evening be anything less than perfect for him. He was grateful. Immeasurably so. Something that he would eventually regret not telling her.

One of her hands was placed insecurely on the sleeve of her dress, covering the stitching repair that she had speedily mended mere hours before their evening outing. Executed to perfection as always, but despite her fine skills, Camille still insisted on covering it up, mortified at the prospect of showing Etienne up on this important evening.

'This will not do!' Camille had repeated to herself as she scurried around the kitchen grabbing her sewing supplies.

'Maman, no one will care about the dress,' Etienne argued, as he floated around his mother, impatiently waiting for her to fix his tie.

The tear had been minuscule, no one would ever have noticed. But this was Camille Touelle, always in a hurry, always trying to fix things as soon as they became broken. Etienne would never forget the moment that his mother paused at his protests, rushed to his side, and held his face in her hands. He was surprised to see her eyes brimming with tears as she held his stare with her large beautiful blue eyes.

'Ma pêche,' she almost whispered, 'have you ever thought that something so important to you, may also be very important to another? Maybe even more so?'

'No Maman,' Etienne replied.

'Your happiness my son, is my happiness. Do you understand?' She asked, almost pleadingly.

He did not know what she meant, nor what to say, instead, he continued to watch long after his mother's gaze had left his, trying to work out the meaning behind her words as Camille once again sat at the kitchen table, fixing what was broken.

Minutes continued to tick by which felt like an eternity for Etienne, he longed for that haunting warmth from the first clear note caressed from the violin strings. The breaking of that eerie suspense. The space completely overwhelmed with the sense of great expectations. The feeling that a wonderful journey is about to take place. Everything, and everything all at once.

The applause of the audience signalled the entrance of the conductor. But Etienne's attention was on the three young, rather studious-looking violinists who had seated themselves in the front row of the orchestra on the right-hand side of the stage. One of the males adjusted his tie; the second of the trio tapped his foot ever so slightly, no sound escaped under the sole of his shoe, but Etienne could not help but keep the timed beat in his head. The only female of the group however was not fidgeting, she sat as still as a statue, staring steadfastly ahead, not daring to move a muscle.

Silence descended. The conductor raised his baton as if to assemble troops to attention.

The violinists dutifully positioned their bows, and as the conductor's baton issued the signal, the first hums of the strings sang out. Each musician moved precisely and maintained perfect timing. Etienne marvelled at how such graceful movement could produce such a warm and gentle atmosphere, as they began to build suspense in the opening section.

The violin's big protective sibling in the form of the cello performed its protective duties by giving the piece its firm foundation and sustaining every other instrument throughout. Now the violins started to sing, adding the next layer of the story, the higher notes carrying a notion of hope, of brightness. Suddenly the tempo was changing left, right, and centre, the mind not knowing where to concentrate, with so many things happening at once how was it at all possible to appreciate the full picture that was unfolding? Everything, and everything all at once.

Then in amongst the chaos, the low bass statements of the sturdy cellos could be heard once again, bringing the story back to centre once more. The violins re-assembled to commence the next stage in the story, but it was more sombre, more compelling. Then just one focus, coming from the sole female violinist, the solo mournful sound of her tune glided through every captivated ear. But almost as if this burden was too much to bear, her fellow violins rallied around this lonely sound, the crescendo further reflecting this turmoil, which just seemed to keep tumbling and tumbling. And yet, the reliable cellos, continuing to return to maintain order, paving the way for the violins to pick up the narrative, this time choosing to run at pace, daring the audience to keep up with them.

Suddenly, the cellos dropped out, the violins were given free rein to do whatever they pleased. As the final crescendo continued to build in might, sound, and power, it physically pushed people back further into their chairs, overwhelmed at where this beautiful chaos may take them. Then finally, an eruption of sounds coming from every corner of the group created the last triumphant climax, and then just as they had started, the strings ceased their song and story together in perfect harmony.

The audience broke out in rapturous applause, many rose to their feet, as if the taller you stood, the more entitled and worthy your admiration was. But Etienne remained firmly seated, still in awe of the talent of this remarkable group of people who were now gleefully accepting their praise. He was astounded by the ability of people to break hearts, stir hope, and overwhelm the senses to the point of total submission, all through their talent and passion reflected on their faces, as they simultaneously balanced losing themselves in the music, but also maintaining the perfect concentration on the tale the music told.

Hot tears streamed down Etienne's cheeks once again. His mother was lost in her own admiration for the performance, and Etienne was glad that she did not notice him. He had never been so happy.

**

In years to come, Etienne would cling to the memories of that evening, not only to bring him comfort but as a stark reminder that when the atmosphere is overwhelming, there is undiscovered and unspoken beauty in the chaos. When one is unable to focus on all the different noises coming from every corner, the bass sounds of the foundation remain. Although drowned out at times, they prevail to bring the story back to the centre. Even if that may take longer than expected.

ADA

Stuttgart, April 1925

The drizzly April rain pattered against the window, its constant tapping distracting Ada to the point where all she could do was watch the droplets race each other down the pane. Despite the refreshing breeze from the seasonal springtime rain, the packed classroom remained incredibly stuffy and thick with the smell of damp grass and the sweat of half of the football team, who had marched in triumphantly after lunch declaring a joyous victory over Frau Sauer's class.

Ada understood then why the other boys had all worn such murderous looks. She subconsciously started to rub the sensitive spot on her arm that was slowly forming into a bruise, after one of the boys had barged into her so roughly that it sent her sprawling hard against the wall. She couldn't forget the thunderous look of the boy staring menacingly into her eyes, the way he spat viciously at her feet, before turning sharply on his heels and marching away. Too stunned to speak, Ada had been left thinking, *humiliation brings out the worst in people.*

Increasingly sickened by the odours of sweat and damp clothes, Ada reached out to the edge of her desk and picked up a textbook. It was old, the binding was loose, Ada inhaled its dry musty scent and felt immediately comforted. To her, it smelt of knowledge,

15

and she was hungry for knowledge. Most of her hours at home were spent buried in a world of words absorbing information, the fantastic imaginary worlds, and the complexities and resolve of the human character. Although too young at this stage to fully comprehend what it all meant, the relentless desire to consume it all burned brightly within her.

As students, they were persistently told of the great victories of the German people and the eternal greatness of the nation. Ada heard conversations at home between her father and grandfather reminiscing about Germany's dominance and influence when they were young men, they never mentioned the Great War, and she knew better than to ever speak of it. Besides, the past days of glory were bound to return. This is what she had been told, and she believed it.

'Fräulein Stein!' thundered Frau Bauer, startling Ada from her reverie, and she leapt to her feet in fright. Frau Bauer was a formidable woman, and for a woman who couldn't have been much taller than five feet, she still had a way of towering over a person and making them feel like the smallest person in the room. The long frown lines on her face never budged, even when she was furious all they seemed to do was outline the bulging anger in her eyes.

'Es tut mir sehr leid!' Ada exclaimed and gulped as Frau Bauer strode towards her desk, her dark hair pulled back into the tightest bun did not move an inch, and neither did the ferocious scowl that was pressed firmly into her lips.

Without hesitation, she grabbed Ada by the bruised part of her arm, making her wince, which only added to the choir of sniggers that were rippling around her. She was marched towards the front desk right by Frau Bauer, and next to Bruno Müller, the boy who always thought it hilarious to let off the most horrifying-smelling farts whenever he felt like it. When Frau Bauer returned to her position at the head of the room, Ada placed her hand on her arm, willing away the throbbing pain, and tried to ignore the eyes boring into the back of her head. She took a deep breath and tried to focus on her mathematical equations. Feeling her cheeks flush with heat, she moved her short braid around the side of her face in a feeble attempt to hide the pink humiliation.

Ada hated this about herself, her inability to hide anything that she thought and felt. She feared having to explain the day's events to her father. She could never get away with lying, her cheeks burned with the fire of dishonesty that gave her away every time. Even if she was completely innocent, her face seemed to tell a different story, one she did not intend to tell.

At class dismissal, Ada grabbed all her belongings and ran out of the room. She sprinted across the grounds without looking to see if anyone was following her to torment her further. When she reached the main streets, she finally took a moment to catch her breath and mop her sweaty brow. Downcast, she stared at the ground, kicking the loose stones ahead of her as she paced along angrily. However, it did not take long for company in the form of her best friend Liselotte to find her.

'Fräulein Stein!' She laughed mockingly.

'It's not funny, Lise,' Ada grumbled.

'Oh, come on Ada, I'm only joking!'

Ada grunted and continued to pace. But Liselotte, athletic and tall, the opposite of Ada, caught her up immediately with her long strides. Blocking the path in front of her, Ada was now resigned to see what ploy her best friend had to win back her affection.

Liselotte squatted down, did a tiny march in a circle swinging her arms by her sides in a stiff motion, and pulled an exaggerated frowny face.

'Hey! Who am I, Ada? *Your eyes must only look at the page in front of you! Look anywhere else and feel my wrath*!'

Betrayed once again by her cheeks, Ada could not conceal the giggle that was rising in her chest.

'You're laughing, Ada Stein,' Liselotte smirked. 'All forgiven, yes?'

'Sure,' Ada laughed.

'You can't stay mad at me!' Liselotte chimed, bounding up

towards Ada and linking their arms together as they continued the short journey back home.

Liselotte had been Ada's best friend for as long as she could remember. They had grown up in neighbouring streets, and always felt safest in each other's company.

'Those füβball boys are getting worse,' Liselotte stated.

'You're telling me! One of them knocked me into the wall after the game this afternoon,' Ada proclaimed, revealing the enlarged red patch on her arm that continued to pound painfully under her sleeve.

'Savages. The lot of them,' Liselotte snorted.

'You could get away with calling them that to their faces and they would still find you the most beautiful girl in the world,' Ada teased.

'I certainly would not be interested even if that were the case,' Liselotte said proudly, nose high in the air.

'Sure, sure,' Ada muttered.

'I mean it, Ada!' Liselotte asserted, untying her plait, and letting her long, silky golden hair unravel down to her waist. Ada couldn't help but admire her best friend's beauty, in comparison to her own perceived plainness. Where Liselotte was tall, shapely, and athletic, Ada was short, round-faced, and plump. She found herself reaching around for her braid, only to find that it had become tangled, she pulled at it to try and free it.

'Here, let me,' Liselotte said, as she carefully prised the tangles apart, delicately running her fingers through the knots until Ada saw her own wavy dark brown hair fall past her cheeks.

'Beautiful,' Liselotte smiled.

'Danke, Lise,' Ada replied. When Liselotte smiled, it was always genuine, she really did make it impossible to harbour any bad feelings towards her. She felt silly for feeling so self-conscious around Liselotte when she knew perfectly well that there was

18

never any opposition between them, no jealousy, no unnecessary drama. Liselotte was the only person in Ada's life that provided her with any sense of calm and reassurance.

'But I do wonder what has made those hooligans so angry, particularly in these last few weeks?' Liselotte said, continuing to voice her pondering, a puzzled look drawing her perfect freckles together.

'Who knows?' Ada shrugged.

'I heard that Alexander's father has just had to let another twenty employees go.'

'Another twenty? I thought he was starting to get back on his feet!' Ada exclaimed.

The Beck family owned a brewery on the outskirts of Stuttgart, which employed many men from the nearby towns and villages, many of whom were fathers to the students at the school.

'Apparently not,' Liselotte frowned.

'It can't be easy on the families,' Ada sighed, thinking back on her own family's experience when her father could not return to work at Schulmann's car factory, despite news of the supposed '*economic miracle*' by Chancellor Stresemann that was frequently serenaded on the front pages of the newspapers that they often walked past. Not everyone could be happy.

As they neared the fork separating their two streets, Liselotte turned to Ada.

'We'll be alright though, won't we?' Liselotte asked.

Ada was taken aback by Liselotte's uncertainty. Liselotte was always the more self-assured of the two of them. Why did she seem so insecure? Her father worked in the bakery in the centre of town where the divine scent of freshly cooked strudels, meat pies, biscuits, and loaves of bread would waft down into every street, alleyway, and any open window it could claim, leading the entire town out in a salivating trance towards the source of the delicious aromas. Ada's stomach growled at the thought of it. But even though their workforce too had been cut, Liselotte's father had been kept, his skills too valuable and essential to the business to part with. And even though they were forced to just cover the essential bread supply, they were still in business, and therefore extremely fortunate. So, why could Liselotte be worried?

'Of course!' Ada beamed, irked at her hesitation that could cause her dear friend to worry.

Liselotte smiled, but not convincingly, Ada knew her too well.

'You're right, you're always right,' Liselotte said.

Say it again and I'll believe you, Ada thought.

Liselotte stepped towards Ada pulling at her sleeve, tugging it down over the angry red mark that was growing in fury.

'So that your father won't see,' Liselotte said.

Liselotte knew all too well how volatile Günther Stein could be. The number of times that Ada had sat in her arms and cried, hurting all over, and not just emotionally. In those moments, no words were needed, Liselotte was Ada's safety, and she would dutifully, and gently hold Ada until she could summon up the strength to put her faith in anyone again.

'Danke,' Ada replied, before enveloping her closest friend in a tight squeeze.

They parted, and Liselotte was smiling once again, all seemed right.

'I'll see you tomorrow. No more run-ins with Bauer now, do you hear me?' Liselotte giggled.

'I promise,' Ada laughed.

Ada watched and smiled as Liselotte waved and skipped around the corner. Not until she was completely out of sight did she turn and start towards her own home.

The Stein household was the final house on the row, overlooking the alleyway which connected another neighbouring street. It was tall and thin, which gave it an almost dominating presence until you came up close to it. Huge cracks ran along the brickwork like a twisted evil maze, the jaggedness of the edges casting menacing shadows in the late afternoon sun. They beckoned passers-by to look and feel uneasy. The wooden frames were noticeably rotting away, forming gaping holes that resembled terrified faces crying for help. Each of the windows was either smudged with grime on the outside or displayed target-shaped holes that punctured the panes. It wasn't for lack of care, the repairs were just too expensive, and Ada knew never to talk about such things. Even though her parents faced troubles, she loved them deeply, and would never deliberately try to wound their pride. But they stood out, it couldn't be hidden, not when other houses looked so smart and presentable. People gossiped; Ada knew this. If the nosy peeks from behind the curtain were not enough, the whisper of '*the poor Stein family*' seemed to resonate around the neighbourhood like a haunted tale.

As Ada approached the building, she tripped on her shoelace, placing her hands out to break her fall, she collided with the door at force. Wide-eyed she looked up at the wonky latch. *Still there! Thank God!* Ada breathed a sigh of relief.

Before Ada could re-position herself, the door swung open to reveal a very cross looking lady.

'What on earth do you think you are doing girl?' She barked as she shoved Ada forcibly through, 'Are you trying to knock this house down?'

'No Mütter. I'm sorry,' Ada replied with a fearful quiver.

Her mother's large, murky green eyes, identical to her own, softened ever so slightly. Her hands moved from their stiff position on her wide hips down to her sides, before pointing her finger at Ada's feet.

'Shoes off! And re-braid your hair!' She ordered, before turning to the right and walking the short distance to the kitchen adjoining the living room to busy herself with the food bubbling on the stove.

Ada watched momentarily as her mother tucked a strand of grey hair behind her ear that had come loose from her bun. She constantly looked concerned, Ada pitied her, but it was always impossible to know if she should help her or stay away from her.

Ada dutifully removed her shoes, placing them gently by the door. She hastily braided her hair and roughly secured it before removing her satchel from her shoulder, plucked out a book, and settled in the worn armchair. Her nose wrinkled at the pungent smell of damp and stale tobacco that permeated throughout the house.

'No, Ada!'

Her mother's shout caught her by surprise, and she flinched as she wondered what she had done wrong now.

'Your father and grandfather will be home any minute,' she warned.

Ada sprung up out of the chair immediately, cursing herself quietly for her lack of vigilance, grabbed a grubby dust cloth, and began to dust around the picture frames. She had only cleaned them the other day but showing that she was busy would hopefully keep her out of trouble. It was well known that if her father and grandfather had not returned by the time she was back from school, then it meant that they had gone out to drink.

Unable to find steady work in the last two years, Günther had been doing odd jobs for any business that would accept help - collecting and disposing of refuse, delivering, and collecting supplies, and even washing windows at some points. But despite his dedication, the contracts were short, or businesses failed, and he was forced onto the scrap heap time and time again. A fiercely proud man, all he wished to do was work and provide. He was an engineer by trade, highly revered by the regiment in which he served during the war. For a time, he was able to showcase his skills working at the Schulmann's car factory and proved himself to be a hard-working employee. But times got hard, really hard. Günther's ego, his pride, and his purpose, were deeply damaged. They had already been through so much as a family.

His angry outbursts cursed the '*November Criminals*' for ending the war which Germany was assuredly going to win. The war that he and his sons had fought so passionately for, before losing, so much. The government was to blame for everything.

'He claims he is helping the cities!' *Stresemann,* 'But I don't see any improvements, do you?'

Her grandfather only spurred him on. A strong patriot himself, he echoed Günther's ramblings usually over a bottle of whisky, not that they could afford it, but it kept a peace of some sort. And that's where they would both be now, drowning their sorrows and squandering the little money they had.

Sure enough, ten minutes later the door burst open, and Günther and Walther stumbled through the rickety door. His increasing frailty had made Walther more reliant on his walking stick over the last few years, Ada had tried to feel sorry for him, but his quick temper and habitual bitterness frightened her. Unaware of just how much space she had instinctively put between herself and the men of the household, she glanced up to see her mother gesturing with her eyes at Walther's persistent stumbling. Stepping forward with trepidation, Ada shakily put out her hand.

'Let me help Grandfather,' she pleaded. Walther glared at her, grunted in disgust, and swiped at her with his stick before losing his balance, but mercifully fell into a chair.

'Are you alright Father?' Gisela screeched, rushing in from the kitchen.

'I'm fine!' Walther barked. 'The sight of this one made me lose my footing,' jabbing his stick accusingly at Ada.

'It's all fine Gisela,' Günther mumbled, 'stay out of the way Ada,' before succumbing to hiccups. Ada wondered if he deliberately meant to hurt her the way he did. But she was relieved that she only smelt a hint of booze on his breath, she hoped that tonight would be more bearable.

Gisela quickly intervened.

'Ada, will you carry out the potatoes?' It wasn't a request, but an order, one which Ada was happy to uphold. She shuffled along the wall, keeping distance between her and the men of the house. Gisela handed her the bowl and pushed her back towards the table.

Günther made his way over to their scratched dining table wedged in the small gap between the living room and the kitchen. He sat huddled over, head placed in his hands, a man who looked crushed by the world. Ada wanted to hug him, hold him, and do anything she could to make things better.

'Whatever happened to that strange fellow from 1923?' Walther grumbled as he fell clumsily into the free space next to Günther, fiddling with the tobacco in his pipe.

Ada carefully approached, placing the potatoes down gently in the centre of the table, she then hastily retreated to the seat opposite her father, next to her mother, well away from her grandfather. She was closely followed by her mother, who set the plain looking stew down in front of them, the odd stray stringy pieces of leftover meat bobbed on top of the strange skin that had formed and coated the dish. Made from the cheapest cuts, and any precious vegetables they could get their hands on, it was all they could afford, but Ada knew to count her blessings and she smiled gratefully at her mother, who curtly nodded her acknowledgement.

'He got released just at the end of last year' Günther grunted.

'Remarkable really, seeing as they wanted to kick-start an entire revolution,' Gisela commented.

'At least they know what they want and are willing to do something about it,' Günther snarled. Walther cackled in response, baring his disgusting rotting teeth for all to see. Ada averted her gaze.

'Please eat, everyone,' Gisela announced hurriedly sensing the brewing anger in her husband's tone.

Ada knew the event they were referring to; the news had spread widely over the country at the time. But she remembered it as a crazy man who fired a gun in a beer hall, kidnapped some important men, and said he was taking over. How was that impressive?

Günther and Walther both spooned watery stew onto their plates and talked hungrily between mouthfuls.

'Great speaker he is,' Walther mumbled, his mouth full of food, specks of spit flying across the table.

'He believed in Germany,' Günther said. 'But I haven't heard much about him in some time,' he sighed.

'Germany will be great again Father,' Ada said, trying to make her sentiment sound as confident as she could but she choked on a piece of potato that lodged in her windpipe.

'You know nothing my girl,' Günther grunted. Ada bowed her head to hide the tears that had sprung to her eyes.

Günther said nothing more and gazed into the middle distance, his hand clutched his water glass. His silence paved the way for Walther to unleash his own torment.

'Don't talk of things you know nothing about,' he said, waving his fork at Ada. 'You have no idea what it means to be a proud German.'

Ada remained motionless.

'A real German is brave and proud, not like you, sat there whimpering in your chair.'

She didn't realise that she was crying.

Walther continued in his rage. 'Your brothers, and your father, too, were brave, true Germans. They fought for Germany, and for what? For weak, useless, cowardly people like you.' He rose from his chair, fists clenched, face contorted. Ada could not hold back the sob that was bubbling in her chest from escaping. But the abuse came to an abrupt stop at the spraying of glass all over the table.

'Günther! Your hand!' Gisela gasped, leaping up from her seat.

Ada saw her father, white in the face, his hand hadn't moved from where he had squeezed the glass so tightly. Was he even aware of what was happening? He had a large gash in the centre of his hand that was pulsing out streams of bright red blood, scattered red dashes adorned his index finger and thumb, and small shards of glass stuck out of them.

Gisela was now running around frantically, retrieving tweezers, and wet and dry cloths for cleaning and bandaging.

'Sort this out, Ada!' Her mother shrieked.

Ada leapt up and grabbed the plates, bowls, and crockery from the glass-strewn table, cautious not to cut herself on the stray pieces. Placing everything on the kitchen worktop, she picked up the brush and started clearing away the smashed glass. All the while her grandfather sat in silence, no expression on his face, unfazed by the distress he had caused. Why did he have to bring up her brothers? Not when the pain of their absence still weighed heavily on their hearts.

Gisela helped her husband over to the armchair, where she busied herself tending to his wounds. She diligently removed each shard of glass and mopped away the blood, not caring if any got on her. She smoothed a strand of hair away from Günther's crestfallen face, now that he had finally come to his senses, and lightly placed her forehead against his. Her parents did the best they could to uphold each other, and Ada took small comfort in their strangely tender moment considering the chaos that had ensued minutes before. But all too quickly she was plagued with the constant question in her mind as to why her parents seemed unable to show her the same level of care.

Ada sneaked back into the kitchen, not wanting to disturb this rare second of peace, and started on the dishes, scrubbing everything until her hands were raw. Gisela took her by surprise as she started putting plates away behind her. Ada peeked around the corner, relieved to see her father with his eyes closed, in sleep or contemplation, she wasn't sure, but she was not going to find out.

'I didn't mean to upset him,' Ada whined, turning back towards her mother.

'I know,' Gisela replied, monotone, unmoving.

Ada knew by this point that she was better off out of sight and out of mind. Without a word, she climbed the narrow, creaking stairs, just as broken as everything else in the house it seemed, before entering her bedroom and shutting the door firmly behind her.

The room was tiny, but a safe place where she could be alone with her thoughts. But solitude wasn't so welcoming tonight, all she felt was loneliness. She pulled her blouse over her head, removed her skirt and socks, and placed them at the end of her bed. She examined the bruising on her arm, thank God it didn't draw any attention this evening. But it would be harder to hide as it developed its colour over the next few days. She tugged her nightdress on, spun around to make sure no one had followed her upstairs, made her way over to her small chest of drawers, and loosened the wood panel on the wall to retrieve her French language book. It was still light outside as she crawled into bed, gently opened the page to her current learning stage, and began to read, mouthing words and phrases so as not to be heard. French came very easily to her, and she could imagine herself transported to a time and place where she could share this passion with others, and dare she dream, with French friends. It was crazy to even fathom these days when even her own people couldn't settle a disagreement without either getting shot or injured.

When tiredness overcame the ability to see the words properly, she placed the book back in its hiding place, but not before catching a glimpse of the inscribed name on the front page, *Heinrich Stein,* the rebellious brother. His name reminded her of how it felt to be curious about the world. But he couldn't teach her that now. She would have loved to pick his brains for wisdom, take him on in a debate, theorise, and just talk together. She had found a load of Heinrich's old books in the attic. Ada was never allowed to go up there, but on the rare occasions that the ladder was left out, and no one was around, she would seize her opportunity.

There were three boxes in a row up there, all labelled with a single letter 'K', 'W', and 'H'. Ada was surprised that her mother had kept so many belongings. She was drawn to Heinrich's box purely for the number of books contained in there. But she vowed that she would eventually go through each of the boxes, to try and understand who her brothers were, why she could never live up to their brilliance, and maybe understand her role in the family who seemed to despise her.

PHILIPP

Berlin, June 1920

'You're a proper man now, Johann!'

'Doesn't he look wonderful!'

'You must be so proud of him, Felix.'

'Finally, you can take him on as your official business protégé now!'

For months this was all Philipp had heard in the lead-up to his brother's big day, and it wasn't that he wasn't pleased for him, he was delighted. Johann would step into his new responsibilities with great care and consideration, of which he had no doubt. But this was always the case with Johann, beloved by everyone he met, and adored by his father because of their shared interests. The eldest automatically had a special place in the family and wider community. It was just never the same with Philipp.

The whole morning had been filled with extended family members bustling around the small space of their home. His aunts feverishly pressing their suits, any slight movement that caused a crease to form was forbidden.

'Where's his shirt, Liesl?'

'Gretchen had it last!'

'It was on the hanger by the door!'

'Get out of the way Philipp! You are always under everyone's feet!'

Maybe it was a combination of this nagging reminder of inadequacy, his aunts being a nightmare, and sleeping right next to Johann for the last week and enduring his sleep twitching every five minutes, that made Philipp feel on edge. He was doing his best for the sake of his brother and the family, he was all too aware of the day's significance, and he didn't want to let them down, but it seemed that no matter what he did, he was always in the way or not doing enough to help.

He took a deep breath and moved away from his aunt's incessant fussing, headed to the kitchen, and started to make some coffee. As he put the kettle on to boil, he realised that he was alone, a blissful moment's peace that he had been craving all week, away from his crazy aunts, his lazy uncles, hyperactive cousins, overly concerned father, and most of all his self-righteous brother. He set out mugs on the table and spooned the ground-up coffee into a jug, he poured in the hot water carefully and placed the full jug on the side of the table. Angling himself to grab the last of the mugs, Philipp suddenly tripped and bumped into the side of the table the jug sloshed steaming hot coffee all over his clean shirt.

'AH!' Philipp yelped as he sprang back from the mess, pulling his shirt away from his body to stop the heat from scalding his skin.

Then he heard laughing, his glare slowly met the beaming face of his brother.

'You've got a bit of a stain on that shirt there, Philipp.'

'This is my only one Johann!' Philipp growled.

'Oh dear, Aunt Liesl will not be pleased,' Johann smirked.

'Don't you dare,' Philipp threatened, the last thing he needed was his Aunt Liesl to give him a slap around the ear and blow the situation out of proportion.

'AUNT LI...'

Before he could finish, Philipp sprinted away from him to the back door by the kitchen, out of the house, down the street, and towards the shop. His father had forbidden him and Johann to be down there by themselves, but all Philipp wanted to do was get away. He knew the shop would be open, Felix would often pop in and out on days that he wasn't working to drop off documents or move the stock around.

The shop had been in his family's possession since the mid-eighteenth century when many members of his family had relocated to what was then part of Prussia. It had always been an antique business. Different generations had varied the types of goods bought, target clients, and dealership contracts and relationships, but the shop itself remained almost exactly the same as it had done since Philipp's great, great, great, great grandfather had founded the family business all those years ago.

Philipp eased the door open and angrily strode in past the large shelving units containing trinkets, goblets, and pots. Magnificent art pieces were displayed above them to add to their grandeur. Looking to his right, Philipp was temporarily blinded by the sunbeams reflecting off the sea of glass cabinets that extended to the middle of the room. The twinkling from the array of pocket watches, jewels, and vases that they homed confounded him even more. When he was able to finally see clearly, it was too little too late. In his angry pacing, he collided hard with a plinth display and the vase it hosted fell to the floor, shattering into hundreds of pieces.

Oh, no! What have I done?

Philipp stood alone on the shop floor, unable to move away from the carnage that he had caused, and now he was going to be in so much trouble.

He glanced around desperately trying to find something, anything to hide what he'd done. The store cupboard! His mother had always kept a broom in there, and no one had ever questioned her resourcefulness, so he had heard. Her gentle gaze from the large photo frame on his father's desk followed Philipp around in his attempts to make things right. Every time he looked at her face he was always struck with a strange mixture of love, loss, and overwhelming guilt. He knew in his heart that what happened to her was not his fault, his father had reassured him of this on many an occasion, but somehow, he couldn't escape the feeling.

He darted over to the other side of the shop, carefully weaving between the new beautifully varnished cabinets his father had just brought in. The door had a sticky lock, so it took all of Philipp's strength to heave the door open, when it finally gave way Philipp's leg buckled and he tumbled backwards, colliding with the coat rack and the rounded point of the metal hanger dug into his back making him yelp in pain. He prayed silently as he gathered himself up that everyone was too busy to hear the commotion he was causing. Spotting the broom at the back of the cupboard he clambered into the maze of mess, knocking over cloths, a mop, dusters, and polish in the process until he finally grabbed the handle of the broom and leapt out as quick as a flash.

A fresh pang of terror and nausea washed over Philipp as he was re-acquainted with the ruins of the vase he had just destroyed. And not just any old vase, a Qianlong Dynasty vase, circa 1755, his father had been extremely lucky to find one of these. He had been so happy the day he arrived home from the auction with it in his hands.

'We finally got one, boys!' He had proudly announced as he burst through the door three weeks earlier.

'Let's see it Father!' Johann had replied, jumping off from the seat at his father's desk. Johann was the spitting image of their father in more ways than one. They shared the same thick dark brown hair, which was almost at shoulder length but swept tidily to the side of their round faces to reveal dashing smiles that matched up perfectly with their gentle blue eyes which made people feel completely at ease. Unlike Philipp, who was instead the spitting image of their mother. With his golden hair, short stature, slight frame, hazel eyes, and even down to the strangely shaped birthmark on his upper left arm, he was a permanent visual reminder of the loss they had all suffered. Not only that, but

Johann shared his father's passion for antiques. The two of them would sit for hours admiring and examining the pieces that Felix brought back from auctions, discussing the history, craftsmanship, and beauty in such fine detail.

This particular vase had a long neck, which split into three sections of colour. Each section was decorated with beautiful ornate flowers and patterns and bordered with gold. Along the side of the spout were two golden handles, each displaying magnificent cylindrical patterns that complemented its opposite side perfectly. The body of the vase portrayed a scene of villagers sitting near the base of mountains, overlooking a running river where the trees bowed over the top of the rushing of the water almost in awe of its grace and power. Felix and Johann would understand and talk about the significance of each detail. Philipp could not, he couldn't see what his father and brother could see. He could appreciate the history but could never look beyond what was in front of him. His imagination simply didn't run as deep despite his best efforts.

But none of that mattered now that it was completely ruined. Newer stock always remained uncovered for a time in the shop, as Felix liked to experiment with displays, giving careful thought as to where each item should be placed to draw the most attention from prospective customers. That's why the vase had been there that morning, and Philipp in his frustration had walked straight into it. If only he had just brushed it, it would have wobbled at best, but no, he had to storm in, change the angle of his stride just enough that his shoulder would hit the vase with enough force to send it crashing down to the floor before he even realised what he had done. Now here he was sweeping up every shard he could find, trying to get his story straight, there would be no getting out of this one, but if he grovelled enough maybe Felix would be understanding and wouldn't be so disappointed, but he would have to come clean. It had to remain between him and his father and...

'Oh, no,' said a smug voice drifting in from the shop entrance.

Philipp froze, cursing himself for not shutting the door behind him, he would have been alerted to the loud creak that announced a new presence. He now turned around to face his older brother standing in the doorway, arms crossed, with an arrogant smirk that at that moment Philipp wanted to punch clean off his face. It was his fault that he was even in the shop in the first place.

'Father's going to be so mad when he finds out what you've done,' Johann gloated as he slowly sauntered his way towards his brother.

'It was an accident, I swear!' Philipp pleaded. 'Please don't tell him! I.. I'll tell him the truth, I promise!'

He knew he had to get Johann out of there and quickly; people were drawn to him like a magnet. Where he went, others were not far behind. After all, it was his Bar-Mitzvah today.

'You're so selfish Philipp. It's my celebration and you have to storm off and cause more drama!'

He couldn't tell if Johann was teasing, or whether he was genuinely mad, either way, it was disconcerting.

'I promise you; it was an accident!' Philipp cried. 'If you want your day to be perfect then please just go! I'll sort this out! Just pretend like you haven't seen anything. Please, Johann? They'll all be looking for you and I don't want people to see this mess.'

He was going to cry; he didn't want to start blubbing in front of his brother. Philipp looked to the floor, praying that his brother wouldn't notice the tears welling up in his eyes. But he must have and realised what he could do.

'Hmmm okay,' Johann chuckled, 'I'll go. Make sure that it all gets cleaned up.'

The tone of the chuckle unnerved Philipp. He glanced up.

'Thank you?' He said tentatively.

Johann smiled a wry smile and left the shop, only for Philipp to hear him call out.

'Father! There is a customer in the shop to see you!'

Philipp broke into a run to give chase to his brother.

'You bastard, Johann!' He yelled, just to be greeted by his brother's smug laughter carrying up the street towards their house.

Realising that his efforts were futile with Johann, he raced back to the shop, grabbed the wastepaper bin, and started to scoop the broken shards of the vase into it as quickly as possible. His breathing was ragged, and his heart was pounding, which nearly burst out of his chest when he heard a deep voice coming from the doorway.

'You shouldn't say such things to your brother.'

Philipp jumped and spun around to face his giant of a father whose usual smiling eyes were fixed on him with a look of concern that made Philipp avert his gaze, he already felt guilty enough.

He pulled at his shirt, still damp from the coffee stain, and instinctively shifted his body over the remaining shards under the illusion that his father hadn't seen them.

'I..I... I'm sorry,' Philipp stammered.

For everything, he thought.

Felix took a further step in, his gaze not leaving his son, had he noticed the vase?

'Your mother would not like to see you two arguing this way,' he said gently, Philipp felt his heart squeeze slightly.

'I know, but he drives me crazy! I tried to be good to him on his special day, I really did...'

Felix put his hand up to shush him, ran a hand through his beard, stepped towards his son, and knelt. Philipp felt the hot rush of guilt run further up his neck into his cheeks.

'Families are crazy, Philipp,' Felix said. 'But you love them no matter what. It is easy to love someone who is kind, but you are to love everyone.'

'He makes it tough to do, Father,' Philipp whimpered.

Through his tears, he could see a large smile underneath his father's bushy beard.

'Siblings have an innate sense of how to provoke each other,' he chuckled. 'You have to learn not to bite so easily!'

Philipp nodded. His father made him feel so safe, yet so guilty all at once.

He hadn't realised that Felix had had his hand behind his back the entire time, he brought his arm around to reveal a fresh, white, pressed shirt. Philipp breathed a sigh of relief. Felix smiled and winked at him.

'Don't tell your aunts,' Felix chuckled 'Now get yourself cleaned up, your brother needs you on this day, and you are going to play your important role. Do you understand me?'

'Yes, Father,' Philipp said.

'Good,' Felix smiled, looking at the broken pieces by Philipp's feet before squeezing his son's shoulder lightly and walking out of the door.

***

The walk to the synagogue from their house was a short one. His aunts exited the house first, each followed by a long chain of screaming cousins. Johann walked behind at a distance, being careful not to get a toddler's sticky hand all over his best suit. Felix remained close to his elder son's side, and Philipp watched them closely from the shop door, distinguished men of the community and they certainly looked the part. Johann was beaming up at his father, and Felix returned his adoration with his twinkling, smiling kind eyes. At that moment, Philipp felt a bigger sense of pride for his father than his brother, for he knew he had suffered but endured and never let any circumstance get the better of him, and to see his son take his first big steps into the wider world was a day that Philipp knew he had longed for. He allowed his family's procession to pass by, before stepping out into the street and joining the crowds of people who were beginning to assemble.

Philipp hung back, just enough to keep his father and brother in his eyesight, all the while people were approaching Felix and Johann, shaking their hands warmly with good wishes and congratulations, the pair of them receiving them graciously as they walked alongside each other.

The next street was wider, and their amassed following sprawled out to fill the space. Soon the grand rounded turrets of the synagogue came into view, towering over the neighbouring buildings, its presence unmistakable. As they began to draw closer, Philipp noticed a group of teenage boys standing in the alleyway on the opposite side of the street. He didn't mean to stare, but Philipp found himself perplexed by the way that they glanced up and down at everyone who headed towards the synagogue. They almost seemed as if they were sizing them up. Something in their glare and the way they slowly moved their cigarettes towards their lips in an almost calculating manner, unnerved him.

'Philipp!' Felix's voice rang out from the excited chatter that encircled them. He didn't realise how far back he had fallen.

The teenagers' gaze snapped straight at him, he averted his eyes as quickly as he could, but they had seen him. He picked up his pace, eager to distance himself from the boys and now to escape from the looming dark rain clouds making an unwelcome return, forming at a rapid rate behind him.

He took the hand of one of the youngest cousins, who had stopped to suck his thumb and observe the passing people with a wholehearted childlike wonder. He suddenly felt a light touch on his arm, he looked up to see his Aunt Liesl by his side, a look of wariness causing her to frown.

'Stay well away from the likes of them, young man,' she warned.

'What do you mean, Aunt Liesl?' Philipp asked, puzzled at the seriousness of her tone.

'There are many people across our country who do not take kindly to people like us,' Liesl said, but with almost a sense of trepidation.

'Like us?'

'Because of our beliefs, our traditions, our heritage.'

'But we are just like everyone else?'

'There are those who do not think so Philipp.'

'Have we done something wrong?'

'No, my dear boy no, but war changes people, it changes how they think about people, it changes how they treat people. There are those who think that we pose some kind of threat to their way of life.'

'But how?'

'I do not know my dear nephew. You can never truly know when the seed of hatred in someone's heart starts to take hold.'

She turned her head slightly, straightened her back, and lifted her head high, almost as if she were trying to shake off an unwanted thought.

'No mention of this conversation to your father and brother, not today, you hear me, Philipp?'

Aunt Liesl looked stern, but there was noticeable panic behind her eyes, and Philipp obediently nodded, he knew when to not dig further.

Yet he still didn't fully understand exactly what his aunt was referring to. Had she seen this before? Philipp wondered. Should he be worried? Liesl shot him one last warning look as they climbed the steps together to the synagogue. The dark clouds had now nearly fully encompassed them, but mercifully it wasn't until they were all inside, contained inside their jubilation that the rain was unleashed.

ETIENNE

Avignon, July 1914

'What is he looking at?'

'Don't look at him!'

'The weird boy in the corner?'

'The one who doesn't say anything?'

Etienne ignored them, as usual. He had grown bored of their same old taunts and drowned them out with the melodies that captivated his mind. He was seated on the dusty side of the school grounds, none of the other kids usually bothered him here, they were too worried about getting dust in their eyes and hair. With one hand he drummed a gentle beat, and with the other, he strummed the accompanying melody along the aged creases of the tree. The delicate rise and fall of the crescendos extended further up the trunk as he followed the melody's story, the softest notes represented by the lightest brushing of his fingertips.

A light breeze caught the edges of the dust piles lifting the particles so that they lightly swirled around the stump of the tree to accompany his musical storytelling.

'There he is!'

Etienne kept his back turned and imagination engaged as a small gang of boys started to form from the other side of the yard. The melody shifted unexpectedly in dynamic, Etienne drummed heavier and pressed his finger hard into the bark, the pinch almost bursting the skin.

'Hey, freak!' A loud, aggressive voice called out and stood alone in amongst the buzz of threatening distractions.

Now Etienne paused and swallowed, he silently wished he had not heard him.

'How are the fairies today?' The same voice continued.

Again. Not a new one, and not one that bothered him, but from Marcel, he knew that taunts were never just it. He was smaller than any of the other boys in their year, but he had the biggest mouth on him. Wherever he was, he had to be heard, and what he had to say was far from impressive. Vulgarity and insults seemed to be his only two repertoires, yet this seemed to win him more followers. However, Etienne understood that he did not want to be on Marcel's bad side. The other children either laughed along or stayed away. Etienne chose the latter but his quirks, as his beloved mother lovingly called them, made him always stand out in a way that he did not want to.

'Is he playing a song on a tree?' Laughter ensued from all around, unnervingly loud, they must be moving closer towards him.

'What do you call this piece of shit?' Marcel jeered.

That's what made Marcel's words different from the other insults, he knew where to hit the nerve. Etienne never cared much about what people thought about him, he was different, maybe even odd, but that didn't make him a bad person and it was the only way he knew how to accept that; he couldn't pretend to be someone that he wasn't, even if he tried.

'You should create music and call it 'Down in the crap' because that's where it belongs!'

It was now all too much, Marcel's yells were getting closer and clearer, and the flutter of fury that was burning inside his chest was now spreading like wildfire. He fought to contain his erratic breathing. But he made the mistake of turning to face his foe, where he was met with a stabbing sensation in his arm as a sharp stone cut him just above his elbow. Marcel was grinning with sadistic glee as he reeled his arm back from his successful aim.

Etienne glanced down at his arm to see a small pool of blood growing across his shirt sleeve; wincing at the prickle of pain that resonated across his forearm praying that Marcel wouldn't see. Instinctively he inspected the wound, and bravely - or stupidly - he wasn't sure, he then turned to face Marcel once again. But forgetting about the stray root of the tree stump, Etienne caught it with his heel, stumbled backwards, and fell onto his side throwing a large cloud of dust up in the air on landing.

The horde was ablaze with laughter now, swarming him, attacking him.

Why won't they just leave me alone?

'Did the fairies push you?' Marcel wheezed in between cackles.

Etienne hastily pulled himself to his feet and frantically began brushing the dust off his shorts which by now were completely covered.

'You're an embarrassment you know that?' Marcel barked coldly, his tone had shifted, he was no longer teasing, he was mad, threatening, and unpredictable, this is when he made Etienne particularly nervous.

'Men need to be brave. Our country needs that. And because you are not, you bring shame.'

Everyone was on edge nowadays, war was coming, and they all knew it. There was no stopping it, and no one was unaffected by its looming presence. His own household was suffering, not in the same way, but suffering all the same. Late at night when his parents thought he was sleeping he had heard them arguing.

'Please don't do this, Pierre!'

'I have no choice.'

'There's always a choice!'

'We all have to make sacrifices, Camille.'

'Please don't make this one.'

Marcel's family had a reputation for being the rough and tough type. There was a rumour that his father used to be involved in a gang and that the yelling and crashing that could often be heard ringing through the street on which they lived could be attributed to them, but no one could ever prove it. Etienne was far more astute than other children his age, despite his awkwardness he could see through situations that others couldn't, which is why in that moment instead of feeling humiliated or embarrassed by Marcel's insults, he felt pity for him.

His silence seemed to irk Marcel more, because now he was striding forwards, drawing up to his face, but Etienne's feet remained frozen to the ground, he couldn't back away.

Despite Etienne being over an inch taller than him, Marcel's intimidation was still palpable. His gang didn't say a word. Etienne caught a glimpse of the looks on some of their faces - some were egging him on with eagerness in their eyes, some looked unsure possibly even scared, and others were stone-faced giving away nothing.

He could feel Marcel's breath now, thick with heat and unsettled rage. His small dark eyes darted around Etienne's face studying every little detail of him, Etienne was determined that he too would give away nothing. But Marcel continued to stare, ponder, and judge for what seemed like an eternity.

'You will be the downfall,' he finally whispered.

Etienne didn't understand and searched Marcel's face for understanding but to no avail, suddenly he heard a big intake of air followed by a large splash on his cheek that sent him reeling. The roars of laughter exploded again.

'Oh, you got him good Marcel!' One voice called out.

42

'Right in his stupid face!' Shouted another.

Tentatively wiping away the sticky spittle from his face, Etienne caught one last sight of Marcel chuckling and strutting away. He felt violated, and disgusted, but the worst of it was over, for now.

Etienne cautiously remained in his spot for a while longer as Marcel led his gang away from the scene, before trying to compose himself. He scooped up his satchel which he had tactically hidden behind the tree, one of many lessons he had learnt the hard way. He turned his attention to the wound on his elbow, rolling up his sleeve he could see that it was bigger than he first thought. He sighed knowing it would only worry his mother if she saw it.

As he plucked his handkerchief out from his pocket to blot the rest of the fresh blood he jumped at the sudden breaking of the silence.

'Oberon.'

For a moment he thought he had misheard and continued to tend to the wound. But the lone voice repeated:

'Oberon.'

Etienne looked up and noticed a skinny, blonde, freckled young boy approaching him from the other side of the grounds from the direction of the school hall.

'Pardon?' Etienne asked confused.

'Oberon. You know like king of the fairies? In Shakespeare.'

Another mocker. Great.

Etienne stiffly nodded at him and turned back to adjust his clothing.

'I didn't intend it in a mean way!' The boy called out.

Etienne grunted his dismissal.

43

'Well, if you think about it… Oberon's a king. And kings rule over people, so you know, lots of power and control.'

Surprised at the profound nature of the boy's knowledge and sentiment, Etienne was once again stunned into silence.

'So, um yeah,' The boy spoke shyly and took a step back to walk away.

'I…I guess I never thought of it that way before!' Etienne hastily replied, for once noticing that he was missing a social cue.

The boy stepped towards him again, smiling, encouraged.

'Yeah, so if you think about it, when that ant insults you about fairies just think about Oberon, and you're actually more powerful than him. I'm Gabriel,' the boy beamed, extending his hand, Etienne took it lightly and gave a gentle handshake in return.

'Etienne. I… I haven't seen you before,' Etienne stammered.

'We only moved a few weeks ago, from Paris, we um… needed to get away from there.'

His mother had taught him not to pry. Etienne simply nodded a sympathetic understanding.

Seemingly grateful for his silence, Gabriel continued.

'You're Pierre Touelle's son, right?' He asked.

'Yes,' Etienne replied.

'He is a very good man.'

'I know,' Etienne said.

'Our house was smashed up after we had been there only for a few days. Everything was destroyed, tables, chairs, clocks, beds, you name it.'

'I'm so sorry.'

'It had to be fixed, and people say your father's skills are amazing. You only live around the corner from us, so we came to him to ask if he could help. We went round and explained what had happened, and he just ran out of the door with some tools and a notebook.'

Etienne smiled, that was so typical of his father, completely dedicated and focused on the job.

'He went straight round to our house, measured everything up, wrote down the materials he needed, and then spent the afternoon carting all of the pieces back to the shop.'

Etienne remembered this case well; the broken pieces were piled up almost to the ceiling of Pierre's workshop and he had worked tirelessly day and night for a week. His mother had worried incessantly that he would burn out.

'A week later we headed out to go and pick everything up, but your father was at the door with everything brought back looking perfect. It was incredible! He moved it all back into the house, and when my father went to pay him, your father said he wouldn't hear of it. I don't think I have ever seen my father cry before, and that day he cried like a baby.'

This came as no surprise to Etienne, these kinds of actions defined who his father was. Camille had come home that evening to see his father looking very sheepish, he tentatively explained what he had done, only to be met by her huge embrace and his face covered in affectionate kisses. It was embarrassing to watch at the time, but now he realised that this was how they assured each other that all would be well, and they were thinking alike.

'I'm really glad he could help,' Etienne smiled, adjusting the satchel on his shoulder as he began walking. But Gabriel ran in front of him blocking his route.

'We owe you!'

'Oh, no, that's not necessary.'

'It is. That kind of work was not cheap, and it was probably costly to your father too. But he would rather do a favour than care about money. I don't know many people like that.'

'That's just how he is.'

'It is how you all are.'

'How do you mean?'

'Your father talked so fondly about your mother and you; you mean everything to him.'

Etienne shifted awkwardly; his parent's fierce love could be overwhelming sometimes.

'You like music, right?'

Etienne's head snapped up.

'Yes. The violin.'

Gabriel beamed. 'My mother used to play the violin in an orchestra when we lived in Paris. But her circumstances… changed,' he stopped suddenly, biting his lip, as if he had revealed too much.

Etienne nodded his understanding.

'She doesn't play in an orchestra anymore. But she can still teach, she has students on Tuesday and Wednesday. She wants to teach you.'

For a moment, the jubilation in Etienne's gut rose to his chest spreading in warmth as he relished even the thought of being able to play his most beloved instrument.

But the harsh nature of reality hit him right in the heart and it sank.

'We can't afford it,' Etienne said, averting his gaze.

'She still has her violin. Most of her students can't afford their own, they practise on hers.'

'We still couldn't afford the lessons,' Etienne's eyes remained fixed on the ground.

Gabriel lowered his head to try and meet Etienne's eye, he was smiling knowingly.

Etienne's eyes bulged in excitement.

'Really?' He nearly screamed.

Gabriel laughed. 'Yes, of course! After the kindness your family showed mine, it is the least that we could do!'

This time Etienne grasped Gabriel's hand in a firm grip and shook his hand vigorously.

'I don't know how to thank you!'

'You don't need to! Really, Etienne, it's our pleasure.'

He could not wipe the smile off his face, his breathing was erratic, and his heart was pounding so hard that he thought it would burst through his chest.

'When would she like me to come round?' Etienne finally gasped in a moment of composure.

'Thursdays. Five o'clock?'

'I'll be there!' Etienne exclaimed.

He was so wrapped up in his joy that he didn't notice his teacher coming out of the building, didn't hear the playtime bell ringing, and didn't notice the other kids filing back inside.

The rest of the day did not even register with Etienne, he was able to hide away at the back as he usually did. It wasn't exactly out of character so it wasn't as if anyone would suspect him or guess that anything was different. But of all days, and in his excitement, it was the only thing he wanted to fixate on, and today he wanted to be ignored.

He never ran, he never hurried. He organised his time to the point that he didn't need to hurry. But today was different, and today he ran home.

He raced out of the school gate, his satchel lightly beating against his leg. He steadied himself as he descended the small hill, darted round the sharp corner by the butchers, and skidded across the smooth cobbles nearly colliding with old Madame Jaminet.

'Pardon, Madame!' He called out, placing his hands out in front of him to stop his momentum.

'What's the rush young Etienne?' She laughed.

'I just need to get home!' Etienne replied as he picked up his pace again. 'Enjoy your evening Madame!' He called back over his shoulder, never forgetting his manners.

The farmers were still selling produce in the old town that day, and a small number of customers convened around the stalls huddled over in hushed conversation. He didn't pick up too much but the phrase 'President Poincaré is scared' was uttered a few times in the moments that he tried to squeeze past them in the narrowed street.

'Etienne?'

'Monsieur Auclair.'

'Is your mother making her famous tarte tatin for the fête?'

'Oui, monsieur.'

'Well, she'll be needing the best ingredients, won't she?' He winked, as he placed several large apples in a bag, slipping the bag underneath the table into Etienne's hands.

'I'll be sure to place the highest bid on it.'

'Merci, Monsieur Auclair!'

The weight of the apples hindered the rest of his race home, and he was careful now to avoid every uneven nook and cranny in the cobbled stones as he made his way back towards his house. He stumbled slightly as he neared the final corner but made no effort to plant his feet because he could feel the heat hit his nostrils before he even had a chance to see what had happened.

Etienne felt the apples tumble out of the bag as he lost his grip, and he watched as one by one they rolled down the street. He tried to take a step forward, but his knee buckled, and he sank to the floor. His eyes started to sting with tears from the smoke which helped disguise the huge lump in his throat and the welling sob in his chest. He could just about see the outline of his parents clinging to each other at a safe distance as the firemen doused the flames. The smell burned his senses with as much intensity as the remaining blaze that consumed the outside of the door frame.

He could see his mother crying, his father holding her tightly against his chest. Etienne wanted to run to them, he tried with all his might to stand up, but his shock rooted him to the ground. He watched through blurred vision as an apple bounced against his mother's leg causing her to look up. Within moments they were by his side, the three of them enveloped in a protective embrace, the pungent smell of smoke and scratchy fabric pressed firmly against Etienne's face overwhelmed his senses. His mother's tears soaked through his hair as she kissed every part of his face.

'Thank you, God!' She gasped between sniffles.

'For this, Camille? Everything needs to be rebuilt, the workshop, the goods, our *home,* the cost will be ridiculous!' Pierre exclaimed, gesturing at the burnt remains of the building.

'For *this,* Pierre,' Camille replied grasping onto both Pierre and Etienne's shoulders for dear life.

'It didn't spread to the other houses,' Etienne finally spoke.

Camille and Pierre glanced up and down the street, to affirm what Etienne had said. Not a single other building on the street had the slightest bit of damage.

'Now that is a miracle,' Pierre breathed, holding onto his wife's hand tenderly.

'Monsieur Touelle?' The chief fireman asked.

'Yes,' Pierre said rising to his feet.

'I'm sorry to tell you this but it looks like this was an act of arson.'

'Arson?' Pierre gasped.

'Yes. We found two areas where the fire burned most intensely. By the open shop window and the back window in your workshop. My best guess is that someone threw two lit matches onto the tables on the display at the front, and onto your workbench in the workshop. I have to ask you, where were you when the fire started?'

'Me and my wife were upstairs, we were gathering up some bills to send out to our customers.'

'Are you having financial trouble Monsieur Touelle?'

'You can't seriously think my husband had anything to do with this?' Camille exclaimed with a threatening look in her eye.

The fireman cleared his throat, 'Not at all Madame, we are just trying to ascertain how the opportunity would have arisen to light the fires.'

'At the moment things are okay, the best they've been for a while, we saved some money after a large payment from many years ago. But we're still cautious you know; we can't spend on extra luxuries.'

'I understand,' the fireman replied sympathetically.

'It was two people, wasn't it?' Etienne asked.

'Etienne! You can't make those kinds of accusations!' Camille chastised.

'No, he's right. At least that's what we think. One targeted the front whilst the other targeted the back.'

'Zut alors!' Pierre gasped, running his hands through his hair.

'Do you know of anyone who holds a grudge against you?'

'No, no one would do this to us,' Camille said determinedly.

'Maybe now is not the time for these kinds of questions,' Pierre said.

'Very well Monsieur, we will come back again tomorrow. Do you have anywhere you can stay tonight?'

'What about Georgette's townhouse?' Pierre asked.

Camille froze, her face etched into a hard line.

'It won't be for long, I promise! I will start sorting everything out in the morning. I can fix this ma chère; you know I can. I just need a bit of time.'

'I can't Pierre,' Camille replied, her lip wobbling.

Pierre came round to face her folding her into his arms and stroking her hair as she cried.

'You know I would not ask you to do this if it wasn't necessary.'

'I know,' she whimpered into his shirt.

Etienne reached up and took his mother's hand.

'Let's go, Maman,' he said.

Camille took a deep breath, squeezed Etienne's hand, and slipped her other hand into Pierre's.

'Do you know the largest townhouse over the bridge, overlooking the river?' Pierre asked.

'The Beaufort residence?' The fireman asked.

Camille winced. Pierre rubbed his thumb reassuringly over her knuckles.

'That's the one,' he replied.

'We'll see you there in the morning, Monsieur.'

Pierre nodded his thanks, clasped Camille's hand in his, and led his family down the street, now surrounded by the sight of nosy neighbours wanting to get a glimpse of the commotion. Some called to them, asking what had happened, and if they could help. Pierre gestured with his hand that all was well, enough to get them to stop prying for now.

The walk to the townhouses usually took around half an hour. However, they walked slowly, mournfully, silently, but in deep thought. In the end, it took them nearly an hour to get there and it was almost completely dark. When they eventually strolled onto the street, Camille hesitated.

'Ma chère?' Pierre asked, his intonation filled with concern.

'It's been a long time Pierre,' Camille whispered.

'I know,' Pierre sympathised. 'It will be okay.'

Camille nodded, trusting her husband completely. She turned to Etienne, her eyes lighting up in alarm as she caught sight of his shirt sleeve.

'Ma pêche, your arm! What happened?'

The stain had dried now leaving a noticeable dark red mark.

'Oh, I think I caught it. On, on some of the damaged wood outside the house.'

'You need to be careful my darling!' She said as she hugged him tightly.

Over her shoulder, he could see the look on his father's face, concern, and disappointment.

'Um… Maman we should knock on the door. I'm tired.'

Camille let him go, stood up, and straightened her skirt.

'Yes, of course, ma pêche.'

They joined hands again and took the steps up to the grand front door in unison. Pierre lifted the hefty knocker in his hand and rapped it three times against the door.

A light went on in the living room, then there was a moment's pause as the sound of locks shifted around, before the door was opened revealing a statuesque woman, draped in a fine silk robe. Etienne was struck by the familiarity of her appearance, especially by the long, shiny, mousy brown hair.

'Bonsoir, Georgette,' Camille said coldly.

'Sister!' She gasped, rushing down the steps and enveloping Camille in a vice-like grip.

Eventually, she let her go for long enough to see Pierre and Etienne standing there looking bemused in the doorway.

'Pierre, my darling brother!' She exclaimed cupping his face in her hands.

'And this must be Etienne!'

Etienne shuffled behind his father's leg.

'Etienne, this is your Tante Georgette.'

'Enchantée,' she gleamed, offering him her hand.

Etienne touched it lightly in politeness.

'Come in, come in! I can't believe you're all here!' She squealed.

Camille rolled her eyes as Pierre ushered her gently into the house, whilst Etienne was left standing by the door wondering how much a single day could change everything.

ADA

Stuttgart, May 1932

'Où est le magasin le plus proche, s'il vous plaît?'

'Where is the nearest shop, please? Bon!' Liselotte applauded.

'Great!' Ada beamed.

'Shhhh! Keep your voice down!' Liselotte warned.

Not too many would react too well to hearing two German girls practising another language, and the language of an enemy no less.

'I think maybe we should stop for today with the practice. You're a natural at this Ada, you pick it all up so quickly!'

'You help me out so much Lise. I know it's risky.'

'Ada, you are practically my sister, of course I'm going to help you in any way that I can.'

'What did I do to deserve you?'

'Our mothers helped each other give birth, we're bonded for life Ada, so I'm afraid you're stuck with me,' Liselotte teased, pushing Ada's shoulder playfully.

Ada giggled, seated herself behind Liselotte on the grass, untied her beautiful, glossy hair, separated it into three sections, and began to plait.

'If ever you have a daughter, she will be lucky to have a Mütter who does the best hair plaits.'

'I know,' Ada joked.

Ada and Liselotte would venture out to the park on a different day each week, Liselotte would attach her favourite indigo blue hair ribbon to the lock on her front window which Ada could see from her bedroom. They couldn't risk having a regular pattern should they be seen or overheard. Their girlish aloofness was long gone, they had been forced to grow up far too quickly. At seventeen, they watched in despair as their country slowly destroyed itself, now giving into more unhelpful influences, the agenda of which had taken hold of their community, and for Ada, her own household.

As she finished securing Liselotte's hair Ada shuddered at the memory of the night that the Nazis gained over one hundred seats in the Reichstag. How her house had celebrated. There was dancing, and cheering accompanied by the consumption of large amounts of alcohol. They were overjoyed, and Ada was not, her lack of enthusiasm for the occasion had been enough for violence to ensue. She had turned up at Liselotte's house in the early hours of the morning, the gash on her arm had taken a long time to stop weeping.

As Ada lay huddled up against Liselotte that night, they made a pledge.

'No matter who shouts the loudest. We refuse to accept what they are saying.' Liselotte stated.

'Agreed,' Ada said, nuzzling into her best friend's comforting arms.

Now as they sat together on the grass drinking in the fresh spring air, it was their opportunity to talk plainly.

'There are rumours that Bruning is going to resign,' Liselotte sighed.

'Mmm hmmm,' Ada grunted.

'He's pissed off a lot of people.'

'He's trying to stand up to bullies, and thugs, and actually help the people!' Ada spat.

'Hey, I know, I'm not fighting against you,' Liselotte hushed her, rubbing her arm, her fingertips brushing over the faint scar.

'Sorry, Lise,' Ada sighed.

'Don't be, Ada. That anger is good, it shows that you care. Besides, you're the brave one.'

'Brave? Me? I'm always the one who comes to you in pieces.' Ada gasped in disbelief.

'But you carry the anger day in and day out, and I never see you snap at anyone, you have the purest heart I know, Ada Stein. I'm scared every day, but then I see you. You give me strength.'

Tears were in Liselotte's eyes as she spoke, she wasn't teasing or joking.

'Lise?'

Liselotte turned her face away furiously brushing away the tears. Ada shuffled closer to her, drawing her into her arms, and stroked her hair.

'What happened, Lise?'

Liselotte sniffed hard before clearing her throat and speaking.

'It's Thomas,' she gulped.

***

Stuttgart, March 1932

Thomas was the dashing new apprentice from Frankfurt at Herr

Krause's bakery. Artur Krause was hard going on him, but Thomas rose to each challenge, respected Artur's mentorship, and was grateful for any opportunity that came his way. Ada had been with Liselotte the day she first laid eyes on him; and when she had nearly fallen over in shock, Ada had nearly fallen over with laughter. He had been placing fresh bread loaves out on the counter, he was tall, well over six feet, with thick strong arms with muscles that were tight against his shirt. His long light brown hair swayed across his neck gracefully.

'Now that's what I call falling head over heels in love,' Ada wheezed as she tried to catch her breath.

'Shut up, Ada,' Liselotte threatened.

'Is everything okay out here?' Thomas' gentle, charming voice rang in the air.

Liselotte's eyes were bulging, her cheeks flushed pink. Ada rarely saw her in such a state.

'Yes. Yes, all is fine. I am fine. I mean *we* are fine,' Liselotte gestured towards Ada who was still leaning against the lamppost, trying to compose her breathing between giggles, who haphazardly raised a hand limply in greeting.

Thomas smiled a dazzling white smile that formed small crinkles at the sides of his deep brown eyes.

'Well, I'm glad,' he chuckled 'You looked like you were going to go down hard for a second there.'

'Excuse me?' Liselotte demanded, hands on her hips, she looked ridiculous. Ada doubled back over in a fresh fit of giggles.

'Oh! I didn't mean anything crude Fräulein!' Thomas responded, genuinely horrified at his insinuation.

'It's Fräulein Krause for your information,' Liselotte commanded.

'Fräulein Krause,' Thomas smiled, 'You are the famous Liselotte.'

'That's me,' she asserted, but her hands started to lower from her hips.

'Your father is my boss. I'm Thomas, his new apprentice,' he beamed, stepping forward to shake her hand.

Liselotte took it tentatively, and Ada saw her quiver, ever so slightly. But what she couldn't ignore was the way that they couldn't take their eyes off each other.

'Um… this is my best friend, Ada,' Liselotte spluttered breaking away from their enchantment.

'Hello, Thomas,' Ada said, stepping forward, and shaking his hand curtly.

'Herr Krause, makes the best apple strudel, doesn't he?' Ada interjected, desperate to continue the conversation.

'Oh yes, he definitely does! But I don't start training on that for a while,' Thomas replied, not taking his eyes off Liselotte for a second.

Liselotte made a funny noise, a small gasping noise as if she was trying to say something but couldn't, she looked to Ada for help.

'W...well… that would be because of the ingredients shortage! Right, Lise?' Ada said, nodding towards Liselotte.

'Uh… yes, exactly,' Liselotte stammered.

'Maybe one day. It certainly won't happen if we hand our country over to those insane Nazi maniacs.' Thomas sighed.

His honesty seemed to suck the air out of their lungs, rarely did anyone express such a strong opinion when thugs could be anywhere these days.

'You should watch your tongue,' Liselotte warned.

'You're not a supporter, are you?' The blood from Thomas' face drained, the consequences even now to cross a Nazi supporter were severe, Ada knew that all too well.

'No. Neither of us are,' Liselotte whispered. 'But you need to be careful what you say around here. People are desperate.'

'I am well aware,' Thomas sighed. 'There were two brownshirts in here today. They threw flour all over the floor and turned over a table before Herr Krause came out from the kitchen, and they ran off.'

Liselotte swallowed hard. Thomas noticed.

'But don't worry, Fräulein! He was unharmed.'

'Liselotte, bitte,' Liselotte pleaded.

'Liselotte,' Thomas exhaled, smiling another dazzling smile as he did so.

'Uh. Ada, we should go, we'll be late.'

'For what?' Ada asked.

Liselotte shot her a dangerous glance; Ada knew better than to cross that line with her.

'Oh, yes! After you.'

Liselotte's eyes calmed; she craned her neck slightly to regain her composure.

'It was nice to meet you, Thomas,' she said curtly.

'It was very nice to meet you, Fräulein Liselotte Krause,' he said slowly, it was sexy, Liselotte felt it, and Ada knew she did.

Ada came to her friend's side and lightly took her arm.

'Good day, Thomas,' Ada smiled.

'Good day!' Thomas called back as the two girls walked back down the street.

They passed at least two streets in silence until Ada couldn't hold back anymore.

'So…'

'So?'

'Thomas. He seems… nice.'

'Hmm.'

'Hmm? That's all you have to say about him?'

'What else is there to say about him?'

Ada stepped in front of Liselotte, crossing her arms in frustration at her best friend.

'Oh, come on Lise! Every boy who notices you can't take his eyes off you, neither could Thomas!'

'What's your point, Ada?'

'You tell me that every boy you see is too immature, you don't give them a second glance. But Thomas, you couldn't take your eyes off him.'

'He.. he threw me off guard. That's all!'

'That's all?'

'Yes, Ada, that's all! He's arrogant. How could I be interested in someone like that?'

'Lise, he's not arrogant, he's passionate. You and he are like-minded, you heard how he spoke! He thinks as we think!'

'Ada, he works for my father. He would be furious to hear that one of his employees was involved with his daughter. Besides, there is nothing between us.'

They started courting a week later. Ada of course was their go-between, delivering notes to arrange their romantic rendezvous. Thomas fitted into their dynamic perfectly, he was so in love with Liselotte and Ada was so happy to see her best friend so happy. They had another ally, someone who shared their ideas and kept their secrets.

***

Stuttgart, May 1932

'What happened to him, Lise?'

'Those thugs that keep harassing the bakery. They came back, normally they just make a mess and then run off like the cowards that they are. But Father had just left for a couple of minutes to run an errand, Thomas was on his own...' her voice trailed off, Ada squeezed her hand. 'Ada, they were armed this time.'

'Meine Güte! Where is he now?'

'In hospital. My father said that he was unconscious, but he was going to be fine.'

'Thank God!' Ada exhaled, relieved.

'I can't go and see him, Ada. When Father told me what had happened it took everything within me not to faint. I had to pretend that I just have a healthy concern for his employees. This pretence is horrible.'

'You can't tell him, Lise, not yet,' Ada muttered, ashamed that she couldn't comfort her at that moment.

'I know, I know,' Liselotte sniffed, rubbing her face in frustration.

'Why did you arrange our meet-up today, Lise? We didn't have to do this.'

Liselotte's head snapped up.

'It's *exactly* why we had to meet today, Ada. Don't you get it? The reason Thomas was beaten up by those bastards was because they are trying to beat out every last bit of good that this country has to offer! If we want anything we do to matter, we have to keep going!'

She was yelling now; Ada was acutely aware of a few people in the distance turning their heads towards them. Their spot was secluded enough so that they couldn't be heard, but public enough so that they could be seen and therefore wouldn't be suspected of doing anything untoward.

'Lise, please!' Ada begged.

Liselotte glanced around, fresh tears spilling over her cheeks.

'I'm sorry,' she breathed.

The city bell began its chime. Ada counted in her head one, two, three, four, five… *fuck.*

'Lise, it's five o'clock!'

'Oh crap, we need to get you to the line!'

The girls leapt up, brushed the grass off their skirts, and began to sprint. The soup kitchen wasn't far away from the park, but the queue grew very quickly, people didn't dare miss their slots. Even if people were on time, scuffles would break out frequently and it could get ugly.

They crossed the park within seconds, swinging around the lampposts to turn them sharply east towards the bridge. They could see the tunnel entrance and Ada's legs were pumping hard as she desperately tried to keep up with Liselotte's athleticism. Liselotte leapt down the incline into the tunnel entrance before coming to a sudden halt. Ada frantically tried to slow her momentum but skidded straight into Liselotte, causing them both to sprawl out on the wet floor.

'What the hell…' Ada began but fell silent at the look of concern in Liselotte's eyes. She glanced up and caught the sight of two brown-shirted men standing at the other end of the tunnel, she didn't need to be warned twice.

'Whoa! Need some help there, ladies?' One of the men shouted, stumbling slightly.

Oh crap they're worse when they're drunk.

Ada disentangled herself from Liselotte, jumped to her feet, and offered her hand to help her up. Liselotte gave her only one hand.

'Lise, come on,' she whispered.

But Liselotte still only gave her one hand.

'What are you doing?' Ada hissed.

She finally looked downwards to see Liselotte tugging slightly at her jacket with her other hand.

Her French phrasebook.

She was sure that she had placed the book in its usual place, in the tear in the lining of her favourite jacket. Or was she? They had been in a rush to leave; she hadn't done her usual checks.

Ada's cheeks flushed, and she started to pant, but she nodded her understanding to Liselotte. Liselotte dutifully gave Ada her other hand allowing her to pull her to her feet, making sure that she stepped far enough in front of Ada to conceal her tucking the book firmly into its place.

Her skirt was soaked and stained from the muddy water, but it was better to suffer her mother's disappointment than any encounter with one of Hitler's thugs. Liselotte was breathing heavily, fists clenched, and her jawline twitched tightly. Ada felt the panic rise in her throat as she tried to measure up the situation. She knew what these men were capable of, and they were two young women at their mercy. They had to pass them, the only alternative was to walk an extra fifteen minutes in the other direction, and they didn't have that kind of time. Carefully, she took Liselotte's arm, who flinched at her touch.

'Head down. Not a sound,' Ada whispered.

Liselotte's eyes were brimming with tears, Ada could feel her friend's fury. They could have been the men who assaulted Thomas for all they knew, Ada fought to push the thought to the back of her mind to suppress her own anger.

Together they started to take small steps forward, Liselotte's face remained staring at her feet.

'Where are you heading?' One of the brownshirts called out.

It took Ada by surprise; their paths had nearly come together already.

'T..t..to the market square,' Ada stammered.

They were right in front of them now, Ada wanted to just keep walking, but they were both broad in stature, something she didn't notice in the distance. Both of them were tall and looked rough. One of the men had patchy stubble growing over his chin, when he grinned, he bore the missing space of a tooth, and there was bruising around his lip. Ada silently hoped that Thomas had delivered the blow responsible for his injuries. The other man's face wasn't beaten, but Ada couldn't help but stare at the knuckles on his left hand, three were out of place, they had been broken multiple times. To her disgust, he noticed.

'Don't worry sexy, they don't hurt that much, you know what would make them better though?' He sneered.

Ada's cheeks flushed again, and she visibly flinched at his inference.

'Oh, she's an innocent one!' The other man jibed. 'Look at her face! She hasn't tasted the delights of a proper German man.'

He stepped towards her; she could feel his breath on her face as she turned away from the stench of beer that permeated the air. Suddenly, Liselotte started to heave and convulse.

'She's sick!' The bare-toothed one yelled.

'Eugh, get her out of here!'

With widespread hunger, mass unemployment, political chaos, and public unrest, there was only one other thing equal to people's fears, and that was getting sick. Many more were dying of the smallest ailments nowadays.

Before she had a chance to think, Ada lifted Liselotte's arm around her shoulder and hastily hauled her past the two brownshirts towards the end of the tunnel. Liselotte was coughing hard, but Ada didn't dare stop moving, she was sweating with the effort, yet her blood ran cold at the resounding echo that was left behind.

'Isn't that the baker boy's girl?'

Ada carried Liselotte until they rounded the corner into the market square. Only there did Liselotte finally stop heaving and began to breathe steadily.

'Oh, thank God,' she gasped.

'That was all fake?' Ada asked.

'Ada, they were going to…'

'I know what they were going to…' Ada trailed off. 'Thank you.'

Liselotte smiled in relief, and Ada threw her arms around her squeezing her tightly.

'They know about you and Thomas,' Ada whispered into her ear.

'Oh, please God, no,' Liselotte whimpered.

Before Ada could reply there was a loud shout from across the square.

'Ada, where the hell have you been? Get here right now!'

More wrinkles now etched her mother's face, from hunger or stress, Ada couldn't tell.

'Coming!' Ada called back.

She could see Clara and Artur standing beside her family; she guided a speechless Liselotte towards them.

'There you girls are!' the always cheery voice of Clara Krause rang out. 'You two are so inseparable that one day I'm worried that you will both run off and never return!'

'And you would find a way to get by! Thick as thieves the pair of you!' Artur teased, winking at both of them.

The girls offered up a smile, convincing enough to hide the toll of the afternoon. Ada gave Liselotte's hand one last squeeze before joining her family in the line.

'What happened to your skirt, girl?' Her grandfather questioned, deliberately too loudly.

Ada closed her eyes, wishing that he would just disappear.

'I slipped,' she replied.

'Stupid, ugly, and clumsy,' he scoffed.

'And how do you expect to get that dirt out of it?' Gisela asked.

'I've got some left-over soap at home that will do the trick, Gisela, don't worry,' Clara chimed.

'Make sure that *she* cleans it though, Clara.'

***

The soup they ate that evening was barely edible, yet they all downed it within seconds. You had to be grateful for what you did have, even if that was hardly anything at all. With the taste of what Ada was pretty sure was soil lingering on her breath, she walked back home with her family, picking up her feet to keep up with them so that they couldn't berate her.

Dusk was setting in by the time they returned, Gisela took out the key to carefully unlock the fragile door. But to their shock, the door swung open, and a tall man with sturdy black boots, long black trousers, and a partially unbuttoned white collared shirt stood in the doorway. His dark brown hair was smoothly slicked back, he had a button nose not too dissimilar from Ada's, and murky, green eyes just like hers. As Ada studied him carefully, he looked more and more familiar, the mole on the right side of his neck, the one wonky canine on the left side of his mouth.

'Ernst?' Gisela gasped.

Günther stepped forward bumping past Ada's shoulder putting distance between them, and removed his cap, out of respect or shock, it was hard to tell.

'Son? Is that really you?' Günther asked.

The strange man took a confident stride forward and blew a neat line of cigarette smoke in the air, before throwing the butt on the floor and stamping it out hard with a menacing authority that suddenly made Ada feel nervous.

'Hello, Mother, and Father. Grandfather.' He said slowly, nodding at each person in turn.

Gisela and Günther burst forward, enveloping Ernst in their embrace, with gasps of shock and jubilation. Ada felt a sharp poke in her leg as Walther prodded her with his stick to move her out of the way. She obediently stood aside and watched as he took a firm grasp of Ernst's hand.

'Welcome back my boy!' He chortled, his rotting teeth sticking out against his thinning skin which clung tightly to his face.

'So, this is what home is like now?' Ernst remarked, glancing around, his nose wrinkled in disgust.

Gisela went quiet and stepped back in resignation.

Ernst chuckled a low chuckle. 'Oh, come on Mother, you think I haven't heard the whispers before?'

'Why didn't you tell us that you were coming back, son?' Günther asked, practically bubbling over with glee.

'It would have ruined the surprise!' Ernst replied, opening his arms again to embrace him again.

He's a son. A Stein son is the pride of the family. He keeps our brothers' memories alive. I am a reminder that everything is different. Now it makes sense.

Ada hung back, and looked away, feeling like a loose piece in her own family. When she looked up again, she jumped at the sight of Ernst's beady eyes fixed on her.

'Well, well, well,' he spoke slowly, 'Ada, my baby sister. All grown up.'

Her cheeks flushed; he was making her feel uncomfortable.

'I know I haven't seen you since you were small, but you've really got nothing to say to your big brother?'

'She's not worth your breath my boy,' Walther spat, Gisela and Günther averted their gaze away from Ada.

Ernst laughed. 'I'm sure that's not true Grandfather! She's just a bit lost for words, aren't you?'

His condescending tone made her bristle, but he stuck up for her, sort of.

She finally took a tentative step forward, placing her hand out as firmly as she could for him to shake. Instead, he swept her up in a big hug, hoisting her off her feet, and crushing the air out of her lungs.

'It's been a long time sister, we have a lot to catch up on,' he smiled, this time more earnestly, Ada eased slightly as he released her.

'I hope you don't mind, Mother and Father, but I've brought a guest home. We're both stationed here on a project, and I invited him to stay.'

Ernst ushered everyone inside the house. In the living room stood a tall broad-shouldered young man, dressed in the same attire as her brother, his hair smooth and slicked back in the same style, except his hair was bright blonde. He was younger than her brother, he couldn't have been much older than twenty-one. He was clean-shaven and undeniably handsome, and when he smiled Ada couldn't help the small feelings of desire flutter in her stomach.

'Nice to meet you, everyone. My name is Otto.'

PHILIPP

Berlin, October 1927

He was trembling as he held the letter in his hand. He couldn't believe it; all of his hard work had paid off. Philipp scrambled out of the kitchen and raced down to the shop to share the good news with his father. He flew through the door in such a rush that he clattered straight into Johann, knocking them both to the floor.

'What the hell, Philipp?' Johann grunted as he pulled himself up.

'Sorry Johann!' Philipp shouted as he sprinted over to his father's desk.

Felix looked up from his papers and chuckled at the commotion.

'You have news, my boy?' Felix smiled, his eyes sparkling in anticipation.

'I got in! *The* Professor Bergmann has accepted *me!*'

Felix rose to his feet, hurrying round to meet his son, and embraced him tightly.

'All that time making notes of our customer's symptoms and all of those diagrams you drew whilst you were supposed to be working have paid off.' Felix chuckled.

Philipp blushed, but he mostly felt relief. It had taken a lot of convincing by him and his schoolteachers to persuade Felix to let him pursue his true passions.

'The business is set up and ready for you here my boy,' he would say, 'you and your brother will take this place from strength to strength.'

But after a while, even Felix couldn't ignore what made his son the happiest and soon became his biggest supporter.

'My brilliant boy! I knew you could do it!' Felix said warmly, still holding Philipp close to him.

'Thank you, Father!'

And then Felix did something that took him by surprise, he placed his hands over Philipp's cheeks so that he was looking straight into his eyes. His father's eyes were filled with tears, more than he had seen on the day of his own Bar Mitzvah years before.

'You are going to do amazing things as a doctor. Change the world, my boy.'

Philipp placed his hand on his father's wrist.

'I promise I'll make you proud,' he said.

'Wait, what?' Johann exclaimed.

Philipp had almost forgotten that his brother was in the room.

'The medical professor I was telling you about. He runs exclusive classes here in Berlin every year for six months. Students only get in through teacher recommendations and glowing ones at that. Anyway, I've been accepted!'

'I know about the damn classes!' Johann barked.

'Johann,' Felix spoke slowly and calmly, 'This is a huge opportunity for Philipp, you should be delighted for him.'

'I thought this wasn't serious! That it was so exclusive, that there was no chance that he would actually get in.'

Philipp's jaw dropped.

'You thought I wouldn't get in?' Philipp gasped.

'No, I didn't think you would,' Johann admitted, too coldly for Philipp's liking. 'When were you planning on dumping the business on me and not telling me about it?'

'This isn't about you Johann,' Philipp growled.

'Why are you walking away from everything we have built?'

'We're more than this shop Johann,' Felix interjected. 'You are both destined for great things, but your paths are different.'

Johann gave Philipp one last disgusted look, before storming out of the shop.

***

Berlin, December 1927

'This seat is free, yes?'

Philipp heard her before she spoke, the stomping of her big clunky boots made sure of that. He looked up to see a short young woman with a vast mane of curly, auburn hair staring at him intensely through her huge, unflattering, circular glasses. She was the only female in their class, and everyone had done their best to avoid her, and Philipp for that matter, despite his efforts to befriend them.

'Sure,' Philipp replied politely, moving his books as far over onto his desk as possible to give her space.

She nodded with what he perceived as a thank you and promptly sat herself down next to him, not giving him a single glance.

'Philipp Blau,' Philipp said, offering his hand.

She looked almost horrified by his initiation of conversation, and

71

her response matched.

'Well, Philipp Blau, I am not here to make friends. I am here to be the best. I assume that's why you're here too.'

'I want to be a doctor,' Philipp replied.

'If you're sure about that then you need to spend more time focusing on your studies instead of pathetically trying to get people to like you,' she snapped.

A few sniggers could be heard at the back of the classroom, where they watched the rebuttal with keen interest.

'Sorry I bothered,' Philipp sighed.

***

Berlin, January 1928

As the weeks went by, Philipp started to understand her frustrations more. She was consistently overlooked for giving answers to the questions Professor Bergmann posed, and she was right more times than the other students ever were.

In their first class back after the Christmas break, Philipp had been running a high fever all day and was struggling to concentrate on any of the words that were coming out of Professor Bergmann's mouth, let alone offer a cohesive answer.

'Exciting new medical breakthroughs are happening around us all the time. In rather recent times, Albert Hustin made vast improvements in which area?'

'Blood transfusions,' she muttered. She had become progressively more withdrawn, tired of being overlooked and her constant sniffs indicated a weariness from flu symptoms also.

'Herr Blau, did you say something?'

Everyone was now looking at Philipp, he swallowed hard, his throat scratching horribly as he did so.

'Erm, blood transfusions?'

'Sehr gut, Herr Blau!' His professor sang.

Philipp didn't even need to look at her to feel her hot glare on his face, he was already feeling the pressure from the unbearable headache that had been pounding since that morning.

Before Professor Bergmann could change the subject, Philipp raised a weary hand in the air.

'Yes, Herr Blau? Do you have something more you would like to share?'

'My classmate here told me the answer, I apologise,' he admitted.

'Oh, well, sehr gut Fräulein Keller, make sure you know yourself for next time, Herr Blau.'

'Danke Professor,' she replied, her face a vision of surprise.

The professor promptly turned back to his blackboard drawing out diagrams that they all started dutifully copying into their books.

Philipp ran a hand across his burning brow and sighed in exhaustion.

'Feeling pretty rough there, huh?' A raspy voice asked.

Philipp jumped, nearly falling out of his chair in shock at hearing her address him. She laughed at his reaction.

'Oh, um yeah, sorry, I'm coming down with flu. Looks like you are too,' he said.

'Is that your official diagnosis, doctor Blau?'

Was she teasing him?

'It is?'

'You should have more confidence in yourself Philipp, because you're correct,' she smiled.

'Well, thank you,' Philipp replied, unsure of what else to say.

'My name is Celine.'

From then on, they helped each other with their studies, in between helping at the antiques shop and school. Celine would come over to study, and they soon became an unstoppable force of knowledge in their class, giving each other the voice they desperately needed.

***

Berlin, February 1928

'Coffee?'

'Celine, you are the best!' Philipp gasped, as Celine pressed the small cup into his hand from her thermos flask, his shivering ceased almost immediately.

'How much longer do we need to wait? It's freezing out here,' she moaned, her teeth starting to chatter in the bitter cold.

Fifteen minutes later, the train slowly rumbled into the station. The entire class dashed to get onboard only to be immediately disappointed that it wasn't much warmer inside. Philipp was seemingly the only passenger smiling when the train finally heaved forward across the frozen tracks and started its journey towards Leipzig.

'This is taking *so* long!' Celine grumbled as the train continued to struggle, causing further delay to their excursion that they were all eagerly anticipating. But nothing could dampen Philipp's spirit; he was relishing every moment of being away from the shop, and particularly away from Johann.

He had become more unbearable since Philipp had accepted his place on the course. Whenever Philipp was around to help out at the shop all his brother would do was point out every little thing he did wrong- missing undusted areas, positioning the plates wrong, even closing the door too hard behind him, it was tedious.

On their arrival at the university, the students were escorted to the laboratories. Celine grabbed Philipp's hand and raced them towards the front to get the best view of the cadaver lying on the table. When the buzz of excited chatter died down, the university professor proceeded to pick up the scalpel from the array of instruments lying before him and made the first incision. Starting at the thorax he extended down the sternum and stopped mid-torso before unveiling the chest cavity. The slate grey colour of the lungs stood out underneath the laboratory lights. Philipp quietly observed no visible mottling, they were well-proportioned and identical in size.

'This patient died of lung-related causes; can anyone identify what it was that killed him?' the professor asked.

Every student leaned forward craning their heads around every possible angle to make their assessments. Many seemed to be trying to look at the largest area on the surface of the lungs, eyes frantically scrutinising every millimetre in fine detail, breath held in frustration. Celine was one of them, her head bobbed around hastily as she tried to piece the mystery together.

'Gah! I can't see it!' She whispered agitatedly.

But Philipp wasn't listening to her, he too was scouring over every detail of the lungs in front of them, but something was bothering him. He rose from his seat and moved around to the left of the room, not taking his eyes off the cadaver. It could have been a trick of the light, it was tiny, but he could have sworn that he saw something that wasn't right.

'You see something there?' the professor asked.

Philipp snapped his head up, immediately embarrassed at the attention that he had drawn to himself. Butterflies swarmed around in his stomach, and all he wanted to do at that moment was bolt right out of the door.

'I... um...' he stammered.

'What do you see, Philipp?' Professor Bergmann said softly.

'I… I can't be sure. But here,' he pointed to the left-hand side of the left lung. 'There's a nodule, a thin one, there's no mottling, and the colour shows that they are healthy, but the nodule, that shouldn't be there.'

He stepped to the side, breathing heavily, and sweating furiously even though the laboratory wasn't much warmer than the freezing conditions outside.

The professors in the room were looking at each other, Philipp couldn't read their expressions. Were they impressed or bemused at what he thought he had or hadn't seen?

'So, what did this man die of?' Another professor asked, who had a very long white beard, that reminded Philipp of his late grandfather.

Philipp swallowed. A diagnosis with limited information was challenging for any doctor, let alone a student who still had vast amounts to learn. He looked back at the body, trying to process each fact that came to mind. He was male, he looked quite young, maybe around thirty years of age, and his hair was light brown- *irrelevant Philipp come on,* but there was a very slight stain on the edge of the man's mouth.

'I don't think it's cancer…' he murmured.

'Why not?'

'He's young, there's no clear damage that would be caused by bad air or factory conditions. That stain on his mouth… blood? I think this patient died of tuberculosis.'

There was a wall of warm smiles from each of the professors. And Philipp finally exhaled.

'What's your name young man?'

'Philipp Blau,' he replied.

'We'll be keeping our eye on you.'

Philipp smiled and nodded; it was all he could do to contain the overwhelming joy that wanted to burst out of him.

Back in Berlin, Philipp's confidence only increased; he finally started to find his voice.

'How is it possible to twist our palms to face up or down?'

Philipp's hand shot up in the air.

'Herr Blau?'

'Because of the pivot joint,' he answered confidently.

'Sehr gut, and how is the joint able to perform its function?'

'It lets one bone rotate around the other.'

'Sehr gut, sehr gut!'

'Nice one there, Philipp,' Celine whispered, playfully nudging him in the ribs.

'Ha, danke Celine,' Philipp replied.

'Do you have something you would like to share there, Fräulein Keller?' Professor Bergmann asked.

'Only that we have a pivot joint in our neck as well, it is what allows us to turn our head from side to side.'

'Sehr gut Fräulein Keller! Make sure you speak up next time.'

Well maybe, the competitive edge hadn't completely fizzled away. Philipp rolled his eyes in jest at her ambition, she playfully kicked his foot in return.

At the end of their evening class, Philipp and Celine quickly tidied away their books and diagrams and wrestled on thick coats, scarves, and gloves.

'Study at the shop tonight?' Philipp asked.

'Sounds good,' Celine replied.

Celine always came over to the house or the shop to study, but Philipp never went to hers. He knew that her mother wasn't around, it was just her and her father living in a small apartment in a block of flats, around half a mile away from where Philipp lived. Celine could be secretive at the best of times, and they had formed such a good working partnership in the last few weeks that he didn't want to give any reason for their relationship to sour. So, he kept his mouth shut on the matter, never asking too many questions.

The last of the freezing winter still clung onto the city with a vice-like grip. Snow lay thick on the ground and the trodden paths had already frozen over, making them treacherous to walk on. It was only a mile away, but the thick snow and icy conditions made the journey exhausting. Celine struggled on her short legs to find a consistent tread pattern, she kept sliding into Philipp who courteously propped her back up time and time again.

'Sorry Philipp,' she harrumphed. 'I hate the snow.'

'Really?' Philipp laughed. 'I think it's beautiful.'

'It is when you're nice and warm inside!' Celine barked, but soon she was laughing too.

They stumbled on for half of the journey before Celine signalled that she needed to take a break. They brushed the fresh snow off their clothes and sat on a bench.

'Do you think you will stay in Berlin for medical school?' Celine asked.

'Where did that come from?' Philipp questioned.

'Well, we need to think about it, it's coming around quickly,' Celine stated.

'I think so,' Philipp admitted, 'my father won't want me to be too far away from home. I can be close by to help out in the shop too.'

'You think you will have time to help out in the shop when you're there?'

'I barely have time as it is,' Philipp sighed, 'I feel like I'm letting them down.'

'No, Philipp! Only a few students get selected for this program. You and I are extremely lucky. We're setting ourselves up for our future.'

'I think in their minds they already had my future planned,' Philipp confessed.

'But your brother is a partner in the business now, right? Won't he be able to run it by himself when your father eventually retires?'

'There is a lot more to it than you think. He will need help.'

'But he can hire an apprentice?'

'Sure, but I think I know who he would rather have.'

Celine bit her lip in frustration.

'That's not fair on you Philipp.'

'I know,' he sighed.

Philipp and Celine resumed the rest of the trudge back to the shop; it took them well over an hour to finally approach the street. Philipp heaved the door open; its usual loud creak was accompanied by a high-pitched squeal from the frozen hinges. A trail of snow hurried in behind them. They had barely taken a step into the building before they were confronted by Johann.

'Why are you so late?' He growled at Philipp.

Johann was fast approaching twenty years of age now, he was broad and muscular, with a line of stubble scattered across his cheeks and chin, his hair was unkempt and long, and he already had the frown lines of a man ten years his senior.

'If you haven't noticed, it's pretty bleak out there!' Philipp argued.

'You're supposed to be working,' Johann grumbled, thrusting a broom into Philipp's hand.

'Hey, you don't decide my hours! I agreed with Father that I would sort out the remaining stock and clear up when I got home from class. And the last time I checked, he was still running this place, not you.'

Celine briskly walked over to the middle of the shop, out of earshot of the two brothers, and pretended to occupy her attention looking at the coin collections.

'Well seeing as you brought your girlfriend back with you, I think work is not what's on your mind right now,' Johann continued.

'She's not my girlfriend Johann. Just because I can speak to women, doesn't mean you should get so jealous.'

'Me? Jealous? Of a self-entitled brat like you?'

Johann squared up to Philipp, 'Do you have any idea how hard Father has worked today? The client and auction meetings have been non-stop, and I have been overwhelmed here at the shop, and you're off doing whatever the hell you want.'

Philipp fought hard to control his temper which was starting to bubble in his stomach.

'How is that fair, Johann? I must take this opportunity, you know that.'

'You're turning your back on us!' Johann struck back.

'Johann, I don't want to work here! This is *your* dream. Not mine. Why can't you understand that?'

Johann took another step towards him, to tower above him and make him feel intimidated.

'You bring shame on this family,' Johann hissed.

The gravity of his words took a moment to hit him. He and

Johann had always fought, but he had never hurt him so deeply that it made him question everything about himself. Philipp knew he would regret what he was going to say, but his anger was burning so hot within him that he couldn't hold back. He glared at his brother and hissed back,

'And you brother, are bitter, jealous, and rotten.'

Johann's eyes widened in horror, but before he could react, Philipp strode angrily away from him into the middle room.

'I'll walk you home Celine,' Philipp said coldly.

'What about our studies?' She asked.

'Not tonight,' Philipp barked, far too harshly, Celine flinched.

'Okay,' she squeaked.

They exited quickly, crossing the shop floor without glancing up in every effort to avoid Johann. They stepped out into the snow, Celine slipped on an icy patch colliding with Philipp who grabbed her and the lamppost to steady their fall.

'Whoa, slow down!' Celine protested.

'Sorry,' Philipp sighed.

'Philipp, what happened in there?'

'Nothing, don't worry.'

'Look I know you two argue a lot, but it seems like that was a particularly bad one…' Celine said tentatively.

'You think Celine?' He exploded.

Celine blinked at him, shocked by his outburst.

'I'm sorry,' Philipp pleaded, 'it's just, you don't understand what it's like.'

'I know,' she said, 'but just because I don't have any siblings doesn't mean I don't recognise when two people deeply care about each other. You are lucky to have him, Philipp.'

'How? He makes my life a misery.'

'That's not true, he loves you.'

She was right but he was too mad to admit it. Philipp harrumphed and carried on walking.

'I don't understand why you two fight so much. Your Father adores and supports both of you.'

'Johann doesn't understand me. He never has.'

'He doesn't understand your ambitions?'

'It's more than that.'

'Then what? What can you two possibly need to fight about all the time?'

Philipp paused, he was so tired of explaining, tired of justifying, tired of arguing. Finally, he blurted out what he had known for so long but never spoken out loud, let alone confide in anyone.

'Because he's convinced that I killed our Mother.'

ETIENNE

Avignon, August-October 1914

True to his word, the day after Georgette had taken them in, Pierre had set to work contacting his suppliers trying to get his hands on any materials possible to start renovations; seemingly trying to ignore the reality that the attack had been confirmed as arson, and someone out there wanted to cause them harm.

His parents' denial had sent Etienne into a silent, reflective stupor. It had taken him over a week to tell them about Gabriel, his family, and the offer of violin lessons. As much as his parents had been delighted for him, it had also created new suspicions. Etienne couldn't help but wonder why Gabriel's house was vandalised, and why their house was attacked so shortly after his father's charitable gesture.

But to their relief, most of the community had rallied to their aid. When Pierre had returned to their home, every neighbour on their street had been outside, tools in hand, an array of building materials at their feet, and they had got straight to work restoring the home. Camille would stay up all night cooking and baking for the large numbers of people who were showing them this huge kindness. The foundations of the house were restored in no time, it was basic but that was all that they needed.

'Not long now ma chère,' Pierre had shared with Camille excitedly. Camille had had the small number of possessions they had packed up and ready since the moment they had arrived, she simply couldn't wait to leave, despite Georgette's generous hospitality.

But then the call came. The call they had all been dreading. The sacrifice that his mother had begged his father not to take. The whispers, the fantasising, the fearing, the panicking had all fed this powerful foe and spoken it into being. The world was at war, and its impact was inescapable.

Pierre, along with many others took up the call of duty, and gradually they left one by one. By October 1914, their once vivacious, chatty neighbourhood which once hosted carefree children running, skipping, and playing, the travelling accordion player, the calls of the market sellers, the smells of home-baked goods by family members old and new, singing, and laughing, was all reduced to a mournful silence.

As a result of his father's hasty call away, their house remained in need of essential installations, and furnishing. They couldn't move back, and they didn't know when it would be possible to do so, and it was tearing Camille apart.

***

Avignon, June 1915

Etienne's vacant stares out of the shutters inside the drawing room were returned by a sea of emptiness from the streets below. He withdrew inside, crossing over to the burgundy chaise longue where he teetered on the edge watching the hands of the magnificent grandfather clock tick by slowly. Now that city-wide alerts and curfews were in place, there wasn't much to look forward to. Camille felt it too unsafe for Etienne to go to school, but she had agreed to let Etienne continue his violin lessons on the condition that she accompanied him and that they took place in the morning.

But now it was Thursday, lesson day, and the plaintive sounds of the violin were crying out in his head, Etienne couldn't wait to wield the bow in his hand, to be the one to control the pressure on the strings, to swim along in the heights of the dynamics, but most importantly, to tell *his* story.

It was now 8.25, Camille was usually downstairs putting her shoes on at this point, getting ready to walk him to his lesson. But he hadn't heard a sound from her all morning. They had to leave by 8.30 otherwise he would be late, she knew that. Etienne hopped off the edge of the chaise longue and wandered towards the staircase, the steps were so smooth that he struggled to maintain a steady grip as he ascended the steps. He walked over to Camille's room and gently knocked on the door.

'Ma pêche? Is that you?' A quiet raspy voice called out.

Etienne eased the door open as delicately as he could. His mother lay still in her bed, her breathing was heavy, and her hair and face were soaked in sweat.

'What's wrong, Maman?' he asked.

'Don't you worry, my darling,' she wheezed before she was taken over by an uncontrollable hacking cough. Etienne took a tentative step back.

'It's flu my darling, I will get better.'

'Can I help you, Maman?'

She smiled weakly at him.

'All I want right now is to hold you in my arms, but you need to stay away from me, I don't want to make you unwell.'

She looked so helpless, and it wasn't just from feeling unwell, his mother had found the adjustment to living with Georgette and her lavish lifestyle extremely difficult. Their arguments that Etienne overheard whilst hiding away in his uncle's office revealed plenty.

***

Avignon, May 1915

'You, Pierre, and Etienne should visit us more often!'

'You have always had the option to visit us too.'

'Oh, but we didn't move here all that long ago Camille, as you would know if you read my letters. There has been a lot to unpack, things to arrange, you know how it is.'

'Maybe once I did Georgette. And I did read your letters.'

There had been a long awkward pause between the two sisters at that moment before Camille finally asked the significant question.

'Why did you and François move here, Georgette?'

'It's a beautiful city, why would I not want to move here?' Georgette said airily, almost laughing off Camille's question.

'Paris is grander, François has many connections there for work, you have your house there, why here?' Camille asked slowly.

'Paris is grand. You are right. By the way, you must come and visit us there sometime too, they have the most exquisite boutiques that I am simply dying to take you to!'

'Georgette,' Camille interrupted, firmly and decisively, her tone immediately stunning Georgette into silence.

At this point, curiosity got the better of Etienne. He had never understood why his mother had been so deliberately hostile since arriving at Georgette's house, this was not who she was. He nudged the door open the tiniest crack to listen in closer.

He heard Georgette sigh heavily. He got the impression she was about to say something important, and not necessarily a good thing. He found his aunt Georgette pleasant enough, and she was very sweet to him, but she was precious about the luxurious items that she owned, and the lifestyle she maintained.

'We knew that *this* was coming...' she began, 'Mother and Father were... worried about you. Me and François have been coming to Avignon for the last couple of years. For weekend trips, not to check up on you, I promise. But we did ask around after you.'

Her response had been left hanging in the air and it was unnervingly quiet, it felt like an eternity before Georgette resumed.

'When the war looked more inevitable, Mother and Father asked if we would buy a property in Avignon… we said yes. We do really like it down here Camille. But you are my baby sister. I have to look out for you.'

Camille's silence was almost unbearable, even Etienne held his breath in anticipation of her reaction, his sweet, gentle, loving mother, now he was second-guessing her and he suddenly felt a feeling of shame wash over him.

'I have Pierre and Etienne,' she finally said in a controlled and calm voice. 'I do not need Mother and Father to be sending you to look out for me. I can look after myself.'

'But, Camille, you don't need to! You know they want you to return home.'

Return home? Etienne was confused.

'You want me to return? Back to a place where I never fitted in? A place where I will be watched and judged for everything I say and do. A place where I can only talk to certain people because we stupidly believe that anyone with less money than us is beneath us. And let me guess, it will once again be under the condition that I left Pierre.'

Etienne swallowed hard. His mother had never really spoken about her family to him, and now he was starting to understand why.

'Camille…' Georgette whispered, trying to soften the blow, but to no avail.

'This is my home, Georgette! When are you, and François, and Mother, and Father, and the whole damn Duplantier family going to realise that?'

'You would curse your family's name like that?' Georgette shouted, equally as agitated as Camille now.

'I am a Touelle. Pierre and Etienne are my family,' Camille spat through gritted teeth.

That was the last thing he heard before angry footsteps started to stomp up the stairs, Etienne moved away from the door quickly, retreating to his study space. He had never been so shocked at his mother, but equally, he had never loved her so much. But her words still hit hard, and he couldn't help but think back to his confrontation with Marcel.

You will bring shame.

Judging by what his mother had said, the life she left, and what important people now thought of her, did he add to this shame that was hanging over their family?

***

Avignon, June 1915

It wasn't long until his mother slipped back into a feverish sleep, so Etienne slowly backed out of the door and quietly shut the door behind him. But now he was stuck without a chaperone. He hadn't seen his aunt Georgette since last night, she had been sitting alone, and not her usual vibrant energetic self. It seemed that the rift between her and his mother had taken its toll on her too. Etienne shuffled across the landing towards his aunt's bedroom, the heavy pine door was shut, Etienne traced the length of the panel with his fingertips. He leaned against the door listening out for his aunt's steady snoring, which he had heard a few times when he had caught her snoozing in the living room. But to his surprise, the door swung open, and Georgette appeared looking very bleary-eyed, her usually immaculate long shiny hair was knotted, frizzing in its mid-section, her face was drawn, and she had large bags under her eyes, no sleep, and her eyes were bloodshot, *the constant crying*. Etienne remembered that his mother had looked the same way when his father first left to go to war.

His aunt blinked at him as she squinted at her first glimpses of

88

the morning sun.

'Etienne?' She rasped, clearing her throat hurriedly. 'What are you doing up so early my sweet?'

She had taken to giving him her own term of endearment, which only added to his mother's disdain.

'It's my violin lesson today, Tante.'

'Oh! How lovely!' She said trying to muster a smile.

'Maman's sick,' Etienne stated.

'Oh… oh dear… well um, she needs to rest. Will you let me know if I need to call someone to help her, my sweet?'

'She's asleep right now. I need to go to my violin lesson now Tante Georgette. Maman says I can't go alone. Can you take me?'

'Oh. No, I can't my sweet I'm sorry. Can you miss it this week?'

'But I promised Madame Penaud that I would be there. She will be confused if I don't show up.'

'I'm sure she would understand, Etienne.'

She was getting annoyed now, she only used his name when she wanted him to go away.

'Okay,' Etienne mumbled.

'Good boy. Now go run along and play. Use the drawing room, and don't go into the living room. Please.'

Etienne nodded whilst his aunt turned around and shut the door firmly in his face.

He knew he shouldn't do it, but without his violin lessons, there was no sense of normality. He knew the way there; he had walked the route many times with his mother. But times were dangerous, the rules were in place for a reason.

Etienne glanced around the landing and wandered back to his uncle's office to gather his sheet music before slowly tiptoeing down the varnished stairs being careful not to slip. He scooped up his shoes by the front door, meticulously tying his laces before slowly turning the door handle until he felt a small click.

Why were all of the doors in his aunt's house so heavy?

He pushed with all his might against the frame before it finally yielded. He descended the steps, put his head down, and started walking at a brisk pace. For once, he was running late.

The river was calm this morning, and small waves lapped against the shore. Its calmness seemed oddly out of place considering the days they were living in. He followed the path away from the river up towards the familiar cobbled streets. Everywhere was eerily quiet as he meandered down each street. People weren't even hanging their washing out on their balconies anymore, for fear of making themselves a target should the enemy turn up on their doorsteps. The only sound he heard was the scuffing of his shoes against the uneven stones.

As he walked, Etienne couldn't help but think of his father, and how unwanted he was by his mother's side of the family. Well, Etienne wanted him. He missed him and his calming presence. His heart ached without knowing if he was safe, or even coming home at all.

His thoughts were finally stilled when he turned the corner of a familiar street. The outside of their house was well patched up, but as he peered inside, his heart sank with the memories that were locked up inside the vacant space. He found it difficult to tear himself away, but he could hear the clock chiming in the distance, it was nine o'clock and now he was officially late.

Etienne hurried up the street past the seamstress shop and made a sharp right at the end before he finally reached the house, it was the smallest one on the street, but that made it surprisingly eye-catching. He knocked a little too frantically, reflected by Gabriel's confused face as he let him in.

'Hey, Etienne! Where have you been? Maman was getting

worried. Where's your mother?'

'Sorry!' Etienne panted. 'Maman's sick.'

'Oh, did your aunt walk you here?'

'No, I came by myself,' Etienne admitted.

'Hey, I know it's daytime Etienne, but you need to be careful.'

'I know.'

'Anyway, Maman's waiting for you upstairs.'

Etienne ascended the staircase and walked down to the right to the smallest room in the house, he knocked loudly and called out.

'Madame Penaud? It's Etienne Touelle.'

'Come in,' the voice responded.

Etienne entered the room and saw Madame Penaud seated at her small table near the window. She used to sit right by the window so that she could hear the chatter on the streets and feel the breeze carried in by the river. She couldn't sit so close now, just as a precaution. Etienne approached her slowly making sure that he made his steps audible on the floor, he extended his hand to lightly touch hers, she always jumped slightly at his touch but smiled reassuringly when she knew it was him. Her milky glazed eyes passed over his figure, he knew that she couldn't physically see him, yet she was probably the only one who could fully see him for who he was.

'How did you get on with the sheet music I gave you?' She asked softly.

'Yes fine, thank you,' Etienne replied.

'Did you practice the note timings, tapping it out like we did last week?'

'Oui, Madame.'

'Great! Let's see how you apply it to playing the music,' she said gesturing her hand to the beautiful violin that was resting on its stand in its displayed glory.

That same rush of excitement that he had felt the first time Madame Penaud had invited him to take up her treasured violin in his hands had never left him. His fingertips tingled to the point that he would nearly shake, the first time he actually did, his breathing heightened, and his palms would sweat slightly, thankfully this had become more controlled.

He placed the sheets onto the music stand before stooping down to disturb the violin and bow compatriots from their peaceful rest. He gently took the neck of the violin and gracefully swept the instrument up underneath his chin, leaning on the magnificent ash wood rest. He would always close his eyes to relish the moment. Etienne drew himself up to the stand, and studied the first few notes on the page, measuring out the timing and formulating the melody in his mind. Once he was satisfied with his preparations, he stroked the bow across the strings and the first notes rang out, but it was too loud, and he paused.

'Why did you stop?' Madame Penaud inquired.

'I started it too loud; I need to start again.'

'Oui, but even if you make a mistake at the start, keep playing, it can still sound beautiful in its entirety.'

That thought hadn't occurred to him before, the violin players he had heard were perfect in timing and dynamics. He strived to be just as good as them, it was frustrating not having his own violin to practise with outside of lessons, this was the only precious time that he got to apply his studies, and when it didn't come together as he imagined, he would get deeply discouraged. Madame Penaud sensed this.

'Don't put so much pressure on yourself, Etienne. It doesn't always need to be outstanding. As much as learning an instrument is about getting the technical aspects right, it's also about the joy that music gives you. I know that it brings you joy Etienne, it defines you, don't suppress that joy by trying to constantly be perfect.'

She understood, and for a moment Etienne thought if her not being able to see had suppressed any of her joy, or if somehow, she had managed to create new joys in her life. He hoped that she was aware of how much joy she brought to him. And with only that thought in mind, he began to play, and he didn't stop for the duration of the lesson.

The hour they had together always seemed to fly by. The end was signalled by Madame Penaud raising her hand to halt him. He obediently stopped and placed the violin and bow back in their rest with the utmost delicacy, before loudly pacing over to where Madame Penaud was sat. She reached into the bag beside her and pulled out some new music, Etienne's heart fluttered in excitement.

'We're not going to play through this one today. I want you to take this home, read it carefully, study the melody, and then before we properly get started in next week's lesson, I want you to hum the tune for me. Can you work on that for me?'

'Oui, Madame,' Etienne replied.

'Wonderful!' She smiled, 'by the way, where is your mother? She usually comes in to say hello.'

'Oh, we need to be on our way, she has to go and check on something on the house.'

His cheeks burned with his deceit; lying didn't come naturally to him.

'That's a shame, I will see you both next week.'

'Au revoir, Madame.'

He slowly paced back down the stairs; he peered around the corner to see Gabriel sitting on a chair reading a book.

'What are you reading?' Etienne asked.

Gabriel glanced up and smiled, 'A Midsummer Night's Dream.'

'Oberon,' Etienne chuckled.

'He's the best character for sure,' Gabriel laughed.

Etienne left the house and started his walk back along the street, his joy restored. He had only been walking for a few minutes when he heard a distant cry, he paused momentarily thinking it to be a cat meowing, but then he listened harder, and he could hear wailing. It was coming from the direction of Gabriel's house, he turned back and headed along the path. As he drew closer to Gabriel's house, he could hear the wailing becoming more desperate, it was coming from the old chapel at the end of the street. He wandered up to the doors pulling them open, the wailing was ringing all around, echoing off the cold stone walls, but he couldn't see the source of it.

The altar space was bare, and the chapel was empty, it wasn't unusual for the chapel to be open, but usually the chaplain was close by to offer prayer and advice. Etienne figured that he would get a better vantage point from above, the small set of stairs led to some higher pews, he climbed up and made his way along the seats. He reached the far-right-hand side of the row and inspected the seats below and that was where he spotted him. A young boy was on the other side of the chapel on one of the lower pews, he couldn't have been more than five years of age and he was curled up on the floor.

'Bonjour,' Etienne called out; his voice carried further by the echo.

The boy's cries stifled, and he unravelled himself to look towards Etienne's voice.

'Are you lost?' Etienne asked.

The boy sniffled and nodded.

'Where is your mother?'

The boy shrugged and his lip started to wobble again.

'It's okay, don't cry, my name is Etienne. Do you remember where you were last time with her?'

'She said my clothes needed fixing. I didn't want to go. I walked off, and then I couldn't find her.' The boy whimpered.

'It's okay, I think I know where you were. Were there dresses in the window?'

The boy looked up, eyes wide open, and he nodded enthusiastically.

'I know where it is, I'll take you there, give me a minute.'

He stood upright and started making his way back towards the stairs when all of a sudden, he heard a loud creak, the floorboard felt unstable, and a crack started to form. Before he could react, the crack grew along the length of the pew giving way completely and Etienne with it. He couldn't panic, all he could do was fall, and brace himself.

He hit the floor hard. His left leg had landed first. The pain was fierce and burning. He tried to move but he doubled over in pain. He screamed. He had been so stupid to go by himself. Now his leg was broken, he knew that, but his hip didn't feel right, and he was scared. As he lay there, he began to feel woozy, the pain was too much, and he could feel himself starting to slip out of consciousness. Through blurred eyes he could make out the young boy running through the doors, he was calling out, but his ears were ringing, and finally, the world went black.

ADA

Stuttgart, June 1932

Otto resided with them for a few weeks. Gisela was delighted because it gave Ernst an excuse to stay, she could mother her precious last remaining son. The house was always loud, Ernst and Otto also liked to drink, and her father and grandfather would join in their sessions with equal vigour. Their joy took over from the anger and resentment that had run their household for years, and Ada was grateful for that. But it didn't take long for her to find out the real reason why Ernst and Otto were there.

At first, she pretended not to notice. But the steady stream of pamphlets and posters that kept appearing in their satchels and the way they were able to easily converse with the thugs in brown shirts with merry smiles was all too revealing. They weren't just supporters, they were members.

Whilst they were in the family home, she couldn't meet with Liselotte as often. They had to keep each other safe now that there were watchful eyes everywhere. But what was worse was that despite the threat and the fear that had Ada looking around every corner, Otto was incredibly charming, handsome, and flattering, and Ada couldn't help the butterflies that flew around in her stomach furiously whenever he was around her, and he was around a lot.

Not even her book could keep her attention as she stole a glance at him as he walked in through the door that evening.

'What are you reading there, Fräulein Stein?' Otto asked with a sweet intonation.

'Oh, the… The Magic Mountain,' she stammered, flushing bright red.

He leaned in close to her, and a small strand of his immaculate blonde hair trailed above his eyebrow, and she felt her heart beat faster.

'Lots of disease in that book, right?' He said with a wry smile.

'It's also a lot about life, and that life exists outside of war,' Ada replied brightly.

'You are a smart girl, Ada Stein,' he smiled at her gently, his blue eyes sparkling as they gazed at hers.

***

Stuttgart, July 1932

'I don't know how you do it, Ada, living with those pigs.'

They had all managed to meet in the park about a month after Ernst's return, when Gisela had gone to bed, and the rest of the household had drunk themselves into a snoring stupor.

'Lise, he's my brother. What can I do?'

'He's working for *them,* Ada.'

'You think I don't know that?'

'What's his friend like?' Thomas asked.

He had made a full recovery from the beating, and Liselotte had barely left his side. Artur must have found out about their relationship by now, Liselotte never said, but if he did, he must have given them his blessing, some good news at long last.

'Who, Otto?' Ada remarked, feigning ignorance, 'he's… um… dedicated, he works a lot with Ernst promoting the Party.'

'It's been weeks, why is he still staying with you?'

'He and Ernst are good friends, I think the Party feels like their work is needed strongly here, and wherever they're told to go, that's where they go.'

'*The Party?*' Liselotte hissed. 'Are you even listening to yourself right now? They are *animals!* How can they be thought of as anything else?'

'Liselotte, love, please,' Thomas said placing a protective arm around her shoulders.

'There's more, isn't there?' Liselotte said suspiciously.

'No,' Ada answered, her cheeks began to burn.

'Don't lie, Ada.'

Ada stared at the floor.

'Oh no. Please no. You don't like him, do you?'

'Lise…'

'Ada, he's one of *them!*'

'I know, but he's kind! He shows interest in me. Maybe he doesn't believe in all of it? You have seen what desperation does to people, maybe I could help him.'

'We're all desperate Ada,' Liselotte stated coldly. 'But no matter how desperate it gets; we all have a *choice.* I don't see any of us signing up to be part of their spectacle and delusion. He has made his choice; you need to stay away from the likes of him.'

'You deserve better than him, Ada,' Thomas agreed.

She wanted to believe them, but it was difficult to find clarity in her feelings. She had been overlooked by so many people in her life, by both her family and any man she found remotely attractive, there was always someone better than her. Liselotte and Thomas headed back to the bakery, so Ada walked home by herself.

She avoided the tunnel this time, deliberately taking the long way around, the trauma of her last encounter was still fresh in her mind, and still caused a pang of nausea to hit her whenever she thought about it.

For the first time, she found herself feeling bitterness towards the two people she treasured so dearly. She rubbed away the angry tears that were stinging her eyes. But then, to her horror, she heard an unnervingly familiar voice.

'You okay there?' A slurred voice drooled.

Her heart dropped and she picked up the pace of her steps.

'Don't I know you?' The voice persisted.

He was close.

Ada walked faster.

'Hey, I'm talking to you!'

Ada was now running, her heart pounding, she was desperately trying to get away. But now she could hear another set of footsteps pattering quickly behind her, alongside her. He cut her off. The streets were dark and strangely quiet.

He sauntered confidently up to her, swaying slightly and he grinned that grin, the one that bore his missing tooth.

'Did you miss me, darling? It's been a while.'

'I… I don't want any trouble,' Ada stuttered.

'Who said anything about trouble?' He laughed.

'What do you want from me?' She whimpered.

'You're so sweet. Not many like you anymore. The innocent

99

ones taste the best.'

Ada stepped back. 'Please don't,' she pleaded.

He moved quickly towards her, pinning her arms to the side as he pushed her hard against the wall, her head struck it hard, and everything went fuzzy. She could feel his hands move across her skirts, she struggled against his body weight on top of her, his stubble scratching her neck and chest as he hungrily smothered her in uncomfortable kisses. She pleaded quietly as she tried to fight back against him.

'Rolf!' A voice called out.

The brute paused his assault, to look up.

'Otto, come on, get your own girl!' He spat towards him and resumed his grip on Ada.

'You don't want her Rolf. She's spoiled goods.'

'What?' Rolf spluttered.

'She's been with loads of us, trust me she's not going to bring you any joy.'

'Is that true?' Rolf's attention was turned on Ada once again, his eyes burning with fury now.

Ada was wide-eyed in terror; she shot a glance at Otto who gave her a small nod.

'Yes,' she gasped underneath Rolf's tight grip.

'Whore!' Rolf yelled, before slapping Ada hard in the face, she fell to the floor shielding her face and bracing herself for more.

But all that came her away was a huge ball of spit which landed at her feet, followed by the harsh sound of footsteps gradually getting further and further away. And then Otto was there, cradling her in his arms, and suddenly she felt safe.

'Shit, Ada! What were you doing out here by yourself at this time?'

She couldn't speak, she just cried into his shirt.

'Shhhh you're safe now,' he hushed. 'Did he?...'

'N...n...no, ahhh my head!' Ada cried.

'Can you walk?' Otto asked.

Ada tried to pull herself to her feet but was hit by a wave of dizziness, she stumbled, and Otto caught her. He placed a supportive arm around her waist and draped her arm over his shoulder, and they slowly made their way back to the house.

'Otto... please don't tell my parents,' Ada begged.

'Don't worry, I won't, I'm going to make sure that you're okay.'

Her family was mercifully sound asleep when Otto managed to ease the door open in relative silence. He prepared a cold cloth and held it against her head, she winced with the pain, but the fuzziness had gone now much to her relief.

'I'm so sorry,' she whispered as Otto tended to her.

'It's okay Ada, you just need to be careful. You need to stay away from people like Rolf, he's a mean bastard.'

'You talked to him like a friend. Why are you friends with people like him?'

Otto sighed. 'He's not a friend of mine, but we are compatriots, we work towards the same goal, but not the same way.'

Ada's heart sank at his response, he was too kind and sensitive for this.

'You are innocent, Ada Stein and you are smart, and kind... and beautiful.'

Ada glanced up at his confession, her heart could have beaten right out of her chest.

***

She awoke the next morning in her bed, Otto must have moved her in the night. She was fully clothed, and her blanket was draped lightly over her. She picked up her hairbrush and crept out of her room to the landing. In the grimy mirror, she inspected her face relieved to see that there was no bruising. Her hair was a mess, brush in hand, she started to pull it through the knots. As she moved the brush around to the back of her head, she found the small lump that had risen during the night, she yelped slightly when she caught it, slapping her hand over her mouth to mute her cries. Gently, she began to braid her hair, deliberately leaving it untidy enough to hide the lump.

Looking back at the mirror, she addressed the rest of her body. At seventeen she had fully blossomed into womanhood, she was short but shapely, heavy-chested, and maintained a stubborn plump belly, it had never gone away. She continued to keep her hair at shoulder length, it frizzed more now, much to her annoyance, she could never keep it neat. Her high cheekbones showed a bit more, but her chubby cheeks still succeeded in keeping them mostly concealed. Sighing heavily, she stretched out and immediately felt the ache in her arms. When she glanced down at them, she could see that the bruising from Rolf's grip was extensive and illustrated a brutal pattern.

A small thud startled her, someone in the house was stirring, she hurried back to her bedroom, shutting the door firmly behind her, listening closely to hear if anyone was following her. Happy that she was alone, Ada looked around her room, relieved to see a clean flowery blouse hanging off the edge of her bed. As she unbuttoned her dirty, cotton dress the memory of Rolf's hands grappling her breasts and tugging at her shirt flashed in her mind. She fell back onto her bed, pulled the blanket back over her bareness and desperately tried to get her erratic breathing under control.

There was a light knock at the door, she wasn't prepared, or ready, she wiped her face, but the tears wouldn't stop.

'Ada?' A soft voice called out.

The door slowly opened, and Otto entered the room.

'Are you okay?' He asked as he approached her bedside, leaning down to her.

'I…I'm okay,' Ada stuttered.

'How bad is it?'

He looked concerned, but she didn't want him to see her like this. He rose to shut the door, before coming back to her side.

'Let me see.'

She let him ease her to a seated position before he pushed the blanket down over her arms, it was soft yet the sensitivity to touch was painful, and she winced. He studied the damage, tight-lipped and serious. Ada was embarrassed, but as she tried to look away, she could have sworn that he had stolen a quick glance at her chest, her heart fluttered.

'Oh, Ada,' he whispered, 'I'm so sorry.'

She looked up at him tearfully, and he placed a reassuring hand on her cheek, his touch felt nice, and she leaned into it, and he smiled at her.

'Can you pass me that blouse on the edge of the bed, please?' She asked timidly.

He did so, and respectfully turned away as Ada slid out of her dress, pulled on the blouse, and fastened the buttons before quickly grabbing a crumpled black skirt off the floor and tugged it on, fighting to get it over her stomach.

'Thank you,' she gasped, as she finally secured the fastening on the skirt. Otto turned back towards her, giving her a small smile.

'I came to see how you were doing. But clearly, you're not doing so well.'

'I'll be fine. I can handle it,' she replied hastily.

Otto nodded at her and headed back towards the door.

'Otto.'

He paused and looked at her again.

'Thank you.'

He faced her, stepping towards her he took her hands lightly, his touch was warm, and it spread up her wrists, she shivered but not because she was cold. He was closer to her now and she could smell his musk, she closed her eyes as she breathed him in, and felt her whole body let itself go as she felt his lips brush against her forehead. She looked up at him and met his intense gaze, he brushed her hair away from her face and leaned his face in close to hers, she held her breath as she tilted her face, and finally, their lips came together.

His kiss was so light at first, then firmer, he placed his hand on the back of her neck pulling Ada closer to him. Ada returned his kiss with fervour, she wanted to savour every bit of him. Her stomach was on fire with desire. Otto's mouth feverishly explored hers, his tongue slipped in, causing her to moan with longing. It was over too quickly, and Otto pulled her away gently, accidentally holding a bruised part of her arm, but the pain was nothing compared to the yearning that was overwhelming her.

'Ada,' Otto whispered against her hair.

Liselotte just couldn't understand, despite his beliefs, this man wanted to protect her, he respected her, he wanted her, and for Ada, that was all that mattered.

***

Stuttgart, August 1932

For weeks their relationship was nothing more than stolen moments of passion. Otto would nibble hard on her lip, it wasn't something she particularly enjoyed but he was passionate, and he was expressing that on her, and that alone made her feel excited. She breathlessly pulled away from him as she smoothed her hair down, Otto was doing the same, laughing lightly.

'Ada Stein, you are incredible,' he chuckled.

'You're not so bad yourself, Otto Neumann,' she purred.

Otto tucked his shirt back into his trousers, smiling up at Ada with desire. She both loved and hated when he looked at her that way, everything inside her melted but she couldn't have him fully much to her frustration.

'Ada, please? I want you,' Otto begged.

'I can't,' Ada whined, 'not until I'm married.'

'Oh, you don't know what you're missing,' he teased as he started kissing her neck, weakening her inhibitions even further.

'Hey, you may have sinned,' Ada teased, 'but I want to do this properly, my love.'

'My love?' Otto raised his eyebrows in surprise.

Ada flushed bright red.

'I... I mean...'

'Your cheeks give you away all the time,' he laughed.

'Eugh, I know,' Ada sighed, burying her face in her hands.

But Otto's hands were there prying them away from her face so that all she could do was look upon him.

'There's something so special about you, Ada Stein.'

'But?' She asked as panic rose in her throat, she had said it too early, he didn't feel the same way, how could she have been so stupid?

'But nothing. I love you.'

'W...what?' She stammered.

'Is that so hard to believe?' He chuckled as he kissed her softly.

Ada felt like a light had been lit inside her, and everything had faded into insignificance.

'We need to tell them,' Ada gasped as she leaned into his shoulder.

'Your brother is going to kill me.'

'I won't let him, I promise.'

Otto pressed his forehead against hers, just as her parents did in their own stolen moments and she felt so certain of him and for the first time in her life, completely secure.

***

Otto wasn't wrong, Ernst had been furious when they told him. He went to swing a punch at Otto and had only been saved when Günther had intervened. Oddly, it had been Walther of all people who had swayed their feelings.

'A well-bred German man through and through, what more could you want for her? She'll never get anyone better than him.'

Gisela had been delighted from the start. After the news had broken, she hugged Ada tightly. Ada was too shocked initially to return the embrace, her arms had stayed glued to her side, before awkwardly placing them around her mother's waist.

'I am so proud of you, Ada.'

Ada felt a lump rise in her throat. 'Thank you, Mütter,' she said. Finally, she had given her parents something to be proud of her for at long last.

But then her mother said something which put her on edge.

'Be careful not to move things along too quickly.'

Gisela affectionately squeezed Ada's shoulders, but hard enough to heed a sense of warning too. But she was so secure, so loved, Ada questioned what could possibly be wrong with that.

Otto proposed two months later. Ada accepted without a moment's hesitation.

***

Stuttgart, December 1932

Liselotte flew into a rage when Ada told her about her engagement. She didn't speak to her for nearly two weeks, until finally, Ada saw the ribbon in Liselotte's window.

Ada waited nervously outside of the bakery. She didn't know what to expect, but she knew she couldn't lose her.

As soon as they saw each other they embraced, clinging tightly to each other as if their lives depended on it.

'I'm still mad at you, you know,' Liselotte mumbled into Ada's ear.

'I know.'

'But if anyone can change someone like him, you can.'

'Thank you, Lise.'

They stood in the warmth of the bakery for a long time, away from the bitter winter chill.

'They made von Schleicher chancellor,' Liselotte said, 'he thinks the Nazis are on their way out!'

'Believe me, I heard,' Ada harrumphed.

Ernst and Otto had come back seething that evening, so much so that Ernst had thrown a plate at the wall showering the floor in shards of pottery.

'The choice is so obvious!' He thundered.

'We are not down and out brother. We recruit more people every day. Von Schleicher has no support anyway, he will be defeated,' Otto had stated with unwavering confidence.

Ernst had stormed out of the room slamming the doors behind him. Otto had gone to follow him, and when Ada placed a comforting hand on his arm to console him, he shrugged her affection off immediately followed by a glaring stare that rendered her motionless. It was at that moment that Günther entered the household, proudly showing off his papers to say that he had officially joined the Nazi Party.

***

Stuttgart, January 1933

The following month brought about even more change. There was strong speculation that von Schleicher was already on his way out, and it was now inevitable that Hitler would be given the role of chancellor of Germany. The thought made Ada feel sick to her stomach, but she couldn't show that, she knew the consequences of defiance all too well, especially now as she prepared for her nuptials.

Otto had been distant with her in the last month with all of the rapid political changes, his mood seemed to change with them, when he was happy, he was the charming protective man she loved, but his dark moods were extreme, threatening, scary.

But he too sensed that a big change was coming, and he wanted the month to be highly commemorated for it. He had announced unbeknownst to the family and even Ada herself that they would wed that month. At first, she had been so excited, she longed to be with him and get out of her home. But as the day drew nearer, she couldn't escape the feeling that Liselotte was right and that she hadn't heeded her mother's warning. It had all moved so quickly, and they barely had any time to prepare for it. The guests would just be Ada's family, Liselotte's parents, Thomas, and of course Liselotte, and Otto's cousin who lived in one of the towns not too far away from the main city, Otto never said which one. It was only then that she realised that she knew barely anything about his family.

It was 30th January 1933, and Ada was being fastened into Gisela's old wedding gown, it was too tight on her curves. Gisela had clearly had a much more slender waist than she did at her age.

The dress had long sleeves which felt like they would cut off her circulation, the neckline covered her entire chest up to her neck, and the bow in the middle at least went some way in covering her stomach which was poking out more than ever under the restraining fabric, the rest of the skirt flowed down to her feet. She was touched by the sentiment, but she felt frumpy, but more than that she felt so ill-prepared for what lay ahead.

'You're all grown up,' Gisela said triumphantly as she forcefully secured the last button.

If grown up feels like trying to catch your breath all the time. Then sure. I'm definitely grown up.

'Thank you, Mütter,' Ada wheezed.

There was a small knock at the door and Liselotte stood in the doorway wearing a light pink small puff-sleeved gown that cascaded down to her feet. Her hair had been rolled into little ringlets that lay beautifully on the sides of her face. Ada felt a flash of envy for her best friend's beauty when she felt far from beautiful, and far from being a bride. Liselotte was frowning, not even a twitch of a smile crossed her face. Ada knew her objections, but she could at least pretend to be happy for her.

'Let me go and help Ernst bring the car around,' Gisela announced.

The borrowing of the car had been a gesture on behalf of the Nazi Party in recognition of all of Otto's hard work. When he had announced this, Ada had wanted the ground to swallow her up and she hadn't escaped that feeling since.

'Okay Mütter,' Ada replied, trying to smile.

'It's just nerves, Ada, it will be okay,' she reassured.

Ada smiled tightly, dropping it as soon as her mother left the room.

Liselotte crossed over to her, extending her arms and drawing her into a light hug, before starting to arrange the flowers in Ada's hair.

'Smile,' Ada said gently.

'Tell yourself that,' Liselotte replied.

Her friend held her at arm's length, Liselotte's frown was now a scowl, something was very wrong.

'You should know now before we go,' her voice was solemn and emotionless, 'President Hindenburg has just announced *him* as chancellor.'

'No, please no!' Ada pleaded.

'I'm so sorry to tell you this now, but you needed to know,' Liselotte said.

But they couldn't be seen worrying about it now. Liselotte carried Ada's train as she descended the stairs. Her father stood by the front door, dutifully extending his arm for Ada to take as he led them out towards the car, a fresh wave of nausea hit Ada as they sat down and started the short journey to the church.

They sat in silence for most of the way there, until the church started to come into view. Ada felt the grasp of her father's hand on hers, he looked at her intensely.

'You make me proud my girl.' It sounded like a command rather than a sentiment.

I try all the time. Why have you only noticed now?

'I will, Father,' she replied.

The rest of the ceremony had been a blur, she had focused so hard on making sure that she planted her feet firmly on the ground, her husband-to-be at the altar beamed the biggest smile she had ever seen. She wanted to believe that it was for her, but she knew even then that marrying her was not his biggest joy on that day.

PHILIPP

Berlin, June 1928

June brought an end to Professor Bergmann's classes. It was very bittersweet for Philipp, the lessons had been life-changing for him, his passions had truly been ignited and his medical knowledge and experience had grown exponentially. With the progress he had demonstrated he was sure he would get a glowing recommendation, at long last he could see the pieces falling into place for his future. It filled him with an unrelenting optimism, a feeling of invincibility that nobody was going to stand in his way.

Celine came by most evenings to work on their applications for schools. It was easier to outline each other's strengths so that they could get it down on paper.

'Philipp, if you are not going to say all the good things about yourself, then who is?'

He sighed, he didn't mind her being right, but it made her smug.

'You're saying nothing because you haven't got an argument to come back with,' she taunted.

Philipp chuckled, he removed the cushion from behind his back and lightly threw it across the room hitting Celine in the face, skewing her glasses.

'Hey!' She laughed.

'You will have to deal with patients flailing around all the time when you're a doctor, you have to get used to these things,' Philipp teased.

'So will you! Anyway, my patients will be impeccable, and listen to all of my advice, any troublesome ones I'll just refer to you.'

'Clearly, I'm more up for the challenge.' Philipp smirked.

**

Berlin, August 1928

Eight weeks went by agonisingly slowly as they waited and waited. Even though the applications had been sent off, Celine still came around regularly, which Philipp attributed to her nerves.

The middle of the month had seen the temperatures rise dramatically, making shifting heavy furniture and re-arranging the cabinets unbearably exhausting work. With more time available due to no classes, Philipp dutifully carried out more responsibilities in the shop. Johann's words from all those months ago still twisted in the pit of his stomach, and with full-time studies and medical school on the horizon, he didn't want to leave his family on bitter terms.

'Philipp! The crystal tumblers go in the cabinet closest to the door, not in the middle!'

Johann was still as bossy as ever, Philipp couldn't fault him for being responsible: his ability to register and organise the stock was impeccable, and his customer service skills were charismatic and welcoming. He was just like their father. He was doing an amazing job, and Philipp was proud of him, but he could never bring himself around to tell him.

Philipp pulled a handkerchief out of his pocket and wiped the pouring sweat off his face, he was too tired to argue with his brother today.

'Sorry Johann,' he said earnestly.

'That's okay, just make sure you change them over, oh and wear the gloves so you don't get marks all over them.'

It was as good as he was going to get in terms of an olive branch, which he willingly accepted.

'Sure. I'll go back to the house quickly and get a jug of water.'

'That would be great, thank you.'

Philipp carefully reassembled the tumblers and swiftly left the shop. The sun was directly overhead and blazing down on the street below, somehow it felt hotter outside than being cooped up indoors.

He walked the short distance briskly, not caring if it made him sweat more to get out of the sun. Philipp quickly filled a jug full of water, grabbed two glasses off the shelf, and made his way back to the shop. When he returned, he saw that the door had been propped open, usually Johann would only open the windows on days like today, since he argued that it looked more professional that way, even though they were almost unable to stand in the imprisoning heat. Philipp wondered whether it had more to do with the handful of vandalisms that had taken place. He was suddenly reminded of his aunt Liesl's words from years before, and a disconcerted feeling pricked his conscience.

Curious as to what had changed his brother's mind, he stepped into the shop trying to avoid spilling the water anywhere near the stock, when he was met with a sight that shocked him to his core.

Celine had been coming around earlier and earlier lately, her father was a brilliant man, a mind as sharp and as intelligent as his daughter's, but that meant that they butted heads frequently, and she needed to put space between them. At least that was what she had told Philipp, and it was what Philipp had believed. But there she was standing in the middle of the empty store, held tightly in Johann's embrace, their lips pressed together, eyes closed, and lost in the magic of the moment. All Philipp could do was stand aghast, his jaw dropped, he felt hurt, angered, and betrayed.

Celine was the first to open her eyes, catching sight of Philipp's horrified stares she hastily pulled away from Johann. She opened and closed her mouth a few times before a small gasp left her throat. Johann turned to speak, but there was no way he was going to get the first word in.

'What the hell?' Philipp yelled.

'Shhh Philipp keep your voice down!' Johann pleaded.

'Keep *my* voice down?' Philipp continued, 'Why is *this* happening?' he shouted, gesturing wildly with his arm.

'Philipp. We're sorry, we didn't want you to find out this way,' Johann stated with way too much confidence, he sounded more proud than sorry, which only added to Philipp's burning rage.

'Find out? Were you ever going to tell me?' He shouted, directly addressing Celine. Her lip quivered as she stared at the floor. A part of him was glad that she understood how costly her betrayal was. His closest friend, the neutral figurehead he could talk frankly to, the only one who truly understood and shared his ambitions. But what really stung was that he was now second to his brother, yet again.

'Don't speak to her like that!' Johann barked.

'*You* don't get to say anything right now!' Philipp hissed. 'Why do you feel the need to ruin everything in my life?'

'Philipp, I get that Celine is your friend, but I'm sorry, things between us, they just happened! I can't help how I feel about her.'

He placed a protective arm around Celine's waist drawing her in close to him, she looked up at him, giving him a small smile. But their display only enraged Philipp further.

'I've put up with so much of your crap over the years Johann. And I've lived in your shadow, you the perfect son, the eldest, the one who will take over this proud family business, your father's son through and through. You hate me and my dreams, and now you have to take away my friends too!'

'And you,' he glared at Celine, 'I trusted you; I confided in you, you know how much grief he causes me! Yet you wanted him all this time? You were my friend, Celine, I thought we understood each other.'

'I'm still your friend Philipp!' Celine cried out.

'No. Friends don't do this to each other.'

She started to cry, and that's when he noticed that she had been holding a letter in her hand. Philipp angrily strode towards the door.

'I got into Leipzig,' he heard Celine mutter.

'Well, that's just great,' Philipp sighed.

He could hear her sobbing even after he had walked out of the shop. He was halfway down the street when a firm hand dragged him to the floor.

'You're a real piece of work Philipp,' Johann growled, staring down at him from a height.

'Go fuck yourself, Johann,' Philipp spat as he rose to his feet.

'What do you want from me Philipp?'

'To disappear.'

'It's a good job Mother didn't stick around to see what you've become.'

'Our Mother is dead Johann, get that into your head.'

'She's only dead because of you!'

And there it was, the unspoken suspicion, the taboo, that they had held against each other their whole lives. Philipp couldn't fully recall the moments that followed, it was almost as if his brain consciously blacked out because the next thing he saw was Celine screaming and crying uncontrollably. He felt his father's huge hands hauling him away. Ahead was a blurred scene; Johann lay limp in the middle of the street and there were patches of red spotted all over his face.

Philipp glanced down at his own hands as his vision slowly came back into focus, there was a hot pain searing up his hand and into his wrist, something was horribly broken he knew that much, but it was the vast amounts of blood that was concerning him the most, and that he couldn't tell how much of it was his and how much of it was his brother's.

***

Berlin, September 1928

Weeks continued to drag by, and still, Philipp heard nothing from medical schools. His heart was heavy, and he felt completely crushed.

Johann had been holed up in recovery the entire time. Multiple cheek fractures, a broken nose, and jaw had left him unable to speak and eat, and in a great deal of pain. Philipp hadn't spoken a word to Johann, his father, or Celine who had been by nearly every day to tend to Johann and help get fluids and watery soup down his throat.

His hand was set in a splint, with broken knuckles, and a broken wrist, but this hadn't stopped Felix from working him hard. He knew this was his penance, and he carried out his orders in furious silence. Felix had had to return to oversee the running of the shop, away from his client meetings, and auctions, and they had lost business as a result.

This silence continued for two weeks, until one day when Philipp was struggling to unload fine china plates one-handed, Felix was organising order forms at his desk, he raised his large, bearded face from his work and finally spoke.

'Are you ready to talk about it?'

'No,' he replied sternly.

'Well, I am,' Felix replied.

Felix rose from his desk, placed the closed sign in the window, and locked the door. His large frame sauntered over to Philipp, easily engulfing his smaller stature.

'Sit down,' he ordered. Philipp obliged.

For a moment they stared at each other in stand-off. But it wasn't in anger, it was almost as if they were trying to rediscover each other.

'What makes you think you have the right to raise your hands against another human in that way? And not just any human, your brother! Your flesh and blood!'

'I don't,' Philipp sighed, defeated.

'So, explain to me why Johann has been rendered speechless by your actions?'

'I can't,' Philipp inhaled deeply, the tears that had been repressed for a while were finally welling up, the exhaustive toll finally showing.

His father wasn't angry which made it worse, he looked confused and deeply saddened. He was looking at him in a way that confirmed what Johann had said, that he was a piece of work, someone he didn't recognise anymore.

'You have to believe me when I say I don't know what came over me.'

'Philipp...'

'No! I know it's not an excuse, but I just can't explain it!'

'What did he say to you, son?'

Felix's question floored him. 'Say to me? I was mad about him and Celine, that they didn't tell me, that he has to interfere with everything in my life.'

Felix put his hand up to shush him, even after all these years it was still effective.

'I know all of that,' he said gently, 'I'm asking you, what did he say to you?'

Philipp swallowed as the first hot tears streamed down his cheeks.

'He told me that it was my fault that Mother died.'

Felix reeled, tears sprung to his eyes, he cleared his throat, before moving around to pull Philipp into his warm embrace, to absorb his son's sobs that were now cascading out. Philipp felt like a little boy all over again, it's what he deserved after his actions, but it felt oddly comforting, letting all of his brokenness out next to the man he loved and admired the most.

'What happened to your mother was awful,' Felix began.

'It was my birth that killed her.'

'No one could have foreseen what was going to happen, son.'

'But it doesn't change the fact that because of me she died.'

'She loved you, more than you will ever know! Even though our hearts were shattered, they were also full because of your arrival. Do you have any idea how much of a blessing you are? You were not the end of a chapter, but the start of a new beginning.'

Philipp mulled over his father's words, trying his best to believe them and ignore his doubts.

'Can I go and get some air?' He asked.

'If that's what the doctor thinks is best,' Felix winked.

Philipp grabbed his jacket, carefully pulling it over his tender hand, exited the shop, and started walking. He had no route planned, he placed one foot in front of the other as he tried to collect his thoughts. He walked at pace for at least half an hour before he looked up and realised that he was walking in the direction of the school building. There was a thin figure, with a large white bushy beard, standing against the charcoal grey stone.

Philipp slowly approached until he was within earshot of the old man.

'Professor Bergmann?' He asked.

The man startled before smiling brightly at him when he recognised who he was.

'Philipp Blau! How are you doing boy?'

'As well as can be,' Philipp replied.

'Any news on medical schools?' Bergmann asked curiously.

Philipp shook his head.

The smile dropped from Bergmann's face. 'It simply isn't fair,' he sighed.

'Professor?' Philipp enquired, confused as to what he meant.

Bergmann extended a long bony finger and gestured to Philipp to follow him closely.

'Let's take a walk,' he whispered.

Philipp obliged, curious as to what Professor Bergmann knew. The lack of response from his applications was breaking his heart, if Bergmann could shed some light on the situation, he would at least be a step closer to understanding.

They walked back in the opposite direction at a brisk pace, Philipp was impressed at how sprightly Professor Bergmann was in his senior years. For a while they said nothing, Philipp noticed many eyes watching them suspiciously from a distance. When they finally stopped, they had walked at least a mile, maybe further, and Philipp was becoming impatient.

'Professor, what's going on?'

Bergmann looked at him solemnly, almost sorrowful in his demeanour.

'Things in Germany are changing, and not for the good, I fear. People like you are going to find life incredibly difficult. I hope and pray there will be a day that you will be recognised for the brilliant doctor you are destined to be. People can't see past their hatred and fear, Philipp.'

'People like me, Professor?'

Bergmann's eyes glanced down the street, Philipp's eyes followed, the synagogue was in view. Aunt Liesl's warning started ringing in his head.

'I had hoped that I would run into you at some point, Philipp,' Bergmann admitted.

'I submitted my highest recommendation of you to your chosen medical schools.' His words faded as he looked sadly up at Philipp. 'I want you to hold onto this,' he said, as he pulled a brown envelope out of his coat pocket. 'One day I hope it will help you achieve your dream. I'm just sorry that it can't be now.'

Philipp took the letter from his hand, quickly placing it in his jacket pocket, he could feel the hairs on the back of his neck standing on end.

'Thank you, Professor Bergmann,' he whispered, extending his good hand towards him for a handshake. Bergmann grasped it firmly, and leaned in close, he whispered hurriedly.

'Get out while you can, Philipp. Be careful, and good luck my boy.'

Professor Bergmann quickly turned away, and within seconds he was gone.

With Bergmann's words firmly etched in his mind, and the uncertainty he felt stirring in the pit of his stomach, he rushed back home as fast as he could. When he reached the front door, he burst through it and made straight for the stairs, unlocking the door to Johann's room. Celine was at his bedside, rising in shock as Philipp entered, Philipp put his hands up as a sign of peace, and she nodded at him.

Johann's entire face was bruised and swollen, the rush of guilt that Philipp felt almost made him turn away, but he had to do this. Johann was weary but awake, he groaned in discomfort as he turned to face Philipp.

'I'm so sorry!' Philipp cried, as tears gushed out. 'Please forgive me!'

Johann grunted; his swollen eye darted to his bedside.

'He wants to write something,' Celine muttered.

'Thank you,' Philipp said gently.

Celine looked up at him and smiled, Philipp returned it warmly. He picked up the paper and pen and handed them to Johann who started scrawling out a note, when he was done, he pressed the note firmly into Philipp's hand.

I'm so sorry. I love you.

Philipp gasped in relief, tears ran down his cheeks, and he could see tears forming in the corners of his brother's eyes too. Philipp reached out with his good hand and Johann gripped it tightly as the brothers began to heal their bond.

***

Berlin, September 1933

'Where is he?' Celine cried as she flew through the shop door.

'Hey, slow down!' Philipp cautioned as he ran over to her. 'Why aren't you in Leipzig?'

'Where's Johann, Philipp?'

'He's off sick, he told us not to disturb him.'

She burst into tears in front of him, a small crowd of people had gathered outside the shop and were trying to get a peek at the commotion, thankfully they couldn't see much under the paint that now covered the front window.

'Come this way,' Philipp whispered, ushering her through to the middle room, away from prying eyes.

'Celine you can't be here,' Philipp said, despair gripping his voice.

'They can't tell me what to do!' Celine asserted as she gasped for air between sobs.

'That's technically true, but there's too much at stake.'

Celine started to shake as she continued to weep. Philipp put his arms around her.

'He wrote to me,' she whispered against his chest.

'He ended the relationship, didn't he?'

'He said he didn't love me anymore, that he had a new girl.'

'He's lying, you know that he loves you.'

'Then why would he say those things?'

'Celine. Look around. It's for your own safety that you don't come around here anymore. He's protecting you.'

She looked around, taking in the emptiness of the shop, the star, the writing on the door, and the snooping presence outside.

'I can't accept this, Philipp. You can't not be in my life.'

He took her face in his hands. 'I know. But this is how it must be.'

She threw her arms around his neck, holding him tightly.

'He can't bear to say goodbye to you this way. You need to know that. He loves you, and so do I.'

Celine glanced up at him and kissed his cheek softly.

'Don't ever give up,' she commanded.

'Yes boss,' he replied.

***

Berlin, 15th September 1935

- Jews are German 'subjects', not citizens.
- Jews lose the right to citizenship, the right to vote, the right to hold government office, and hold German passports.
- Jews must wear a yellow star patch on their clothes so that they can be recognised.
- Jews are forbidden from having sexual relations with German citizens.
- Jews are not permitted to marry German citizens.

***

Berlin, November 1935

They came in the night. Philipp was shocked awake to the sound of the door being knocked off its hinges, and taunts being yelled up the stairs. He sprung up out of bed running towards the sound, almost colliding with Johann and Felix on the way. Felix stepped between them both.

'Father, what's going on?' Philipp asked.

'Hide,' Felix ordered.

'I'm sorry, what?' Johann demanded, 'We're men, Father.'

'You are my sons, and I am ordering you to hide.'

'What about you?' Philipp pleaded.

'Trust me, let me handle this, now go.'

The brothers watched as their father descended the stairs, before helping each other crawl into the small attic space, where they crouched together in the corner and held onto each other for dear life.

Philipp shivered against Johann, as daylight crept through the window. Johann shook him gently stirring him from his sleep.

'It's dawn Philipp,' he whispered.

They untangled themselves from each other, manoeuvred out of the cramped space, and started to frantically search for their father.

'Is he in his room?' Johann called out.

'No! Is he in the kitchen?'

'No!'

They rushed back to the remnants of the front door which lay in pieces at their feet, the cold bitter wind made them shiver all over.

'He never came home, did he?' Philipp asked, looking to his older brother for reassurance. Johann could only manage a worried glance back in return.

They grabbed their coats and hurried outside. They split up and searched opposite ends of the street. Philipp looked left and right, down every alleyway, his father was a big man, he would be easy to spot, but there was no sign of him anywhere. They had heard no words spoken between Felix and the aggressors, they didn't know if they were in imminent danger, they didn't know where they had taken Felix, they didn't even know if he was still alive.

After what felt like an eternity, Philipp finally heard a distant call.

'Philipp! I've found him!'

Thank God. Philipp prayed as he charged back down the street.

When he saw them, he nearly collapsed in disbelief. His brother struggled under the hunched form of their father, he dashed towards them, hauling up his father's other arm over his shoulder and together they pulled him into the house, summoning every ounce of strength they had to get him into bed.

'Go and make him some coffee, he's as cold as ice,' Johann

ordered.

'Of course!' Philipp replied.

He brewed it as quickly as possible, there were precious grounds left. The boycotts meant that there was no longer any business, and no money coming in. He carried the warm mug upstairs and placed it in his father's bruised hands. Felix winced as the warmth ignited the sensitive spots.

'Shhhh, get some rest Father,' Johann said quietly.

They both waited at his side until the sounds of Felix's snores echoed off the walls. Johann looked up at Philipp and together they left the room, quietly shutting the door behind them.

'There's grass in his beard.' Johann said.

'Grass? Where would they have taken him?'

Johann couldn't look him in the eye, 'I've heard rumours,' he began, 'where they round Jews up in the middle of the night. They take them to fields and order them to cut the grass... with their teeth.'

'Meine Güte! He can't hide us forever, Johann.' Philipp gasped.

'It will be me next time. I will not let him go,' Johann said determinedly.

'Johann, no! They can't get you too! We need to get out! We all need to go!'

'And go where Philipp? They'll track us, and these fucking things make us stand out just a bit!' Johann barked, angrily gesturing at the patch on his shirt.

'We have to try! What's the other option? Let them destroy us?'

'I don't know Philipp, but we need to stay together.'

***

RACHEL WELLAND

Berlin, November 1938

They would remember it as the night of broken glass. There was some sort of poetic beauty in that name. It was anything but. Philipp had sat in the attic space all night with his father and brother, hands placed firmly over his ears as the rest of their home was ransacked. He could hear smashing in the distance, which he knew in his heart was coming from the shop. People were screaming, embers of flames drifted up to the windows from the street below, and the cold made the smell of the burning crisper, assaulting their senses.

He was angry and scared, many a time he had tried to convince Felix and Johann to run away with him. But they refused.

When the height of the violence finally subsided, on a still winter's night, Philipp silently picked up his packed bag, placed his unpicked patches on his bedside, and rose from his bed for the last time. He placed a note under his father's door and one under Johann's. He had quietly cried every moment he could be alone to prepare himself for what he was about to do. But now he physically couldn't cry anymore, as he planned to make the exit as quiet as possible. He nudged the broken door open wide enough to squeeze through and slipped out into the night. He stared straight ahead and fought every temptation not to turn around and go back.

ETIENNE

Avignon, June 1915

When he finally stirred from his morphine-induced slumber, his mother and aunt were arguing once again, but this time they were screaming at each other.

'He could have *died!'*

'But he didn't Camille, I told him to stay here! He went against what I said, it is not my fault that he broke the rules!'

'Don't you *dare* blame him for this! This is entirely your fault! On the *one* day I couldn't go! You couldn't just do a simple favour to help someone else out for once in your life!'

'I let you in when you had nowhere else to go!'

'If we had never come here, Etienne would still be able to walk.'

The yelling was bombarding his senses, his head felt fuzzy and extremely heavy as he tried to lift it to peer down at his injuries. He was lying flat out on his bed, back in his aunt's house, the strange Parisian art pieces were blurry and moving around in strange shapes as his eyes fought to readjust to the surroundings. The room smelt strange, a mix of mustiness, plasters, and chemicals, the combination of which made Etienne feel sick.

When he gathered enough strength to hold his head in position, he caught a glimpse of the bandage that was hiding a large amount of the bruising which felt more sensitive as the painkillers started to wear off. His whole leg was secured in a splint, he shuffled to test his mobility which he regretted immediately as a fresh shot of pain fired up from his shin, blazed all over his leg, and nestled in his hip. He whimpered loudly and his mother was by him in a flash.

'Etienne! Ma pêche! Oh, ma pêche!' She cried out.

'Maman, I'm sorry.'

'Shhhh my darling, it's okay!'

'I shouldn't have gone by myself. The boy needed my help!' Etienne blurted before dissolving into tears.

His mother's face was against his, her hot tears merging with his as she ran her fingers through his hair.

'You don't need to explain ma pêche, it's all going to be okay,' she said, trying to reassure him as best as she could.

'It hurts, Maman,' Etienne moaned.

'I know my darling, I know.'

He had missed Pierre since the day he left, but at that moment, Etienne missed his father more than anything. Also, he was scared, because he seemed to have been the only one who noticed that despite the heavy bandaging, a small jut remained near his left calf, and the intensity of the pain had not subsided in his hip.

***

Avignon, November 1918

Now aged fourteen, he had grown substantially but so very painfully. Etienne retrieved the walking cane that was still far too big for him and manoeuvred his way out of bed. His hip throbbed horribly as it always did first thing in the morning, and he eased his way towards the upstairs landing window that overlooked the river.

Across the city, there had been jubilation at the announcement of the war's end. People left their homes with no fear, and the streets were once again filled with people singing and dancing excitedly as they celebrated victory and eagerly awaited the return of loved ones. Trumpeters had convened at the edge of the river every evening to resound in joyous song, and even though it was bitterly cold outside, the sound of splashes and yelps of enjoyment rang out from the banks once again. Despite the comfort that was felt in the return of normality, something still felt tainted and violated. There was a strange guilt attached to people's efforts to start again.

Both his aunt's and his mother's bedroom doors were open, they must be downstairs in the parlour, Etienne thought, but strangely, there was no arguing. Etienne wobbled awkwardly on the stick as he hobbled towards the staircase, he leaned heavily on the banister as he eased his way down step by step. It had been over three years, but he still struggled with his mobility, and the stiffness and aching in his joints was almost unbearable.

As he got closer to the parlour he could hear quiet voices, but this time there was a male voice with them. His uncle had sent news that he was returning to Paris before convening with Georgette in Avignon, but he wasn't due for at least another two weeks. Even though the voices were hushed, they sounded animated. Etienne curiously peered around the doorway, his aunt stood by the sink in her long silk robe, a mug of precious coffee cradled in her hands, and a small smile etched on her face. His mother was desperately clinging onto the hands of a thin, dishevelled man, her eyes wide with relief, a huge grin plastered to her face as if she was trying to make up for the lack of smiling, from years of frowning.

He saw the shaggy dark hair, a hint of the furrowed brow, and the way he was gently caressing his mother's hands under her tight grip.

'Papa?'

The man turned immediately to the sound of his voice, and Etienne stumbled back knocking into the cupboard behind him. It was his father, but his beard was patchy, his hair long and unruly, and deep cuts decorated his cheeks and split his lip. His cheeks were severely drawn, and the outline of his skull was impossible to ignore. His eyes weren't sitting right, his left eye leaned more to the left, his right eye more central, they weren't even shadows under his eyes, they looked more like huge purple bruises that had been robbing him of sleep for years.

'Etienne, my boy is that you?' He wheezed.

Etienne looked up at his mother, she smiled reassuringly at him gesturing to him to come closer. He limped towards the shell of his father. Pierre clattered out of his chair to meet him in the middle of the room, they both caught each other as they fell into each other's arms.

'You have grown so much my boy!' Pierre did his best to muster a smile, but it was tinged with an unmistakable sadness.

He knew his father was delighted to see him, but when Pierre caught sight of his leg, Etienne all of a sudden felt ashamed. So many of the city's finest men had lost their lives, and the bright buzz of the city was dimmer as a result. Etienne had seen with own eyes men returning to their loved ones after four unimaginable years, haunted for a lifetime. It should be his turn to look after his father, but Etienne felt like he was the liability.

'Papa, I'm so sorry,' he said.

***

The weeks following Pierre's return were extremely difficult. No one knew how to react around him. He insisted that he was fine and would snap if anyone questioned him. He had set to work immediately creating a better suited walking cane for Etienne and had demanded that Georgette pull strings and arrange to have the best chestnut delivered to craft it. He had measured his disjointed leg with the utmost care. A project like this would have taken him no time at all, but Etienne couldn't be sure if it was because he wanted to take care of his first woodwork project since coming home, or because of the slight tremor in his hand that he tried to hide.

'Thank you, Papa,' he said hugging his father tightly, now able to reach around his shoulders. But when Etienne released him, Pierre ruffled his hair before promptly walking off and locking himself away. He barely said a word to anyone. Etienne wondered whether it was because he didn't want to, or whether he couldn't.

But the finished project had been perfect, he could walk with much more balance in his steps, and as a result, he held his head a little bit higher. Etienne's features were more angular now, he was broodingly handsome. His sharp cheekbones jutted out against his thin face, his hair was long and dark like his father's and swept over neatly on the left side of his face. His eyes were narrowed and perceptive, a brilliant blue just like his mother's, and he now had a hint of stubble forming on his chin. A few girls had noticed him at school, and not in the way people usually did when they taunted his habits, but he could only go as far as noticing their attention. Other boys his age were fawning over girls, their early desires overwhelming their senses and actions, Etienne thought they were all ridiculous.

'What about that lovely girl, Josephine?' His aunt said wistfully. 'She's got those adorable freckles, beautiful golden curls, and that dashing smile is meant for you, my sweet!'

Etienne knew at least six boys who would have wanted nothing more than to hear those very words spoken to them. Josephine was pretty in a conventional sense he supposed, but the only thing that stood out to Etienne about her was the loud grinding of her teeth in the middle of class, which always set him on edge.

'I don't think so, tante Georgette,' Etienne said.

'Aww, well one day someone will capture your heart, my sweet.' She said, squeezing his hand in encouragement.

'He's fourteen, Georgette!' Camille exclaimed.

'You weren't a great deal older when you married, dear sister,' Georgette teased.

Camille smiled warmly at her sister; the first time Etienne had seen her do that in the entire time they had been living there.

His father emerged from the kitchen, his face was finally clean-shaven, Etienne felt relieved, it was another small step back to reality. But Pierre looked uneasy and out of place. Etienne watched as his father drew in a deep breath and levelled his stance; something was bothering him.

'I want to return to our home,' Pierre declared.

Camille and Georgette's heads snapped up in surprise.

'It's empty, Pierre,' Camille said gently.

'Well, we need to fill it again!' Pierre exclaimed.

'There's no money, ma chère. It all went on repairs. The materials…'

Pierre put his hand up to silence her.

'We need to move back, Camille.'

She rose to be close to him, Etienne saw his father hesitate as his mother approached him but softened when she affectionately laced her hands behind his head.

'I want that too, more than anything, but we just can't, not right now.'

Pierre looked at Camille in a way that Etienne had never seen before. He looked like a wounded animal, betrayed by his pack. He shook himself out of Camille's embrace, stormed over to the other side of the room and slumped into a chair, burying his face in his hands.

The subsequent days followed a similar pattern of dead-end arguments, all with the same outcome. Between school and his beloved violin lessons, Etienne found himself playing cards with his aunt in the drawing room. The sound of his aunt's aimless waffling was much more pleasurable to listen to than his parents' repetitious rantings.

***

Avignon, January 1919

Ringing in the New Year was a quiet affair for the joint Beaufort/Touelle household. Large-scale parties could be heard across the city to serenade new beginnings for a new France. Georgette had frequently expressed her desire to celebrate in Paris, but at long last her husband François had returned, who had insisted that it was paramount that the family remained together; and despite the endless drama, Etienne was grateful for some extra cheerful company.

On New Year's Day, he was once again sat in the drawing room with his aunt as she puffed away on her fancy cigarette, one just like Madame Lavigne's from years before. Pierre and Camille had gone out for a walk to try and settle another heated argument. Etienne and Georgette had been intensely focused on their game when François quietly entered the room, Etienne jumped at his sudden presence.

His uncle was much older than his aunt, he had a thick moustache that was turned up neatly at the edges, his receding hairline sported only a thin covering of golden-brown hair, and he was stout, but not fat. He had been heavily involved in the war, but not in the same capacity as Pierre. François had returned immaculately dressed in the finest tailored suit, adorned with his fancy pocket watch dangling from its designated pocket. He had a twinkle in his eye which suited his charms, Etienne could see why his aunt was so enamoured with him.

'I've heard a great deal about you, young Etienne,' he said fondly.

'All good things my sweet, I promise you!' Georgette quickly added.

'Tell me, Etienne, have you ever met your grandparents?' François inquired.

'No, sir.'

'That is a shame. He's a good man your grandfather. He let me marry his wonderful daughter for one thing,' he said glancing down affectionately at Georgette who swayed with a girlish glee. 'He also cares deeply about you, my boy,' he stated, turning his attention back to Etienne.

'But he's never met me?' Etienne replied confused.

'You are family nonetheless my boy, and that carries a lot of importance.'

Etienne nodded, feigning understanding of what his uncle meant.

'You are fourteen years of age now, I believe?'

'Fifteen this year, sir.'

'Practically a man.'

Etienne glanced down shyly.

'As a man Etienne, you will have to learn to handle a lot of responsibilities.'

'Yes, sir,' Etienne agreed.

'Before returning to my beautiful wife, I met with your grandparents in Paris. Your grandfather believes you are ready for such a responsibility.'

'What kind of responsibility?' Etienne asked.

'Financial.'

Etienne gulped. Money was to be used wisely, and to have lots of it was evil, at least that's what he had overheard from his mother.

François brandished an envelope from his inside pocket and handed it to Etienne. Etienne took it in both hands, scrutinising the fancy looped scrawl of his name on the front. He carefully peeled the wax seal on the back and opened the letter. Enclosed was a note that Etienne read through diligently.

Dearest Etienne,

It is difficult to know where to begin. I will start by formally introducing myself, my name is Antoine Duplantier, and your dearest mother Camille is my daughter, making you my beloved grandson.

We cannot begin to express our relief that you are all safe.

It is hard to believe how quickly the years have passed, and how grown up you are. Our darling Camille remains close to our hearts. We miss you all so dearly.

Who was 'we'? His grandmother? More aunts and uncles that he knew nothing about? His grandfather's words overflowed with affection, but it was difficult to see how this could be genuine when they had never met, that they disapproved of his mother and father's marriage, and as a direct result of that, his very existence. Etienne continued to read.

We are greatly gladdened to hear that you have been reunited with Georgette, and in times as uncertain as these, it is necessary that you all stay together.

I am aware that the arrival of this letter will come as somewhat of a shock to you, and you must have many questions. I fear that our dear Camille has not been forthcoming with information about your wider family. Your mother is an extraordinary woman, headstrong, determined, and compassionate. Without her permission, I did not want to indulge in details that she would see as unwanted. But now that you are now a young man, I have no issue in asking permission to tell you about your family. It would please me greatly to keep in regular contact with you Etienne, the address to which to send your correspondence can be found at the bottom of this letter.

As a young man, you will start making decisions for yourself, and some of these decisions are not to be made lightly, they will have far-reaching consequences, therefore you need to consider them carefully and choose wisely. I have come to one such decision.

Your mother would never allow me to make such a gesture, therefore I am entrusting this to you, my dear grandson. Along with this letter is an enclosed cheque that I have addressed to you, for you to invest in your future. I trust that you have a good head on your shoulders and that you will make us proud with your decision.

With love,

Antoine Duplantier

Etienne sat back in his chair, awash with mixed feelings. He was flattered that people of high esteem would consider him mature and wise enough for such big decisions, but equally, he was puzzled, and couldn't escape the feeling that this was some kind of test. There was clearly a reason why his mother had spent so long trying to distance herself from her close family, to lead a life completely different from the one she grew up in. Etienne trusted her completely, so why would she give him any reason to doubt her now?

He tucked the letter behind the accompanying piece of paper and shot up in shock at the sight before him, his hip fired up in pain at the jolt, and he buckled over as his aunt rushed to his side to settle him.

He had never seen so much money in his life.

'There must be some mistake, Uncle François!' He gasped, still reeling from the pain.

'No mistake my boy. Now what you do with it is your sole responsibility. Do you understand?'

For the first time today, he did.

***

Etienne lay wide awake in bed that night, he waited patiently until he was sure that Camille was fast asleep. He knew that his father would be awake, sat in the main living room, and would stay up until the early hours of the morning before falling into a heavy slumber by the fireplace. Etienne fumbled around in the dark desperately trying to muffle the click of his cane on the floor as he sneaked out of his room and down to the living room.

Pierre's patchy beard was growing in again, and his hair had grown even longer, his eyes still looked burdened and heavy, and Etienne's heart sank at the sight of his sorry state.

'Papa,' he whispered.

Pierre grunted as he stirred from his sleep.

'Etienne? Are you okay?' He croaked.

Etienne placed the letter into his father's hands. Pierre squinted in the low light to read, reeling as he got towards the end. His fist clenched, and Etienne swept in to remove the letter from him, folding it up neatly. Even though he knew that the contact with his grandparents would not be well received by his parents, and he couldn't hope for them to understand, but this was important to him. He wanted to help, and this was the best way he knew how.

'Home. The shop. Don't tell Maman.' Etienne said with confidence he did not know he had.

ADA

Stuttgart, January 1933

Everything went wrong right from the start.

It was late by the time they had gotten into their new apartment after the wedding. Ada was exhausted and overwhelmed, she wanted time to process everything that had happened, but at the same time, she needed to sleep.

She wandered into the bedroom, where she found the bed neatly made up and her belongings placed in the corner of the room. She knew that Gisela and Liselotte were planning to do this together, mainly because she had begged Liselotte to find hiding places for her precious language book.

Ada threw her arms behind her back and feverishly wrestled with the buttons on her dress, simply so that she could breathe properly for the first time that day.

'Whoa! Steady there,' Otto slurred as he slipped into the room, 'isn't it me who should be doing that?'

Ada giggled but suddenly felt panicked. She had wanted him in this way for so long, but so much had changed, and now that she was here, she didn't know what to think or expect.

Otto spun her around so that her back was facing him, she had to steady herself. He fumbled with the buttons, and Ada prayed silently that he wouldn't damage her mother's dress, he was incredibly drunk and unpredictable which always set her on edge. She wanted to be with the man who made her feel protected and secure, that was when she was on fire for him.

Otto's voice was harsh and his breath was hot in her ear.

'You belong to me now, Frau Neumann.'

This was normal, right? This is just flirting.

He was being rougher with the buttons, she felt his impatience and agitation, and before she could try and calm him there was a loud ripping noise and she drew in a sharp breath as Otto tore the dress from seam to seam, buttons showering the floor.

'Otto!' She gasped.

He turned her to face him, pushed the remaining material off her shoulders and let it tumble to the floor.

'You can fix it darling, that's what good housewives do.' His tone was still harsh, and Ada shuddered.

Otto stepped towards her, swiftly unhooked her bra, and yanked her underwear down, he was still fully clothed. He started to study her carefully, his eyes passed over her disdainfully, he said nothing as he led her to the bed. Ada lay on her back and watched as Otto began to remove his shirt and tie, she felt a small flutter arise in her stomach as his bare muscular torso was displayed in front of her. She propped herself up on her elbow and extended her hand towards him, keen to run her hand over his chest and up through his hair.

Instead, Otto directed her hand down to his belt, Ada obliged, she sat up, undid the buckle, and pulled the belt out along the top of his trousers. Otto lowered her back down onto the bed, more gently this time and Ada felt a little more at ease. He quickly undid the clasp and drew the zipper down; his trousers and underwear came down in joint succession. Ada barely had time to admire him before he was on top of her. She took in a sharp breath, she knew he was experienced, but he also knew this was her first time, he had to go easy on her.

He stared at her intensely, Ada arched her back up to get closer to him. Otto leaned down, kissing her firmly on the mouth, all force and no feeling. She felt his teeth graze along her jaw, moving down and exploring her collarbone, she shifted uncomfortably at the sharpness of the pain. His hands moved up the length of her body coaxing her arms above her head, as he tightened his grip on her wrists.

'Otto?' Ada whispered as her wrists started to cramp under the pressure.

'Shhhh,' Otto hushed.

His erection was hard against her leg, the sensation surprised her, and she felt a fresh wave of nerves flood her stomach. She didn't want to do this, not tonight, not when Otto was so drunk and rough. Any excitement she had felt had waned completely, she could feel Otto pushing her legs open, and she tensed. The loosening of his hands on her wrists was a welcome relief, but only briefly as he guided himself inside her and she felt a sharp tear. The dryness made it so much worse, and tears sprang to her eyes as she muffled her cries. Otto had either not heard or mistaken it for pleasure as he continued to thrust harder and deeper, Ada tensed with each beat, each one more uncomfortable than the last. She closed her eyes and willed it to be over, until at long last Otto filled her with his satisfaction, groaning loudly as he did so.

He pulled out of her quickly, rolled onto his back, breathing heavily, he lightly brushed Ada's arm, the only affection he had shown her the entire time. Ada lay awake for a long time, feeling completely exposed, silent tears ran down her cheeks. Everything hurt as she delicately drew her legs back together. She wondered what she had entered into; it was a matter bigger than she had ever anticipated, and she was terrified.

***

The following morning Ada had made sure to wake up before her husband. She scrambled around on the floor grabbing the precious buttons. She had just collected them all when she heard Otto stir and saw him swing his legs over the side of the bed. He paced around the corner colliding hard into Ada's side knocking the wind out of her. 'Get out of the fucking way, Ada!' he grunted, stepping over her and out of the room.

Ada stared up in horror at her husband, who didn't even hesitate, he never glanced back. She had done well to hold onto every button as she fought to catch her breath as pain resonated all the way up her ribs. Who was Otto? Who was this man that she had married?

Ada briefly pushed her thoughts to the back of her mind as she hurried over to her dressing table and deposited the buttons into a small drawer before turning her attention to the torn remains of her mother's dress on the floor, her warning ringing loudly in her ears.

Be careful not to move things along too quickly.

But how could she not when they were the proudest they had ever been of her? She gulped hard to hold back the tears that were forming, which wasn't helped by the state of the dress making her sick with worry.

That's what good housewives do.

Cooking and cleaning were no issue, her mother had taught her well. But sewing, God knows she had tried but she just couldn't do it. Her fingers were too clumsy, she didn't have the patience for the finer details. She knew she would have to hide the dress away until she could figure out what to do with it. Something that she couldn't help but feel was going to be a regular pattern in her life.

***

Stuttgart, March 1933

Ada hoped that things would improve, but eventually, she couldn't tell which was worse, day or night. When it wasn't rough and painful sex, it was brutal and demeaning beatings. Otto's care, passion, and patience no longer existed. She initially blamed the

Party for influencing his behaviour, but now she questioned everything. Why had she married someone that she barely knew?

When the Party wanted Otto to come back and take on more responsibilities, Ada was glad to see him go. Promotion and recruitment demands had increased dramatically since Hitler's appointment as Chancellor, and Otto had been called upon to lead campaigns in Stuttgart. Ada knew what he meant by 'campaigns' of course, if he wasn't brutalising her then he was brutalising someone else. The more successful the 'campaign', the more gleeful he would be when he returned home.

He left early in the mornings so Ada could pretend that she was asleep long enough for him to leave. She would get up and go straight to the bathroom and start applying powder to the worst-looking marks. She had never been interested in make-up, but now it was a necessity, and Otto preferred her all made-up, it was one less way to aggravate him.

It was a beautiful spring day and Ada decided to visit her family and Liselotte. Their apartment was only a fifteen-minute walk away. Despite the sunshine, there was still a slight chill in the air, so she grabbed her coat, grateful for the secrets she could hide underneath it. She breathed in the fresh air with huge relief, she had barely left the house since the wedding, and only then it was to get groceries. Ada plodded along slowly down the eerily quiet streets until she had gotten past the apartment blocks and headed towards the main part of the city. The dark beams of the houses stood out prominently in the morning sunshine as they framed the high rise of the clock tower of the town hall looming in the distance. Eventually, she turned onto the familiar corner, spotting the tall, run-down, yet domineering building, with its menacing edges.

She gently knocked on the fragile door frame, Gisela answered almost immediately taking Ada by surprise.

'Ada?' She asked, looking confused by her appearance.

'Hello, Mütter.'

Ada stepped inside; the living room was in disarray. Books were strewn all over the floor and several smashed mugs led an incriminating trail back to Ernst who was snoring loudly in the chair still dressed in his uniform. Her grandfather was sitting in the adjoining chair, he craned his crooked neck up to glare at her.

'What are you doing back here? Otto already bored of you?' He snarled.

'Just thought I would pay you all a visit,' Ada replied as brightly as she could through gritted teeth.

'Coffee?' Gisela asked.

'Ja, danke schön.'

Gisela ushered her into the kitchen holding Ada's shoulder which ached uncomfortably, she tried not to wince, but she failed, and Gisela saw.

'What's wrong?' She asked, eyeing her with suspicion.

'I...I... just lifted something heavy the other day. It's not quite healed yet.'

'Otto should lift those things, Ada.'

'I know, but he's been so busy lately, I didn't want to bother him,' her deceitful blush threatened to give her away.

It was certainly a more satisfactory tale, rather than the real one that involved being slammed into a wall and the accompanying fall resulting in Ada's shoulder popping out of place, all during one of Otto's drunken rages. Mercifully, it went back into place, but two weeks later it still ached horribly.

'Rough night?' Ada asked, changing the topic quickly.

Gisela peered over at Ernst who was still fast asleep.

'They have been doing reviews of every institution you can think of,' she said in a hushed voice. 'He was mad when he found so many didn't match the Party's requirements,' directing her eyes towards the littered books, 'make sure you sort through yours.'

'They aren't in power yet.'

'It won't be long, Ada.'

She knew that her mother was right, but it did nothing to halt the wave of nausea that had her running to the bathroom in haste before vomiting profusely.

When she finally lifted her head from the bowl, she was embarrassed to see a family audience all looking down on her with a mix of concern, annoyance, and disgust.

'Did Otto put a baby in you *already?*' Walther sneered as he slumped back down the stairs, Ernst followed him closely, leaving Gisela standing in the doorway white as a sheet.

'Ada, when did you last bleed?' She asked.

'A few weeks ago, I think? I can't be pregnant, not this early,' she said, but not confidently enough to disguise the terrifying doubt that her grandfather had planted in her mind. She stayed for a further awkward hour where not a single word was uttered between them.

By midday Ada was restless. She hastily bid her family goodbye and tried to run the short journey to the Krause household, but the pangs of nausea had her stopping to take deep breaths until it subsided. When she finally reached the house she rapped vigorously on the door and was greeted with the beaming smile of Clara Krause.

'Precious Ada!' She squealed with delight. 'Liselotte! Ada's here!'

Liselotte bolted down the stairs, her loose, silky blonde hair flowing wildly behind her, she hadn't had a chance to braid it yet, and she launched herself into Ada's arms squeezing her tightly. The pain in Ada's shoulder was pounding but she pushed through it, squeezing Liselotte back as hard as she could.

'Well, hello there stranger!' Liselotte teased.

There were leftover buns from the bakery on the table and they were all soon tucking into them, talking and laughing as if not a single day had passed since they had last seen each other. Clara excused herself to start washing clothes, leaving Ada and Liselotte to properly get caught up.

'I've missed this so much,' Ada sighed.

'Me too Ada, why don't you come round more often?'

'Things are… busy,' Ada muttered, nervously scratching at her hand.

'So, Frau Neumann, I want details of married life.'

'It's interesting,' she said, trying to smile.

'I know it can't be easy with his ties to *them.*' Liselotte said taking Ada's hand in hers, tears welled in Ada's eyes.

'Hey, what's wrong?'

'Nothing. It's just hard as you say, and I miss you so much,' Ada sniffed.

Before she allowed the tears to flow, she once again hastily changed the subject.

'So, what about you and Thomas? Are things good between you two?'

'Yeah, things are great,' Liselotte smiled, 'we've talked about getting engaged.'

'That's wonderful Lise! You two will be a wonderful married couple.'

Ada knew they would have a beautiful marriage, but she couldn't help the pang of envy and sorrow that struck her hard in the pit of her stomach.

'I love him, Ada, so much.'

'I know you do,' Ada smiled warmly.

'We tell each other everything, we have no secrets, when we're together it's like a fire that I can't control.'

'Disgusting,' Ada winked at Liselotte.

'You know what I mean!'

I thought I did once.

'Sure,' Ada smiled.

Liselotte pulled her into a tight hug again, Ada let out an exasperated breath this time.

'Oh sorry! Too tight?'

'No, never too tight.'

'Please come around more often, I miss you.'

This time Ada let one solo tear roll down her cheek.

***

The dark clouds had rolled in by the time Ada left the Krause household, the rain hammered down on her as she ran as fast as her short legs would carry her. She slipped on the smooth concrete paving slabs as she neared the apartment complex, her make-up had all run off and her marks were visible again. She fumbled with her keys as she tried to pluck them out of her pocket. But then to her shock, the door opened, and there Otto stood with a look of fury on his face, he grabbed her by the hair and dragged her inside.

'Otto, please! You're hurting me! Stop!' Ada protested.

'Where the *hell* have you been?' He screamed.

'I… I… went to see my family,' Ada whined.

'Your place is *here*!'

'I need to see them from time to time, Otto.'

He threw her away from his body, she turned around to face him,

146

and he struck her hard across the cheek.

'Give me your keys,' he growled.

Shaking violently, she dropped the keys out of her hand into Otto's.

'If you want to go out from now on, you need to ask my permission, and then you can have these.'

Ada whimpered but managed to nod.

'By the way, I have sorted out the books, you are to throw the ones in the bag away,' he ordered.

***

Stuttgart, May 1933

Liselotte was coming around that day. The first time that she was going to visit the apartment, Otto hadn't said anything about other people coming around to the house.

An enthusiastic knock at the door signalled her arrival, Ada hastily made sure her make-up was in place before answering, desperately trying to repress the nausea that was still running rampant in her stomach.

'Hello stranger,' Liselotte beamed.

'Hey Lise,' Ada beamed back, embracing her tightly.

The two of them sat together drinking coffee, sharing the excitement of Liselotte's engagement which was now official as of the previous week.

'So, I was thinking lavender in the bouquet.'

'Such a beautiful smelling flower, and such a lovely colour. I think it will be perfect.'

'Obviously, you will be my maid of honour.'

Ada swallowed. 'Of course! But I will need to talk about it with Otto.'

Liselotte looked at her confused. 'He will be invited Ada… he is your husband.'

'Oh, I know, but I will still need to discuss it with him.'

Liselotte laughed, 'Ada. You and I are like sisters, you have to be there.'

'And I will be! I promise! Forget I said anything.'

'Okay, you had me worried.'

Ada hoped she had done enough to convince her.

'Speaking of weddings Lise…'

'Go on?'

'I need your help with something.'

'Sure, anything!'

Ada led Liselotte to the bedroom, wandered over to the dressing table and retrieved the buttons.

'Are they the ones from your mother's dress?' Liselotte asked peering over Ada's shoulder.

Ada nodded and placed the buttons into Liselotte's hands. Ada proceeded to walk over to the wardrobe, and she retrieved the torn dress from the box that she had stored in the corner.

'Woah! Looks like you and Otto went a little crazy,' Liselotte teased.

'Something like that,' Ada sighed.

'What happened Ada?' Liselotte inquired.

'Nothing. Don't worry. I have the sewing supplies, I know we won't be able to fix this all today, but you're so much better at this than me, can you help?'

'Well sure, but Ada this is really damaged, it will take a while.'

Ada couldn't hold it back any longer, not in front of Liselotte, and she crumpled onto the floor sobbing.

'My dear Ada, you have to tell me what's going on!'

Liselotte rubbed her friends' arms in comfort, shifting the material of Ada's blouse, to reveal a long pattern of fresh bruises that painted Ada's upper arm.

'Oh, Ada! Shit. He did this, didn't he?'

Ada nodded.

'Ada, I'm going to kill him! How could he do this to you?'

'Lise, you can't.'

'Ada, there's a way out of this, we'll work something out.'

'Lise…'

'You can leave him, people will understand.'

'Lise…'

'You can come and live with me and Thomas when we're married!'

'*Lise!*'

Liselotte fell silent.

'I'm pregnant.'

'Ada… that's…'

'A nightmare. But also, a miracle.'

'When did you find out?'

'I've suspected for a while. But Lise, it's my baby, I have to do the best for him or her.'

Liselotte sniffled, 'I know. You're going to be a wonderful mother, Ada. But *him* a *father*?'

They protectively huddled together as they had done so many times, Liselotte delicately stroked Ada's hair before she spoke softly.

'I can't believe my godson or goddaughter is in there,' she grinned, gently placing her hand on Ada's tiny, but noticeable bump.

'That's rather presumptuous of you,' Ada winked, 'But I can't believe it either.'

They spent the rest of the afternoon trying to reconstruct the dress, their conversation focused on the wedding, it was the best distraction, for both of them. Their bliss was interrupted by the turning of the key in the door signalling Otto's early arrival. Ada grabbed the dress and stuffed it back in the box throwing it into a cupboard before he came in.

Otto entered the room calmly, approached Ada, and gave her a swift kiss on her cheek.

'Hello, my darling,' he purred.

'Hello, my love,' Ada replied.

'Liselotte, it is lovely to see you again.'

'You too Otto,' Liselotte said tightly.

Ada nudged her leg underneath the table.

'Busy day, Otto?' Liselotte asked, more sweetly this time.

'Always, much work to do and for the good of the country, wouldn't you agree?'

Ada knew he was taunting her, hoping Liselotte would bite, but to her relief and gratitude, Liselotte held firm.

'Of course,' Liselotte smiled.

Otto smirked, placing a hand on Ada's shoulder causing her to flinch slightly. Liselotte continued.

'Me and Thomas are engaged. We would love to have you both at the wedding, with Ada as my maid of honour.'

She was bold, Ada wished she had half as much of Liselotte's bravery.

'We would be honoured to be there Liselotte, congratulations to you both,' Otto said sweetly, increasing the pressure of his squeeze on Ada's shoulder.

'That would be wonderful. Anyway, I must be leaving, I will come and visit again soon.'

'We would love to see you.'

'Can I give Ada a hug goodbye?'

'Of course,' Otto said, releasing his hold on Ada.

As they embraced, Liselotte leaned close to Ada's ear.

'Stay strong, I will come back for you I promise, I love you.'

They released each other, and Liselotte slowly headed to the door, flashing a final concerned glance at Ada before the door shut behind her.

Otto switched the second the latch clicked. He grabbed a book off the shelf and hurled it towards Ada's head, she ducked in time before it hit the wall.

'You have the *audacity* to go behind my back yet again!'

'Otto, please!'

'And with that bitch? She stands against everything we are trying to build, Ada! Why can't you see that?'

'Otto, she's my best friend!'

'She's poison, Ada!'

'But if she's here more then maybe you can change her mind?'

'Shut your mouth!' He yelled as he raised his hand to slap her.

'Otto, please! Not the baby!'

His hand froze mid-air, and the colour drained from his face.

'Baby?'

PHILIPP

Berlin, November 1938

Even when he would look back on all he had to endure, the first night he walked away would always be the toughest. Now that *they* were running the country, they didn't bother to hide in the shadows anymore, their presence plagued each street, carrying their intense darkness wherever they went.

Philipp tugged up the collar of his coat as much as he could to shroud his face and stuck close to the buildings, and against his instincts, dived down every single dark alleyway. He headed southwest of the city but knew that there was no way that he would be able to escape the city that night. Tired, and freezing cold, the bitter wind made Philipp's eyes feel heavy as he pressed ahead. He walked on determinedly until he could see a slither of light break through the black skyline, he had walked all night just as he had planned. With the Nazis seemingly hunting them in their own homes at night and targeting them in public in the light of day, he hoped that they wouldn't suspect one of them to be on the move. He had already taken a huge risk by leaving his star at home. If anyone asked for identification he would surely be found out, getting caught simply wasn't an option.

He could just about make out a park down the street, the open scenery would at least provide a better perspective from which to check out his options. His feet were refusing to obey him as he mustered all his strength to try and drag one in front of the other the last couple of yards. Luckily, he was greeted with the sight of a bench as soon as he entered the perimeter of the park, where he slumped down heavily, rubbing his eyes trying to revive energy back into them. He had been so focused on getting as far away as quickly as possible, that he hadn't had a single moment to reflect on what exactly he was doing. His father and Johann would be waking up in just a few hours and would find him missing, he prayed that they found the notes that he had left. When he was sure that he was completely alone, he let himself cry.

Daylight was streaming through the bare twisted branches of the trees by the time he awoke. How long had he been there? He couldn't allow himself to fall asleep and in such a public place.

Stupid Philipp!

He frantically looked left and right, it must have still been early, the park appeared deserted. But then a voice from behind him made him leap up in terror.

'You're on the run, aren't you?'

Philipp scurried back, tripped over his feet and fell flat on his back. He crawled backwards trying to get away until his hand enclosed over a branch, he grabbed it and thrust it in front of him.

'Stay away!' Philipp shouted.

The figure edged closer, his hands in the air as if in surrender.

'Whoa! Easy, easy! And stop that shouting, you never know who could be watching.'

Adrenaline was pumping hard through Philipp's veins; he rose to his feet still extending the branch out ahead of him.

'Who are you?' Philipp demanded.

A small, thin man with wispy hazel hair came into view. He didn't look much older than Philipp, but his cheeks were deeply sunken.

Malnutrition

'My name is Max. I'm trying to get out of here too, and judging by the fact that your eyes are red from crying, you look completely exhausted and scared out of your skin, I think I am right in my assumption, yes?'

Philipp hated Max's perceptiveness, if anyone wished him ill and had an eye as good as Max's he would be doomed, and it only increased his terror.

'Why are you running away?' Philipp asked suspiciously.

'Because I dare to believe in the exact opposite of what those fuckers believe.'

Philipp couldn't see a Star of David patch or an area where one would have been. So, what had he meant by opposite beliefs? Philipp thought back on all that had happened since the Nazis had come into power, whom they had targeted, and 'proved' a threat to society. And then it came to him, he remembered the Reichstag fire five years ago, and the hatred that it had unleashed.

'You're a communist?'

'Aren't you a discerning one?' Max chuckled, 'What's your crime?'

'My entire people are responsible for the downfall of this country apparently; our beliefs seem to sicken those 'fuckers',' Philipp replied with as much wit as he could muster.

'You're Jewish,' Max stated, with a tone of pity in his voice that annoyed Philipp more than it eased him.

'Where's your star?' Max asked.

'I got rid of it.'

'Are you trying to get yourself killed?'

'It's no better than having it displayed for all to see.'

'But… your papers?'

'I'll figure something out.' Philipp asserted with as much confidence as he could fake.

Perceptive as he was, Max didn't see through this one.

'You're shivering. Have you been out here all night?'

'I travel at night.'

'You must be freezing, tired, hungry?'

Philipp didn't need to respond; his growling stomach did the job perfectly for him.

'Come with me,' Max gestured.

If he didn't look so beaten down, Philipp would never have trusted him, but exhaustion clouded his judgement, and they had been talking long enough that if Max was some kind of undercover Nazi, chances are that he would have been surrounded and arrested by now.

'My name is Philipp,' Philipp muttered.

'Pleased to make your acquaintance, not so pleased that it had to be under these circumstances.'

Philipp scooped up his bag over his shoulder and followed Max over the frosty ground. They walked in silence, both warily sticking to the shadowed parts of the street. Around twenty minutes later they reached a gated shabby-looking alleyway where Max paused.

'Max, there's nothing here?' Philipp said confused.

'Shut up and help me with this,' Max ordered.

He was on the floor pulling at the fence, Philipp crouched down to get a better look at it and saw that a line had been cut. He immediately started to help Max pull it open until there was a gap big enough for one of them to fit through. Max took the lead kicking aside the debris that was stacked against it. He threw his small satchel over the top before scrambling inside, gesturing to Philipp to hand him his bag. Philipp obliged and then squeezed himself inside catching the edge of his sleeve on a sharp piece of the wire whilst Max kept the gap pried open. They wandered around to the other side of the building where the high-rising chimneys and darkened steel frame indicated exactly where they were.

'Don't worry, it's been abandoned for years.'

'You're living in a factory?' Philipp asked, baffled at Max's unorthodox resourcefulness.

'It's shelter, for now.'

Max rapped five quick knocks on the door, before pausing and repeating it. They waited a minute before the heavy door squeaked open, revealing a small, grubby girl, with beautiful stony blue eyes, and a crooked nose, it looked like it had been broken several times. She stood aside to let them both in, warily staring at Philipp as he entered, he tried to smile at her reassuringly.

'You're late Max, we were getting worried,' she grumbled.

'I'm too smart for them Marta,' Max said smugly as he drew Marta into an embrace, lightly kissing the top of her head.

'Who is he?' Marta asked, directing her attention to Philipp.

'This is Philipp,' Max replied.

Philipp tried a half-hearted wave, he could feel warmth emanating from somewhere in the building and all he wanted to do was run towards it, away from Marta's judging eyes.

'Is he like us?' She asked.

She couldn't even question him directly; Philipp couldn't tell if it was out of rudeness or self-protection but sensing that this was his best opportunity for safety right now, he would play along.

157

'In a way,' Max chuckled, 'he was bold enough to rip his target off his chest.'

'Jewish, eh? I'm sorry for what's happening to your people.'

'Likewise,' Philipp replied earnestly.

'How long will you be staying with us Philipp?' Marta asked.

'Who is *us*?' Philipp inquired.

'There's five of us, me, Marta, Georg, Kurt, and Eva,' Max informed.

'And we're all waiting for you,' Marta crowed as she tugged impatiently on Max's hand.

'I would like to think it's because they missed me, but it's only because I have food,' Max laughed.

Philipp smiled as he followed Max and Marta in the direction of the enticing warmth, where he saw the others huddled close together under blankets around a wastepaper basket that contained a steady crackling fire.

'Max! Thank goodness!' One of the men called out, 'We thought we would waste away with the amount of time you were gone for.'

'Don't joke about those things, Kurt,' snapped the young woman seated next to him, she must have been Eva.

'Who's the new one?' The other man asked, he must have been Georg, he had a stern look which was obvious even through the thick hair on his face.

'I'm Philipp,' Philipp said tentatively.

'Who did you piss off to end up with the likes of us, Philipp?' He laughed.

'Who do you think, dumbkopf?' Kurt grunted.

'How long are you joining us for, Philipp?' Eva asked.

Philipp felt himself starting to relax, their acceptance was touching. It didn't matter why they were all there, or what they had done at that point. When under the hand of someone or something far worse, what makes people different can be the element that brings them together.

'Just tonight. Sorry, today,' Philipp corrected himself, they all laughed with him, and he stood a little taller.

'Where are you heading to?' Eva continued.

'I am meeting someone near Leipzig, and then I will head on to France.'

They all nodded along quietly; did they think he was crazy? But crazy had got him this far.

'Well, good luck to you Philipp, I think we could all do with a bit of your bravery,' Kurt commended.

'Or insanity?' Georg snorted.

'Okay, okay, enough of this interrogation guys, let's eat!' Max announced.

The group gathered around as Max emptied out two apples, a cabbage, and a small loaf of bread.

'A feast fit for kings Max! You've done well my friend,' Kurt declared.

Philipp wondered how long they had all been living here, depending on each other for survival, and with such meagre supplies. The three members of the huddled group disbanded to move closer to the food, and that was when Philipp noticed fresh blood on Eva's shirt.

'Eva, you're bleeding,' Philipp stated.

She looked confused and then looked down at her sleeve.

'Oh damn,' she cursed, 'I must have caught it on the fence when I came back from foraging yesterday.'

'Foraging?' Philipp asked.

'We like to call it that, instead of what it actually is, which is technically stealing,' Eva smiled.

'It's shit enough here; we try and make it sound like a challenge or adventure instead,' Georg said proudly.

'Can I take a look at it? If it's still fresh from yesterday, there's a risk it could get infected,' Philipp said.

'And you have the equipment to treat it, doctor?' Eva scoffed.

Philipp lowered his bag down and rummaged around until he picked out some bandages and large plasters.

'Where did you get those?' Max gasped.

'Before I was declared a non-human, I was trying to start training as a doctor. I may have taken a few souvenirs from some lessons.'

Philipp kneeled close to Eva's arm, he gently folded back the material that was already hanging loosely from her tiny arm. The blood had stuck the material securely to her skin, she flinched as he slowly tried to peel it away.

'I'm sorry Eva, I know this is uncomfortable.'

The gash was pretty nasty, it was still quite moist, but he couldn't see any noticeable signs of infection.

'It needs cleaning, but it's not infected. Does anyone have any alcohol?'

He looked up at a series of blank faces, before catching Marta deliberately averting her gaze. Max noticed it too.

'Marta?' Max asked.

She sighed, shrugging off his protective arm around her shoulder, and paced over to a shaded corner of the warehouse room, reached behind a pillar, and pulled out a half-full bottle of vodka.

'Fuck! Marta! Where did you get that?' Georg exclaimed.

'I…I was foraging the other night. One of them was just slumped over asleep in the corner, snoring away like the pig that he is.'

'Marta, are you crazy? We use the night to stay away from them, not rob them!' Kurt shouted.

'I know that! I'm not an idiot! I don't know why I did it, but I just wanted to take something from them, when they've already taken so much from us!'

'You could have been caught love,' Max said quietly, placing his arms around her, she buried her head into his chest, and he held her tight.

'I'm sorry,' she whimpered, 'I won't do it again.'

'You're damn right you won't, you risked exposing all of us!' Georg exploded.

'Enough, Georg!' Max threatened.

Georg grunted his displeasure, yanked off a cabbage leaf, shoved it into his mouth, and chewed loudly.

'Marta, may I?' Philipp asked tentatively.

Still pressed close into Max, Marta placed the bottle into Max's hand who promptly handed it over to Philipp.

Philipp's shirt was long so tearing off a piece of it was no issue, he doused the cloth in the alcohol and set to work cleaning the wound, placed the plaster on, and secured the bandage around it.

'The gash isn't too deep so you don't need stitches, it should heal on its own, but you will need to re-dress it. I'll leave a few more of these with you.'

'No! You will need them, what if something bad happens to you?' Eva protested.

'Then I will just make sure that that doesn't happen,' Philipp assured her.

***

Even after he had eaten, Philipp's stomach still growled as he lay down to rest. The group took it in turns to keep watch whilst the others slept, changing over every couple of hours.

He was awoken by soft shaking; he opened his eyes blearily to see Marta kneeling beside him.

'Philipp?' She whispered.

'Marta? Are you okay?'

'That was a kind thing you did for Eva, thank you.'

'It's no problem, but I don't think that's why you woke me up?'

'I… I just want you to know. The others, they ended up here because of me.'

'What do you mean?'

'They were all members of the KPD, I wasn't. I was just in love with one of them,' she looked affectionately over at Max who was sleeping soundly under a thin blanket.

'I wasn't a target, so those scumbags talked to me, at least I didn't think they were scumbags at the time. Max would tell me the location of his meetings; he knew I wouldn't tell a soul. Even though I don't agree with his politics, I still love him. I would go and meet him after the meetings a whole street over so that they wouldn't suspect anything. But I guess these ones had more brains than I gave them credit for. They followed me and put the pieces together, the meeting got stormed and so many were arrested, we were lucky to escape.'

'You can't blame yourself, Marta. Anyone could have given them away.'

'But look what we're reduced to!'

'But you're together, like a family, they stick together,' Philipp said, his voice catching at his last words.

'Where's your family, Philipp?' Marta asked.

'Somewhere not safe,' Philipp replied breathing in sharply.

He could see the realisation hit her as her eyes brimmed with tears, she placed her hand on his shoulder.

'I hope God brings you all back together someday,' she whispered.

'Me too,' Philipp replied.

He must have fallen into a deep sleep as the next thing he felt was another shake, rougher this time. Philipp awoke to see Max's face staring down at him. Dusk had fallen across the city signalling his time to leave. Philipp groggily pulled himself to his feet, and stretched out, every part of his body cramping from lying on the cold hard floor. He started to fold up his blanket and passed it back over to Max.

'No, you keep it. You already gave Eva the bandages. Besides you have a long journey ahead of you.'

'Danke, Max,' Philipp said warmly, extending his hand in gratitude, instead Max pulled him into a tight hug.

'Survive. That's how we'll win Philipp,' he whispered into his ear.

They drew back from each other, and Philipp clasped Max's arm firmly.

'Good luck to you, my friend. To all of you.'

Max helped him out through the fence, and without turning back, Philipp set off once again.

***

He did well over the next few days to avoid detection. Inspired by the group, he dipped into abandoned buildings to sleep in during daytime hours, there were many to choose from, so many hadn't recovered from the troubled years after the war.

The night air was so beautiful as the snow glittered in the starlight of Leipzig. Snowflakes hung in the air as if they were frozen in time. Philipp's visible breath guided him step by agonising step. He definitely had a torn tendon in his foot, the swelling and pain made it almost unbearable to put weight on it.

He wasn't far away now. He took a quick glance before stepping into an alley to check the location scribbled on the back of Bergmann's letter for what seemed like the millionth time.

Elias Schafer

Leipziger Stadtische Bibliotheken

Wilhelm-Leuschner-Platz 10-11, 04107

The public library of all places, it made him uneasy being so visible, but Professor Bergmann must have had his reasons for sending him here. Philipp hesitated as the library came into view, he hoped that people studying there had left by the time he arrived. It was a Thursday when the library stayed open late, the crucial time to go, at least that's what Bergmann's scrawled instructions said.

Philipp started to ascend the steps, each one taking immense effort. He was almost at the door when he heard a flurry of loud voices rounding the corner, he spun around and pressed himself against a pillar keeping his head down and pretended to furrow around in his bag.

'Got an entire family of them this time! The father got it good.'

'Made the filthy mother watch as I messed up the daughter!'

'It's what they deserve!'

Philipp suddenly didn't feel the cold so badly, the anger burned through his veins, and he fought every temptation not to launch himself at these animals. He obeyed his better judgement and remained rooted to his spot, not daring to breathe as their haunting laughs drifted away into the wind.

Confident that they were gone, Philipp pushed the heavy door open and started to look around. Elias Schafer: he must have been a friend of Professor Bergmann's, likely to be senior in his years, he must have been an important figure at the library for Bergmann to send him here. He felt exposed, and uneasy underneath the bright lights, he dragged his feet as quickly as possible to the stairs leading down to the library basement, it would be darker down there and it would give him time to think. In the coolness of the basement, his breath surrounded him.

An echoey voice rang around the deserted room.

'Can I help you, young man?'

Philipp spun around startled.

'Sorry, I didn't mean to scare you!'

He could have been Bergmann's twin by the impressive beard alone.

'Are you, Elias Schafer?'

'Who's asking?' The old man croaked.

'I... I'm a friend of Professor Bergmann's, he left your name and address on an important document of mine. I think he meant for me to be here?'

Sudden panic arose in his conviction, what if he had got this all wrong? The man had looked suspicious, what if he was contemplating reporting him? How would he explain himself?

The old man stumbled on his frail legs; his bushy eyebrows shot up in surprise.

'Good Lord! You made it!' He gasped.

'You know who I am?' Philipp breathed a sigh of relief.

'This way Herr Blau,' Elias whispered, gesturing him forward.

The two of them hurried along to a small office at the far end of the basement. Elias grabbed a gnarly-looking key from his pocket, glancing left and right before unlocking the door, pushed Philipp inside, and locked the door behind them.

A large bookshelf took up the entire width of the back wall which Elias strode towards and started to remove handfuls of books.

'Here, let me help sir,' Philipp said, placing his hands out for the books.

'No trouble my boy, no trouble.'

Finally, there was a hollow click and Elias removed the loose shelf, Philipp peered in and saw a stash of blank cards. Elias selected one and placed the shelf and books back as if nothing had been disturbed. Turning to his desk, he opened a drawer and selected an elaborate, artistic-looking pen.

'Do you have a photograph of yourself?'

'Pardon?'

'A photograph.'

'Sir, I don't understand, what is happening?' Philipp asked.

'You are leaving Germany, yes?'

Philipp's heart began to pound. 'How did you know?'

'Alfred Bergmann is a very astute man. He's been watching carefully, and he's seen what's been happening to your people, you are in grave danger.'

Philipp gulped, he had been right, but it did nothing to quell the terror he felt inside.

Elias continued, 'Alfred wrote to me about this amazing student, with so much promise, but your chances would be cruelly ripped away and you were going to have to do everything you need to do to survive.'

Philipp hung his head.

'I can help you.' Elias said gently, 'I know how to make a whole new identity for someone.'

'You're a forger?'

'I am a research associate, my boy! But I have interests on the side,' Elias remarked with a crafty smile.

Philipp had taken few precious items with him, but he allowed himself one sentimental item, a family photograph. He tentatively handed it over to Elias.

'This will do nicely,' he stated, as he sat down, carefully cutting Philipp's face out of the scene.

Philipp slumped down into an armchair in the corner of the office, its immediate comfort on his exhausted body caused his eyelids to droop.

'Rest Philipp, you will need your strength.'

'Won't people wonder where you are?' Philipp asked groggily as he fought to keep his eyes open long enough for Elias to respond.

'It's not unusual for me to camp out down here,' Elias smirked.

Finally, he closed his eyes and dreamed fitfully, flashes of his father, Johann, Max, and Marta raced through his mind.

When he awoke it was morning and Elias was sitting writing at his desk.

'I'm so sorry!' Philipp exclaimed.

'Nonsense my boy, Friday is a research day for me, so my schedule is clear. You stay as long as you need to.'

'Why are you helping me so much, Elias? You could get into

serious trouble for aiding Jews.'

'You think attitudes like theirs haven't poisoned this society before?'

Philipp stayed silent, looking intently at Elias for more information.

Elias' face was sombre, the charming twinkle vacant from his eyes. 'Frida Weber. My teenage love, she was so beautiful, vivacious, the love of my life. She was Jewish.'

'Was?' Philipp asked unnervingly.

'People in my neighbourhood didn't take too kindly to her and her family. They hated that we were together, they thought she had brainwashed me.' He took a shuddered breath before continuing. 'One night a group of boys, teenagers, slaughtered the whole family, but with my Frida, they took their time. She was found the next morning naked, beaten, and stabbed. There was so much blood.' Elias' hands were shaking, his eyes staring at the floor.

Philipp couldn't say anything; nausea churned in his stomach.

'I made a vow to myself to do whatever it took to stand up for those who were brutalised like she was.'

Philipp didn't notice the silent hot tears rolling down his cheeks, 'I'm truly sorry for your suffering, sir. I don't know how I can ever repay your kindness.'

'Think nothing of it. But once we part ways, we can never see each other again. It's for our own safety do you understand?' Elias said sternly.

Philipp nodded.

'Now I cannot give you a French identity, your accent is too thick. But I can give you a German citizen identity and pray that they will be lenient towards you.'

A German citizen's identity. The words stung harshly; he *was* a German citizen. Only short-sighted fools believed otherwise, but unfortunately, it was those fools who were in charge.

'Your name is now Edgar Meyer,' Elias stated, handing over the new identification card.

'Edgar Meyer,' Philipp repeated.

***

Strasbourg, January 1939

His hands were almost a blur in front of him as they shook violently. Snow was falling thick and fast, and he could barely see anything in front of him. He tugged his coat tight around him and felt the comforting crumple of papers in his inside pocket.

It had been weeks, and it was dark by the time he finally crossed the border. Only a small sprinkling of lights dotted the landscape which shone on a handful of shadowy silhouettes in the distance. He trudged slowly towards them, the wet snow seeped into the now remarkably thin soles of his boots that he hadn't taken off since leaving Berlin, He repeated the name over and over again through his chattering teeth.

'Edgar Meyer, Edgar Meyer, Edgar Meyer.'

'Excuse me, sir? Identification please.'

'Name?'

'Edgar Meyer,' Philipp said confidently.

'German?'

'What's your business here?'

'Work travel.'

'Whereabouts?'

'Bordeaux.'

The guards looked at each other suspiciously, turning their backs to confer.

'We have transport heading there, come this way.'

Something about their tone and glances wasn't right, but he had no choice but to follow. He allowed them to lead him to the station where several other guards boarded the train with him, and they set off. Philipp didn't dare fall asleep, not whilst the guards watched him closely.

He lost track of the number of train journeys, confused when they finally came to a stop seemingly in the middle of nowhere and he was hauled into various cars, always under guard. He felt sick to his stomach, but he couldn't run. They were past Bordeaux now, that much he knew. The final sign he remembered said Pau, and not long after passing it the commune came into view, Gurs.

ETIENNE

Avignon, April 1920

Etienne had done exactly what his grandfather had instructed him to do, invested. There was only ever one choice, and he would always choose to invest in his family. The money covered everything and more.

Pierre almost singlehandedly refurbished the entire shop and home; he was finally acting like his former self. Etienne smiled as he watched his father assess the wood even though he always knew exactly what was needed for each project. He could see the gleam return to his father's eyes as his hands glided over each piece, shaping, sanding, varnishing. He had new vigour and enthusiasm, and he was thriving.

Etienne was now his father's official assistant and the work flooded in. After the restoration work on the shop was complete, Pierre had wasted no time in training Etienne in carpentry, he was a natural, entrusted to work solo on commissions very quickly. His dependency on his cane prevented him from being able to work on larger projects. Etienne felt guilty for the extra demands it put on his father, but he never grumbled once.

Despite their success, Etienne was aware of the lingering feeling of loss across Avignon. Some citizens chose to leave for good, and others rarely left their houses again, unable to face society without their loved ones. Their neighbours, Monsieur, and Madame Auclair had left without even so much as a whisper. But the business expanded quickly, so much so that it infringed on their living space. Riddled with guilt, Pierre bought the Auclair property, which not only became more workspace but also became Etienne's home. Etienne liked the independence and the space, but guilt and loss haunted the property.

It had never been the same for his mother. There had been no fooling her, she knew exactly where the money had come from. For the first month back in their own home, she didn't speak a single word to Etienne or Pierre, instead spending more time in their small garden re-planting flowers. Etienne had tried to apologise, but he knew that it wasn't sincere, he was mad at her. This was what they all wanted; she should have been grateful.

***

Avignon, October 1938

As the years went by, he didn't stop corresponding with his grandfather. He did it secretly, of course, knowing he was betraying his mother's trust. His grandfather had invited him to Paris on many occasions, but the work demands made it impossible to go. Antoine provided useful business advice that Etienne implemented to great success, but he was demanding, domineering, and forceful in his opinions. It was clear that he had a vision of what Etienne's life *should* look like, and it made Etienne feel uncomfortable. One thing that he had been adamant about, was for Etienne to start courting with the intention to marry. His Aunt Georgette had taken on managing this task with overbearing enthusiasm, much to Etienne's dismay.

He now stood in front of the mirror adjusting his tie that was constantly skewing to the side, getting ready for the third date in two weeks. At thirty-four years of age, he looked incredibly distinguished; his hair was parted and swept neatly to the side, his face was long and sported a prominent chin, he now stood at over six foot. He sighed heavily, he didn't want to disappoint anyone, but this was one expectation he worried he could not fulfil.

All the ladies that his aunt had set him up with had been

interesting, pleasant, and pretty enough, but the romantic spark remained dormant inside him. Etienne took another resigned breath and felt a fresh wave of guilt wash over him in anticipation of letting this poor new girl down. A soft knock on his door distracted him, as his mother entered the room holding a small bouquet of fresh lavender that she had picked from the garden.

Lines of wrinkles lined her cheeks now, and her hair was tinged with a breathtaking glossy white. She had done enough worrying to last a lifetime and it had caught up with her, but if anything, her maturity made her look even more beautiful.

'For your lovely lady,' she said warmly, placing the bouquet in his hands.

'Thank you, Maman,' Etienne said tightly.

'What is it ma pêche?' Camille asked, patting the space next to her on the bed.

Etienne sat next to her, exhaling heavily, and placed his face in his hands, his mother rubbed his shoulders reassuringly.

'Your aunt does it because she's worried, Etienne.'

'I know, but she's not my mother, you are, and I don't see you getting so worried about this.'

Camille sighed. 'It's the proper thing to do my darling. I would love nothing more than to see you fall in love with a lovely young lady.'

'You and Papa were married at nineteen and twenty! I'm thirty-four, Maman.'

'Because it was the right time for us Etienne. Your time will come ma pêche.' She rose steadily, patted his knee, and left the room.

'I don't think that will happen, Maman.' Etienne whispered after her.

***

Light raindrops pattered soothingly against the window as Etienne twiddled his thumbs and fidgeted uncomfortably in his chair. Villiere's Bistro overlooked the river, and Etienne relaxed a little at the sight of the small swells in the river flow peeking into view every few seconds, the raindrops made its movement and shimmers even more enchanting.

Elise Cartier. The *lucky* lady he was dining with tonight, so everyone had said to him repeatedly. The elder daughter of Benoit Cartier, a high achieving banker in the city, with business associates located all over the country, including his grandfather. But he was desperately trying to restore his family reputation after his younger daughter Odette had eloped with a young farmer the previous year, according to Georgette's gossip. Maybe it would be best to avoid that avenue of conversation, Etienne thought. Any discussions of marriage would trigger anxious heart palpitations, and he would find himself formulating the most ridiculous excuses for him to escape. Fortunately, that had only happened once, and he hadn't seen the poor lady since.

Etienne muddled over some potential conversation starters in his mind. His grandfather and uncle were both high achievers in their respective businesses, which could be impressive. The Great War was always something that people reflected on, different experiences had shaped lives dramatically, but the loss was still so tough to comprehend. Plus, there were the heated, panicked conversations about activities taking place in the country next door. One thing that he felt marginally positive about was the fact that Elise was a rather good pianist, at least that is what he had been told.

'Bonsoir, Monsieur Touelle,' a lilted voice wafted over the sea of chatter in the crowded room.

'Bonsoir, Mademoiselle Cartier,' he replied rising in his seat to take her hand, knocking his knee clumsily on the table, making the glasses jump and jangle in unison.

Her chaperone, her younger brother, sighed heavily in irritation as he nodded towards Etienne before hastily leaving them.

Even amongst the heavy smoke in the air courtesy of the

customers sitting at the adjacent tables, Etienne could still see that Elise was absolutely gorgeous. Radiant ringlets of silken auburn hair framed her perfectly heart-shaped face, and her sparkling sapphire-like eyes dazzled in the slightly dimmed restaurant lighting. She wore a short-sleeved dress, which cinched in at her waist, and a large bow was attached. The skirt flowed just beyond her knees, and the outfit was completed with a pair of black court shoes with a small heel. She flashed him a stunning smile revealing perfectly straight teeth, her dimples giving her an air of innocence.

'Thank you for coming,' Etienne said pulling out her chair chivalrously, waiting for her to take her seat.

They sat in awkward silence for a moment, Etienne tried to keep his face relaxed as he repressed the shooting pain in his knee that had made his way up to his bad hip.

At long last Elise broke the silence.

'Are those for me?' She asked, her eyes diverted to the small bouquet of lavender still in Etienne's hand.

'Oh yes, of course!' Etienne grinned, handing them over to her.

'They're lovely, thank you,' she smiled.

'Homegrown,' Etienne said with pride.

'How... wholesome,' Elise replied, Etienne chose to ignore the disdain in her tone.

Further silence dominated the air between them until it fell to Elise once again to speak.

'So, your aunt is... enthusiastic.'

'Yes, she is,' Etienne sighed.

'She spoke very highly of you.'

'She is very kind.'

Elise smiled and nodded in agreement.

'Erm, so how well does your father know my grandfather?' Etienne asked, out of inclination more than interest.

'They have done business together in the past. My father always speaks so highly of Antoine Duplantier, you have quite the impressive family.'

Etienne smiled tightly.

'You must see him a lot, I imagine he has a lot to offer you and your business,' Elise said.

'My business? What exactly did my aunt tell you?' Etienne questioned, confused.

'That you run your own business here in the city? That your grandfather helped give you the funds to set it all up and it is rather successful.'

Omitting his father yet again. He was finally understanding why his mother harboured so much resentment for her side of the family. Pierre was a cornerstone in the community, the business that *he* had built had served and helped so many. It made no sense as to why they were so determined to eradicate his influence.

'Sorry Elise, I think my aunt has got it wrong. Yes, my grandfather gave us money to start up the business again after the war. It is my father's business; I have been his associate for nearly twenty years now. Charpentier Touelle, his workshop is in the old town.'

'Carpentry?' Elise spluttered, rather too incredulously for Etienne's liking.

'Oui.'

She glanced dismissively to the side, and Etienne quickly signalled the waiter to order wine. He could feel the heat rising up his neck and he adjusted his tie in discomfort, the urge to bolt grew stronger with each passing minute.

'I am told you like the piano,' Etienne said trying to offer up more conversation, and one that he was more comfortable with at that.

'Hmmm, in a way. I've been playing since I was a little girl. My father likes to impress his clients by bringing me out to perform for them.'

'Isn't it so enjoyable! The way you control the flow of the music, the emotions you convey, how you can captivate an audience.'

'Um, I guess so?' Elise shrugged.

Etienne's heart sank, he knew deep down that not every music player shared his exact passions, but to see someone whose passion had completely died saddened him.

They continued their date in patchy silence. Etienne poked around at the fish he had ordered, willing the night to end soon. He took his mind off Elise for the time being, whose wine glass was being refilled every few minutes. He began to think about how he was going to explain to his family that a romantic connection was not something that he wanted, and he could not even consider getting married. Was he broken? Why didn't he want what so many did? Did this make him as weird as so many made him out to be? All these thoughts plagued his mind, as he took a sip of wine to try and still his anxieties.

They were halfway through dessert when Elise piped up once again. She swayed unsteadily in her chair, gesturing to Etienne's side with her glass and perfectly manicured hand.

'I say, Etienne, why do you carry that cane with you? Isn't that what older gentlemen do?' She giggled, hiccupping at the same time.

'Oh, it's for my leg,' Etienne replied.

'What's wrong with it?' Elise asked.

'I had an accident when I was young. During the war. It's never been right since,' Etienne said, keeping the details brief.

'Tha's no good,' Elise slurred. 'Does that mean you have problems performing?' She asked, rather loudly.

'The violin? Oh no, I usually sit on a stool if the pain gets too much. It doesn't affect my ability to perform at all.'

Elise laughed, it sounded more like a cackle, a few glances flashed their way from the irritated and nosy customers. Etienne tried to look away from their accusatory glares.

'Not the violin you fool! I mean *perform,*' she purred, winking at him flirtatiously.

'I'm sorry?' Etienne asked, starting to feel panicked as a bead of anxious sweat ran down his back.

'Oh, come on now, a man of your age knows how to treat a lady, and how to *treat* a lady,' she grinned.

'I'm afraid I don't know what you mean Elise,' Etienne protested.

He could feel her toes fishing at the bottom of his trouser leg, followed by her foot slowly edging its way up until she got to…

'Elise. Please.'

'I like it when they beg,' she teased.

'No, Elise stop, please I don't want to do this.'

A deep scowl formed on Elise's face, her perfect features now all knitted together in fury. She wasn't so flawless now.

'You don't say,' she said coldly, as her foot slid away from Etienne's crotch. 'You must be the only man in France who is not even the slightest bit interested.'

'You are drunk.'

'So?'

'I don't want to see you embarrass yourself.'

'You care far too much about what people think.'

Even though Elise was being completely inappropriate, she made a good point. Everything he did in his life was borne out of trying to please people, to do what *they* thought was the right thing to do. Etienne signalled to the waiter that he required the cheque.

After paying, he escorted Elise out of the restaurant as quickly as possible, her endless giggles continued to increase in volume. With each diner he locked eyes with Etienne raised an eyebrow in apology, some nodded in return. When they were finally outside, he could catch his breath, now that the rain had finally cleared it had left a freshness in the air and the smell of dew in the orange and red autumnal leaves was familiar and reassuring. He offered Elise his arm and she stumbled into him, grasping his elbow tightly.

It proved to be more difficult than he thought, trying to maintain his own precarious balance as well as supporting someone else's. They clumsily meandered through the streets towards the grand townhouses along the riverside.

Night had fallen across the city, and the dim streetlights did little to reveal their path home. Elise had not stopped rambling in her inebriated state; Etienne remained steadfast, looking straight ahead as he ushered her forward.

Fortunately, the tallest of the townhouses came into view in the hazy light finally signalling the Cartier residence. Etienne eased away from Elise to knock on the door, but before he could reach the knocker, he was tugged back, and Elise planted her lips hard on his. She wrapped her arms around his neck and hungrily explored him. With regret, Etienne allowed her to, trying to match her passion. But despite his attempts, she must have been able to feel his reluctance, as she pulled away hastily, that same disappointed look flashed in her eyes.

'I'm sorry Elise. I shouldn't have done that.'

'They can't resist that usually,' she smiled, twirling a perfect ringlet around her finger.

'Thank you for tonight,' Etienne said with haste, desperate to leave.

'That's your problem Etienne Touelle. You're the perfect gentleman.'

'I don't understand?'

Elise threw back her head, letting out another laugh, Etienne took a fearful glance around, but still, no one was there. *Thank God.*

'Give in to your passions! Let them rule you for a change! Life is more fun that way!'

There was no point in arguing with her now, so Etienne merely nodded politely, which seemed to frustrate her more.

'Euugh forget it. Goodnight, Etienne.'

She stumbled up the stairs, and Etienne waited patiently until the door was opened by their maid. She waved shyly to Etienne before quietly closing the door and with that the chapter of Etienne's courting attempts.

She was wrong about him, he thought. Passion played a role in his life; it just wasn't where people would think to find it.

***

Etienne kept to himself over the following few days, mainly to avoid any invasive questions. Feigning that he was feeling unwell, he used the excuse to move his work to his house, opting to work from the desk space on the lower floor so that he could still see outside of the window whilst he worked.

Many mothers and daughters crowded the streets during this time. Young ladies would be getting engaged and visiting the seamstress shop on their street to start planning the designs of their dresses in preparation for their inevitable summer weddings, all of which always fell on the same day. It was an amusing spectacle to behold, the mothers often looking like they were on a mission, whereas the expectant brides, were still lost in the airy magic of it all where everything was beautiful and perfect, the look was identifiable from a mile away. Etienne smiled to himself in the relief that the city had some continuity in its seasons and perks. But the next time that he looked up from his writings, he saw something that puzzled him, or rather someone.

This girl was on her own. No mission-oriented mother by her side. No fairy-tale twinkle in her eyes. She didn't walk as if she were on air. She didn't smile and giggle at every person that looked her way. Her dark brown hair was knotted, bedraggled, and falling just beyond her shoulders. A dark green dress hung loosely from her short frame, but as the autumnal breeze swept the skirt around her it clung to her body to reveal a slight hint of stomach. Her face was round, but lifeless, the bags under her eyes looked like they carried years of heaviness. She was out of place, and it seemed that she knew this, her quick paranoid head jerks hinted that she was on edge, and Etienne was intrigued by her.

Over the next few days, he continued to notice her a lot in the old town. He couldn't help it, but he would simply observe her, confused by her behaviour. She seemed to converse well with people, who would point her in various directions which she would follow obediently, and Etienne would watch her intently until she was out of sight.

***

He had been at a violin playing session late into the evening. He was so good now that he would go round to Madame Penaud's to play purely for entertainment. The family liked his company, and he theirs. Whenever Gabriel was in town with his new family, it was always an added joy to see him. It was gone half past ten by the time he left, and he glanced up in the direction of the old chapel. It was a habit now, and a painful reminder in more ways than one. He snapped out of his reverie when he felt a large thud fall into him, knocking his cane out of his hand, and sending him sprawling for balance.

'Pardon, Monsieur!' A panicked shrill voice rang out.

Etienne glanced around, ready to chastise the person for their clumsiness. But when he looked around, wide-eyed, murky green eyes met his, and intrigue got the better of him. *It was her.*

She quickly regained her own balance before tugging at Etienne's hand to pull him to his feet. He put his hand out to slow her down, the familiar pain extending up in his leg and hip stopping him from moving.

'Did I hurt you? I am so sorry!' She gasped.

'No, no, I'm okay!' Etienne pleaded. He didn't want her to leave, she was so fascinating to him, he didn't know why, and it bothered him.

She gulped and nodded, she noticed his cane and bent down to retrieve it, easing it gently back into Etienne's hand, which he used to gather himself back up.

'Merci, Mademoiselle.'

She looked taken aback by his address, and before he could say another word she hurried away to the top of the street, round the corner and out of sight.

'Wait!' Etienne called out but in vain.

Her French was good, but there was something unfamiliar about it, and he couldn't put his finger on it. He fell asleep frustrated that night.

***

A week went by and there was no sign of her. Etienne looked out for her every single day, both from his desk and on his walks around the city- the market town, riverside, the opera, everywhere.

He dug his cane into the floor heavily as he arrived back at his parent's house.

'A long day, ma pêche?' His mother's sweet voice called out.

'Something like that, Maman,' Etienne replied.

'Come in, come eat with us.'

She ushered him into their small kitchen area which hosted a tiny kitchen table. But tonight, it was set for four.

'Maman? Are we expecting company?' Etienne asked.

'Oui ma pêche, I want you to meet a new young lady from the church, she will be staying with us for a while until she gets on her feet. She's just moved to the area.'

'Ahem.'

Etienne spun round, and there she was standing before him. Her hair had been brushed out, braided, and secured back with one of his mother's hairbands. She wore a floor length blue cotton dress that flowed around her shapely curves. She looked a little more refreshed, but Etienne saw her tense at her recognition of him.

'My name is Marianne,' she said softly, almost indecisively.

'Etienne.'

A small smile formed on her thin lips as their eyes met. They shared a puzzled look, but they were captivated by each other, burning with an eagerness to uncover each other's mystery.

ADA

The train shuddered to a halt waking her with a start. The conductor opened the carriage door announcing their arrival. She was groggy with the intermittent sleep she had gotten over the last few days, but when she realised where she was, she was conflicted by feelings of relief and gut-wrenching guilt.

She stooped to pick up the tiny bag with the few items she was able to grab and stepped out of the carriage. She was doing this, she was being brave, she had to be here, she had done the right thing... she was a terrible daughter, a terrible wife, a terrible friend, a terrible mother, she was... going to be sick.

***

Stuttgart, January 1934

The two extra weeks had been a mixed blessing, she could barely stand under the weight of her enormous bump. She was so ready for the baby to be born, but at the same time, she knew that the safest place for them was inside, at least she could protect them in there, from their father and the world.

She was eighteen years old and perpetually frightened of everything. Despite Otto's violence quelling at the news of her condition, she knew that she wouldn't be able to control what happened after the baby arrived.

Liselotte and Thomas' wedding had been the only helpful distraction throughout the entire period. Otto had allowed Ada to see Liselotte more regularly to help with preparations. Picking out fabrics for dresses, perusing flower shops, and finalising cake designs with Liselotte's father, was the most joy she had felt in a long time. They had laughed to the point of tears at the fourth amendment of Ada's dress to accommodate her growing stomach.

'How many are you having Ada?' Liselotte gasped as she fought to loosen the waist seam.

'Only one!' Ada gasped, finally able to breathe comfortably.

'Honestly, I wouldn't be surprised if there's three in there.'

'You had better be wrong, Lise.'

'Hey, this is *your* child. Therefore, he, or she, will be wonderful.'

Ada sighed. 'I hope it's a boy.'

'Really? Having a little Ada would be so sweet.'

'No Lise. It *has* to be a boy.'

'Oh.' Liselotte trailed off, and the laughter ceased.

Boys were the light and joy of her family, she knew that now, and she did not want her child to suffer the way she had.

'That's my son in there!' Otto had proclaimed many a time, both drunk and sober, to the amusement of others. But at home, those same words were a threat, and it kept Ada wide awake at night worrying about the future consequences if she did not fulfil this command. She prayed earnestly every day, on her knees, begging God for a son.

***

But the time had finally come, for hours now she had been lying on the bed screaming in agony and was completely exhausted. Liselotte diligently pressed cold cloths against her sweaty brow and her mother kept checking on her progress.

'How much longer?' Ada wailed helplessly.

'It's impossible to tell Ada, I'm sorry,' Gisela said.

'I can't do this anymore,' Ada moaned, briefly catching her breath before being overcome with an intense twisting sensation as if something was pulling everything inside her with all its might.

Otto had walked out the moment the pains started, and now he was sitting in the living room with Ernst, Günther, and Walther, their raucous drunken cheers irritating Ada's every nerve, and she threw her head back onto the pillows in frustration.

'Don't listen to them Ada,' Liselotte whispered soothingly.

'You know that me and Clara helped each other give birth,' Gisela smiled.

Both Ada and Liselotte knew the story in part, they had both been surprise pregnancies at the start of the war. Liselotte's family had only recently relocated to Stuttgart when Artur was offered a job at the bakery; but like so many, he was soon called up to the army.

'Your mother would not leave me alone,' Gisela chuckled addressing Liselotte. Everyone knew that if Clara Krause wanted to make someone her friend, she would make it her mission, and she succeeded every time.

Gisela continued, 'The winter felt like it would never end, of course, we were trying to keep as many provisions back as possible. I had never been so tired during pregnancy. A part of me was glad that your father wasn't there to see me like that, he would have been disappointed.'

Ada's heart sank for her mother, Gisela chose to live her life to serve others, and she was so good at it. If she felt like she had let anyone down she would take it out on herself the hardest.

'It was February, and I had never seen such impressive icicles hanging off every house. I knew it was risky when the snow had frozen over from the previous night, but I went to go and visit Clara. The walk took so long.'

Ada listened attentively, transfixed by her mother's tale, their conversations had never lasted longer than a few minutes, let alone her confiding personal details of her life with her.

'By the time I reached the house, I could see that the door was slightly ajar, we were all having to do what we could to keep the warmth in, so I immediately assumed something was wrong. I pushed the door open to find Clara hunched over by the fireplace. The poor girl had been there for hours in agony, screaming for help. By the time I had put down towels and got fresh water ready, she was ready to push. Liselotte shot out so quickly I barely caught you in time, you were like a bar of soap.'

Both Ada and Liselotte giggled. Gisela smiled, it warmed Ada's heart.

'Clara stayed with me for the next few weeks so that I could help her with nursing. You weren't due until May, Ada, but you wanted to see the world immediately, as soon as April arrived, so did you. I should have expected it with you being my fifth baby.'

Gisela paused and sighed, still smiling. 'All of that chaos, stress, and pain, it melts away the moment you hold your baby in your arms.' She looked directly at Ada. 'The love is instant, and you will feel the same too, Ada.'

Ada exhaled, mostly in relief, she had received few words of affirmation throughout her pregnancy. Otto paid little attention to her, only concerned that she stayed healthy for the sake of *his* son. It meant the world to her that these calming words were coming from her own mother.

'There you go Ada, you just need to have five and by the time you get to the last one it will be easy!' Liselotte teased as she nudged Ada lightly on the shoulder.

'I hate you,' Ada groaned.

Liselotte giggled, 'That, my friend, you do not.'

At that moment the pressure inside her changed, Ada tried to shift but couldn't, Gisela noticed and immediately looked underneath to check.

'Ada, my girl, you need to push.'

The stinging was horrendous, and she could barely catch her breath before exerting every single last bit of strength she had down into her body. She could feel something stretching, instructions being yelled from somewhere, and loud voices coming from outside the door, but she couldn't focus on anything else other than the excruciating pain. Finally, there was a release, and everything stopped. Ada fell back in exhaustion, Liselotte left her side and rushed around next to Gisela. At long last a croaky cry rang out; it was the most beautiful sound Ada had ever heard. Somehow, she found the strength to prop herself up on her elbows, peering over her arched knees she could see her mother and best friend gleaming down at the face of the baby, *her* baby.

'Ada. You have a son,' Liselotte breathed, making no attempt to wipe away the happy tears that were streaming down her face, as she nestled the precious life into Ada's arms.

'He's perfect!' Ada gasped, staring down at a tiny pink face, scrunched up in bemusement, wondering what had just happened to him. She kissed the top of his head tenderly, and as soon as her lips met his soft skin, he opened his eyes and looked directly into hers with fascination and total trust, Ada thought her heart would burst with fullness.

They had a mere five minutes of precious time alone before the men in the adjoining room sauntered in. They were clapping Otto heartily on the back, handshakes going around, before Ernst left to find more drinks for even more toasts.

'My son Erich,' Otto announced.

'Erich?' Ada asked quietly.

'Of course, after my grandfather,' Otto stated, with a subtle undertone of threat that Ada had become accustomed to.

'It's a fine name,' Ada hastily agreed.

She was relieved to be able to lie back and watch with happiness as Erich was passed around, cooed over, rocked, and *approved* by the family. She thought of her mother's story, and how circumstances drew people together in the most unlikely manner. Gisela was a proud woman through and through, family was everything to her, and the delight she could see in her face as she cradled her grandson filled Ada's heart with hope.

Dealing with loneliness, uncertainty, and a newborn would have been difficult enough, but Ada had worked out it, and her mother would have faced the unimaginable. In her brother's boxes, she had found the telegrams, the first one arriving not long after her own birth.

```
The Secretary of War desires me to express
his deep regret that your son Kristian Stein
was killed in action.
```

The first of the beloved sons. In 1916 it was Wilhelm, and in 1918, Heinrich was cruelly taken just before the end came. The loss must have been devastating, unimaginable, maybe it was simply impossible for her mother to put into words, which is why she never did.

***

Stuttgart, March 1938

'Zoom!' Erich squealed in delight as he ran around the room, Ada chased after him with a cloth trying to wipe off the porridge plastered all over his face and hands.

'You are a little rascal, Erich!' Ada toyed playfully, as he hid behind the sofa.

Erich's delightful giggles lit up the room as he continued to race around, his thick, curly blonde hair bounced behind him, and his green eyes, just like Ada's, shone with glee. He was so pure and wonderful, he made it easier to ignore the bad things that were happening around them.

She had been relieved when Erich fussed in the night, it kept her away from Otto. She had had three exhausting but glorious weeks at the start, where she did nothing but tend to Erich, but that time went too quickly and soon Otto was back to his usual self. She couldn't hide the pain anymore; she was still torn badly from the birth, and everything was incredibly sensitive, the bleeds were getting progressively worse the rougher he got.

Some nights he returned, drunk, shirt buttoned up incorrectly, collar askew, stinking of cheap perfume. Ada knew that he was keeping other company, she was ashamed that she felt more relief than outrage. When he was with them, he would return satisfied. When he was with them, he wasn't hurting her, and she could protect Erich.

Their game of chase was soon interrupted by a knock at the door.

'It's open, Lise!' Ada called out. Now that she had given her husband a son, there were a few relaxations to the rules.

'Tante, Ise-lotte!' Erich squawked as he galloped towards Liselotte's open arms as she stood in the doorway.

Liselotte came around as much as she could during the weekdays when Otto was at work. As well as his administrative duties, he was now also part of the security of some of the highest-ranking Nazi officials. Keeping him busy was a relief, but his level of trustworthiness within the Party now meant that everyone around him had to be even more careful of what they said and did. Ada didn't doubt for a second that he would turn her in if she did anything out of line, and she knew how much he disproved of Liselotte and her outspoken nature.

'How's my favourite little one today?' Liselotte said squeezing Erich tight and whirling him around the room.

'Covered in porridge,' Ada laughed, even harder when she saw the look on Liselotte's face as she set Erich down precariously wiping off the oats from her now sticky hands.

'Ah, so he is.'

Once they had all cleaned up, Erich stood between Ada and

Liselotte placing his hands out for both to take. Together they set off for the market, lifting Erich up to jump over every crack in the pavement as they strolled along.

'Me and Thomas would love to have you over for dinner sometime.'

Ada sighed regretfully, 'You know I would love to Lise, but I don't think it would be a good idea to have Thomas and Otto together in the same room.'

'I'm not inviting Otto, I'm inviting you,' Liselotte snapped.

'Lise?'

Liselotte glanced down at Erich, making sure that he was blissfully unaware of their conversation before turning back to Ada.

'You do everything that man tells you to do, Ada.'

'That man is my husband, Lise. Remember that.'

'Well, he certainly doesn't treat you as a man is supposed to treat his wife. You do everything he asks of you, and still... that happens,' she hissed, glaring at a fresh bruise on Ada's arm just visible under the cuff of her blouse.

'It's only dinner, Ada. How can he possibly object to that?'

'It's not as simple as that, Lise.'

'What's going on, Ada?'

Ada took a deep breath, and looked down at her precious son, when she looked back up Liselotte met her gaze and nodded her understanding.

'Around him too?'

'That's what I'm trying to prevent.'

The hustle and bustle of the market provided a momentary

distraction as Ada and Liselotte picked out fruits, vegetables, and meats. Arms full they started making their way back to Ada's apartment in relative silence, only breaking it to humour Erich as he pointed to every detail in his surroundings.

'Star!' Erich called out, pointing diagonally across the street.

'Stars come out at night darling,' Ada said.

'No! Mütter, a star!'

Erich had come to a complete stop and was gesturing wildly with his little hands. Both Ada and Liselotte glanced up to see a grubby young girl stumbling down the street, her large eyes nearly bulging out of their sockets, attached to a gaunt-looking face. Her limbs were as thin as sticks, and underneath the grime lay sickly pale-looking skin, and on her torn, tatty shirt a large yellow star was displayed.

Ada's heart immediately dropped, she couldn't have been much older than Erich, seven years old at most. She was on her own, with no adult in sight to claim responsibility for her. It wasn't long before the girl noticed Erich's pointed finger at her. She frantically tried to hide her face and hurry away, but the weakness of what looked like months of malnourishment caused her to trip and fall onto the hard concrete floor.

'Erich, stop pointing now!' Ada whispered harshly at her son; his lip wobbled as he brought his hand back down to his side.

Liselotte wasted no time hurrying over to the girl, gently helping her back to her feet.

'Step away from her!' A severe loud voice barked, as three officers came into view.

'She's hurt,' Liselotte protested.

'You shouldn't concern yourself with such matters,' another said threateningly.

'Please, she's just a child!'

'We'll take her from here,' the third one said coolly, Ada shuddered.

'Where are you taking her?' Liselotte asked.

'As I said, you shouldn't concern yourself with such matters.'

The third officer placed his sturdy boot between Liselotte and the girl, before reaching down and yanking the girl up forcefully from the ground, a spine-chilling crack rang out and the girl roared in pain. Ada averted her eyes, the twisted knot in her stomach grew tighter, and she could still hear Liselotte's protests.

'You're hurting her! Let me take her somewhere where she can get help! Please! Ahhhh!'

There was a loud slap and Ada spun round to see Liselotte clasping her face and collapsed on the floor, as the heavy thud of the boots and continuous cries of the young girl became more distant.

'Lise! Are you okay?'

Liselotte pulled herself up, spitting out blood as she did so.

'Lise, what were you thinking?'

'What was *I* thinking?' Liselotte groaned.

'You don't want to make an enemy out of them!'

'You are a *mother!* She was just a child! How can you just stand there and do nothing?'

Ada stepped back, stung by Liselotte's words. Anger burned deep inside her, but if there was one thing she was good at by now, it was keeping her emotions hidden. She grasped Erich firmly by the hand, so much so that he whimpered in discomfort as she marched him off down the street.

'Ise-lotte!' Erich called back.

'That's it, Ada! Walk away! Pretend nothing terrible ever

happens! It's what you're good at!' Liselotte's angry words carried on the breeze as Ada tried to pace further and further away. She was so mad, mad at Liselotte's insults, mad at the atrocities that were being carried out in the name of 'national interest', but mostly she was mad at herself, and how right Liselotte was.

***

Stuttgart, August 1938

Months went by, and not a word was spoken between Ada and Liselotte. Instead, Ada threw herself into carrying out Otto's house-making visions. She scrapped the original furniture that had been there when they first moved in, almost single-handedly moved the new sofas in, and arranged them in the formation that he wanted. She re-painted all of the rooms and hung up pictures of the family and the Führer ignoring the nudges of disgust from her conscience. Her efforts were rewarded with no gratitude from Otto, he found fault with everything she had done, and with the absence of a child in her womb, his sexual aggression had returned and become much worse.

'Otto please, it hurts,' she would cry as night after night he would forcefully bend her over the table, kick her legs apart and enter her from behind. The tearing never stopped being painful, and she would spend hours after the ordeals quietly sobbing on the sofa.

It was approaching the end of August, the temperatures continued to soar and the humidity in the apartment was unbearable. Yet Otto still insisted on hot stews for dinner. As the evening drew in, Ada stood at the stove, sweating relentlessly as she chopped meat and vegetables, made up the stock, and stood over the hot bubbles. Otto sat quietly in the corner reading his newspaper, ignoring Erich's requests to play. Ada took a small step back and lowered the heat for the food to simmer.

'Erich darling, go and find a book. I'll come and read with you in a minute.'

Erich flashed her an irresistible grin that always made her heart melt and rushed off in a hurried search. Ada removed her apron, splashed cold water on her face, and mopped it with a spare cloth.

'This one, Mütter!' Erich chirped in triumph.

As she turned around, the sight she was met with made her heart sink and panic rise in her throat, a stifling small whine escaped from her lips. Erich was waving her French book in the air for all to see. She slowly glanced towards Otto, who was leaning forward in his chair, his eyes full of fire, and a small pulsing vein was visible on the side of his head.

'What the *hell* is that doing in our home?' He roared.

'Erich, go into your room darling,' Ada ordered.

He toddled away obediently, and Ada caught a glimpse of his little face peering out from underneath his bed as the first punch caught her in the jaw.

When she finally regained consciousness, she could barely breathe, her throat was on fire, and her whole body was throbbing in agony. A handful of words were fuzzy in her mind. *Traitor. Disgrace. Example.* His hands had been around her neck, she hadn't been able to breathe, and the room had gone black. How long had she been out? The charred smells coming from the stove suggested a while.

She looked around, the room was spinning but she could just about get enough clarity to see that both Otto and Erich were nowhere to be seen. She closed her eyes desperately trying to piece the events together. As the words continued to whir around, the flashbacks of each hit came into view.

I will make an example of you!

No... please!

My son does not deserve a mother like you! You are a disgrace! A traitor to this country!

He had gone to report her. She was sure of it. She couldn't think straight, but all she knew was that she needed to get out. What if they came around tonight? What would they do to her? She crawled towards the stove, reached up, and fumbled with the hob, successfully turning it off before collapsing back on the floor in exhaustion. But she had to keep going, she had to move, she started to panic. Somehow the adrenaline gave her the motivation to get to her feet, as she stumbled towards the door she saw the book, miraculously intact, she grabbed it and shoved it down the side of her boot, nudged the door open, and sprinted out into the muggy night air.

She was sobbing in desperation as she pounded on the door until finally a surprised face appeared in the doorway.

'Ada?' Thomas asked.

'Thank God!' Ada cried as she leaned against the doorframe. She felt Thomas take her weight, propping her up under his arm and steering her towards the kitchen table. He left momentarily but returned quickly with a young lady with an untidy braid.

'What do you want, Ada?' She asked sternly.

'Help. Please?' Ada cried.

'Ada, what did he do to you?' She gasped, pointing a bony finger towards her neck.

Ada tentatively followed her direction, lightly touching the skin, she immediately cried out as pain radiated everywhere.

'He's going to kill me, Lise,' Ada trembled as she dissolved into tears, Liselotte's arms were around her in an instant, disputes forgotten, bond unbreakable.

Over the next few hours, Ada gradually recalled the events of the evening, Erich, the book, and the beating.

'He is in so deep. He won't hesitate to report anyone. Not even me,' Ada concluded.

Liselotte and Thomas were stony-faced, they looked at each other expressionless before turning their focus back on Ada. Liselotte took Ada's hands in hers and stared into her eyes with a ferocity that Ada feared.

'Ada. My dearest friend. You have to get out.'

'I can't just leave him, Lise. Where would I live? What about Erich?'

Liselotte squeezed her hand urgently.

'No, Ada. You have to get out of Germany.'

***

Stuttgart, September 1938

Liselotte was right. But how could she even try to leave everything she knew and loved behind?

Thomas revealed that he knew of people who had already left and settled elsewhere around the continent, some living under new identities. He sent off correspondence immediately asking for their help, meanwhile, they formulated a plan to relay information to each other. Every few days Ada had gone to the bakery with Erich to see Thomas. For the first three appearances, it was the same response.

'I'm sorry, Frau Neumann, we don't have the specialist loaf that you ordered, there is a delay with the ingredients.'

Until finally.

'Frau Neumann, the specialist loaf has arrived, I shall get it packaged up for you immediately.'

She was almost shaking as she took the loaf from Thomas' hands, but she steadied herself to keep up the pretence. When they were home, she carefully removed the loose slice at the top of the loaf where inside was a slip of paper with an address on it, Ada wept with relief.

'Mütter? Why are you sad?' Erich asked, snuggling close to her.

'I'm not sad my darling, I'm very happy,' she smiled pressing her lips against his forehead and squeezing him tight.

'Blue,' Erich chimed.

'What was that darling?'

'Blue,' Erich repeated, pointing to the strip of blue ribbon that was also inside the packaging. Ada picked it up in her hand, small lettering was visible at the end of the strip, which was fraying slightly, *10 am.* The signal? But why now?

Ada did as she was instructed. Quietly leaving the house after Otto had left for work, she had been sure to check her surroundings every fifteen seconds to make sure that she wasn't being watched or followed. Otto hadn't uttered a word to her since his return after that fateful night. It was just another way to torture her, the constant unknowing of how much trouble she was in.

When she finally arrived at Liselotte and Thomas' house with Erich in tow, she burst through the door. They were both in the kitchen awaiting her arrival as planned.

Liselotte distracted Erich with some wooden spoons and a pot to use as a drum whilst Thomas delivered the news.

'They have agreed to help you. You are to meet them in a week at that address in Paris.'

'I don't know how I can ever thank you Thomas,' Ada said reaching for his hands, but he did not budge, and she withdrew them slowly.

'What's wrong?' Ada asked.

Thomas sighed, hanging his head. Liselotte turned away.

'This group is limited in resources. They can only procure documents for one person.'

'Y…you mean?'

'Erich,' Thomas finally said, 'can't come with you.'

PHILIPP

Gurs, July 1939

It was even more unbearable in the heat. Hut 184 lay at the far end of the camp, the last time he counted, there were fifty-seven men in there, all of them were Spanish. Many of them were noisy, and they never seemed to stop speaking, even at night, making the unbreathable stuffy heat, and the foul stench of vomit, waste, and sweat secondary reasons as to why it was impossible to sleep. At least he could keep track of the rats surrounding his feet.

The midday sun bore down overhead, and every single bit of shaded shelter was occupied by an unfamiliar group, Philipp assumed they all knew each other. Being the outsider kept him out, but he was glad to see that communities had found ways to stay together through the toughest times, it gave him a glimmer of hope.

He wandered over to the edge of the camp, the sunlight burned his eyes as it glared off the barbed wire fence. Settling in a corner with the tiniest sliver of shade, he tugged at the collar of his shirt, trying as hard as he could to get as much coverage on his already badly burnt skin.

Here he just existed. He had been here for months, for no other reason seemingly that he was German, not that he was Jewish, his documentation must have been convincing enough, that was at least something to be grateful for. He had been there a lot longer than some of the other inmates. Some hadn't survived the winter, others had succumbed to illness, and the rest were like him, wondering whether they would ever escape this strange limbo.

A small scrap of material floated into his lap, the brush of it against his skin startled him from his thoughts. Philipp shielded his eyes from the sun as he looked around, he was surprised to see a man standing a few yards to his left watching him curiously. Philipp took the material in his hand and offered it to the man who shook his head vigorously and gestured draping around his neck. Philipp noticed his uneven shirt and the ripped seam along the edge, he nodded his understanding and draped the material around his neck, any extra coverage from the sun was highly appreciated. The man slowly approached, Philipp had not seen him before, he was likely from another hut.

When they were within earshot of each other, the man placed his large bony hand on his chest,

'Carlos', he said, his intonation inviting Philipp to replicate.

Philipp placed his hand on his own chest, 'Edgar,' he replied. 'Danke schön,' he quickly added, pointing to the material gift.

'De nada,' Carlos smiled.

'Es aleman?' Carlos asked.

Philipp had heard some of the other inmates say this word around him a few times, at least he thought it was to him they were referring, but he couldn't be sure if it was good or bad.

'Germany,' Philipp replied.

Carlos nodded, Philipp was relieved to see him respond this way, it wasn't difficult to see that Germans were carrying a distrustful reputation these days.

'Hitler?' Carlos pressed further.

Philipp hung his head and nodded sadly. When he was on the move, he had to plan everything so carefully, each day, each hour involved looking out, procuring food, and finding shelter. Now that he was locked up, all he could think about was home, how leadership wanted him and so many others hunted down and beaten, even killed. If he was a blight on Hitler's journey, then Hitler sure as hell was a blight on his. Philipp found himself tensing.

'La guerra viene, es verdad?'

War. Philipp knew what that meant, it was the most uttered word around the camp. Poor folks like Carlos had already fled from one war because of politics, now they were on the cusp of being dragged into another. Philipp looked up at Carlos and shrugged.

***

Philipp lay wide awake in his bunk that night, his stomach churned from the foul smells exacerbated by the heat that was also causing a river of sweat to flow down his back, and he tried to drown out the incessant chatter with his own thoughts.

Thoughts of his family and friends plagued him night after night, but tonight his usual feelings of guilt and worry were intermingled with something else. All the talk of war had Philipp thinking realistically and forced him to plan ahead for the first time in months.

Hitler would invade. That much was inevitable. The question was, how long would it be before the army reached France? Surely, they would target places like this in the hunt for people like him. Philipp could feel the target on his back growing weightier by the second.

He had to get out of Gurs to stand any chance of surviving. But he felt weak, physically, and emotionally from the scarcity of food and the lack of strength to venture out into the unknown once again. But despite this, Max's words were a constant and poignant reminder of why he was doing this.

Survive. That's how we'll win, Philipp.

***

He spent the next few days scouring around every inch of the perimeter, desperately looking for a slight hole in the fence or ground that he could dig up, but to no avail. The ground was tough and the fence was too deep. He sank into the dirt, angrily throwing debris into the corners.

'Edgar?'

Philipp ignored the sound as he rubbed his eyes.

'Edgar?'

Oh, shit that was him!

Philipp looked up this time, embarrassed by his current state as Carlos peered at him.

'Está bien?' He asked.

Philipp waved his hand dismissively.

Carlos crouched down beside him and without saying a word, he began to draw a scene in the dust, Philipp leaned closer. He could see a crowd of people, they were running, and behind them were more figures, chasing them possibly. They looked like they were holding something.

'A gun?' Philipp asked.

Carlos nodded slowly, he pointed to the fleeing crowd.

'Familia,' he muttered.

'Guerra?' Philipp asked.

'Si,' Carlos answered, before shaking his head solemnly and wiping the scene out with his foot.

'Y tú?' Carlos said, pointing at Philipp.

He had already lied about his name, and Carlos had shown him kindness and vulnerability. Philipp glanced around cautiously, and when he was happy that the coast was clear he started drawing. Not a scene, but a symbol. The Star of David. He pointed to his chest; a burning sensation ran over his breast. Carlos' face sank in realisation, and he placed his hand on Philipp's shoulder.

'Lo siento.'

Philipp sighed and quickly rubbed out the image.

'Intentas a huir?' Carlos asked, curious rather than interrogatory.

'Escape,' Philipp whispered.

Carlos started to speak enthusiastically, gesturing to the other huts emphatically, but Philipp didn't understand. Philipp blinked at him with a blank expression on his face. Carlos started to draw again; it looked like a box. He drew wheels, followed by a plus sign, an ambulance. Aid workers! Of course!

***

A sharp nudge woke him up a week and a half later. Hot, sour breath made his nose wrinkle, and he was suddenly wide-eyed and alert. A heavily bearded scrawny man stared at him. Philipp shuffled back in his bunk startled.

'Alemania?' He asked in a low gruff voice.

Philipp nodded, and the stranger gestured to him to follow. He obediently jumped down from his bunk, the hard ground bruising the soles of his feet as he did so. Despite it being summer, it was still dark outside, it must have been extremely early. The man led him down the sides of the huts, the months of near starvation allowed them both to easily slip down the narrow gaps. They crept along silently, careful not to alert anyone to their activity.

They eventually found a group of four men by a makeshift shelter located by the huts north of the camp. They were huddled closely together.

'Edgar!' Carlos called out, before being hurriedly shushed by his accomplices.

'Llegarán hoy,' another said.

Carlos quickly got to work illustrating his friend's explanation in the dust, Philipp leaned in closely to make out the etchings in the darkness. He smiled at how innocently childlike it was. It reminded him of visiting his cousins in Hanover. His uncle Paul owned a huge property on the outskirts of the city where they would stay nearly every summer. Paul also had six children, each more chaotic than the last. Johann was able to tolerate them for longer than Philipp; but eventually, they would both end up retreating to the end of the long garden, where they could hide in the tall hedgerows using the brambles to communicate silently in the dirt as they hid themselves away from the madness of their extended family.

'Alemania?'

Philipp snapped his head up; they were all looking at him intently. He swallowed; his throat was unbearably dry. He studied Carlos' sketches closely. They detailed the arrival of the vans, men exiting them and talking with the guards, and the assistants spreading out around the camp. Carlos pointed to each phase in order, Philipp nodded his understanding at each stage until he hovered over one particular scene. It showed a group banded together; one person lay on the ground. Philipp pointed to it confused. His hut mate pointed at Philipp making small choking sounds.

'Sick?' Philipp asked, making a low gargling sound.

The men nodded. He was going to be the bait. Then one man pointed towards the clock face overlooking the courtyard, and Carlos wrote the number eleven.

***

10.50 am

He couldn't stand still, he tried to stop his hands from twitching.

His hut friend, whom he believed was called Marco, remained close by. Everyone was out in the yard, making it easier for the group to keep in sight of each other.

Ten minutes to go. They were all on high alert, every scrape of gravel underfoot, every slight movement of a guard, and every muffled sound that came from the office had their ears prickling. The door had been left slightly ajar, men were coming in and out in preparation for the first aider's arrival, meaning they could listen in easier. Two members of the group were stationed nearby, they looked up occasionally, nodding to confirm that the schedule was running to plan.

Philipp rubbed his clammy palms on the thinning material of his trousers.

'Alemania, estás bien?' Marco asked.

Philipp smiled tightly.

The distant sound of engines got them all standing to attention. The group instinctively started to move closer together. They waited, silently, and patiently as the medical teams started to filter through the doors.

'Edgar, ahora!' Carlos called.

The urgency in the tone snapped him out of his doubts, that was his cue.

His own medical experiences would help make this look convincing, but he still felt ashamed.

Forgive me.

Philipp groaned as loud as he could, before flinging himself to the floor and began to shake violently. He leaned back trying to roll his eyes back as far as he could and tried to push out every last bit of drool from his dry mouth. In the meanwhile, one person stepped out, and the others stayed watching over him.

'Ayuda!' One of the members called out.

A flurry of worried voices immediately started to drift towards them, suddenly Philipp felt himself being hoisted up, he counted ten hands on his back, they had all managed to regroup. Someone was pinching his side hard, Philipp assumed he was to keep going with the pretence as long as possible, and he obediently continued to convulse with every ounce of energy that he had.

They moved away from their position, up some steps, they must have been heading for the office, gosh it felt cooler in there than the unbearable stuffy heat that permeated through every nook and cranny of the camp. He could hear two French voices calling out, they were going to have to lose them somehow. Before he knew it, he could hear the click of the van door opening and he was being lowered down onto something spongy, he had not felt comfort like it in so long, and for a moment, he wanted to stay there.

No one was giving him any indication as to what was happening, he continued to convulse, gargle, groan, and drool. But then he could hear choking, he snapped out of his act, leaned up on his elbows and saw two of his accomplices with the two accompanying medics in tight chokeholds, their faces flushed red as they desperately tried to gasp for breath.

'No!' Philipp shouted.

His accomplices looked at him with a mix of confusion and irritation. Philipp knew that he was ruining the plan, but he refused to have men's blood on his hands. He had to think quickly. Philipp saw a stethoscope hanging on a hook on the wall of the van, he grabbed it, frantically gesturing to himself and the instrument, praying that they would make a connection.

'Edgar, es medico?' Carlos asked as he peered around the side of the door.

'Doctor!' Philipp exclaimed.

That seemed to do the trick, the two men handling the medics started to release their grips, and both medics crumpled to the floor coughing and wheezing heavily. Philipp rushed over to them, giving them enough time to catch their breath before he did what he had to do.

'I'm sorry,' he whimpered, as he struck both the medics in the side of the neck, both quickly fell to the floor.

The group was in an uproar.

'Asesinato!' They cried.

'Sabia que no podiamos confiar en este hombre!'

Carlos frantically tried to calm them. Philipp now angered by the ruckus they were causing, shushed them, placed his hands together, and leaned his head on them.

'Dormido!' Carlos exclaimed.

'Asleep! Yes!' Philipp shouted. The group looked at each other in bemusement.

'Vamos!' Marco ordered, tired of waiting around. If their absence hadn't alerted anyone, then the prolonged period of the medics being away was going to capture attention very soon.

Marco and Carlos moved the unconscious medics out of the vehicle whilst the others jumped in and seated themselves. Marco and Carlos were not far behind them as they burst into the van, keys in hand.

'Vendran! Id!'

Marco jumped into the driver's seat and fired up the engine. He stomped on the acceleration, throwing everyone forward, crashing hard into each other, this time it was Philipp's turn to lose consciousness in the process.

***

He had no idea how long he blacked out for. He had no idea how far they had travelled. But when he awoke it was pitch black, and they were in the middle of nowhere. Half of the group was nowhere to be seen. Marco was in the driver's seat, Carlos was looking down at Philipp, a worried expression creased into every line in his face.

'Edgar!' He smiled as Philipp's eyes fluttered open.

He could see Marco smiling in relief as he pulled the van over and swiftly exited the vehicle. Carlos helped Philipp up on his feet, thrusting a cup of water in his face.

Philipp spluttered and laughed as the water splashed against his skin and sank into every parched pore. He couldn't believe that they had done it.

Marco sauntered around the side of the vehicle with his small bag slung over his shoulder, he pulled Carlos into a tight hug, and they exchanged words that Philipp couldn't understand, but it wasn't difficult to understand that this was goodbye. When they released each other from their embrace, Marco turned to Philipp and grasped his hand firmly in a handshake.

'Muchas gracias, Edgar,'

'De nada,' Philipp replied.

Marco chuckled and gave a final wave before disappearing into the night.

'Lo hemos hecho!' Carlos exclaimed, raising his hands in the air.

Philipp nodded in disbelief, he couldn't stop himself from smiling, he had no idea what lay ahead, but this moment of victory he would cherish. He helped Carlos stash medical supplies into a backpack before filling a borrowed sack for himself, and when their final task was completed they turned to each other.

'Good luck, Carlos.'

'Buena suerte, Edgar.'

They started to pace away from each other, drawn-out goodbyes were too painful. But Philipp still felt guilt gnawing away at him, Carlos had entrusted everything to a complete stranger. He had risked everything to involve him in this escape, he deserved to know some truth. Philipp turned back, relieved to see that Carlos had done the same.

'Philipp Blau,' he uttered, placing his hand on his chest.

He smiled back at him. 'Alejandro López,' placing his hand on his own chest.

***

THE PLIGHT OF OTHERS

August 1939-March 1940

Hide. Move. Look. Survive.

***

Avignon, March 1940

His feet were bleeding all over. Words were coming out of his mouth, but he didn't know what he was saying. People were staring.

He stumbled on a cobble and felt a sharp fire burn through his ankle, and darkness started to encircle him.

A shadowy figure was in front of him, grasping his shoulders. He felt for sure that his luck had run out, his eyes rolled back as he began to embrace his fate, drifting in and out of consciousness.

An arm was around him. There was a voice, but it was light, concerned, female.

'Hier entlang.'

German?

Between the blurriness in his vision, he could just about see that she wasn't dressed smartly, rather raggedly in fact. The Nazis paid informants well. Unless she was disguised? He couldn't think straight, let alone fight back. She ushered him into a small building.

'Etienne! Viens vite!'

French? What was happening?

A loud clunk signalled the man's entry. He was tall and stern, he edged towards him, and before Philipp could react, the darkness overtook him completely.

ETIENNE

Avignon, September 1939

It was all happening again. But this time it felt different. As soon as the official announcement came on the 3rd September when all of the gunfire was about to start again, Pierre fell silent, and Camille tried to remain optimistic. Etienne held the violin gently underneath his chin, took a deep breath, thought deeply, and began to play.

***

It was now their turn, his generation, everything fell on their shoulders to deliver a nation. Gabriel had been one of the first to sign up, and it had made no sense to Etienne, he was a married man with three young children.

'What do you have to prove?' Etienne had asked him.

'It's my duty, Etienne.'

Etienne had heard the words before, and still, he wasn't convinced by them. He thought back to his childhood, and what Marcel had said all those years ago.

Men need to be brave. Our country needs that. And because you are not, you bring shame.

Some didn't want to fight, and some couldn't, like him. It was the only blessing that his injury had ever given him. On the outside, people showed sympathy, but deep down Etienne could sense their resentment.

The streets were once again haunted by the eerie silence that screamed of turmoil, grief, and despair for the loved ones who had left, and no one knew if they would return. Everyone was terrified. It felt like they had just rebuilt, they had all given everything to return to a new normal. Now the threat of it all being ripped away and taken over by something far worse kept Etienne wide awake at night.

***

He caressed the last mournful note from the violin.

'What pain are you in Etienne?' Madame Penaud asked, her face tilted towards the open window.

'Madame Penaud?' Etienne asked, confused by her sentiments.

'Your interpretations of music are magnificent Etienne. But they are filled with such pain.'

Although Etienne adored his family, and Gabriel was his closest friend, none of them could ever fully understand him. But Madame Penaud came close, someone who could translate and be transformed by music the same way he was. For others, music kept them guessing, but for Etienne, it was the only way he could be completely honest about anything.

'I cannot tell what kind of pain. Only that it is heavy on you.' She continued.

Etienne sighed, he felt lost in a world that didn't make any sense to him, even when there wasn't a war on, how could he communicate that?

'The music tells our stories, but it also reveals our plight.' She whispered.

She could not see his physical afflictions, and he could not see through her eyes, yet they felt one and the same.

'I will be praying for Gabriel, Madame Penaud.'

'Don't stop until he is returned safely to us, Etienne.'

'Oui, Madame,' Etienne promised.

***

He felt troubled as he walked home. Was Gabriel right about the notion of duty? Was the only way to show it to sign up for war? If so, then Etienne had failed. He was doing his country a disservice. He was not rich, he was physically damaged, nuances went over his head, he was not married, and he did not have children, it left him wondering what his contribution to the world was. These thoughts swirled around his mind right up until he got to the front door of his parent's home. His cane buckled at an awkward angle, entangling his feet, he was about to lose his balance before *she* stepped in to help.

'Bonsoir, Etienne,' she said brightly, beaming up at him. Despite her smile, she was difficult to read. Etienne never knew how to feel around her.

'Bonsoir, Marianne,' he replied curtly.

Marianne. She had made herself incredibly useful over the last few months whilst lodging with his parents. Camille was putting her impeccable sewing skills to practice, picking up work at the seamstresses after the last of the owner's daughters married and moved away. Marianne had consequently taken over the bookkeeping for the carpentry business. She was intelligent, accurate, polite, punctual, and hard-working. Furthermore, she would often help to cook and clean the house, Etienne couldn't fault her attitude and work ethic. But still, something wasn't right about her.

She was trying too hard to please people. He noticed that she never spoke about herself but spoke effortlessly about anything else. There was something strange about her accent, it was very alternative sounding, but he couldn't pinpoint it specifically. He also knew that she had nightmares, her mournful screams would penetrate through the walls separating their two houses. At times when he was working late in his father's workshop, he ventured upstairs out of curiosity and saw her clinging to Camille's safe embrace, knuckles white, and eyes full of terror. His heart sank for her, and he hated the part of him that made him so suspicious of what she was holding back. Maybe coming here had been a fresh start for her? But he couldn't help but question, why Avignon? And why had she encountered Etienne and his family in particular?

'How is Madame Penaud doing?' She asked as she untangled her hand from the crook of his elbow to prevent his fall.

'She misses her son,' Etienne replied bluntly.

Her reaction caught him off guard. Marianne swallowed a lump in her throat, and she quickly turned away from him, as if he had scorned her. When she looked back at him slowly, Etienne refused to break his stare. She hesitantly stepped back, unnerved by his suspicious gaze, and knocked into the umbrella stand by the door, jumping as she did so. Etienne eased himself down uncomfortably to her level as he helped her rearrange the stand.

'What happened to you, Marianne?' He asked gently.

Before she could answer him, Camille appeared in the room.

'There you two are. The food is ready on the table, please come and eat.'

Etienne and Marianne glanced awkwardly at each other before Marianne dashed to the kitchen. Etienne looked on after her as her dark hair, which had grown further down her back, swished behind her as she exited his view. Etienne tried to hide his frustration as his mother helped him back to his feet, placing his cane in his hand.

'Merci, Maman,' he grimaced as he waited for the discomfort to ease in his hip.

'There is something between you two ma pêche,' Camille said, smiling knowingly.

'No, Maman,' Etienne insisted.

'It wasn't a question my darling. I have seen the way you two look at each other, it's a look of pure fascination.'

She was right. Marianne did fascinate him. Only in the sense that he didn't understand her, or why people had accepted her with no questions asked.

He sighed as he followed his mother to the kitchen, the delightful aroma of the roast chicken wafted through the house, his mouth began to water, and his stomach growled, and he only realised at that moment how hungry he was.

He made no eye contact with Marianne as they sat down to eat, he could feel his mother's watchful eye over him, and he refused to give her the satisfaction of looking up. Even though Marianne remained the subject of all of his thoughts.

'Etienne?' His mother interjected.

'Pardon, Maman,' Etienne apologised.

'I asked what piece you played tonight at Madame Penaud's?'

'Oh. Mainly the Chaccone. But some improvised pieces too.' He replied.

'How wonderful!' she chimed, 'do you like music, Marianne?'

He could see what his mother was doing, inside he was begging her to stop, he shot her a warning glance across the table, she didn't take it seriously and drew her attention back to Marianne's drawn-out pause.

'Oh… well… my family were never very musical, so I never really heard much growing up.'

'Well, you simply must hear Etienne play sometime! His gifting and passion is truly inspiring!'

Etienne couldn't tell if this was exaggerated to impress Marianne, or whether she truly meant it, but it always made his heart sing whenever she told him she was proud of him, he smiled gratefully. He felt even better when he could see his father smiling underneath his shaggy beard.

'I should like that very much,' Marianne replied.

Etienne nodded and averted his eyes to disguise his frustration. He sensed that she had felt it, as out of the corner of his eye, he saw her head bow down, in shame or hiding, he wasn't sure, but somehow, he had to find out.

***

Avignon, November 1939

As the weeks went by, the city got emptier. The air was thick with a sombre demeanour. Etienne ventured down the vacant streets to the butcher's, coat wrapped tightly around his slim shoulders, collar pulled up around his long neck.

'Bonjour, Monsieur Vernier,' Etienne said as brightly as he could.

'Oh! Bonjour Etienne!' Monsieur Vernier replied, stunned out of his reverie.

'Do you have any beef, monsieur?' Etienne asked, not sure whether to keep the conversation fixed on professional matters or to address the very present elephant in the room.

He had made that mistake at the seamstresses' last week when he had asked after Charlotte's son, and she had burst into hysterical tears right in front of him. Thankfully his mother had been at the shop that day and was on hand to console her. He may have been thirty-five years of age, but Camille still didn't hold back in giving him a clip round the ear and scolded him harshly for being insensitive. It was never deliberate; he was able to see what others refused to see yet could never seem to act appropriately in social situations.

After that incident he tried to avoid talking about the war with anyone, he could see how much people were burning with the need to speak about it, yet they dared not. Being brave was the only way they were expected to feel right now, but how can one be brave when everything was falling apart?

'Only a little bit I'm afraid, Etienne. More supplies are being sent to the army. I know your mother still likes to cook for your neighbours, but you need to get her to understand that the rations will return like they did last time.'

Etienne nodded, paid the money to Monsieur Vernier, tucked the parcel under his arm, and leaned heavily on his cane as he exited the shop. It was starting to get cold again, which always made his pain worse. Even though the walk was difficult, it was better than sitting in the draughty workshop. Moving generated some warmth and made it a little better, but there was little he could do about it at night. The aching made it unbearable to lie down and often woke him up in the early hours of the morning.

That night was no different, admitting defeat, knowing that sleep was not happening, Etienne decided to sort through some papers. He paced around his small workshop in his house for a while before settling as comfortably as he could at his office desk and got to work. He worked by candlelight so as not to disturb anyone or make his parents worry, should they see. The work was a welcome distraction from his discomfort as he scrawled away making lists of commissions, required materials, and estimates for bills, Marianne would sort out the final figures, and there she was, on his mind once again.

They hadn't been able to stay in the same room as each other since their awkward dinner. Marianne would hastily leave, or busy herself with something else. He didn't mean to make her feel scared, but at the same time, if she did pose danger, he didn't want to take any chances.

Etienne tried to shake her from his mind, by continuing to bury himself in words and numbers until he could see the sun starting to rise over the horizon, but then he saw her. He quickly blew out the candle and shifted towards the wall, out of sight of the window. She had a shawl draped around her shoulders and a pair of his mother's sturdy gardening boots on. She peered around cautiously and shivered in the cool morning air before making her way past the house up the street, Etienne moved around slowly to spot her heading in the direction of the chapel.

***

Spying on her made him uneasy, but not understanding her was driving him crazy. He rose early every morning over the next week to watch her leaving. She did not vary from her routine, and finally, he could form a plan.

On a quiet Monday morning, he waited in the darkness, not daring to breathe. The edge of her nightgown swept out into view first, before she noiselessly left the house. Etienne carefully watched to make sure that she was out of sight before sneaking inside. He was having to do it without the cane, it was too loud, and he could not afford to cause any disturbance. Etienne bit his lip hard as he winced through the pain whilst manoeuvring his way quietly through the house, up the stairs, and into Marianne's bedroom.

It was wrong, and violating on so many levels, but pushing past his disgusted inhibitions, Etienne began searching. The bedside drawer, the wardrobe, under the pillow, under the thin mattress, nothing incriminating. He didn't even know what he was looking for. He felt foolish and his heart raced knowing that Marianne could return at any minute.

He lowered himself to the floor and jumped when a loud creak emerged from beneath him. He steadied his breathing, bracing himself for the worst, but when no one came he breathed a sigh of relief. Something felt strange beneath him. This had been his room for many years, he remembered it well, and the floorboards were never this bad. Etienne budged the culprit floorboard with his foot and saw that it wobbled. He crouched down to lift it, and there a tattered book lay concealed. Etienne plucked it out and inspected it. A French conversation and grammar book? Why would Marianne have use for this? She was French? There was an inscription on the first page, *Heinrich Stein.* Who was he? It was a very German-sounding name… and Marianne's accent was strange…

She's a German spy!

'Etienne?' A harsh whisper emerged in the darkness.

Etienne dropped the book in shock, unable to move quickly from his crouched position, he desperately tried to pull himself to his feet.

Marianne was standing in the doorway, her face as white as a sheet in the flickering candlelight, her eyes not moving from the book that had clattered down in front of her.

Burning with adrenaline, Etienne managed to haul himself to his feet, he cast an accusatory finger at Marianne.

'Who the hell are you, Marianne?' He hissed.

'Etienne… I….' she began.

'Give me one good reason why I shouldn't go to the gendarme right now and report you,' he threatened.

'Wh…what for?' She stammered.

'Even now you are trying to lie. Tell me the truth!'

'Etienne, I promise you I have no idea what you are talking about!'

'You are German! You arrived here before the war began. We all know that Hitler has been preparing for this, we are not stupid! You are one of his spies!'

'What? No, Etienne, you have got it all wrong!'

'Oh really? So, who is this Heinrich? Your contact?'

She stood in stunned silence, trying to gasp for breath. Her eyes pleaded with him, but he was not fooled anymore. Etienne made for the door, but she was faster, she closed it behind them and grabbed his hand.

'Etienne, please,' she begged, 'just listen to me.'

The adrenaline coursing through his veins urged him to defy her, but it wasn't in his nature. He had desired to expose her lies, but his deep-rooted fascination towards her since the day he had first laid eyes on her burned stronger. He relaxed his hand long enough for Marianne to compose herself.

'I am German, that is true. Heinrich was my brother, he died during the Great War. I found this when I was a young girl. Material like this was frowned upon even before Hitler and his animals came to power. I learned in secret; it is what I am good at.'

Etienne looked desperately for any tells of lying, a twitch of the eye or the lip, but she spoke earnestly. He believed her.

They sat together on the floor for some time as she told him about the awful things that had happened in Germany, how living there was unbearable. Etienne was wracked with guilt and surprise. It had never occurred to him that his assumed enemy would be living so wretchedly and was just as much in need as anyone else.

'I ran away Etienne. Things at home were bad, really bad.' She shuddered. 'I was in danger, I had to get away. But I had to do some terrible things to do that.'

'The chapel?' He asked gently.

She nodded, 'I go there every morning to pray for the ones I had to leave behind. My son mostly.'

Etienne raised his eyebrows in surprise. *She was a mother.*

'How old are you, Marianne?' he asked.

'I am twenty-four,' she replied.

Etienne exhaled, she had been through so much and at such a tender age. But he had to know more, and this time he didn't care if it wasn't appropriate.

'What's your real name, Marianne?'

'Ada,' she replied, smiling slightly as if a huge weight had lifted from her shoulders.

'How did you arrive here under your new identity?'

'My dearest friends defy the Nazis in whatever way they can,' she smiled, 'they have contacts here in France who are creating papers for people fleeing danger,' she stated, plucking crumpled sheets out the back of the book that lay in front of them handing them over to Etienne's trembling hands.

He studied them carefully, and he was struck by how lucky she had been. The workmanship was not brilliant, anyone studying these carefully would easily see how these had been forged.

'What is it?' She asked nervously.

'I worry about this war. I worry about what is going to happen here. I have heard about Hitler's army. These documents are not the most believable. If you are to survive on these, I worry about what could happen to you if you are found out.'

The colour drained from her cheeks, and she shuddered again, Etienne doubted it was from the cold.

She started to cry, Etienne pulled her close to him, to console her, but also to muffle her sobs so as not to wake his parents. How could he help her? Of course, she could stay with them as long as she wanted, but the discovery of these documents would surely be her downfall, they were the problem. She needed more official-looking documentation. Or actual official documentation… it was a mad thought.

'Marianne?'

'Yes, Etienne?'

'Marry me.'

MARIANNE

Avignon, November 1939

'Mütter!'

'Erich, where are you?'

Everywhere was black, she couldn't see a thing, but he called out over and over again.

'Erich!' She screamed.

'Mütter, why won't you find me?' His voice was quieter, thick with tears.

She tried to run but her legs wouldn't move properly. A trickling sound echoed around her. She glanced down at her feet, horrified to see that she was submerged in water up to her waist. She tried to kick her legs frantically, but they simply trod the water which was rising at a rapid rate.

She thrashed about, knowing that she was wasting precious energy, but she couldn't give up. She called out Erich's name repeatedly, but all she could hear was crying.

'Hold on my son, I'm coming!'

She didn't know where the water was coming from, but now it was up to her neck. She had to preserve her breath before the inevitable but if she could just locate him! She gargled and choked on the water that had drifted into her mouth. A rumble ensued around her, and a violent shake sent the water into ripples of frenzy.

'What's going on?' She called out.

The low calculated chuckle rang out, halting her struggle, sending a chill down her spine that paralysed her. She had heard it too many times before.

'Otto?' She whispered.

'I know what you did, Ada. You left him. You won't see him again. But I'll find you,' and with that, he was gone, but more painfully, so was Erich. She resigned herself to her fate, allowing the water to swallow her. Her lungs burned, her consciousness faded, and her heart was breaking.

'No, no, no!' She shrieked, gasping for air, her nightgown heavy on her chest and drenched in sweat. Camille was there in a flash holding her tightly, stroking her straggly, wet hair, humming gently, waiting patiently for her to still.

'I'm sorry,' she sobbed into Camille's shoulder.

'There is nothing you need to apologise for my dear. Your demons run deep. They have been bothering you more lately. Have you been praying?'

Marianne inhaled deeply, 'Everyday Camille.'

'You can call me Maman, my dear,' she smiled as she lifted her chin, gently brushing away the stray tears on her cheeks.

This brought some warmth to her heart. Camille had treated her like a daughter the moment that she arrived in Avignon. Camille was so loving, so attentive, her son Etienne was her pride and joy, and that was plain to see. Her eyes had done nothing but sparkle with glee since they had told them the news. Already she was putting arrangements together, measuring Marianne up for a dress which she insisted that she would make, along with the cake, and arranging the flowers. It brought her so much joy to bring others joy through her works, and Marianne couldn't be more grateful to have her alongside her. But her heart always broke a little bit each time she saw her, knowing that deception was at the centre of their arrangement, Camille didn't deserve that.

She had made that much clear in her shock at Etienne's proposal on that early morning a week earlier.

***

'Etienne, I have already lied enough to you and your family. I can't keep expecting so much of you. This is *marriage* we are talking about! Once we do this, it can't be undone. As Ada, I am already married.'

'But as Marianne, you are not,' he replied so calmly that it dumbfounded her.

'That's not the point, Etienne. We would be living a lie.'

'But what is the alternative, Ada?'

It was so sweet to finally have someone use her proper name. But she knew what needed to be done. He was right, she couldn't take that chance. Etienne was an astute man, there were not many like him, but he also had no experience with identification papers. If he could see through the mistakes, then someone else surely would. She sighed in resignation.

'Are you sure that this is what *you* want, Etienne? You are such a good man; you deserve nothing but love.'

'Ada… I am not… inclined towards romance.'

'What do you mean?'

'I have never had romantic feelings towards anyone. I respect and love people, but not in the way that would be necessary for marriage.'

He glanced at his feet, embarrassed, her heart ached for him.

'You would be willing to go through all of this for me?'

'Oui. You intrigue me, you treat and serve my family well, and now that I know who you really are, I respect you. I want to protect you.'

She knew in her heart that he would treat her well. As wary as they had been around each other in the beginning now that the truth was out, there was a bond between them.

'In which case, you will have to stop calling me Ada,' she smiled.

'Is that a yes?' He asked.

'Yes, Etienne, I will marry you.'

***

Etienne insisted on holding back from telling Camille and Pierre until he had purchased a ring for her; and true to his word, he returned at the end of the working day with a thin gold band, with a tiny blue sapphire in the centre which you almost had to squint to see. It was simple, but it was beautiful, and the gesture was even more so.

'I didn't really know what to look for,' he admitted sheepishly.

'Etienne, it's perfect. You really didn't need to.'

'Everything needs to be official,' he stated, rather seriously but there was a hint of a smile at the edge of his mouth.

He delicately took her hand and placed the band on her finger, she gently squeezed his hand in return. She wanted to do everything she could to show him her gratitude for the lengths he was going to for her. But he hastily took his hand away from her grasp and began to busy himself with the day's schedule.

'When are we going to tell Pierre and Camille?' She asked.

Etienne paused, and straightened his back, wincing as he did so, it was difficult to see him in so much discomfort every day. She knew that he did his best to hide it.

'I was thinking maybe at dinner, remember we have a whole working day to get through first. If my mother knows now, we will never get anything done.'

'That's true,' Marianne chuckled.

Her stomach was in a tight knot by the time the evening had arrived. She triple-checked each of the day's numbers deliberately to slow herself and prolong the inevitable. The band was a perfect fit, but it felt suffocating around her finger. She twisted it round and round, wondering if all the wishes in the world would diminish the guilt she felt. She succeeded in keeping away from Camille for the day, thankfully she had been kept busy at the seamstresses, many brides-to-be were frantically moving their wedding dates up to marry their sweethearts before they were sent off into the abyss of war. She hoped that these women knew exactly whom they were marrying.

Marianne breathed a large sigh of relief when Etienne appeared at the doorway. He accepted her arm as she helped him through the entrance, she could feel how tense he was, his face etched in a strained frown. She held onto him as they tentatively entered the kitchen where Pierre was reading the newspaper, war statistics already scattered the front page. Camille was nursing pinpricks in her thumb from her latest needlework. Her eyes lit up with delight when she saw them arm in arm.

'Maman, Papa,' Etienne began, 'Marianne has done me the great honour of agreeing to be my wife.'

'Ma pêche!' Camille cried out, immediately sweeping them both into the tightest hug, showering them both in kisses and tears of joy.

Pierre rose steadily from his chair and firmly shook Etienne's hand before enveloping him in a firm embrace of his own.

'I knew it, I just knew it!' Camille squealed in excitement, 'a ring

Etienne! Did you get her a ring?'

'Oui, Maman,' Etienne sighed.

The next few minutes were spent cooing over the ring, exclamations of how lucky they were, what a lovely couple they made, and how wonderful it was that they had fallen in love. Marianne's heart both swelled and dropped, it was as overwhelming as she had imagined.

Her newly betrothed seemed to sense her anticipation and quickly changed the subject.

'Maman, it is our desire to be wed soon. Early in the new year, if possible.'

Marianne's heart skipped a beat. So close to her first wedding.

'Of course, ma pêche! We will get you measured up for a dress immediately Marianne my dear! It will have to be basic I'm afraid, there is not a lot of money to spare for materials.'

'Oh, Camille! It's more than enough, thank you!'

'What of your parents, Marianne?' a gruff voice broke through.

She almost jumped at the sound of Pierre's voice; she was so accustomed to his silence that his voice was so unusual to hear.

'They… they are no more,' she replied, dipping her head to hide her deceitful blush, which thankfully they interpreted as a sign of grief.

'Marianne, my dear, it would be an honour to walk you down the aisle and give you away to my son,' Pierre said earnestly, tears sparkling in his eyes.

'Oh, Pierre! Thank you!' She gasped, rushing into his open arms.

The rest of the evening was spent in celebration, the joy overlooked the true nature of their arrangement. Nobody questioned how far they stood apart, their lack of conversation; now and then Etienne gave her a knowing glance. She knew that they would need to put on a convincing show.

But even though it was the safest she had felt since running away, her night terrors had continued, and become worse. Ever since the engagement, the water, and the drowning plagued her dreams.

***

Stuttgart, September 1938

'We will need a reason for your disappearance, Ada. One that will be convincing. Otto won't believe that you just vanished, and worse, he may come looking for you.'

'I don't know what he will believe,' Ada cried, burying her face in her hands, still reeling from the shock of knowing that she would have to abandon her son.

They were all silent for a few moments.

'What if you drowned, Ada?' Liselotte said.

'What?' Ada gasped.

'Not literally, of course! But what if, tomorrow, you leave Erich with your mother, and say you need to run some errands? You come straight here, hand over a few items of the clothes that you are wearing, and I will give you some of mine, and from there we will help you get to the first stage. When people start asking questions, me and Thomas will lay out your clothes in the river, when they are discovered, they will assume the worst.'

'It's all so bleak, Lise.'

'Since when has anything been hopeful in the last few years, Ada?'

Ada looked over longingly at her beautiful son who was happily playing with a rolling pin.

'Only him,' Ada whispered.

***

RACHEL WELLAND

Avignon, January 1940

'I just need to take up that last little bit there Marianne dear.'

Marianne was speechless. She looked long and hard at herself in the mirror, she didn't know how Camille had managed to do it. The crepe material she had procured was simple, yet breath-taking. The beautiful ivory colour was subtle and understated, standing out was far from her intention. The long-ruffled sleeves creased perfectly at her elbow and kept her adequately warm from the bitter winter chill. The sleeves gave way to the simple embroidered high neckline. Marianne couldn't believe how comfortable she could feel in a wedding dress, the memories of her mother's dress clinging to her so tightly subconsciously caused her to hold her breath. The skirt hugged at her curves but flowed gracefully over her belly, which she had come to love. It was her only reminder of Erich; she brushed her hands over it and smiled.

She lifted the bottom of the skirt that spilt over her feet to allow Camille to pin up the hem. As she watched Camille's expert hands work away, she marvelled at how Camille had managed to pull all of it together in just a few weeks. Marianne felt so honoured to become part of her family, making it even more important that she never found out the truth.

When Camille drew herself up, she met Marianne's gaze in the mirror. She squeezed her shoulders tenderly.

'Magnificent, Marianne,' she breathed.

'I don't know how I can ever thank you, Camille.'

'Knowing that you will be a part of our family is more than enough, Marianne, my dear. Take good care of my Etienne.'

'I will, I promise', and she meant every word.

'There's just one thing missing.'

Camille hurried upstairs, leaving Marianne to contemplate. In two days, she would be married, again. The closer the day came the more it gnawed away at her, she felt guilty for robbing Etienne of a life he didn't want, deceiving her in-laws to be, becoming her new identity and burying her past life once and for all. She had barely had a moment in amongst the preparations to grieve.

'Marianne? My dear, what is wrong?' Camille's voice drifted through the room making Marianne jump, she didn't realise that she was crying.

'Nothing, Camille,' Marianne sniffed, 'I just love the dress so much. It's happening so soon and I'm so happy,' she said, pulling Camille into a hug to hide her burning cheeks. The familiar smell of lavender wafted over her shoulder slightly easing the knot in her stomach.

'Anything for you, my dear,' Camille whispered. 'Turn back towards the mirror and crouch down slightly,' she instructed.

Marianne did so, and Camille placed on a small veil and attached the most stunning hairpin that Marianne had ever seen.

'I know that it's not much, but this is the veil I wore when I married Pierre, and this is an heirloom passed down in my family. Will you wear them for me?'

'Camille… they are breathtaking. I couldn't possibly…'

'Of course, you can my dear, you are family, and we do everything for family.'

'That we do,' Marianne sighed, holding onto Camille's hand firmly.

***

Each piece dazzled in the bright sunshine, there could be no more perfect day for a winter wedding. Pierre rubbed Marianne's hands in his to warm them from the crisp chill as they waited outside of the chapel. The guests were few, Etienne's very glamorous aunt and uncle had come to represent Camille's side of the family, the rest were unable to attend, Marianne didn't know why but Etienne had told her not to ask after them. Monsieur and Madame Penaud were there, Etienne's beloved violin teacher whom he had spoken about so fondly. And of course, Camille and Pierre.

As they waited for their cue, Marianne couldn't help but think of her own parents, and how proud they had been of her. She felt like she had done right by them, and she missed them. She quickly smoothed her skirt and fiddled with the hairpin to distract herself.

'You look perfect,' Pierre smiled proudly.

'Thank you for everything, Pierre.'

'Call me Papa.'

'Papa,' Marianne smiled.

They entered through the small rickety door and made their way down the narrow aisle towards Etienne who stood tall and proud in his suit gifted to him by his absent grandfather. His hair was smoothed back, making all his features stand out, his long thin nose, his blue eyes that were steely with determination, and his cheekbones stood out prominently on his clean-shaven face. His navy blue cravat was positioned perfectly against his crisp white shirt and black blazer, he looked the part, and incredibly handsome. The edges of his mouth curved into that small reassuring smile that Marianne had come to know well.

She couldn't help but notice him fidget every now and then and his eyebrows would rise slightly. There were a few small mutterings on the left, and a few fingers pointed towards where Etienne had been looking. They passed by Camille's gorgeous flower arrangements that adorned each pew. She did her best to catch people's eyes and smile at them knowing that good first impressions were vital.

When they finally reached Etienne at the altar, her palms were sweating profusely despite the cold. When Etienne took her hands in his, he could sense her unease, he leaned forward slightly towards her.

'Don't be scared, everything will be okay,' he whispered delicately but assuredly, she nodded, comforted by his certainty.

They both spoke their vows not daring to break eye contact with each other, they both knew what this meant. Forming an unbreakable bond. Whilst they promised to love, honour, and obey, they were silently promising to protect, trust, and support each other in their agreed ways, no matter what. Their light and brief kiss initiated their commitment.

'Presenting, Etienne and Marianne Touelle.'

Marianne Touelle.

***

She had forgotten how exhausting wedding days were. They arrived back at Etienne's house in the early hours of the morning.

She allowed Etienne to ascend the stairs gingerly, she knew he would be hurting after being on his feet all day. She unclasped the hairpin and the veil and placed them both delicately into a small pine wooden box that Etienne had made specially, before placing it all inside Etienne's desk, locking them away for safekeeping. When she eventually ascended the stairs herself and entered the bedroom, she was surprised to see Etienne sitting on the edge of the bed, hands clutching the bedsheets with a pained expression displayed on his face.

'Etienne?'

He nearly leapt out of his skin at the sound of her voice.

'Are you in pain? Is there anything I can get to help?'

'Marianne, I don't know how to do this.'

'Do what Etienne?' She asked.

He looked sheepishly at the bed.

'Oh, that...' Marianne breathed in relief, 'that's okay, we don't have to, tonight.'

He exhaled, but only slightly.

'I don't know if I ever can, Marianne,' he said, staring at his feet in embarrassment.

She sat down next to him, careful not to touch him.

'We don't have to do anything you don't want to do, Etienne,' she assured.

'But won't you want to?'

'My experiences have never been great,' she admitted.

Etienne shuffled his hand next to hers, linking his little finger with hers.

'I will do my best to protect you, I promise.'

'I know you will,' she smiled, 'but Etienne, there is one thing I would like you to do.'

She felt him tense again.

'The violin you finished working on the other day,' she continued, 'will you play it for me?'

Etienne's eyes lit up, she helped him rise to his feet and waited eagerly as he made his way back from his office. She watched him in awe as he gracefully raised the violin rest to his chin, brandished the bow with authority, and began to play. His eyes were closed and focused, in a different world as he glided the bow over the strings, playing the most beautiful melody. All she could do was watch as her husband expressed himself in the truest way he knew how. When the final note faded into the night air, she let out the breath she had been holding.

'Etienne, you are a genius,' she gasped.

Etienne blushed, turning away to set the instrument down safely.

'What was that piece of music?'

'I made it up,' he replied.

'What? It is beautiful! How did you think of it?'

'Good inspiration.'

'What is the piece called?'

'Marianne's song,' he said, smiling warmly at her.

PHILIPP

Avignon, March 1940

The fever was the most unbearable part. He didn't know how many times he had drifted in and out of consciousness. When he started to come around, he was met with the same blurred vision. A small figure was always standing in the doorway of a tiny draughty room. All the colours blurred into one. He had no idea where he was, who he was with, and what they intended to do with him.

It must have been days later when he finally gained enough consciousness to see his surroundings in better clarity. He opened his bleary eyes gently, as the intensity of pain in his head felt like it was going to split wide open. He searched around with his hands desperately trying to utilise his other senses to figure out what was happening. The floor was scratchy and rough, sharp splinters pricked his fingers and he could feel small oozes of blood seep out of his fingertips. He wasn't on a bed; his muscles were stiff and ached like hell. How long had he been motionless? As he continued to search around, his hand finally brushed something slightly softer, a rag or a blanket? Philipp followed the length of material around him, discovering that it had been placed underneath him. His captors had seemed to have gone at least some way to procure comfort for him. He felt around the top of

234

his head, propped up with something chaotically folded, a jacket or coat maybe? The only light that crept in was from some small gaps in the ceiling, the light was a little brighter than before, so it must be daytime.

He needed to know more; it was the longest he had been able to stay awake. Philipp summoned every effort that his body would allow and rolled off the makeshift bed onto his front, his head immediately pounded at the need to support its own weight. Forcing his eyes wide open was met with a sharp intense pain. Reaching out, he could feel that he was almost in contact with another wall, an enclosed space.

It's not a prison cell.

The wood had a familiar smell to it, and the occasional waft of cooking let him deduce that it had to be some kind of residential property. He thought hard, somewhere in the vague recesses of his memory, he had heard clanging, banging, machines of some kind. What the hell it was all for he had no idea. His mind switched to a dark place.

What if this is how I meet my end? At the hands of maniacs?

No. This can't be everything he had fought for, for it all to end now. He had to do something. Anything.

He tried to tuck his legs underneath to pull himself onto all fours but collapsed from the sharp shock of agony that shot through his feet. He tried to cry out, but no sound came, the dryness of his mouth now at the forefront of his awareness.

Severe dehydration. That would explain the unbearable headaches.

He winced hard which dulled the pain in his head for a moment, until he forced his eyes open again. Every part of his body was on fire as he peered down his now almost skeletal like frame down towards his feet which were covered in bandages. What the hell had happened to him?

The fever started to burn fiercely again; he knew he only had a small amount of time before he passed out again. Adrenaline was

235

the only thing that got him back on his knees, wobbling, scrambling, maybe towards a door? His vision blurred. The creak behind him sent him crashing back to the floor. Behind him. His hands had been exploring the walls. The figure was now in the room, standing over him, Philipp tried to flail, but his limbs would not comply, defeated by exhaustion. The shape moved in front of him, and he could just about make out the face of... yes, a female!

'Bitte,' he croaked. The last of the light slowly faded as she finally spoke.

'Etienne! Aide-moi! Il se réveille!'

***

In his dream, he was walking. He was in bad shape. The miles that he had covered coupled with the drastic changes in weather along the way had worn the soles of his boots dramatically, it was like walking on a scrunched-up piece of rag. Every uneven bit of ground, every jagged rock, was torture underfoot. The last of the summer sun beat down on him, he was grateful for the material that Alejandro had given up for him as he mopped a fresh band of sweat from his neck. He had to stop more regularly, he was suffering badly from malnourishment, stealing only what he could from markets much to his discomfort, and trying to make it go as far as possible.

He had lost track of how long he had been on the move; it must have been weeks. The small towns he travelled through had been in a frenzy, something was seriously wrong. People talked frantically, rushed around, some were yelling, and some were crying. Although he couldn't understand what they were saying it didn't take a genius to figure it out. *Guerra,* just as Alejandro said, the word was everywhere. It had finally happened. Despite the amount of stolen goods that he managed to procure that day, he couldn't muster the desire to eat, not when he knew that nowhere in the world was safe now.

Philipp urged his tired feet forward, stumbling further up the beaten track when he at last spotted woodland in the distance. The trees would provide some shade from the sun and maybe there would be a stream running nearby if it hadn't dried up. Mercifully, he didn't have to wander too far before he found a sheltered area that was ideal to stay in, at least for the night.

His feet were sore and swollen, but he had to push through the discomfort as he always did to do his checks, he searched until he was sure that he was alone. Philipp removed his boots and peeled back the socks that had become firmly attached to his feet. He whimpered as he pulled them away from deep, bleeding sores and weeping blisters, set his feet to rest on the grass and breathed through the intense stinging. He sighed knowing they would be hard to treat, his supplies were taking a hit with the number of times he was having to redress the wounds. It was a nightmare not knowing where he was heading, or how long he could keep this up for.

He was so lost in his thoughts that he didn't see the dark clouds forming or hear the first rumble of thunder in the distance. When the first thick teardrop of rain finally fell, it fell directly onto one of the open sores, Philipp cried out but sat back to allow them to be soaked. As the rain lashed down Philipp closed his eyes, a sweet moment of relief, it was as if the rain was cleansing him.

'Thank you, God,' he spoke out into the storm.

***

The same relief that he had felt then was reminiscent of right now. He couldn't tell where it was coming from. Philipp pried his heavy eyelids open to find that he was propped up, leaning against a person, a hand in front of him held a cup, carefully wetting his lips, and tipping tiny drops a bit at a time into the small gap of his open mouth. He flinched as he fully came round, pulling away from the stranger and knocking the cup out of their hand as he tried to scurry away.

'Easy! Easy!' She exclaimed.

'Who are you? What do you want with me?' Philipp gasped, choking on his sharp inhalation of air.

'It's okay!' She exclaimed.

Both were breathing heavily. Their eyes never left each other, fearful that the other would make an unpredictable move. Philipp could feel his heartbeat thumping, he was sure that this stranger would be able to see it almost jumping out from his chest underneath his thin, ragged shirt, and diminished frame.

'My name is Marianne,' she said, calmly.

She was German like him, but what if she was luring him into a false sense of security? Philipp bristled as he fought with his conscience. He remained tight-lipped, pressed up against the wall. To his surprise she lowered herself down onto the splinter-ridden floor, folding her legs beneath her. A sign of submission?

'You were extremely poorly. Do you remember? I found you in the street. You were shouting. Most of it didn't make sense. I tried to keep my distance from you, I thought you were mad. But then I heard your accent, I heard your words, I heard your plight.'

Moments of that day came back in flashes, but he had never forgotten the stranger who took him in. She was convincing, but he wouldn't take the bait, he averted his eyes away from her probing stare.

'This is our home. Me, and my husband.'

Philipp let out a small breath of relief, knowing that some of his deductions had been correct. Marianne's gaze drifted down his body towards the ruined state of his feet.

'I will need to redress them,' she stated.

Philipp could feel every bump, and every open, weeping sore. The anguish was terrible. He knew she was right. She hadn't done too bad a job tending to them, the problem was the infection that had set in.

She rose to her feet and headed towards the door with the empty cup.

'How long have they been like this?' Philipp asked, finally breaking his silence.

Her shoulders relaxed, and she turned back towards him.

238

'I found you like this. You were staggering around the streets. You were so pale, and exhausted. Your eyes looked haunted, and if you don't mind me saying, they still do. Things here are unsafe and people are struggling. Everyone is suspicious of everyone. But you were walking around barefoot, leaving a blood trail behind you. You were fading when I brought you here.'

'Where is *here*?'

'Avignon,' she replied.

There was nowhere he could go in this state. It was so much more dangerous out there now. The Germans were about to make their move, and it was going to be big, he didn't just feel it, he feared it. Philipp shuddered and sighed heavily as he leaned his head back against the wall. He would once again have to have faith in strangers just to survive.

'What is it?' Marianne asked.

'We are both a long way from home,' Philipp mumbled.

It must have struck a nerve with her, every expression on her face dropped, the straight line of her mouth pressed firmer. She scurried to her feet, smoothing her skirt down.

'I... I will fetch you some more water and bandages. Do you think you will be able to eat?'

Philipp nodded absentmindedly as he tried to piece together the rush of memories that Marianne had painted for him. His headache was finally starting to dull, Marianne had done well to rehydrate him, he was still exhausted, his limbs heavy and aching.

Marianne promptly returned with what she promised. She handed Philipp the cup, and this time he drank in gulps, each mouthful replenishing to the soul. When she placed the thin vegetable broth in front of him, his empty stomach howled. Philipp didn't care that the heat scalded his mouth and throat, the immediate strength that he felt from his first taste of proper food in weeks was invigorating. But his blissful moment was interrupted by Marianne's concerned glance returning to his feet. She slowly took the small roll of bandages out from her apron pocket.

'Please,' Philipp begged.

'I'm sorry, but I have to,' she said apologetically.

'No please, let me.'

'Are you sure?'

'Yes. Did I have a bag with me when you found me?'

'Yes, you did! We hid it away.'

'Please could you get it?' Philipp asked.

Marianne said nothing but eyed him suspiciously.

'Look inside it. There's not much left in it. But there may be some alcohol in there.'

Marianne persisted with her stare.

'For the wounds,' Philipp stated, a belligerent tone catching the edge of his words.

His impatience seemed to urge Marianne into action. She obediently climbed down the stairs out of the room returning a few minutes later with the bag.

The strap had become incredibly worn; several of the seams were hanging on by just a few threads. As he suspected, there was hardly anything left in the bag, except for a small bottle of vodka which was a quarter full, the cloth given to him by Alejandro, some small scraps of coarsely cut bandages, and the small bulge in the self-made hidden compartment which contained his identification papers.

He took a deep breath as he started to remove the encrusted, foul-smelling bandages from his feet. When he could finally see the full extent of the damage, he was horrified. Some old cuts had begun to heal but many had fused with blisters to make armies of concentrated infection. Blood and pus oozed out onto his fingertips as he inspected them. He glanced up, surprised to see that Marianne was still standing in the doorway watching him.

'Please could you get me some cloth and fresh water?'

She nodded, seemingly satisfied that neither he nor the contents of his bag posed an immediate threat to her or her household. Philipp continued to inspect in her absence; the abrasions didn't look too deep much to his relief.

No tissue damage. Diligent cleaning and bandage changes should mean they will heal soon.

On Marianne's return, he carefully tended to the worst of the wounds, wincing as the intense stinging raged across his skin. Marianne's face went pale, but she could not tear her eyes away from Philipp's procedure. When he was satisfied with his work, he laid out the fresh bandages. He drew his left foot up close to him, and a different, fresh, sharp pain made him finally see it; the menacing looking bruising that decorated the swollen side of his left foot. Marianne noticed his concern.

'We have barely touched it, I promise. We just cleaned your wounds. We thought that because you were lying down it would heal with rest,' she said quietly.

'How long has it been like this?' Philipp asked.

'The swelling is about three days old. But the bruises have been forming for longer.'

'You did the right thing' he concluded; Marianne smiled in relief.

He quickly bandaged one foot, before turning his attention to the other foot, he glanced up uneasily at Marianne.

'I need you to help me to my feet.'

'What? But they need to be rested, surely?'

'I can't tell if it is broken unless I try and put weight on it.'

Marianne drew back, with uncertainty.

'Please, Marianne,' he begged.

She moved close to him, and draped Philipp's arm over her shoulder. There was the slightest hint of lavender on her clothing, it was immediately calming.

'On three. One, two, three,' Marianne whispered as she lifted him upright, he was shocked at how easily she was able to lift him. She let his feet hover momentarily.

'Now,' Philipp whispered, taking in a bracing breath as he did so, trying to keep his mind clear enough to assess the damage objectively. As his feet touched the floorboards, he felt the sharp pricks of pain from the sores shoot through his feet. Trying to discern what pain was which, Philipp looked down at his swollen foot, gently applying more pressure. He nearly wept with relief at the dull ache that met him.

'What is it?' Marianne asked worryingly, 'Is it broken? You need to sit back down.'

'No, no, it's okay Marianne! It's just sprained, and it's healing.'

'Oh, thank God!' Marianne exclaimed, gently lowering Philipp back onto the blankets, tucking them around him neatly.

'Marianne?' Philipp asked.

'Yes?'

'Why are you helping me? You know nothing about me.'

She paused as she considered his question.

'I have been reliant on the kindness of others for a long time. Both friends and strangers. It is only because of them that I am here. You looked like someone who needed that same kindness.'

Philipp's eyes widened, maybe they had more in common than he first thought? She gave him another small smile and returned downstairs. As Philipp lay back, the fever once again starting to make his body flush all over with heat, he realised that she had never asked him for his name.

***

Marianne came up twice a day with food, water, cloths, and bandages. She would help him onto his feet, and help him walk slowly around the small space, which was just enough for what he needed for now. He could feel himself getting stronger every day. Marianne would try and bring a variety of foods up to him, soups, bread, and very small pieces of meat trying to give him the nutrients he needed to recover. Now that he was able to stay awake for longer, he could spend time conversing. He found out that the noises from downstairs and next door were from the carpentry business that Marianne's husband and father-in-law ran together, that she was originally from Stuttgart and the youngest of five children.

Today it was his turn to confide. He told Marianne of Berlin, his father's antique shop, and his desire to become a doctor.

'That would explain a lot,' she smiled, pointing at his feet, 'you've been taking care of yourself this whole time?'

'Yes, for over a year.'

There was a consistent thud in the background as they talked, but Philipp chose to ignore it.

'You have been on the move that whole time?'

'Not quite.'

'Where will you go from here?'

'I do not know,' he answered truthfully.

The clunking noise was now close, very close... the door swung open making them both jump, revealing a tall, thin man, wearing a thin apron over his dungarees, covered in shavings of wood, stray strands of hair patterned his creased brow.

'Etienne! Qu'est- ce que tu fais ici?'

They exchanged some animated words, Philipp couldn't understand what was being said, but he saw Marianne's lip quiver, they were arguing over him.

Etienne towered above them both, and with that cane next to him he could easily be intimidating, but he made no threatening move towards either of them.

He knew that he couldn't be Edgar Meyer anymore, that man was a fugitive. If people were looking for him then it would be far too risky to use that identity.

'Philipp,' he blurted out.

Both Marianne and Etienne simultaneously snapped their heads towards him. He looked between them, and then just at Marianne.

'Marianne, my name is Philipp. I have been on the run for over a year because I am Jewish.'

Her eyebrows rose in surprise, she whispered the translation to her husband, who immediately drew himself to his full height and without saying a word exited the room, his cane clunking behind him.

Neither Philipp nor Marianne said a word to each other. Etienne's reaction had said it all, he would have to leave, and he feared he wouldn't last long. But then Etienne returned, balancing quilts and a flattened pillow in one arm. He set them down in front of Philipp, looked him directly in the eye, and spoke earnestly.

'Philipp tu dois rester ici.'

'Philipp, you are staying with us,' Marianne gasped.

Philipp wasn't aware of how much emotion he had withheld, but this kindness he could not contain. He wept, he couldn't speak, and the tears did not stop. He extended a shaky hand out to Etienne who grasped it tightly in recognition of their new arrangement.

ETIENNE

News of Hitler's rampage across Europe was all that dominated the news. But in the smaller crowds, there were other whisperings of what was happening to the people that were deemed 'undesirable' by the madman. His thoughts immediately turned to how Philipp looked when Marianne pulled him through the door just a few days ago. Gaunt, skeletal, not far from death's door. He was proud of her, and he admired her desire to help others. But he was also mad at her, for her carelessness and disregard for the risks.

'What the hell were you thinking?'

'He needed help, Etienne.'

'What if you were seen?'

'He needed *help,* Etienne!'

'Marianne, he's German.'

'So am I.'

'It's not the same, and you know it!'

She stormed off.

They sat in stony silence at dinner with Camille and Pierre, the tension between them didn't escape Camille's notice. As they were leaving, she tugged gently at Etienne's sleeve.

'Ma pêche? Is everything okay?'

'It is fine, Maman. We just had an argument.'

'Don't go to bed at odds, ma pêche.'

'We won't, Maman, I promise,' he said before swiftly kissing her cheek, but he could feel her worried stare boring into his back as they left.

Marianne had gone on ahead of him. When he got in through the door, she was already descending the stairs, holding strips of cloth.

'How is he?' Etienne asked.

'Asleep. I've mopped his brow and changed the bandages on his feet. He has a fever.'

Etienne nodded, 'I will get some more bandages when I am in town tomorrow.'

She looked surprised. 'You're not going to throw him out?'

'It's like you said. He needs help.'

Her kiss caught him by surprise as she flew across the room, he did his best to kiss her back, it wasn't unpleasant. As she pulled away, he rubbed her shoulder affectionately but awkwardly.

'I…I'll keep an eye on what people are saying over the next few days. I'll sort things out.'

'You always do Etienne. Thank you,' she said smiling at him before ascending the stairs once again.

For the rest of the week, he found an excuse to go out into the old town and into the city. It was quiet, but a smaller amount of people meant that word would spread faster, particularly if something strange had happened. But by the grace of God, no one seemed to suspect them.

***

Avignon, May 1940

'Once a week only, Marianne. Fetch the groceries and converse lightly with people. They will see you, know who you are, and your work.'

'That's not much Etienne,' she grumbled, swinging her legs childishly from the stool she was perched on.

'It's the safest thing to do for now,' he said, increasingly annoyed at her protests, 'you need to disguise your accent more.'

'Nobody but you notices it, Etienne.'

'If I can notice it Marianne, then someone else inevitably will. What if the Germans invade, and make it here?'

'Okay, I get it,' she muttered, sliding off her seat to busy herself with some account sheets.

He shouldn't have left their dispute hanging in the air as he left to run his errands; they would inevitably argue about it later. He knew that she was bored stuck in the house. But he had to keep her safe, that was his promise to her, and it wasn't just her he had to be concerned about now.

***

Another ball of spit hit him square in the face. He tried to hide his frustration as he wiped his cheek with his sleeve.

'You are an embarrassment!'

'Our sons are off fighting for the likes of you!'

'Useless!'

'Pick up a gun!'

'Be a real man!' voices called out from all around. Another kicked at his cane to try and knock him off balance.

Any man of his age who was still in the city and not on the front line was despised. Especially after the latest news had broken, that covered every front page of the newspapers.

The Germans get past the Meuse River

All within twenty-four hours. They were here. They were even more efficient than first feared. If they didn't need it then, they needed it now, every single available man to defend the country. Even when Etienne had tried to speak to an enlisting officer, he had taken one look at him and sent him on his way.

Etienne wrestled his way out of the mob and found himself walking towards the river instead of to the winding streets that directed him home. He felt vexed and ashamed, why couldn't he be the person that people expected him to be?

He reached the edge of the old crumbling wall where he had stood so often as a child. In the fresh spring air, it was so peacefully tranquil, everything that the world was not. The still water helped him refocus his mind.

Glancing out across the Pont d'Avignon, he took in the luscious scene. The stretches of forest, fern, juniper, and moss green colours from the overgrowth area, blended to paint their picture of harmony. The morning sunshine danced over the loose petals of pale pink springtime blossom that was starting to emerge, the serenity only added to by the chirping of a group of finches dancing around at the furthest point of the bridge.

Maman would love this he thought to himself.

She always kept herself busy, it was difficult to find time to have a decent conversation with her. She was the one who had been with him the evening that his true passions were ignited. But so much had changed since then. Those four long years. Parts of the world had erupted with the sound of gunfire, explosions, and suffering, where other parts fell silent. The silence that they allowed to rob them of joy, family, homes, and peace. Slowly but surely the city was descending into that same silence.

Running his hands back over the uneven pieces of the wall, Etienne plucked out a small, loose piece of rubble and let it tumble over his fingertips. He closed his eyes and made a promise.

I will use the silence to be brave.

Using his free arm, he drew it far back and released the rubble from his hand, and watched it soar over the river and land in a secluded area away from the prying eyes of the shoreline, vegetation, and the nosy wildlife.

The clock chimed in the distance; he was running late getting back to Marianne who was running the shop in his absence. Pierre was busy scouting local areas trying to procure as many materials as possible, they had to be prepared.

***

'Where have you been Etienne? I was getting worried,' Marianne asked, breathing a sigh of relief as Etienne finally limped through the door.

'I went down to the river,' he admitted.

'What happened?'

She knew that it was a special place for him, somewhere for him to gather his thoughts and still his mind. Etienne had taken her there regularly in the early days of their marriage, which everyone else thought was romantic, but it was predominantly done to help Marianne get her bearings, pick out key geographical features, if something happened, and she needed to know how to get away.

'People are angry and scared. I'm okay, you don't need to worry,' he said.

Marianne sighed, seemingly unconvinced by his words but signalled him over to the couple in the workshop.

'Monsieur and Madame Marchand would like a dolls' house for their granddaughter,' she said, tapping his shoulder twice before walking away from him. Their sign that she was going to tend to Philipp.

He knew the exact positioning of the attic, where Philipp was sleeping, every section that creaked, every area where if you listened closely you could pick up hints of conversation. Etienne crossed over to the other side of the room and called his customers to attention.

'Monsieur, Madame, tell me about this doll house you would like.'

***

There hadn't been many occasions where he and Philipp had been alone together, mainly because they couldn't understand each other. Philipp spoke very little French, and Etienne knew no German. Marianne was their go-between, she was good with people and had taken great care of nursing Philipp back to health, and Philipp seemed to trust her.

He was getting stronger every day, he had stopped burning up, the sores on his feet were finally starting to clear, and the sprain had healed enough to allow him to start walking properly again. When the workshop was empty, Etienne would tap his cane on the stairs to signal that it was okay for Philipp to walk around the room.

The following morning was strangely busy, many orders were being retrieved, and carts lined the narrow street outside the shop. Marianne was frantically organising final invoices and arranging payments, whilst Etienne and Camille worked together to carefully move the finished products safely into the hands of their new owners. By midday, they were all drained.

'I will go and make lunch,' Camille announced, 'we have all earned it today!' She smiled as rushed out of the door.

Both Etienne and Marianne were looking at each other in triumph but then Marianne's face turned to one of shock.

'The music box! I was picking up the final pieces for it the other day when I stopped by your Tante Georgette's. She insisted on seeing it, I must have left it there!' She exclaimed.

'It will take me too long to get there Marianne, you will have to go.'

She was almost out of the door by the time he finished speaking.

'Etienne, hold some back,' Marianne instructed, her eyes sought his understanding, Etienne nodded. In their busyness, they had forgotten to give Philipp any food.

Despite Marianne's absence, it was nice to spend some quality time with Camille, even if he was stuffing bread into his pocket when she wasn't looking.

'It is beautiful down by the river at the moment, Maman. The blossom is just starting to bloom.'

'You will have to take me there soon ma pêche. Maybe when the sun is just about to set?'

'The perfect time.'

'You have been such a help to your father ma pêche. I know he does not speak much these days. But he is so proud of you. We both are.'

'Merci, Maman. I do worry about him.'

'You let me worry about him ma pêche. You have enough to be concerned with.'

If only you knew.

'I cannot help it, Maman. What if the Germans get to us? What will that mean for Papa?'

Camille studied her astute son for a moment, Etienne couldn't tell if she was upset or impressed with him.

'You read people so well. But you must also trust what you

already know about them. Your father is struggling to come to terms with what is happening yes. But your father is the bravest man I have ever known.'

'He has seen so much,' Etienne sighed.

'Trust that his bravery will prevail. He is strong, and as his son, you are too.' There was no hint of doubt in her conviction.

He bid goodbye to his mother and watched as she began to busy herself in her garden before going back to his house. It took ages to ascend the small narrow staircase to the attic. When he finally reached the room and opened the door, Philipp scampered back in shock. He had forgotten to tap.

'Pardon! Pardon!' Etienne exclaimed, realising his mistake immediately.

Philipp walked gingerly towards Etienne, and Etienne placed the broken-up pieces of bread and cheese into Philipp's hands.

'Merci beaucoup, Etienne,' Philipp mumbled as he ate hungrily.

Etienne nodded; he never knew what to do now. Marianne could obviously stay and talk with him; he would find out more about him courtesy of her later. Instead, he busied himself with the unsavoury task of clearing away the waste bucket. It seemed horribly primitive, but he couldn't risk Philipp coming downstairs and being seen.

Etienne steadied himself on his feet before heading towards the door.

'Etienne?'

'It's okay Philipp. I have got this,'

'No, no!' Philipp exclaimed.

Etienne paused, shrugging at him to show his confusion. Philipp's face looked puzzled; his gaze was transfixed on Etienne's bad leg; Etienne blushed. He tried to turn away from him, but Philipp's protests persisted.

'No, no! Bein!' he exclaimed again, this time tugging at his sleeve trying to get his attention.

Etienne watched closely as Philipp put his own leg forward, he gestured to his hips, before moving his hands at different heights positioned along his leg, all the while shaking his head. Etienne's eyes opened wide in amazement, was he hinting at what he had believed since he was a child?

'Did the doctor set it wrong?'

'Doktor… set…' Philipp remarked, continuing to shake his head, he pointed towards him emulating the limp.

They had insisted for so many years that his bones simply hadn't healed properly, that it was his fault for resuming activity too quickly, and that he was responsible for his disfigurement.

***

'It was incredible, Marianne! He was looking at it for less than a minute and he managed to see exactly what the issue was, what it's been for so many years!'

Etienne felt liberated, and excited and he didn't hold back in showing it. Marianne had not returned until late in the afternoon, when Georgette started talking there was no stopping her; mercifully she had managed to slip away with enough time to get the music box back before the customer arrived. He couldn't wait to tell her the news.

'Etienne I am so pleased!' She beamed. 'But how could he have known that?'

'I don't know,' Etienne replied, 'but he was born to be a doctor.'

Marianne looped her arm around Etienne's waist and leaned her head against him, he gingerly but affectionately patted her shoulder.

'How can we help him, Etienne?' She whispered.

'I don't know, Marianne,' he admitted.

He wanted to be able to give her absolute certainty, but nothing was ever certain, especially with the enemy snapping closer and closer at their heels, things were only going to become more difficult.

I will use the silence to be brave.

They would have to use the time to plan, and they would have to start putting those plans into action immediately. He was sure that Marianne suspected this, but her plight also meant that she was in danger. It would have to fall to him, but he was resolved to protect everyone.

'We'll do what we can,' he promised, and he meant it.

Marianne loosened herself from their embrace, she smiled at him weakly. She was doing her best to remain strong, and Etienne admired her deeply for it. She gently touched his hand before sitting down at his desk.

'Do you have a violin that you're currently working on?' She asked quietly.

He had been working on it for weeks, lovingly varnishing the exterior, gently manoeuvring the fixed bridge into place, before re-attaching the strings with the utmost care. Etienne had asked diligently about the process his father had undergone when repairing the Belle Rose all those years ago. Fixing violins and restoring them to their full glory was one thing, playing it was a completely different feeling.

'I think it's in the workshop.'

'Will you play it for me?' Marianne pleaded.

'Of course,' Etienne replied. 'What would you like me to play?'

She studied him for a moment before she spoke, 'tell me your story, Etienne,' she said softly.

She seemed to always find ways to take him aback. They were both still trying to figure each other out, slowly revealing more about their lives, but Marianne was good at talking, and Etienne wasn't. It wasn't that he didn't want to tell her, he wanted to be as transparent with her as possible, but most of the time he didn't know how to be.

He dutifully drew the rest up to his chin, rested the bow on the strings, closed his eyes, and began. Loud staccato notes, intertwined with quieter, smoother but discordant melodies. *Show her, show her.* His eyes stayed tightly shut as he rallied all his focus on his communication with his wife.

Tears prickled his eyes when he finally opened them. When his vision cleared, he saw Marianne stood to attention, her expression unreadable, but her eyes wide in wonder. He waited uncomfortably for her to speak first.

'The day we got married. In the chapel. It was just for brief moments, but you looked off to the side, and you were scared. There's no other way to describe it.'

Etienne gulped hard; he couldn't speak.

'What happened there, Etienne?'

He glanced down at his leg, then back to Marianne.

'The pews on the higher level,' he began, Marianne nodded, 'A boy was crying. I couldn't see him. I went up the stairs,' he gulped hard again.

'What happened?' Marianne whispered.

'It gave way... I fell... and all I remember is the pain... my leg, my hip, it all was just... broken. Like me.' He was shocked at his admission, but it was the truth he had been wanting to tell for so long.

'Etienne. I want you to listen to me and I want you to listen to me carefully. We all carry brokenness, but that does not mean that we are broken.'

She was so wise for her young years, and she was desperately trying to understand him. It was all he could ever ask of her, of anyone.

MARIANNE

Avignon, July 1940

'Crayon gris, Marianne, how many times do I need to say?'

'We're arguing over a pencil, Etienne. This is ridiculous!'

'You need to be more convincing.'

'I am trying!'

After they had eaten, and she had tended to Philipp, the rest of their evening would be dedicated to improving her pronunciation, peppering her vocabulary with southern words and phrases. As usual, it had ended up in another argument.

She really was trying. She knew how scared they all were, hell, she was too! It still didn't feel real that the official French surrender had happened just two weeks ago. Etienne's sharp perception had been correct, but not even he could have foreseen that it would all happen so quickly. She would find him sometimes in the early hours of the morning hunched over his desk, his bony hands running through his hair which he did when he was deep in thought. She knew that he was formulating plans and procedures to keep her and Philipp safe, but he kept all his ideas to himself.

He didn't do it to be cruel, she knew that. Involving her and Philipp too early would be too emotionally compromising.

Brilliant though he was, he could not understand that the more she changed, the more distant she felt from Erich, that anything that he may remember about her would become completely unrecognisable.

They glared at each other, breathing heavily before a small smile betrayed Etienne.

'A little softer,' he chuckled.

'You be softer,' Marianne ordered, but she couldn't help the small giggle escaping.

'Do you want to take a break?'

'I don't want to let you down.'

'I think we'll be safe for at least one more night, Marianne.'

'We'll need years at this rate for me to get it right.'

'Don't be so hard on yourself. You are gifted at languages Marianne.'

'It's so confusing! Whenever I speak to Georgette, she has different words for different things, and then I speak to you, or Camille, or Pierre…'

'Tante Georgette has spent too much time in Paris. Besides, we can all understand you.'

'But you can all tell that I'm not from here?'

'We think your accent is peculiar. They don't suspect anything.'

'But you did.'

'You know I would never say anything, Marianne.'

'You would have before.'

'Before I knew who you really were.'

'Then who am I, Etienne?'

He looked taken aback by her question, but she was burning with frustration, why was he so keen to help her? Why was she so worthy of his care and protection?

But Etienne's pause was only momentary, he replied succinctly.

'You are the bravest person that I have ever met.'

His response touched her deeply, but a scoff was the first thing to escape from her lips.

'I ran away Etienne. I left my friends, and my family behind.' She continued. 'I'll tell you what I am Etienne Touelle. Selfish. A liability. Pathetic. Useless. I'm a terrible person. I left my child with his cruel father! His abusive, fanatic, dangerous father. And all of it for what, Etienne? To put you in danger. Philipp in danger. Pierre and Camille in danger. And you think that is brave? It's cowardly is what it is!'

Etienne said nothing. His mouth was agape, and he looked wounded. She couldn't stand to look at him any longer. The adrenaline felt like it was clogging up her chest, and it was getting harder to breathe. She strode past Etienne, up the stairs, and into their room before slamming the door. Collapsing onto the bed, she closed her eyes, pulled the pillow over her face, and screamed.

***

In her dreams, she searched for Erich yet again. He was calling for her, but she couldn't see him.

'Erich, my darling where are you?' She yelled.

The water was about to come flooding in. Otto's malicious taunts would start ringing in her ears, she held her breath trying to speed up the inevitable. But instead, she felt something tickling the bottom of her feet, it wasn't wet, but it felt fresh. Marianne opened one eye to see that there was grass underneath her bare feet, she shuffled slightly and found that she could extend her legs forward, one foot, then the other, and again, and then a little quicker, a bit faster, and then she was running. She ran as fast as her legs would carry her, she passed over fields of long, luscious grass, Erich's voice became clearer the further she ran.

'I'm coming, Erich!'

She felt like her heart would burst with both exertion and hope. She ascended a hill and found him at the top. His beautiful green eyes, glinted in the bright sunlight, and lit up as he saw her coming towards him.

'Mütter!' He squawked in delight as he toddled towards her, his little pudgy arms outstretched as Marianne swept him up into a huge hug.

She could feel her tears seeping into his thick, blonde hair. She inhaled deeply, he smelt just as she remembered, of porridge. He giggled gleefully against her chest, she hoped he could hear her racing heartbeat and know that it was him who made it beat so strongly.

Marianne felt the breeze blow across her skirt, refreshing her bare legs underneath. The wisps of Erich's hair tickled her cheek; she never wanted to leave. She tried to ignore the ominous clunking noise that was slowly approaching, she had to cherish every second before *he* would ruin it all.

'Erich, my darling I want you to listen to me carefully.'

Clunk

'I never meant to leave you. I love you. I will find a way to get back to you someday, I promise.'

Clunk

'But you are here, Mütter?'

Clunk

'I know my darling, but I will need to go away again. I don't want to, but I must.'

CLUNK

She held onto Erich with all her might, her eyes squeezed shut trying to take in Erich's scent, his wide toothy grin, his high-pitched innocent giggle, his curious green eyes, his pinchable chubby cheeks. She heard a familiar voice, but not the one she was expecting.

'He is a sweet boy, Marianne.'

Her eyes flew open. Etienne stood proudly before them, his eyes looking adoringly at both her and Erich locked together.

'Etienne? What are you doing here?'

'Mütter! Etienne made something for me,' Erich squealed as he wriggled out of her clutches and ran towards a patch of long grass.

'A train, Mütter! A train!' He screamed in delight as he whooshed it around in a circle. Etienne laughed and cheered him on, as Erich ran around him diving between his legs and launching himself into Marianne's lap, Marianne couldn't help but laugh and cheer too.

When Erich finally exhausted himself, he fell fast asleep in Marianne's arms as she gently rocked him backwards and forwards.

'You made this for him?' She asked, holding the beautifully sculpted, painted, and varnished steam train in her hand.

Etienne smiled and nodded.

'It's beautiful Etienne, thank you.'

'We're a family Marianne. It's what we do for our loved ones.'

'Well… yes… but Etienne, where is Otto?'

'It's just us now, Marianne.'

'What do you mean?'

Before Etienne could reply the wind began to pick up. The leaves and trees started to swirl into each other, the ground started to get swept away, and before she could say or do anything, both Etienne and Erich were gone from her sight.

'No, no, no!' She cried out.

As the world around her faded, she found herself once again desperately trying to come up for air, gasping as she took in the familiarity of her surroundings. She sat upright in bed, rubbing her clammy hands on her skirt. She was still fully clothed; she must have cried herself into an exhaustive sleep. It was still pitch-black outside, not even the early morning summer sunshine had crept in just yet. Marianne looked over at the other side of the bed, Etienne's side was empty.

I've really upset him this time. Marianne thought to herself as she buried her face in her hands at the memory of her tirade; the cool of her wedding band caught the heat of her cheeks. She looked at it longingly, wondering why it all had to be such a lie, why they couldn't make things right. She also thought back to her dream, Etienne as a father to Erich. He obviously wasn't, but why did everything about that family scene feel so right?

***

As the day dawned Marianne pulled on a fresh light blue cotton dress and secured her hair back in a bun. Her hair had grown since arriving in France, it was fast approaching her waist, almost the same length as Liselotte's, but it remained wavy and wild, and in the summer heat, had gotten frizzy and difficult to tame.

She slowly descended the stairs, unsure if Etienne was asleep or not. But when she reached the workshop, Etienne was nowhere to be seen. Marianne wandered over to the desk where she found a small note.

Marianne,

My father and I have gone to meet a client in Nimes. I will be back as soon as I can.

We need to talk.

Etienne

Always to the point. Marianne sighed as the guilt of what she said made her stomach churn. Etienne was hard-going sometimes, but he didn't deserve her outburst. She wanted to show how grateful she was to him, but it felt like she had thrown it all back in his face.

Trying to put their argument to the back of her mind, Marianne started busying herself preparing breakfast, heating milk, and stirring in porridge oats. She checked outside of the windows and by the front door as Etienne had instructed her to.

'Make sure that no one is watching before you go up to him.'

No one was usually up this early, but Etienne was right, they could never be sure of who could be watching. Satisfied at the deserted street, she carefully ascended the stairs to the attic and quietly knocked on the door.

Philipp was sat bolt upright, stretching his feet out as she entered the room.

'Marianne, you are early!'

'I know, sorry. Etienne had early business to attend to this morning. He and his father are desperate for contracts now more than ever.'

'On a Sunday? But you are closed then,' Philipp said, cocking his head to the side in confusion.

'Yes,'

'Oh, because of the surrender?'

'Yes', she sighed.

Philipp went quiet, drew his knees up to his chest, and diverted his eyes. He had similar ways of showing his discomfort to Etienne.

'I've brought you breakfast,' she announced, trying to change the subject.

'Thank you, Marianne,' Philipp replied, eagerly taking the bowl from her.

Conversation felt impossible today, all she wanted to do was to be by herself, with her thoughts. All she felt like was a burden, causing sadness wherever she went. When Philipp was done eating, she instinctively went to take the bowl from him, but instead, he set it down beside him and pushed it behind his back.

'Philipp?'

'Is everything okay, Marianne?' Philipp asked.

'What do you mean?'

'You, and Etienne... I... heard you two arguing last night,' Philipp admitted.

'Oh Philipp, I'm sorry. You shouldn't have heard all of that,' she groaned.

'I couldn't exactly understand it,' Philipp said half laughing, 'but you sounded annoyed. I just... hope it wasn't over me.'

'Oh, no Philipp! It's... well... to do with everything I suppose', she admitted, 'Etienne is preparing for the worst; and as much as I trust him, I don't think he fully understands the impact that it has.'

'He sees things for what they are, and objectively moves to the best outcome.'

'Exactly,' Marianne giggled.

'What?' Philipp asked smiling.

'You two are both so perceptive. You just see things as they are,' Marianne smiled.

'Hmmm, I have been accused of such things before,' Philipp

chuckled, 'Etienne is doing the right thing you know. But the sacrifices you have to make are not easy, I know.'

'I know you do.'

'I tell you one thing that Etienne and I are very different on.'

'And what's that?' Marianne smiled.

'He's a damn good violin player. I remember a street performer like that back in Berlin, the way she moved to the rhythm of the music. Spellbinding. Were there any like that in Stuttgart?'

'No. My family didn't like music, so we never listened to any.'

'That's a shame. It's the small nuances I miss. It didn't feel like it at the time, but everything before the Great War, before *them,* everything was so much more…'

'Alive?'

'Yes!'

'When did it all change for you, Philipp?'

Philipp paused; he was pensive in his contemplation.

'When the target on our backs became immovable,' he muttered, 'what about you?'

She also hesitated before answering. She thought back to when she believed whom they blamed for Germany's failures, when she thought she could change Otto's perspective on the world, when she couldn't stand up for the poor girl in the street, when she couldn't take a step outside of the house without thinking that someone was out to get her.

'Marianne?' Philipp asked.

She glanced up at him timidly, before responding, 'I could never do the right thing, and stand up for the right people.'

Philipp stayed quiet and stared. Marianne followed his gaze, she realised that it wasn't on her but on the doorway where Etienne stood.

'Etienne, you're back! What happened?' Marianne exclaimed as a strange feeling swelled in her stomach.

'The contract fell through,' he sighed.

'I'm so sorry,' she said earnestly, only to be silenced by Etienne's wave away of her apology.

'I am glad that I found you both here. This evening, we need to all meet downstairs.' He instructed.

Marianne glanced at Philipp who looked every bit as confused as she did. She quickly translated Etienne's orders to him, which only seemed to confuse him more. But before either of them could question anything, the clunk of Etienne's cane on the stairs faded away.

***

She triple checked that she had locked the doors, drawn the curtains, and listened out for any late passers-by in the street. People seldom stayed out late for fear of who was advancing and as a result whom they may encounter.

'Okay, everything is good,' Marianne concluded.

Etienne tapped his cane on the stair three times. Philipp tentatively hobbled down the steps, a look of wonder spread across his face as he stepped into the workshop. He walked across to the cabinets in progress, he seemed to marvel at the craftsmanship. His fascination was disturbed only by Etienne clearing his throat.

'Things are not looking good,' he began, 'I am scared. I think they will come here to Avignon, and we will need to do what we can to survive.'

The strange feeling that she had felt in her stomach earlier in the day started to stir again. Etienne usually kept his feelings guarded; he had never admitted just how frightened he was. But despite his fear, he looked in control, he was too compelling to speak over.

Marianne quietly translated for Philipp.

'Marianne, I would like you to teach Philipp some French.' She nodded and translated for Philipp.

'I want to show you something,' Etienne continued, gesturing to them to follow him. He led them to a clustered corner of the workshop that was littered with leftover materials. He began to move a few pieces to the side, before grabbing his hip in pain. Philipp rushed to his side to help seat him, stretched his leg out and moved it around until the taut muscles in Etienne's face relaxed.

Marianne stepped closer to help Philipp shift the last of the materials until they revealed the wall.

'What are we looking at here, Etienne?'

'Look closely.'

They looked closer, and sure enough, there was an L- shaped crack creeping up the wall.

'Pull it gently,' Etienne instructed.

They did so, and it gave way to a small gap in the wall.

'If it comes to it, this needs to be an alternative hiding place for you, Philipp.'

Marianne obediently translated and Philipp immediately manoeuvred himself in to test it out. It was snug, but amazingly he fitted.

'We will need signals. New phrases every day,' Etienne said.

Marianne and Philipp both nodded in agreement.

'I will arrange this,' Marianne said, 'in accordance with what I teach Philipp.'

'Okay,' Etienne agreed.

She breathed a little easier knowing she was doing right by him. It was late by the time that they rounded up their meeting, and she escorted Philipp back up to the attic.

'Thank you, Marianne,' Philipp smiled when they reached the top of the stairs.

'Get some rest.' Marianne instructed. 'We'll do our first lesson in the morning.'

***

She blew out the last of the candles on the landing, plunging the house into pitch black.

'Shit!' She exclaimed as she tripped on a loose floorboard, only Etienne's hands broke her fall.

'Be careful!'

'You are always there when I need you most, Etienne,' Marianne chuckled as Etienne set her back on her feet.

'That's my job,' he smiled.

He was annoyingly pragmatic, but she couldn't help the feeling of safety whenever she was with him. But she also noticed that he hadn't let go of her arms when she was standing steadily on her feet.

'Etienne, about earlier… I was ungrateful to you… I'm so sorry.'

'You are none of the things you said you were.'

'Etienne…'

'You did what you needed to do to survive. Everyone needs to. Why shouldn't you do the same?'

'They didn't leave their children, Etienne,' her voice caught at her admission.

'I would like to meet him one day, Marianne,' Etienne said

tentatively. The dream came back in an instant, seeing him as a father, Erich so at ease in his presence.

'I would love nothing more,' she whispered as the heat slowly rose up her neck. He stood close to her; she wondered if he could sense her heart pounding in her chest.

'I know you do everything you can to make me happy...' he swallowed, hesitating for a moment, 'I promised to protect you, and I will... but I also want to make *you* happy.'

She wanted to tell him that he already did. He provided so much for her; she was immeasurably grateful to him. But the way that he was now holding her hands loosely, his tenderness and kindness was stirring desire deep in the pit of her stomach, she couldn't deny it.

'Etienne, we don't have to if you don't want to.'

But his mouth was quickly on hers, she took the lead, building the pressure on their lips, moving them together in time, the flutter of butterflies in her stomach drew her closer to him. She linked her arms around his waist, tingles ran down her spine as Etienne untied her bun causing her wavy hair to cascade down her back.

When they eased apart, they looked directly at each other. Etienne's eyes were wide with uncertainty.

'We really don't have to,' Marianne whispered.

'I want to know,' he said defiantly, 'I... I just don't know how.'

'I do,' Marianne reassured, as she took his hand gently and led them to their bedroom. Standing in front of him she slowly unbuttoned her dress and let it fall to the floor. She took a small step towards Etienne, he remained still watching her in fascination, the look of fear gradually faded from his eyes. She unclipped one side of his dungarees as he unclipped the other, the material fell unbalanced as they awkwardly tried to slip it off. Finally, he removed his shirt revealing his slight frame, and a small smattering of hair adorned his chest. He blushed, but before he could turn away from her, she ran her hands over his torso, up his chest, linked her arms around his neck, and kissed him lightly on the lips.

She gasped as she felt his hands move down her back, fiddling with the clasp of her bra, both of them breathed a sigh of relief when it released. Individually, they removed the rest of their underwear and for a moment stood completely bare in front of each other.

Marianne was the first to move, she slowly lay down on her back and nodded towards Etienne to invite him over. He did so delicately, limping lightly towards her, Marianne gave him all the time he needed to settle over her. She smiled at him as he gently smoothed her hair away from her face and gingerly began to kiss her.

'My neck Etienne,' she gasped.

Etienne obeyed, descending his kisses across her jaw and cheek, down towards the sweet spot on her neck.

Oh, I've missed this she thought to herself as she moved her hands further down Etienne's back, gripping lightly. She looked up to see him looking at her.

'Is this okay?' She asked.

He nodded, and this time she rose to kiss him. She could feel him stiffen against her.

'Now?' Etienne whispered.

'Yes,' Marianne gasped, 'gently.'

He did so, and as he moved inside her she felt every single one of her senses come alive with pleasure and desire.

This is what it's supposed to feel like.

When they were finished, Etienne rolled onto his back, not saying a word and breathed heavily.

'Are you okay?' Marianne asked turning towards him. He continued to lie still for a minute.

Did I do something wrong? Again?

At long last he turned towards her, smiling a small smile.

'Everything is okay, Marianne,' he whispered.

'You promise?'

'I will never lie to you. That I promise,' Etienne said, placing his hand in hers in a commitment that they both knew was everlasting.

PHILIPP

Avignon, December 1942

Earlier he had heard the unquestionable sound of children singing carols in the street. It was so out of place, yet so necessary. He had never celebrated Christmas, but this pure, innocent sound had been the only thing to bring some peace to his troubled soul in months.

Now, he didn't dare breathe, if he moved even an inch, he would surely open up the wall. Marianne had haphazardly thrown as many items as she could in front of it in the seconds that they had to act.

He could hear muffled voices in the background. Etienne was talking to them, he was maintaining his calm, steady composure, trying to converse with them the way he would with a client. But these men were not clients.

It was taking every ounce of strength within him not to shake uncontrollably in the ice-cold winter blasts that wound their way through the tiny gaps. He knew that his dramatically diminished frame was struggling to maintain any body heat. Where physicality was letting him down, he hoped that spirituality would win; he closed his eyes and silently prayed as the footsteps drew closer and closer.

***

Avignon, October 1940

'Vous traversez le pont,' Marianne said slowly and clearly.

'I go to the bridge?'

'No, listen carefully,' Marianne instructed, ''vous traversez le pont.'

'I cross the bridge?'

'*You* cross the bridge' she corrected, 'but that's good, you are picking out the keywords.'

Philipp was acutely mindful of Etienne's urgency in making sure they were practised and prepared. They were all terrified. But Marianne was still able to maintain the patience of a saint.

He just hoped that she remained unaware of what happened when the attic door would close behind her at night. How he would stuff his blanket into his mouth to muffle mournful cries from the depths of his soul. In the darkness, and in his dreams, he could still hear the smashing of glass, and with that the destruction of aspirations, livelihoods, and hope. He could feel the heat of the flames prickle his skin as homes, shops, and businesses were torched. He could hear the chilling screams of men, women, and children as they were dragged out of their homes, maybe never to see each other again, he had refused to look. Too many times he had questioned whether it was self-preservation or cowardice to not have stood up for them, stood up for what was right, and every night he came to a different conclusion.

But when he closed his eyes and saw his father, he could almost feel his heart breaking. The jolly, gentle, giant, with his abundant loving heart, the man who returned to them broken trying to protect his sons. It tore Philipp apart knowing that he had not possessed the same strength to put his life on the line for another. He had tried to warn them, but in the end, it was only he who had left. Surviving would be the only thing that would make it worthwhile.

Philipp listened attentively to Marianne as she sounded out each sound, word, and phrase, giving him all the time he needed to take it all in. He was far from natural at it, it frustrated him that it wouldn't come to him quickly, he had always been a fast learner. But learning something new again made him feel alive.

'Where did you learn to speak such good French?' Philipp asked, 'It's not exactly a skill that is held in high esteem back home. Them being the enemy,' he teased.

But Marianne wasn't smiling. The note pages rustled in her hands as they trembled. She cleared her throat before she spoke.

'My brother,' she said hoarsely, 'Heinrich,' she paused as if to organise her thoughts the same way that she was sorting through the papers. 'My family, me included, believed that Germany was the greatest nation in the world. When the Great War was lost, we blamed…' she paused again.

'Us,' Philipp said.

'And others. Communists, politicians, anyone who didn't believe in the greatness of the nation,' she admitted, her head hung low.

'You and many others,' Philipp tried to reassure, but all he could think of was Max and his gang who had set him on the right way. Another group trying to fit into a world that didn't want them, and Marianne had been part of that world. He tried to resist the small seed of resentment that was threatening to sprout in his heart.

'It's no excuse Philipp. I should have known better.' She asserted. Philipp stayed silent, not knowing how to respond.

'I always imagine that Heinrich was rebellious,' Marianne continued.

'You imagine?' Philipp asked.

'He was killed in the Great War along with two of my older brothers.'

273

'Oh Marianne, I'm sorry.'

'I never knew them,' she said sadly, 'I was only little when they died. But my mother kept keepsakes of all of them buried in our attic, and that's where I found Heinrich's French language book. My parents would never have permitted him to have it, so I have no idea where he got it, but I am so grateful that he did. When I picked it up, I found that it came naturally to me, I think it's a beautiful language. My best friend used to test me on phrases. In private of course.'

'Do you miss it?'

She looked at Philipp inquisitively for a moment before replying.

'My heart hurts. But I don't regret it. Do you?'

'Exactly the same.'

Marianne rose to her feet and made a swift exit out of the door. No sooner had she left, she returned, but this time she was lightly holding a battered, sapphire blue book in her hands.

'Heinrich's book?' Philipp asked.

Marianne nodded, extending the book towards him.

'Marianne, I couldn't. It means so much to you,' Philipp protested.

'Please take it. It will help you with your vocabulary, and knowledge is something that they can't take away from you.'

Philipp was too stunned to argue. Her gesture was one of penance as if she was singlehandedly accepting responsibility for all their nation's wrongdoings. He obediently, and delicately took the book from her trembling hands. Despite her past, that people like her had inadvertently been responsible for the hunting of people like him, and the loss they had endured, he pitied her. He hadn't thought it possible to think of anyone like her other than a monster. Naïve she may have been, but at her core beat a pure heart. His hand flew to hers to steady it, she was initially shocked at his touch, but she gave him a small smile.

'What's your real name, Marianne?' Philipp whispered.

Her smile dropped immediately and she withdrew her hand from his.

'That's not important,' she stated.

When she left this time, she did not hurry back.

***

Every two weeks in the dead of night Etienne would summon him with the click of his cane at the bottom of the stairs, and on schedule Philipp would descend the stairs as fast as he could, cross the workshop floor, ease the side of the wall open and contort himself inside the tiny gap. They would time the process, and for a while, he improved. Moving quickly and across bigger areas took some getting used to, but it felt great for a brief rush of air in his lungs. But when the rationing officially began, their progress started to come undone.

Etienne's family were struggling just to feed themselves. Marianne could barely spare a handful of bread a day. Any strength that he had gained over the months that he had been hiding out with Etienne and Marianne slipped away quickly. His figure became gaunt, bones started to poke out underneath his blotchy, pale skin. He could feel strength drain from his body every day. Consequently, his reactions slowed dramatically.

Sleep eluded him. His dreams had become more vivid. He was ten years old again, walking with his family to the synagogue for Johann's Bar Mitzvah. The watchful, accusing eyes of the boys in the shadows bored into him and were as bright as headlights, their blinding, piercing light swallowed up every speck of colour in the streets. Philipp squinted as the brightness burned his eyes, but as the light gradually faded, he could see their forms emerging from their shadowy home. They were bigger, louder, and in uniform. He was so little, helpless to defend himself against them as they marched in unison towards them, their clunky boots made the ground shake beneath them with every firm, decisive step. There was something magnetic about them, he could understand why everyone around him had stopped to stare, but could they not sense the impending harm that was coming their way?

'Run!' Philipp tried to scream, but when he opened his mouth, he couldn't speak. He could see his family ahead if only he could get to them, but he was too far away, the uniforms were getting closer, and time was running out, until finally, it did.

***

'Slower,' Etienne muttered impatiently after they completed their latest drill.

'I'm sorry,' Philipp sighed as he fumbled his way out of the small space. Etienne smiled a small smile of apology. Philipp wished he wouldn't. He had a right to be impatient; the fact that time was running out rapidly scared Etienne as much as it did him.

'We go again?' Philipp asked in his clumsy French.

'Non, il faut le faire quand on ne s'y attend pas,' Etienne groaned as he buried his face in his hands, running them over his prominent cheekbones and forehead which jutted out more now. Etienne always spoke at full speed; he didn't always think to talk slowly and carefully like Marianne did.

'He says that it needs to be done when you're not expecting it,' Marianne said as she emerged from the corner of the room, maintaining her distance from Philipp. Philipp nodded at her, closed the gap in the wall, and moved the leftover wood pieces back in front of the split line.

'Beautiful walnut,' he gasped, as he ran his hands along the edges. The feeling of the notches under his skin brought back the nostalgia, memories that were not tainted with guilt for once, he relished the moment. He didn't realise that Etienne and Marianne had been watching him, he stepped away from the pile blushing.

'Wood?' was the only word that Philipp picked out from Etienne's question as he continued to stare at him inquisitively with his intense blue eyes.

'Er... famille... er... antiques,' he replied awkwardly.

'Of course!' Marianne exclaimed, 'Your father's antique shop!'

She remembered, it warmed him inside to know that she had valued what they had confided in each other, that their co-habitation was more than just a sense of moral duty. But his attention was drawn towards Etienne. He was smiling, genuinely this time. He returned the smile, with a feeling that they were finally building a trust, and not one just founded on taking orders and following a survival protocol. As Philipp started to make his way back towards the stairs, Etienne's voice made him jump.

'Wait!'

Philipp turned to face him, Etienne was steadying himself on his cane and waving him over. There were only a few items left in the workshop now; business had dried up almost completely, and there was far less disposable income left for people to spend on new furniture or large repairs. Most of the available material was being collected for the armies now, for shelters, firewood, and even some medical instruments.

He cautiously wandered over to Etienne's enthusiastic gesture, eyeing him suspiciously as he did so. When he joined Etienne by the side of the cabinets Etienne immediately launched into an excitable flurry of conversation, showing off each crafted piece with pride. Philipp picked up on the wood types, adding his own adjectives to affirm and admire the work. It wasn't difficult to praise. The Touelle's craftsmanship was magnificent, in terms of its precision and finish, but what jumped out at Philipp the most was the way they had kept the pieces of wood that told the most expressive stories. Multiple scenes burst forth; they were captivating to behold. The watchful eyes over the river lines that chased each other in multiple directions, or the satisfying etches that worked together to fan out into a satisfying and beautiful pattern. He knew that Johann or his father would have been able to spin a far more imaginative tale than Philipp was capable of, but thinking of them at that moment filled him with a feeling of determination that had been lying dormant in the pit of his stomach.

***

Etienne became a more frequent visitor afterwards. He would bring up repair forms, a few of them new, most of them were old receipts, Philipp wasn't entirely sure why Etienne held onto them, perhaps he wanted to remember past accomplishments? Maybe it gave him hope for the future? Whatever his reasoning, it felt great to be able to impart his knowledge and feel useful. The two of them would brokenly converse about the mending processes, Philipp recommended wood types to use, and Etienne attempted to explain the skills required for the task.

As happy as it made Philipp that he and Etienne had found common ground, he could see that lately, Etienne had been struggling more physically. Frequently ascending the stairs coupled with the dampness in the October air was giving him more pain. Philipp observed him closely, only on occasion would Etienne allow him to give him some light treatment, his trust won since Philipp identified the source of Etienne's suffering. But Etienne remained ashamed of his condition; he was always grateful for any relief Philipp could provide, but Philipp could tell it made him uncomfortable to address, he respected Etienne and his dignity far too much to press him further.

They finished their notes on the latest commission when Etienne moved to collect the small samples of wood that he had brought up with him. He doubled over in pain from the hasty movement and a deep torturous moan escaped from behind his closed lips as he tried to fight against the agony. This time his medical instincts did not hold Philipp back as he moved towards Etienne, leaning him against the wall so that he could lightly move his leg around until he could see the tension ease from Etienne's face.

'Merci, Philipp,' Etienne gasped.

But Philipp was thinking, he knew that some legs could be shorter than others by mere margins, he had seen it before and was trained to look for it, but it certainly didn't take an expert eye to see just how badly Etienne's legs had fared. He was still in as much disbelief as he was the first time that he saw it. The splint had been done all wrong, they probably missed the break in his hip, and his leg had a strange twist to it, most likely from the way he had walked on it for so many years.

'No, Etienne,' he instructed, as Etienne tried to sit back down again.

Etienne hesitated, surprised by Philipp's assertion, but he obeyed and allowed Philipp to lower him onto his back.

Philipp picked up Etienne's cane and laid it out against his hip, looking closely as it extended down his leg. As he suspected, it was too short.

'What is it?' Etienne muttered.

'Err, short,' Philipp replied, fumbling for the right words.

Etienne sighed, which confirmed what Philipp suspected, Etienne had known for a while.

'New?' Philipp asked, pointing to the cane, but was disappointed at the emphatic shaking of Etienne's head.

'No, no, family, suspect,' were the only words Philipp could identify from Etienne's dismissal, but it was enough to understand. A new cane would attract attention, with few materials available, but also where it would have come from, they couldn't take that chance.

Philipp nodded and turned away to pick up the stray wooden pieces. As he turned over a smooth section of oak in his hand he let the piece knock against his knuckles, an idea came to him.

'Etienne!' He exclaimed as he grabbed the cane; Etienne watched him intently. Philipp gestured placing the wooden piece at the bottom of the cane, extending it. Etienne's eyes lit up.

***

Avignon, December 1942

Everything had gone eerily quiet. He had been holding his breath for so long, he wasn't sure if it was just the blood ringing in his ears that drowned out the sound of each fearful footstep.

What if they had found something?

Had they taken Etienne and Marianne away?

Was he on his own?

Would anyone be coming back for him?

There was nothing in his stomach, but he could feel the bile stinging in his throat as he tried to repress the panic.

'The oak is in short supply.'

Was it just his imagination? He didn't dare look.

Footsteps. Philipp squeezed his eyes tightly shut, sensing the light move over his eyelids.

'Philipp?' Marianne's soft voice spoke.

Philipp crashed out onto the floor, finally bringing up the lingering bile. His lungs burned and he shook all over, but they had survived.

Outside, snow had started to fall, and the carol singers could be heard once again.

Silent night. Holy night. All is calm. All is bright.

ETIENNE

Avignon, December 1942

Vichy.

A nation split in two, supposedly under two methods of control. But that was a lie, and everyone knew it. Petain was no more than a puppet, assuring the people that the collaboration was good, and worked in their best interests. Many were saying that they were fortunate, to be under the French area of control. Somehow word from his grandfather had reached his aunt Georgette agreeing with this sentiment. Especially when the Nazis were swarming all over Paris, causing chaos and misery wherever they went.

'We *are* blessed that we are not in the north' Camille insisted. Etienne was never one to choose confrontation, and he didn't know whether it was the fear-fuelled adrenaline from their close encounter with Nazi officials the other day that still shook his nerves, or whether it was the exhaustion from the constant and urgent changes, but Camille's denial turned out to be his snapping point.

'They are right *here,* Maman! This is not France anymore! *They* run the country now. There is no French control. When are you going to realise that?'

Camille reeled as if he had struck her. Etienne tried his best to keep a straight face. His mother was never one to be bossed around. She squared up to Etienne even though he towered over her and glared at him.

'Why have you given up ma pêche?'

'Because we have lost, Maman.'

She stepped closer to him, he could smell the lavender surrounding her like a halo, it was calming and disarming.

'We have the business.'

'For now.'

'We have our homes'.

'They can take anything they want away from us.'

'And our family?'

This time Etienne was too scared to answer, but his silence said enough.

'You are right Etienne. They can take whatever they want away from us. But our family is rich with love, something they will never understand, nor will they ever be able to take away from us.'

She stepped back, swept her long skirt over her ankles, and walked out of the house. Etienne puffed his cheeks out in frustration. Marianne slowly shuffled out of the kitchen; her blush radiated from her cheeks. She was the last person Etienne wanted to see right now.

'I...I...Erm... Curfew is almost due. She will be freezing cold out there.'

'I know,' Etienne snapped.

She reeled; another one he had stung.

'She will want to see you more than she wants to see me right now,' he said.

'On the contrary,' Marianne replied, assertively. It was humbling. 'Go to her, Etienne, it's not safe out there.'

He hadn't given up, and he knew that he would never stop trying.

I will use the silence to be brave.

Right now, bravery meant keeping his family together when others sought to tear them apart. Etienne shrugged on a small jacket that was in serious need of repair, but it was the warmest item he possessed as materials had become more difficult to acquire.

Marianne handed him his cane, he smiled to himself as he positioned it by his side. Philipp's secret modifications had brought him significant relief. Etienne felt the light brush of Marianne's hand on his shoulder, and he inadvertently arched his back. He appreciated Marianne's patience and consideration when it came to intimacy, but he struggled to reciprocate. He hastily left to avoid yet another uncomfortable conversation.

The freezing fog had become more intense in the last hour. Etienne struggled to see anything as he stumbled out of the shop, the sign frozen in place. It hadn't sung for anyone for some time. The cold bit at his skin the moment he stepped outside, he immediately began to shake, and worry about Philipp upstairs in the poorly insulated attic.

Walking always helped clear his mind, but the streets were so dangerous nowadays, that one couldn't escape the feeling of paranoia. People watched on street corners, rumours were reported, and the consequences of rebellion were unknown.

Camille couldn't have gone far, they all had to walk slower to preserve the little energy they had left. Etienne watched his feet carefully as he navigated his way over the uneven cobbles, only stopping to bask in the warmth radiating from a rubbish bin that had been set on fire by a group of homeless men. The small waves of heat stung against his ice-cold skin, but the pain was worth it. Suspicious eyes watched him warily as he stood parallel to them.

Etienne tightened his jacket around him, which had become saturated in dampness from the fog and lay heavy against his body. All his clothes were looser, and there was not much anyone could do to make any difference. His teeth began to chatter, it was difficult just to put one foot in front of the other, his joints were always so stiff in weather like this, and he grunted with each step.

Challenging as it was to spot her in the elements, Etienne finally spotted his mother standing by the old boarded-up pharmacy. Her hair danced lightly in the freezing breeze; her features were only visible from the dim light of a flickering candle in the window of a nearby house that Camille couldn't tear her eyes away from. Etienne approached her cautiously not wanting to startle her.

'It's so small,' she croaked.

'Pardon, Maman?' Etienne asked as he drew nearer to her side, she was shivering.

'The light. It's so small. But it pierces through the darkness,' she said. She turned to face him. 'I can barely see you without it. But that small flame reveals a lot. Don't you think?'

'Yes, Maman,' Etienne agreed, he knew she meant more by it, but he wasn't sure if he wanted to fully understand. He put his arms around her, doing his best to warm her up.

'Can we go to the river, ma pêche?'

Etienne looked down at his mother, who looked back up at him with huge pleading eyes.

'Maman, it's dark and dangerous, and you are freezing…' he was cut short by her trembling hand placed on his cheek. Her spirit was strong, but it broke his heart to see her physical resilience being chipped away at every day. He took her hands in his.

'Okay, Maman.'

They huddled together as they ambled through the dark side streets of the old town, frantically trying to peer through the fog that seemed to be growing thicker by the minute. They passed the grand silhouettes of the townhouses, and the restaurants overlooking the river. Finally, they reached the shoreline, and together they admired the sheet of ice that extended across the entire body of water which faintly glittered as the bleary light of the moon did its best to expose its beauty. They could hear the muffled sounds of bombing in the distance, they were idiotic to be out there, but they remained secluded in their spot.

'As you promised,' Camille said into the night air, her visible breath carrying its affirmation up into the stars and beyond.

'I'm sorry, Maman,' Etienne murmured, swallowing the lump in his throat.

Sorry for doubting you.

Sorry for lying to you about Marianne.

Sorry, that I am risking our lives by hiding a Jew under my roof.

Sorry for not being as brave as you.

'You always see the good in everything, Maman. I wish I could be more like you.'

'Don't apologise for being you, ma pêche,' Camille asserted.

'I haven't given up, Maman,'

'You are like the moon tonight ma pêche. Trying to shine your light through an obstacle that wishes to block you out.'

'Why do you call ma pêche, Maman?' He chuckled.

He heard her exhale a small laugh.

'In our garden, there is a peach tree. You were an early arrival. When the doctor had finally concluded that you were perfectly healthy you were placed into my arms and slept so peacefully, you never made a fuss.'

'The barren root in the garden? That's a peach tree?'

'It's not barren Etienne. Every year it bears one piece of fruit.

After you were born, I hoped that it meant that every time it bloomed it meant that I would have another child. But the years went by, and it never happened.'

'I'm sorry, Maman.'

'No ma pêche. I have you, and I am never sorry that I only had you, you are everything to me and your father, even though I know he may struggle to tell you.'

She was right. Pierre struggled to verbally communicate anything, but his actions, his practicality, and his consideration, that was how he showed his love, and it was never in doubt.

'I asked your father to fetch me some water, mainly so that I could selfishly spend some precious moments alone with you,' she giggled. 'And that's when I noticed outside of the window, a single peach, vastly out of season, had come out on the tree. God has a sense of humour, Etienne, from that day on you were ma pêche.'

'Why have I never seen the peaches, Maman?'

'I must always pick them before you get the chance'.

'But I will tell you what's funny.' Camille continued.

'Oui?'

'The year you met Marianne, the tree grew an extra peach.'

'You are joking.'

'Never ma pêche. When she came to stay with us, I just got a feeling.'

'She is a good daughter to you.'

'She is. And she is a good wife to you. I have seen the way that you take care of each other.'

'She is,' Etienne agreed. He cared deeply about Marianne, more than he ever thought he could.

They stayed still in quiet contemplation when something solid and heavy struck Etienne in the arm. He cried out as he put space between himself and his mother, both searched the blurry air for the perpetrator.

'Curfew's been and gone frogs!' A man harshly cackled in darkness in an unmistakable German accent.

A chill of fear ran down Etienne's spine. He had been lucky the first time, Philipp was safe, but how was he encountering them again already? They weren't even in the Nazi-run zone. He silently cursed himself for not heeding Marianne's warning, now he was endangering not only himself but his mother.

'Please! We mean no harm!' Etienne called out, holding his injured arm limply.

Another rock whizzed past him; he could feel the small rush of wind it left as it narrowly missed his face.

'Run frogs, run!' The unknown assailant screeched.

'Etienne, this way!' Camille called out as she hurried along the west side of the shoreline. Etienne tried with all his might to scramble after her, he could hear more rocks clattering and shattering on the ground as he forced his stubborn legs to move, all the while the twisted laugh of their attacker lingered in the air. Neither he nor his mother stopped until they reached the bridge. Both were breathing hard as they reached out their hands to find each other in the pitch black.

'Are you hurt, ma pêche?'

Everything hurt. His arm, his leg, his hip, his pride.

'Mmm,' was all he could muster.

She didn't even hesitate to bundle him under her arm, she buckled under the strain on her tiny frame, but she refused to stop. She carried them both back along through the backstreets until the pain was too much for Etienne.

'Maman! Stop! Please!' He gasped.

Camille did so, delicately propping him against a wall. They looked long and hard at each other, grateful to be alive, and although Camille never said it, there was an understanding in her look. There was no more French control. This time it didn't feel good to be right.

***

Avignon, February 1943

The Milice, they called themselves, the secret police. Traitors, parasites, criminals, that's what everyone else called them, behind closed doors, blackout curtains, and in hushed whispers of course.

'We're all desperate. It doesn't make it an excuse to sell your soul to the devil over it,' Marianne said, handing over a tiny portion of ham to Etienne as they huddled together under blankets with Camille and Pierre in the basement of their home as they waited out the current bombardment. Etienne wondered if her suspicions matched his own.

Was their attacker one of them? Did they know who they were? Were they still out to get them?

Camille hummed quietly over Pierre, as he buried his face into her shoulder. When they first started shielding themselves away, Etienne had had to choke back tears when he saw how the terror afflicted his father. He was white as a sheet, eyes wide and alert, trembling from head to foot as Camille guided him down the rickety steps onto the cold stone floor. His cries were haunting, he didn't stop for the whole night.

'Etienne, ma pêche, it does no good to stare,' she had whispered as a warning to him. But he couldn't take his eyes off him, his father, a man he did not recognise. This was the impact of not talking about horrors, eating away at him, and consuming him when he least expected it.

In the basement, he and Marianne would bow their heads together and pray. Camille would say how comforted she felt by it, but little did she know that they were predominantly praying for Philipp.

Etienne started to tremble at the thought of Philipp stuck in the attic, it was always too rushed and therefore too risky to move him to a safer area without anyone seeing him. They hated the thought of him being alone up there, not knowing if it would be his last night.

'But how do you know that it wouldn't be the same for you?' Philipp had said during a late-night discussion.

'The basement will always be the safest place,' Etienne said.

'Even so. We don't know if we will be caught, killed, or arrested from each day to the next. I have made it this far by taking chances with faith. I will take my chances, Etienne,' he had said decisively and said nothing more on the matter.

When the all-clear siren sounded hours later, rousing them from restless and uncomfortable sleep they headed towards the stairs. Pierre and Camille quickly led the way, with Marianne not far behind them, but before she reached the top Etienne grabbed her hand. Startled, she turned to face him.

'I believe myself to be a coward for not being able to fight for my country,' he admitted.

Marianne paused, descended a step to be closer to him, and held his face in her hands before lightly kissing his forehead.

'You are the bravest man I have ever met,' she said earnestly.

'I want to talk about our troubles Marianne. We can't let them defeat us.'

'I agree,' she said softly.

***

The next few days were suspiciously calmer. It gave them a chance to catch their breath. Philipp seemed confident; he had an air of invincibility about him that scared Etienne. He approached all the changes to their escape routes with positive enthusiasm, but Etienne knew it wasn't the time to be complacent.

Marianne was exhausted. She looked frail and had lost a significant amount of weight. Her back was hunched, her eyes were heavy, and her arms hung weightily by her sides. Her hair was nearly as long as Camille's, but it was thin and dry, she had taken to wearing a head scarf to secure it. Etienne knew that she was dividing most of her share of the rations to feed Philipp; he tried to leave pieces of his share on her bedside.

One morning Etienne was sitting at his desk sorting through old newspapers, scrunching them up ready for fire fuel. Bleak headlines met his view. Hundreds of civilians were dying in the bombings. People were publicly executed for resisting. Prisoners of war were being sent to camps along with other 'enemies of the Reich'. Etienne shuddered. He didn't want to have to be the one to tell Philipp.

Etienne looked up to see Marianne sweeping up debris in the house, leaning heavily on the broom. Neither of them had slept much over the last few weeks, alert for the sirens, being attacked, scared about Philipp, and what happened to people who openly defied the regime, the reasons to worry seemed to never end.

They were both disturbed by a gush of cold air that wrapped around their ankles focusing their attention on the door and immediately having to disguise their horror at the sight of the uniformed gentleman who walked in.

'Good day,' the man said steadily. He smiled a small wry smile, a wonky canine stood out prominently. His dark brown hair was slicked back underneath his cap. He had a distinctive button nose and murky green eyes. There was something familiar about him, but Etienne couldn't quite work it out.

They had no warning that they were coming. There was no way that they could alert Philipp now.

'How do you do?' Etienne answered as politely as he could, rising from his chair.

The officer did not hesitate. 'As a carpentry business, you must hand over all your goods and spare wood to the German army. We will be sending men to collect it over the next few days.'

The officer turned sharply on his heel and walked out the door, leaving Etienne in a world of bemusement. He saw the officer join another officer outside who had eye-catching bright blonde hair and flashed a suspicious look through the window before marching down the street with his compatriot.

Etienne turned to Marianne; she was as white as the remaining snow that clung to the rooftops.

'Marianne?'

She said nothing, it was almost as if she were in some kind of trance. She let the broom clatter to the floor. Absentmindedly, she left the room, ascended the stairs, and locked their bedroom door behind her.

MARIANNE

Avignon, February 1943

Her worst nightmares had come true. She hadn't left the bed for at least twenty-four hours. Marianne groggily lifted her head from the flat pillow, heavy with disrupted sleep, her body tense from crying. She precariously rose to her feet, but the pain that hit her in her stomach sent her reeling. Marianne leaned over to try and quell the spasm, a mixture of hunger, dehydration, and despair. She grappled around the top of the drawers unable to stand to her full height. Finally, she knocked a hole-ridden blanket to the floor, which she used to try to cover herself to stop the shivering, not from the freezing chill for once. Curling up on her side she rocked herself lightly trying to shift the waves of pain that kept striking her, silently willing everything to end there and then.

'Marianne?'

Etienne's concern for her was usually such a balm. He made her feel valued and comforted, that she didn't have to endure hardships alone. But right now, she wanted him to leave, or rather she wanted him not to care, he had no idea exactly how much danger they were in. But true to form, Etienne was there, causing pain to himself by struggling to scoop her off the floor. Too exhausted to fight, Marianne allowed Etienne to place her on their bed gently. He tenderly smoothed back her tangled hair from her face, refusing to let her break eye contact with him.

'Marianne, we need to talk,' he whispered softly.

She looked down at her hands where Etienne had placed a small piece of cheese, which she devoured ravenously. The beautiful saltiness and creaminess that she had taken for granted for so long, she now relished as the flavour explored her tastebuds for the first time in days. The spasm in her stomach started to relax and she drew in a deep breath.

'The officer who came in… he is my brother, Ernst.'

Etienne's eyes widened.

'D…Di… Did he recognise you?' He stammered.

'I don't think so. I don't think he saw me at all,' Marianne replied.

'Oh, thank God!' Etienne gasped.

'There's more.'

She didn't dare look at him. Etienne was unnervingly silent.

'That other officer, outside, with the blonde hair, he, and my brother work together for the Party. But that man… his name is Otto… he is my husband.'

The slight touch of Etienne's fingertips on her hand encouraged her to share more.

When Marianne started talking, she couldn't stop. She spoke of their first meeting when she was pleasantly surprised to meet her brother's handsome work associate. She spoke of how special he had made her feel when he took an interest in her, remembering the first time he called her beautiful, how he had protected her, and when he told her that he loved her, but then how quickly it had all changed when they were married.

Etienne's features darkened as she described how Otto would

return home late at night, stinking of booze, and cheap perfume, not caring if his ruckus woke Erich. How he would drain every last drop of brandy that Marianne kept hidden for when Erich was teething.

'Having a son was the only thing that mattered to him,' Marianne said sadly. 'But he didn't want much else to do with him.'

She detailed Otto's drunken rages and recalled the relentless assaults, how she had been left bloody and beaten on so many an occasion, and in so much physical pain for months on end, all whilst trying to hide it all from Erich.

Then she spoke of the girl in the street from that fateful day with Liselotte, how she had done nothing to help her and gone back to the man who she knew with absolute certainty was carrying out similar atrocities. Finally, she told him of how Erich had inadvertently exposed her by finding Heinrich's book, how she had nearly died, that after that incident she knew that she wasn't safe, that Erich would not be safe being associated with a mother, who in a loyal Nazi member's mind, betrayed the nation's ideals.

Etienne's face was crestfallen. Neither of them spoke for a few minutes. Marianne stared at her feet; Etienne paced. Surely, he would be judging her now, surely, he would finally understand why she saw herself as a terrible person. He always said that she was strong, did what she had to do to survive. But now, she had to be seen as nothing more than a coward, how else could she be perceived?

'You saved his life,' Etienne said at long last, the unexpected sound of his voice startled her.

'How can I possibly know? I left him with that monster. And now that he's here, then where is Erich?' She argued, her voice strained with anger.

'It was you he wanted to... destroy,' Etienne said, his voice breaking.

'Why are you taking pity on me?'

'Because no one should ever have to go through what he did to

294

you, Marianne! Why do you think it's your fault?'

'Because I allowed it! I put Erich in danger...' she yelled, bursting into tears, her chest heaved at the weight of her guilt as Etienne pulled her into his arms holding her steady.

'He nearly killed you.'

Too many times. She thought to herself, but she got the feeling that Etienne already knew.

'I miss my son so much, Etienne.'

'That's because you love him and are a good mother. You kept him safe and risked your life to do it.'

'Why do you not hate me?'

'Because there is nothing to hate.'

There was no convincing him, as much as she tried. But inside she lit up, he was her victory.

'There is one thing though.'

'What's that?' She asked.

'You said he was your husband. Not here he's not.'

***

The pressure in her chest was still crushing, but after confessing to Etienne, she was at least able to get out of bed the following day. She carefully brushed through her thinning hair, securing it back with the now tattered scarf that Camille had made for her as a birthday present. Her original false identification papers had at least managed to convince the ones it needed to.

Marianne Rosalie Cardot

16-08-1911

The year they had celebrated her 'thirtieth birthday' back in 1941 felt the strangest, even now when she was still nearly two years away from reaching that milestone. *If I reach that milestone,* she thought.

She continued to dress, pulling the thickest dress she possessed over her awkward, frail frame. She could feel one of the patches that she had clumsily darned start to peel away. There were hardly any supplies of anything useful left, she just hoped that Camille had been resourceful enough to hide some sewing equipment away.

It was still early when she awoke, Etienne was sleeping peacefully next to her. She picked up her bag which she tucked underneath her arm. The strap had broken months ago, and the leather was too thick for any needle she could source. It was small, but big enough to carry their meagre rations home.

The small hallway mirror caused her to catch her reflection in her periphery. She had given up trying to make an effort with her appearance long ago, but it didn't stop her from staring at the strange woman staring back at her. The characteristic plumpness of her cheeks had flattened nearly completely, leaving just her prominent cheekbones sticking out in a gawky fashion. The shadows underneath her eyes complemented the growth of lines on her forehead and the outlines of her mouth. Her face looked sunken like her body was caving in on itself, hiding away from frightening and cruel realities. She brought her bony hands up towards her face, prodding its new unwelcome features, as if she was trying to search for the person who once inhabited this body.

Before she made more excuses for herself not to face the world, she clambered down the stairs and exited the house. Etienne had told her that the only thing she should be going out for was to pick up the rations, any other venture would be far too dangerous; bombs, being exposed, or now encountering her past. She understood, but she missed the freedom. Despite the circumstances that had brought her to Avignon, she truly loved the city. There had been no money for a honeymoon when they first married, but Etienne had given her a personal guided tour. They spent hours wandering around the old town, Etienne talked at length about its history and its inhabitants. They explored the Palais de Papes and the indoor and outdoor markets which were always bursting with the colours of goods and buzzing with the sound of enthusiastic sellers. In the springtime, they would walk through the Jardin des Doms and stroll by the river to take in the beautiful scenery. Etienne would sit in quiet reflection, content to watch the river dance whilst she read books to improve her French. On their first anniversary to escape the inevitable overdone celebrations that Camille would have put in place, Marianne had packed a low-key evening picnic. Etienne had taken her to the Opera d'Avignon, and it was every bit as spectacular as he had said. She sat and listened to Etienne talk for hours about the place, how special it was to him, and how the music made him feel. Music didn't touch her the way it did Etienne, but she felt closer to him for it and was honoured that he would allow her to see that side of his life.

But sadly, that was then, and this was now. As she walked out of the door there was a lingering smell of burning that stung her nostrils on the fresh, crisp cold air. The bombs that had fallen a few days ago were not far away, but near enough that she could smell the devastation as if it were right next to her. Wrapping her arms around herself, she set off as briskly as she could to try and build up some body heat. The first trip was to the bakery, where a downcast teenager slumped over the near-empty shelves.

'Has it all been cleared out already, Juliette?' Marianne asked.

'We've had to cut back more Marianne, I'm sorry,' Juliette Renou replied sadly. She was only thirteen. At the end of last year, Monsieur Renou had been sent to Germany under the orders of Sauckel as part of the foreign labour scheme, and they had not heard from him since. Poor Juliette and her mother were left to try and keep the bakery running in his absence.

'If there's anything we can do, Juliette?'

'Thank you, Marianne,' she said smiling weakly, carefully placing the precious pieces of bread in Marianne's bag. Someone of her age should not be having to lie through smiles to keep loved ones safe, Marianne thought.

Marianne made her way back up the cobbled streets, knowing that she was not to hang around, but she gravitated to the place where she always found a source of comfort, the chapel. It had been shut for some time due to the bombing activity, but today she took a chance. Glancing around to make sure she wasn't being watched, she eased the door open and walked inside. It smelt musty, homely, and safe. She took a moment to take in the familiar sights. She had gone there nearly every day after arriving in Avignon, to thank God for getting her there and to pray for her family's protection. Now she was reminded of her wedding day to Etienne, the promises that they had made to each other not just as spouses, but to keep each other safe, she hoped that she had upheld them as much as he upheld his.

Marianne walked back down the aisle and knelt at the altar, not caring for the discomfort of her bones on the stone floor. She closed her eyes, put her hands together, and took a deep breath, only five words came to mind as she tried to think what to pray, but she said them repeatedly.

Father,

Deliver us, please.

Amen

***

She thought she was imagining the sound to begin with, but then it was louder, an unmistakable sound of a piercing scream. Marianne hurried out of the chapel towards the commotion.

A gang, those thugs, *the Milice,* were beating someone. A woman was crying, begging, but they just kept laughing. It was the young Jewish girl alone in that street all over again. This time she walked towards them, spotting Monsieur Penaud just before an officer struck him hard in the face. She didn't mean to, but she couldn't help it, she screamed. Her reaction was heard by Monsieur Penaud and he stared at her through his swollen eye.

'Marianne!' He gasped.

Madame Penaud also looked towards her, she called out.

'Marianne! Come closer! Please take this to Etienne!' She was clinging onto her precious violin and bow.

Marianne tried to get close to her, but before she got close enough a man blocked her way, whilst another yanked the violin and bow out of Madame Penaud's hands.

'This is official police business; you need to step aside,' a stern voice commanded.

'Sir, what is going on? The Penaud family are good people.' Marianne pleaded.

'Jews can never be good people Madame, surely you know this.'

She never knew. If only she had known. They would have done something, anything to help them. But she knew now it was too late.

'Get the violin to him, Marianne!' Madame Penaud's call faded as she and Monsieur Penaud were hauled into a vehicle, and the door slammed shut behind them.

'Please sir,' Marianne begged, 'it is a beautiful instrument, my husband is an excellent player.'

'I will take it from here, Officer Lehmann,' a sly, chilling voice interrupted, causing Marianne to freeze.

There he was. His brown jacket, his eagle on his cap, and the swastika proudly pinned to his arm. His blonde hair was longer, but still neatly trimmed.

'Identification papers,' he ordered.

She fumbled around in the bag longer than was necessary, she didn't want him to see her hand trembling violently. She handed them over. As she properly met his gaze for the first time in over four years, something changed, a slight shift in his eyebrow, a widening of his eye, he didn't blink as he studied her carefully. She didn't dare say a word.

He looked back and forth at her papers, then at her too many times. All she wanted to do was run but then she would give herself away. Finally, he handed the papers back to her, she quickly tucked them in the bag.

'You know this family?' He asked.

'Oui sir, Madame Penaud is a violin teacher, she taught my husband.' She replied, doing her utmost to make sure her pronunciation sounded convincing. Just as she and Etienne had practised.

'Your husband, you say?' Otto asked with a suspicious tone.

'Oui sir, Etienne Touelle.'

'The carpenter? We know of that family.'

She gulped; she had no idea how to respond. He looked her up and down again disapprovingly.

I've done it. I can leave now, surely?

'You're a terrible sewer, Madame,' he stated.

Marianne glanced down at her skirt and the hole that had split further, 'Oh, yes, not one of my strengths,' she tried to say as jovially as possible.

'My wife was a terrible sewer.'

Chills ran down her spine.

'Oh,' she half whimpered.

'A terrible mother too. Preferred to drown herself rather than fulfilling her duty to raise our son.'

'I'm sorry for your loss sir,' she said hurriedly, not daring to ask after Erich, refusing to play his game despite the fear and anger that was warming her up from the inside.

'Yes. Run along now, Marianne Touelle. I hope your husband enjoys a dead woman's violin.' He smirked, thrusting the violin and bow into her hands.

She nodded and walked as calmly as she could until she rounded the corner, before breaking into a sprint, not daring to stop until she got home.

PHILIPP

Hanover, May 1917

'I bet you can't get to the top!'

'You're probably right, Johann,' Philipp replied, uninterested in his brother's taunts, and turned back to his novel.

The captain had foiled the mutiny, and all the crew were on edge. Some sat back covering their eyes, but peeking through the gaps in their fingers with a twisted curiosity of the gruesome fate that awaited the men, formally their comrades, their brothers. The ringleaders were forced to kneel in front of the man they dared to defy, some chose to look at the decking, possibly out of fear, or showing defiance towards tyranny until the end. The decision gifted to the reader to make for themselves, the element that Philipp always struggled with, seeing beyond the obvious.

He sat and pondered underneath the blossom of the tree in his grandmother's garden. The rain had finally stopped, and they could go out and get some fresh air. Being cooped up with Johann for over a week had felt like an eternity, and being on the receiving end of his antics because he was 'bored' was wearing very thin. But even being outside in the sunshine still hadn't done enough to quell his desire to annoy Philipp.

He could feel him approaching before he saw him. Johann ran past in a flash, yanking the book out of his hands.

'Johann! Give it back!' Philipp called out, chasing Johann down to the end of the garden.

'Come on Philipp, run around with me for a bit! We've been sat down all week because of the rain!'

Philipp did want to stretch his legs and take in the spring air, but he didn't want to admit that to Johann. Johann was also taller and quicker, he made Philipp feel slow and self-conscious. Nothing he did was better than Johann, and Johann had many ways of showing that.

'I want to finish my book, Johann. I was just getting to the good bit!' He protested.

Johann halted and smiled coyly, that was never a good sign. He drew his arm back and threw the book into the tallest tree in the garden.

'Why did you do that?' Philipp whined.

'I want to see how brave you are!'

'Why does that matter Johann? We already know that you're the bravest. Why do I need to prove it?'

His questions made Johann pause to think for a moment before he opened his mouth again.

'Because you're my brother... and brothers do stuff together. I thought it could be like an adventure?'

'By throwing my book in the tree?' Philipp asked, bemused at his brother's logic.

'Climb up there! You can see for miles.'

'Why can't you just ask me what I want to do for fun instead of just being annoying?'

He hit a nerve. Johann's face said it all. The beaming smile on his face dropped.

'Because you never want to spend time with me anymore.'

'You always want to spend time with your friends.'

'But they're not my brother. You are.'

It had been difficult for both of them. But especially for someone as sociable as Johann. For the past two and a half years they had been living with their grandmother whilst their father was away fighting. Johann had to leave his wide circle of friends behind when they left, he thrived amongst large groups of people. He was charismatic, keen to find out about others, and very likeable. Philipp wasn't as outgoing, he felt that he embarrassed his brother, and he preferred to remain tucked away, social situations that Johann loved, were intimidating to Philipp. Changes in school, routine, and rules were all a lot to take in, and their grandmother was a stern woman, who ran a tight ship.

'She would have had to with father and all of his siblings!' Johann had remarked one night as they both lay wide awake unable to sleep. They had giggled a lot that night.

Philipp sighed. Johann's sentiments were touching, but he had a stupid way of showing it. He stepped towards the trunk, took a firm grip on the biggest branch, which also turned out to be the dampest.

'Euugh,' Philipp groaned as he saw bits of mud and twigs start to mark his arms as he ascended his way through the thick, knotted tangle of branches and leaves. The dew soaked him from head to foot and splashed in his eyes, impairing his vision.

'Am I close, Johann?' He called out.

'I can't see you!' Johann shouted.

Holding onto one branch tightly and planting his feet firmly onto a sturdy branch underneath, Philipp used his free hand to blindly swipe around. The sharp bark pierced his skin, and he could feel cuts forming on his knuckles and bare arms. He was about to give up when he struck a branch and felt something fall from it.

'You did it Philipp!' Johann called out, 'I've got it. Climb back down!'

Philipp tried to look around, but the section of the tree was so tangled that there wasn't much daylight that could creep through the gaps. He blinked as much as he could to get the moisture out of his eyes, but it did little to show a clear path back down.

'Johann?'

He heard a rustle, but he couldn't tell if it was Johann or a slight breeze running through the leaves.

'Johann?' He called out again, still no reply.

He shifted his feet along the edges of the branch slowly to find where it ended, and where its thickest and sturdiest points were. Mercifully a group of branches meandered down the tree for part of the way, Philipp followed its path. But before he knew it the obvious path ended, the next largest branch within sight was too far away for him to stretch towards. There was a smaller branch above him which meant using it to swing onto a thicker branch in front of it, but it looked thin and flimsy, but this was the only option. Taking a quick breath, he reached out towards the branch. He gradually leaned more weight onto it before he lifted his feet away from the safety of the lower branch. Now he was dangling, he had no idea how far down the fall would be if he let go now. He started to swing his legs to gain momentum, and as he did so the tree moaned and creaked, he tried to ignore it, just one more swing, and then he could... SNAP.

'JOHANN!'

For those few seconds, Philipp felt every bump and scratch as he tumbled down. He tried to brace himself for pain, and a horrible injury. He squeezed his eyes shut, only to open them wide when he collided with something completely different.

'Oof!' Both boys exclaimed as they fell to the ground.

'Philipp, are you okay?' Johann wheezed.

Philipp gingerly rolled off his brother, he was bruised, and he could feel the cuts on his face, arms, and hands, it wouldn't be fun having to explain it to his grandmother. But he walked around, no harm done.

'You are an excellent cushion, Johann,' he laughed.

'Ha! It's a good job you're so light,' Johann mused.

Philipp walked towards him and pulled him to his feet, before brushing off all the twigs and bramble he had accumulated. When he looked up Johann was holding out the book, he took it gently from his hands.

'I'm sorry,' Johann said quietly.

Philipp turned the book over in his hands.

'Hey, you know this book is pretty damp. It's going to take a while to dry out.'

Johann nodded, still staring at his feet.

'Want to run around and have an adventure whilst we wait?'

Johann's snapped his head up, his features aglow with happiness.

'Let's go!'

They were planes, they were trains, they were pirates, they were cowboys, they were brothers.

'Hey Philipp,' Johann gasped, finally out of breath after hours of play, 'I lied you know.'

'About what?' Philipp asked, puffing harder than his brother.

'Climbing the tree. I said you could see for miles. I don't know, I've never climbed it.'

Philipp opened his mouth to argue, but Johann beat him to it.

'So maybe you should stop worrying about me being better than you. Because today you proved that you're the braver brother,' Johann concluded.

***

Avignon, March 1943

It had been Johann who haunted his dreams last night. Why had he always remembered him for being such an ass? Why had his overriding feeling been one of loathing for his brother? The more time he spent reflecting, he realised that there had been so many times that his brother had been there for him.

Joyful memories tainted with gut-wrenching guilt had not gotten any easier the longer he had been away from home. Each night had the potential to be the last. He was resigned to his fate whatever it may be. He didn't want to die, but living felt like a constant game of roulette, and he felt like his luck would run out sooner rather than later. But the fear gave him adrenaline, and the adrenaline that coursed through his weak limbs and heavy heart was the only thing that reminded him that he was still alive.

Etienne and Marianne had been up to visit him more sparingly. Keeping themselves alive was difficult enough, but they were sparing the little to nothing they already had to keep him alive too. There was more talk of the Milice, it was something he could pick out in their conversations when he dared to pry the door open for a moment.

They were understandably anxious; their close run-in just before Christmas had put them all on edge. He wondered if there had been more encounters with them since then. There was usually a consistent buzz of conversation between them, but now it was an uncomfortable mix of eerie silence and blazing arguments. He wanted to comfort them, talk to them, and help them. Etienne would have a plan, and Marianne would make it happen, at least that's what Philipp kept telling himself.

The sun rose earlier now, and there was finally a warmth to the sunlight that dared to take a sneak peek at him. Slowly but surely his tiny attic room was feeling less like an igloo. He knew that he was unbelievably lucky that he was still there, still a secret. But being a secret had been his identity for over four years now, three of which had been spent with Etienne and Marianne.

How much longer?

He had never forgotten the look on Etienne's face when the officers came around the first time. Whilst Philipp celebrated, Etienne's expression was one of warning.

Don't get arrogant.

Philipp knew that Etienne was right, but time became a strange construct when you spent all your days and nights in one room. Minutes, hours, and days all blurred into one. The only way he could really tell what was happening was through the newspapers that they brought up to him. They were censored heavily now of course, but they still made him feel connected to the outside world, even if they never did much to lift his mood. Sometimes Marianne would stay for a while and help with translation, but her brother's book had been extremely helpful. Finding any medical terminology reignited a spark within him, as he thought back to every procedure he had witnessed, every bodily system memorised in fine detail, every sickness diagnosed, every debate he had had with Celine.

He tried to banish such thoughts from his head, not because he didn't care, but because he knew they would come back to haunt him in his dreams later. Philipp tried to focus on the pages in front of him, both Marianne and Heinrich had left small notes in the margins during their studies, it was comforting. He felt like he was part of a rebellious crew, a German collective fighting against their oppressor, and in a small way they were. It felt like they were all on a continuous adventure. But other than those news headlines, both Etienne and Marianne had been suspiciously quiet on the finer details. Had there been more visits? What was going on outside of the house? Did they know something he didn't? If so, why would they be keeping it from him?

'The shelves need to be varnished.'

Marianne's quiet voice startled him from his thoughts. He crept towards the door, easing it open just a fraction.

'Can I come in?' She asked, so quietly that he barely heard her.

'Of course,' Philipp said.

She looked terrible. Her long hair was now so thin in places that you could see her scalp. She was little more than a skeleton, her eyes were sunken, and no light shone from them. She shuffled to the opposite corner of the room and sat down, stared straight ahead, and drew her legs up to her chest.

'Marianne?' He asked tentatively. No response.

He moved in front of her; she didn't budge.

'Marianne? What's going on?'

She stayed silent, her chest slowly rose and fell methodically, and her gaze didn't change. He didn't know which approach was best, did she trust him more as a friend or a doctor? Or not at all? But he had to try. He crouched down, and slowly stretched out his own skeletal hand towards her until he lightly touched her cold, rough skin. At his touch, she shuddered, her eyes finally met his and he had her attention. But before he could ask her what was going on, she surprised him by speaking first.

'Why did you leave, Philipp?'

She was still so quiet, but there was still a demanding intonation to her question.

'Because the country I call home decided that who I was had to be discarded. But you know this?'

'Did you leave just to save yourself?'

He was shocked at her audacity.

'What?'

'Did you leave just to save yourself?' She repeated, more indignantly.

'I had no choice, Marianne!'

'You always have a choice!' She barked, 'Whom were you helping when you left?'

Philipp was shocked. She had no idea how it felt, to gradually see everything that you worked for stripped away from you, everything that forms your identity decided that it is undesirable, for people to be actively encouraged to beat you, starve you, humiliate you, even kill you. Who wouldn't at least try to run away from that? That was the bravest thing to do, surely? Every single member of his family flashed across his mind, like a photo reel, the guilt would devour him tonight. He knew she wasn't thinking straight but her accusations scratched his guilt red raw unleashing an anger that he had been directing at himself all this time.

'Get out, Marianne,' he growled.

'No.'

'Get out!' He shouted, not caring who heard him.

'I need to know.'

'Know what?'

Her face crumpled into a look of despair, 'That I am not the only one who keeps putting people in danger!'

'You have some nerve, Marianne! Do you think we have common ground with that? You went along with all of it!'

'I didn't believe it was right!'

'But you did nothing!'

She stepped back.

'And when I did something, all I did was hurt more people,' she mumbled.

'How am I able to do anything about that?'

'Survive. Please?' Marianne begged him, before dissolving into huge soul-wrenching sobs.

His anger towards her changed into one of protection, righteous anger, as he pulled her in close, holding her as tight as possible. In his mind, he pictured trying to form a protective shield around her as they stood together in the lonely space of the attic. Maybe some of Johann's imagination had rubbed off on him after all.

'They came for the Penaud family,' Marianne mumbled into the thin material of his shirt.

'Etienne's violin teacher?'

Marianne nodded, as her fresh tears dampened his skin.

His spine stiffened as a chill of horror ran down it. Gurs was awful, but if places like that existed before the war, then who knows how the horrors had escalated across the continent as the Nazis continued their reign of terror. He wasn't naïve, he could only imagine what was happening to people like him, like his family, like Max and his friends.

***

They sat in a mournful silence until Marianne fell into an exhausted sleep. Philipp covered her with a blanket and sat down on the other side of the attic. He watched her for a while as she slept fitfully, even when she was completely drained of energy, her body wouldn't allow her to rest peacefully. Not that his sleep would be any better with the knowledge that the enemy was closing in closer than they had ever been before, that Marianne was at breaking point, and no idea what Etienne was thinking.

'Hey, Johann. We're both brave. How about another adventure? You and me, brother.' He whispered into the night.

ETIENNE

Avignon, November 1939

The rain poured down outside, hitting the windowpane with such ferocity that Etienne was concerned it would punch its way through the glass. But still, that wasn't as distracting as Madame Penaud's silence. No corrections on the dynamics, no comments on the story, no tales of her grandchildren's latest antics.

'Madame Penaud?'

'Oui, Etienne?'

'You are very quiet.'

He had noticed it for a while now, every year it was the same, withdrawn silence, a vacancy in her demeanour.

'I'm sorry, Etienne.'

'No need to apologise Madame. It's just…'

'Oui?'

'It feels like you are carrying a pain,' he said as he slowly approached her in her chair, carefully extending the violin towards her.

'It helps me with my pain.'

The side of her mouth twitched, and she hesitated.

'This is your time though, Etienne. Are you sure you want me to take some of it?'

'I like to think of it as our time, Madame.'

She gave him a stiff smile but extended out her hands where Etienne gently rested the precious violin. When she placed the rest underneath her chin, she held out her hand again for the bow, Etienne obediently lowered it down delicately into her open palm. There was a soft rumble of thunder in the distance.

Etienne limped over to the spare stool next to the piano and shuffled around awkwardly until the aching was bearable.

He watched in respectful silence as Madame Penaud positioned the bow along the strings and began to play. Her song began jovially, with short, cheerful notes that bounced around, life was chaotically busy but happy, the strings sang high, and the scene played out for some time. But then the tone shifted, the strings sang lowly and told a tale of intensity and danger, a large crescendo rounded off in a high-pitched scream from the strings before the sound faded, but it was quick, too quick, it was an unsatisfying way for a piece to end. She paused, her face turned towards the floor lost in thought, or memory of whatever had befallen her.

Etienne shuffled forward, unsure as to whether she had concluded. He jumped when Madame Penaud brought the bow back to centre on the strings and continued, but it sounded like a completely new piece. The next phase of her journey.

It began tentatively, the slow rhythm and lilted melodies didn't indicate happiness necessarily, but a sense of optimism was detectable. The tune was similar until the end, level, balanced, steady. When her song ended, she wiped a small tear away from her eye. Etienne's heart was hammering hard in his chest, she had told him that life had been happy, but something dark had happened and changed everything very suddenly. Things may not have been entirely happy since then, but she still clung onto something, and this in return gave Etienne hope. He manoeuvred his way off the seat, approached carefully to remove the violin and bow from Madame Penaud's hands and placed them back on their display.

'Thank you for sharing that with me, Madame Penaud,' Etienne said gently.

She nodded, 'I trust you, Etienne,' she said, her voice cracking slightly as she spoke.

***

Avignon, March 1943

He presented it with the little materials that he had to hand. A small, feeble, fragile cedar wood frame surrounded the magnificent instrument. No matter what he did, the violin just sat there staring at him. He had tried to put it out of sight, so that he wouldn't keep noticing it, but grew scared that it would come to harm if he could not see it and inevitably brought it back out to display. This instrument that he had played so many times, and adored every experience, had now become the embodiment of guilt and shame.

To play it outside of the Penaud household, without Madame Penaud present, without her permission to play it, was unthinkable. He wanted to play it with every fibre of his being; it took all his willpower not to reach out and touch it every time he walked past it. But how could he ever play it without it reminding him of *this?*

When Marianne had burst in through the door that day, sweaty and flustered, she looked like she was either going to faint or throw up, or both, he knew that something awful had happened.

'Marianne? What happened?' He gasped, rushing over to her as she stumbled into his arms.

Etienne could feel her whole body shaking against his. He placed his hands on her arms to try and steady her, and that's when he finally spotted her gripping the violin and the bow for dear life.

'W... wh...why do you have Madame Penaud's violin?' He stuttered.

Marianne couldn't face him, she stared ahead at the wall, silent tears rolled down her cheeks.

'They just took them, Etienne. Him and his *gang.*'

Otto.

Her voice was little more than a whisper, but she spat the words out with such venom and hatred, Etienne feared her for a moment.

Etienne felt his stomach drop, his heart began to race, and he could feel a small tremble start to creep up from his fingertips. He spun Marianne around to face him, she still wobbled on her feet, but he had to know more.

'Marianne, what is going on?' He asked urgently, as he felt the colour drain from his face.

Marianne swayed, still refusing to meet his eye. He was losing her, he lightly tapped her cheeks, and her eyes finally met his.

'The Penauds are Jewish, Etienne, why did you never tell me that?'

He guided Marianne over to a chair and sat her down gently. Then he started to pace. His limbs, his cane, his heart, and his mind all felt heavier with every step. He had never actually asked her. That was the beauty of their friendship. They never asked each other personal questions, music was always their way of expressing themselves, and they understood each other in a way that no one else did. Should he have asked? What difference would it have made?

But then there was Gabriel, Gabriel's wife and children, and his father. What would happen to them? Gabriel never returned home after the official surrender; Madame Penaud was too grief-stricken to talk about it. He may have died, he may have been captured,

Etienne didn't know. So, he continued to pray for him, as he promised. But now he didn't know what to do.

'I didn't know,' he admitted.

'Why did you never ask her, Etienne?'

'They left Paris to come here when Gabriel was young. Something to do with her blindness. That's all I know.'

She scoffed at him in disbelief; Etienne began to scratch the inside of his thumb in irritation.

'What difference would it have made, Marianne?'

'Difference? We could have *helped* them Etienne! No one else suspected that this would all happen Etienne, but you did. We trusted you, and we prepared. Why the hell could we not help them too?'

'And do what exactly, Marianne?'

She looked towards the stairs.

'No,' Etienne asserted.

Marianne stood up her, energised by her anger, and strode towards him.

'Are you serious?'

'I know you feel guilt over what happened before. But we cannot save everyone as penance for that, Marianne!'

Then he felt the slap on his face, sharp and stinging. He lost his balance, tripped over his cane, and crashed to the floor. The day he fell onto the dusty ground in front of a cackling Marcel and his followers, he felt humiliated, and he felt attacked, just like right now.

It was difficult to move, he couldn't rotate around very easily, and his leg and hip were stiffening, on the brink of spasm. He stretched it out, just as Philipp had taught him, managing to prop himself against a wall and extend. Etienne sat and waited for the pain to stop radiating all over his body, squeezing his eyes shut willing it away as he always did. His vision was blurry when he opened his eyes, but even in his limited sight he could see the horrified expression on Marianne's face.

'Etienne... I...'

'Lay your hand on me like that again and you are on your own,' he growled.

Marianne gulped, nodded, and ran up the stairs. She still had the strength to strike hard if prompted. Wounded as he was, he took strange comfort in knowing that she still had fight left in her.

***

His head was pounding when he finally awoke. His eyes felt heavy from the tears he had shed bountifully in the night, as Marianne's words haunted his mind.

They just took them, Etienne. Him and his gang.

He didn't know how to help them. Heck, he didn't even know how he was going to help his own family. But then it struck him, and he sat bolt right up in bed despite the pain emanating from every part of his body. Marianne had spoken with Otto. If he had seen her at the shop during that first encounter... if she had spoken to him...if he was able to get a decent look at her...

Oh shit.

His silent panic was almost immediately shattered by loud, threatening, hammering at the front door. Fighting through the pain, he shrugged on a patchy, worn woollen jacket as fast as he could. He clambered towards the stairs and waited for the next series of raps to rattle the door frame, whilst they rang out, he tapped his cane on the staircase three times.

'There is much cedar,' he hissed as loudly as he dared, close to the wall, and prayed that he had been heard.

He carefully made his way down the stairs; he didn't need to fully reach the door before he saw them. Their dark, tall, intimidating silhouettes dominated the doorframe, still relentlessly slamming their fists against the wood. Etienne took a moment to collect himself, took a deep breath, and limped towards the door, turned the handle, and let the officers in.

Otto waltzed in, swinging his arms freely by his sides as if he were occupying the entire space, marking his territory. His striking blonde hair was slicked back, apart from one stray hair that floated by his temple. He was proudly dressed in his uniform, adorned with various badges, the likes of which Etienne couldn't understand, nor did he want to. Ernst was closely behind him, and alongside him were Camille and Pierre. They were straight-faced and couldn't bring their heads up. Something was very wrong.

'Etienne Touelle. I presume,' Otto said slowly as he smirked, his beady eyes furiously inspecting him. Etienne shuddered uncomfortably.

'Yes sir. How can I help you?'

'Oh, I don't think there is much you can do to help us,' he sneered.

'Sir?'

'Your carpentry business is under the Compagnonnage guild.'

'Oui…'

'You are no longer to operate. Freemasons are a despicable creed of people. Under official decree businesses under such influence are being shut down.' Behind him, both Pierre and Camille winced.

'But sir, we are no freemasons and no relation to any either,' Etienne pleaded.

Otto was on him in a flash, seizing him by the throat and pinning him hard against the wall, tightening his grip slowly. Camille shrieked, Pierre tried to step forward but was blocked by Ernst, all he could do was look at his son in despair. Etienne desperately tried to pry Otto's strong hands away from his throat as he fought for air.

'I did not ask for your opinion,' his breath was hot, and flecks of spit hit Etienne all over his face. 'I am simply here to carry out orders. You will obey them, or the consequences will be severe. Understood?'

He released him, and Etienne fell to the floor, coughing hard as he tried to regain his breath. The spasm that had been lurking all morning finally unleashed, he grunted in agony as his parents rushed to his side. Otto laughed in exasperation.

'Crippled and pathetic, aren't you an accurate representation of your useless country.'

He turned sharply on his heels, clapping Ernst hard on the back as they headed back towards the door. But then he halted suddenly.

'Oh, and say hello to that wife of yours.'

His chuckle lingered in the air as he headed down the street.

'Ma pêche! Are you okay?' Camille asked frantically.

He tried to lie and say he was fine, but all that came out was a pained groan.

'Why is he asking about, Marianne?' Pierre asked, worry straining his voice.

'He saw her the other day,' Etienne rasped, 'he took note of her surname.'

It was vaguely the truth at least.

'I don't like the way that he spoke about her,' Pierre stated.

Camille busied herself fetching Etienne a glass of water, whilst Pierre stayed with him, propping him up back onto his feet.

'Oh,' Camille's voice rang out.

'What is it, Maman?' Etienne asked as Pierre helped him hobble into the kitchen. She looked sad; her hand placed over her heart as she stared out of the window.

'No peaches grew this year,' she said sadly.

'I'm sorry, Maman,' Etienne said, placing his hands on her shoulders for comfort.

'It is just a silly superstition,' she replied. 'We are all alive, and that's what matters.' She tried a small smile, but it was unconvincing.

As the city grew dark that evening Etienne retrieved his hidden loot, he sliced up the peaches and took them upstairs to Marianne and Philipp, all three peaches.

***

He lay flat on his back in bed that night, unable to sleep. His throat still felt tight from Otto's grasp, he could feel the bruising starting to form, he knew that it would take ages to heal, and he didn't want to look weak.

His parents would not be able to cope with the business officially shut down. How would he console them? And then of course there was Marianne, he was almost certain that Otto knew who she was. He would be back for her, and then what? How would he be able to protect her then? And Philipp? Things had gone from tough to impossible.

He heard the door creak open, his muscles twitched as he craned his neck to see who was there. Marianne crept in through the small gap.

'I'm so sorry, Etienne.'

Her slap felt like a distant memory, but to an extent, he understood now that he had faced Otto's hand. He put his hand up to silence her, and she obeyed. She sat next to him, her face turning to one of shock when she saw him.

'He did that to you didn't he?' She said, as her hand hovered over the bruises.

Etienne nodded.

'I understand, Marianne.'

She held his hands tightly, as tears rolled down her cheeks.

'We need to stick together from now on, Marianne. The business has been shut down. He knows who you are.'

He was surprised at her lack of surprise; she had anticipated this.

'He destroys lives, Etienne.'

He squeezed her hands and pulled her into a forgiving embrace.

'We won't let him. Come with me,' he said gently, taking her by the hand and leading her downstairs.

'Etienne, what are we doing?' She asked.

'Proving that we are not destroyed,' Etienne said defiantly. He strode over to the makeshift frame, pausing as he adored the violin.

'Etienne, it's after curfew. We could get in trouble.'

Madame Penaud used this instrument to tell personal stories, a way of keeping people's memories alive. He had to honour that. He picked up the instrument, closed his eyes, and began to play. As he played Marianne relaxed, she shuffled around in the chair and closed her eyes taking in the music's message.

'What was that song, Etienne?' Marianne asked as Etienne rounded off the song with a flourish.

'It's our victory song, Marianne.'

For the first time in weeks, together, they smiled.

***

Avignon, May 1943

Everything was black. He couldn't see. Somewhere he was bleeding. He didn't know where he was. Shots rang out in the distance, but he couldn't tell where from.

What is happening?

Where am I?

Maman. Papa. Marianne. Philipp. Where are they?

MARIANNE

Avignon, May 1943

Striking Etienne had scared her. When he had struggled to get back up again, she froze, when she should have been down on her knees, lifting him with all her strength, begging him for forgiveness. But instead, she just stood there.

His threat to kick her out hadn't been what terrified her the most though.

You deserve it. You are pathetic, weak, and unworthy. The voice in her head kept telling her.

What she had wanted to say to Etienne more than anything, was the rage that compelled her was not because of him. When she hit him, she saw Otto's face.

***

There was no need for any Nazi officer to remain in an unoccupied zone. He must have pulled some strings to stay in the city. He was staying for a reason, and Marianne knew exactly why.

She could only stay in her own house or go next door to Camille and Pierre, but only if one of them was in to be there with her. A new rule, another adaptation, Etienne did not want to let her out of his sights, and for good reason. Otto's malicious terrorising of their household, shutting down the business, his abuse of Etienne, and his hunting of her had them all terrified. For the tenth time, Marianne checked behind the hazy curtains to make sure he wasn't in sight.

She didn't need to be venturing out into the streets to know what was happening around her. Every day she heard screaming, not out of fear, but out of horror. It was unmistakable. It made her blood chill. The trauma in the cry commanded the hairs on the back of her neck to stand to attention, the invisible punch to the gut was impossible to ignore. 'Enemies' were being shot almost daily. Etienne would arrive home ghostly white, his eyes consumed with distress that ate into his soul.

They had promised to always talk, to confess, they hadn't done enough of it lately and it had taken its toll. She never slept, the fear and graphic nature of Etienne's tales of bodies left hanging in the middle of the street for anyone to walk past haunted her.

She yearned for Etienne's comfort, their lovemaking had always been rare, which hadn't bothered her knowing how uncomfortable it was for Etienne, and not just physically. But Etienne showed her what it was like to be cared for gently and considerately; Marianne craved that feeling more than ever. He couldn't bring himself around to accepting her advances which hurt, but in the middle of the night, it was always Etienne reaching for her hand. She soon came to understand that this was all he was capable of now. He was still showing that they were in this together, and right now, that was enough.

Etienne was finding more solace in the violin. For every horrific sight witnessed, for every moment Philipp's presence went unnoticed, for every bombing they all survived, Etienne would pour all his thoughts, feelings, and his very soul into music. It was as if the violin mourned with every aching heart across the nation, Etienne always managed to capture it so perfectly. Although she was his only visible audience, she knew that Philipp was listening, that Camille and Pierre were in earshot of his mastery and that Etienne was uniting them all in a way that could not be explained.

***

Spring was finally in bloom after the most bitter winter she had ever experienced. The sunshine although welcomed by all, remained a false symbol of hope. But Marianne relished the opportunity it gave her to spend time with Camille.

Around the back of Camille and Pierre's home was a small garden, which Camille had filled with tulips, marigolds, roses, sweet peas, and of course, lavender. Now they were all exploding in a kaleidoscope of colour, and although overpowering at first, the distinct strong aromas blended to give the place a feeling of harmony, and tranquillity, something they had all so desperately been craving for years. The only thing that was out of place was the strange tree in the middle, it had always looked dead, but Camille was adamant that this plant was full of surprises.

'Surprises seem to happen every day, Camille. Just not welcome ones,' Marianne sighed as she clipped back a dead stem on a rose.

'That is the point of the surprise, my dear. You don't know what it will entail, good or bad. But I do feel that you can only get so many bad surprises before the harvest of good ones come in,' Camille gleamed.

'How can you be so sure?'

'I have seen so much good that has come off the back of disappointment or bad situations to not believe it, my dear.' Camille said.

She loved her mother-in-law dearly. Camille was the loving, nurturing mother that she had always sought. But she also made her understand her own mother so much better. When Gisela had seemed cold or distant, she had been trying to protect her. At the time she had seen it as her mother enabling the taunts and abuse to happen, a betrayal of her duties as a mother. It wasn't until she became a mother that she understood the need to do everything it took to protect your child, no matter how strange, desperate, or awful it may be.

As she watched Camille work and hum a cheerful melody,

Marianne was struck at Camille's unfailing ability to see light in the most desperate of situations. Etienne was too realistic to appreciate the optimism, but to Marianne, Camille was inspiring. Even after the attack just a few months ago she had kept going whereas the rest of them had become far more cautious. Where Camille would waltz down the street, the others would be checking behind their shoulders at every turn.

'Marianne, be careful! That's a healthy shoot!'

'Oh, sorry!' Marianne gasped, staring down at her hands. The flower had fought back at her near decapitation attempt. A large thorn was wedged deep in her finger, blood pooled around the epicentre, and the thin skin surrounding it leaked big drops of bright red blood. Marianne heard a sharp tear, and Camille was by her side wrapping torn material from her dress around her finger.

'Wait here, I will be right back. Don't touch it!'

She hurried back into her house, and no sooner had she left than she returned with a makeshift pair of tweezers.

'Is that a sardine tin?' Marianne asked, recognising the faint outline of the old packaging.

'We have to be resourceful, my dear.'

Camille poked around the wound, Marianne didn't flinch at the discomfort, not even when the sharp edges of metal grazed her skin, she found that she was numb to a lot these days. Camille tugged hard, profusely apologising, until finally, the thorn gave way, resisting the whole time as it slid out of Marianne's fingertip, before containing the wound in the material strip.

'That was a deep one! I should know, I've pulled enough splinters out of Pierre's hands to build my own cabinet,' she giggled.

In their line of work, it was impossible not to pick up a splinter here and there. But Etienne never let Marianne tend to his. It wasn't something she envied; it warmed her heart to see Camille blush with young, innocent excitement whenever she spoke of her husband like they had been together for weeks instead of decades.

'You love Pierre very much, don't you?' Marianne said softly, tightening the pressure on her finger.

'I know many don't believe in them, but I believe in soulmates. Pierre is mine.'

'Etienne is lucky to have grown up in a house so full of love,' Marianne remarked, her voice catching as she spoke, she hoped that Camille didn't notice.

'I wanted for him what I didn't have.'

Her comment surprised her; Camille always saw the best in everyone. She never spoke of her family, and Etienne seldom mentioned them.

'Marriage is a financial arrangement in my family. In fact, everything is conducted in accordance with a financial arrangement,' Camille confessed.

Marianne was unsure what to say, Camille chuckled at the puzzled look on her face.

'I know my dear. It's hard to understand when you fall in love.'

'Your family didn't like Pierre?'

'They respected him. He and his whole family worked hard; they had a good reputation. But he wasn't rich, and we were in love, and that was a problem. So, we eloped, and never looked back.'

'Sounds like one of the great love stories.'

'We like to think so,' Camille said winking at her.

Marianne tried to smile, but this time Camille saw through it. She pulled her into a tight hug.

'I'm sure your parents would have been proud of your marriage with Etienne,' she whispered.

Marianne sighed. Her parents may not have been interested in financial prospects, but image and respect, that mattered the most to them. She felt a fresh pang of sadness flood her stomach knowing that her parents would never have understood Etienne's quirks, his interests, and his brilliance like so many didn't.

***

It was early evening by the time Marianne finished in the garden with Camille. She had just walked through the door when she found Etienne in conversation with the church priest.

'Father Joubert! What do we owe the pleasure?' She exclaimed.

The same man who had joyfully married them three years ago, stood before them now with dark circles around his eyes, his hairline dramatically receding. His face told the story of a tormented soul. In his role he had probably overseen the direst of people's circumstances, each experience eating away at him gradually.

'I come here on bleak business I am sorry to say,' he croaked.

'There are still some belongings at the Penaud household. Monsieur Touelle, I am informed that you knew them well. We at the church think it best for you to take ownership of the remaining items before they come to further harm.'

There was an edge in his voice that made Marianne uncomfortable.

'Father, if we are seen near the household, surely we would be suspected of being sympathisers?' Marianne queried.

Father Joubert shook his head sadly. 'If you are there to take possession of the items they will not care. It's not those that they are interested in,' he murmured.

'I want to keep their memory alive,' Etienne said, 'Will someone from the church be there to justify my presence?'

'Oui, Monsieur.'

'Very well. What time shall I come?' Etienne asked.

'I will have one of my men sent there at eight this evening.'

'That is late Father. It is dangerous to be out at that time,' Marianne protested.

'I am afraid that is when these matters are dealt with with the least suspicion, Madame Touelle.' He said hurriedly.

'I will be there, Father,' Etienne affirmed.

'Thank you Monsieur Touelle. Be blessed, both of you,' Father Joubert said as he turned away and exited through the door. Too quickly for Marianne's liking.

'I don't like it, Etienne.'

'Me neither.'

'Don't go.'

'Lock the door behind me and stay inside, if I am not back before curfew, alert my father, and tell him where I have gone. You and Philipp need to be protected.'

'Be careful.'

He kissed her tenderly on her forehead. 'I will. I promise,' he whispered.

***

Curfew came and went and there was no sign of Etienne. The door was locked as he had instructed, but it didn't stop Marianne from pacing around in the workspace. Everything felt empty now that all the goods had been cleared out; begrudgingly handed over to the Milice as supplies for the German army. She jumped at the sound of a frantic knock at the door.

Etienne. Thank God!

Marianne hurried to the door, fumbling with the keys as she tried to unlock it. But as she moved the curtain to the side, she was met with the sight, not of her returned husband, but a white-faced and petrified Juliette.

'Juliette?' She asked as she opened the door. 'What has happened? Where is your mother?'

'Please come Madame Touelle! I didn't know who else to turn to!'

There was a line of dark bruises on Juliette's wrist that were visible in the glint of the moonlight.

'What has happened, Juliette?'

'The bakery is in trouble, my mother is there but she needs help, please come!' She shouted, edging further into the street, gesturing furiously for Marianne to follow her.

Against her better judgement, she found herself rushing out of the door after Juliette, who took off at pace down the streets. Marianne tried to keep up, her aching legs pumping hard as she scrambled down the side streets, trying to match Juliette's pace as she darted around each corner with youthful ease.

'Juliette, wait!' Marianne called out, a stitch stabbing at her sides, her lungs on fire.

At least I know where the bakery is, remember what Etienne showed you, just a bit further down the slope.

She tripped on the cobbles, her ankles ached as they bent at awkward angles. Her mind ran wild with concern. Was the bakery on fire? Had it been vandalised? Was Madame Renou hurt? Why had they asked for her?

At long last she rounded the last corner, running to the last building on the street. She breathed a sigh of relief, to see that there was no damage to the property. Juliette was nowhere to be seen. She hobbled round to the side of the building.

'Juliette?'

A force hit her in the back, knocking her to the floor. Her face hit the cobbles hard, blood immediately streamed out of her nose.

She pushed with all her might on her weak arms until she was upright, shaking all over as she turned to face her assailant. Of course, it was him, standing over her smirking in that awful manner. He dangled Juliette by her arm, as she whimpered in pain.

'Well done. Your mother is in your basement.'

He threw Juliette away, and she struck the wall.

'I'm sorry, Marianne,' she cried.

He grabbed his gun and pointed it directly at Juliette's face.

'GO!' He barked, and Juliette scarpered.

He turned his beady eyes back on Marianne. He stooped down to her yanking her to her feet before placing his hand tightly around her throat.

'Well, well, well,' he sneered. 'When my superiors sent me to this God-forsaken country I must tell you I was furious. A person of my dedication is wasted in this shit city.'

Marianne gasped frantically; her feet kicked furiously.

'But then you appear. My supposedly dead wife is here of all places. Did you really think I wouldn't recognise you? I have seen *all* of you. Do you think a few changes to your appearance is going to make you unrecognisable? You are more stupid than I first thought, Ada.'

He released her, just as he had released Etienne. Marianne coughed hard, choking on the blood that poured out of her nose.

'Sir, I don't what you mean.' Ignorance was her only ploy.

'You think I'm stupid? Don't you dare play me for a fool!' Otto roared as he delivered a hard kick to her side.

'Please!' She gasped, deeply winded by the blow.

'Oh, Liselotte was convincing don't get me wrong. She managed to convince everyone about your pathetic demise. You drowning?

She didn't fool me. She and Thomas got what was coming to them.'

Her blood ran cold. *Lise! Oh, my dear friend!* She winced to hide her shock.

'Broke your mother of course. Her weak heart couldn't cope. All of you Stein children dying and abandoning her, you all killed her.'

Mütter! Please God don't let it be true!

'And of course, there is our son. Erich. He's nine now, Ada. Learning all the time. Far better off without his mother.'

She gulped to contain the rage that was boiling inside her.

'But don't worry, any pathetic traits he got from you have been seen to quickly and dealt with efficiently.'

'If you laid a hand on him,' she growled. She hadn't stood up for the right thing before, she refused to let that happen again, and she realised she was prepared to die for this, die defending her son.

'Ah, so it is you darling!' Otto cackled. 'I just had to be sure that it was you.'

Shit.

'If you've come here to kill me, Otto. Just fucking do it you coward. I love my son more than anything in this world, more than you ever could, and I'll get to tell him that. But you won't, not where you will end up,' Marianne said as defiantly as she could manage.

'You think I'm going to make it that easy, do you?' He snickered.

Her heart began to race. She was prepared. She placed her hands up in surrender. Otto laughed maniacally.

'Giving up as you always do. How predictable.'

'Just shoot me!' She yelled.

'Oh no, no, no,' he chuckled menacingly. 'I have not seen my dear wife in so many years. We need to be reacquainted.'

He overpowered her fast, pinning her down on the uneven ground, she didn't have the strength to fight back. The familiar feeling of dread washed over her as he made short work of pushing her skirts up and tearing her knickers away. She whimpered as he inflicted his ordeal upon her, waiting for it to be over, soon she wouldn't have to suffer any longer.

'You are mine, and you always will be,' he hissed into her ear, before letting out a long groan as he climaxed inside her.

Everything in her was telling her to run the moment he rolled off her, but her body would not obey her. She lay still and defeated. Otto was breathing heavily, and she could hear him re-attaching his belt.

Let it be quick.

He roughly tugged her to her feet again. She couldn't stand, and she fell against the wall.

'Shoot me,' she begged.

'No. I won't give you the satisfaction of a quick death. You betrayed your marital vows. Laying with another man. That's adultery, Ada. The price for sin is death, you know that.'

'There's also such thing as mercy,' she grunted, her head was spinning, and her consciousness was fading.

'Like you deserve any! You are going to die slowly, Ada. And I am going to watch every single moment.'

Her vision blurred, something shiny appeared from Otto's side. It was sharp and cold as he pressed it up against her neck.

'Please,' she gasped.

'It's too late for that.'

'Marianne?'

The instrument was removed from her neck, and she exhaled heavily.

'You have no business here. Go home,' Otto ordered.

'That's my daughter-in-law sir, she shouldn't be out here so late. Please sir, let me take her home, she means no harm.'

Pierre!

'Papa, please go home. It's not safe!'

'I heard the commotion outside the house, I thought you were in trouble,' Pierre called out as Otto still formed a barrier between them.

'You will leave right now. Me and my wife are sorting some affairs out,' Otto threatened.

'Your wife? Marianne, what is going on?'

'Papa, please I will explain, but you need to go home.'

'Marianne, you call her, do you? Well, she's led you all on quite the lie, hasn't she? Haven't you, Ada?'

Her vision came back into focus at the wrong moment, the look of confusion etched all over Pierre's face broke her heart.

'I love the family. Etienne, you, Camille, you are everything to me!' she cried.

Whatever doubt or confusion Pierre was bound to be thinking at that moment didn't stop him from trying to get to her. He shuffled around as best as he could to try and get past Otto, his hand extended out to her for her to take.

'Come, my dear, let me get you home.'

Marianne wobbled on her unsteady legs, desperately trying to move towards him. Every movement required so much focus. So much so that she didn't see that Otto still held the knife in his hand. His huge form moved in front of her once again, blocking her path to Pierre, she tried to see around the back of his head to catch sight of her father-in-law. But then Otto's arm jerked forward, and she was met with the horror of Pierre's wide eyes as he slowly collapsed to the ground, blood poured through his shirt, and he lay with his hand clasped over his heart.

'PAPA, NO!' Marianne shrieked rushing to his side. She placed her hands over his, trying to put pressure on the wound. She glanced around frantically looking for someone, anyone. But all she saw was Otto's intimidating silhouette striding around the corner, out of sight, his satisfied cackle lingered chillingly in the air.

'HELP! PLEASE SOMEONE HELP!' She screamed from the depths of her soul.

'Ma... Mar...' Pierre gurgled. His breathing was laboured, and there was blood in the corner of his mouth.

'Shhh, Papa don't talk, I'm here.'

His shaking bloodied hand caressed her cheek as she wept bitterly.

'T...To...Touelle... always,' he wheezed, smiling tenderly at her.

'Always,' she whispered.

She felt his hand drop from her face; his arm flopped to the side, and his face looked to the sky, unblinking, still, at peace.

The threatening rumble of artillery and exploding bombs echoed from a distance, but even their danger would not move her from the spot. There was nothing left of her now. She looked to the sky and howled with soul-destroying sorrow until the last bit of fight left her completely.

PHILIPP

Unknown

The room was thick with panicked frenzy as people rushed around there. He had no idea how he had got there. There weren't many distinguishing features to identify. The walls were bathed in a bright white light that made him squint every time he looked too long at it. As he slowly paced further inside, obscure shapes started to come into view. Floating circular figures landed securely on the blurred floor, and displays of plates, pocket watches, and coins started to shudder into clarity. The antique shop? But what could have possibly happened to make everyone so frantic?

'Etienne!' a voice called out sharply, resonating on the east side of the room.

'Marianne?' Philipp replied, rushing over to where the sound was strongest, but it faded away by the time he reached it.

Philipp turned his attention back to the room, glancing upwards he saw that there was no roof overhead. Plumes of white smoke coated the area; Philipp wasn't sure whether it was for protection or containment, or whether it meant well or harm. He backed away cautiously, but as he did so he felt a strange pressure pushing down on his chest. Philipp snapped his head to the side, only to notice that he had collided with a cabinet. But he was confused, he hadn't felt it. He touched his side, expecting a tenderness from the impact, but the skin was supple, no pain, no sensitivity, nothing.

Did I?... No, I can't have... Did I walk through it?

'Where am I?' he asked, speaking clearly and loudly. But no answer came.

The pressure in his chest would not ease, and it didn't feel normal. It was like it was digging to his core, looking for something as it intensified with every short breath he could manage. He felt for his heartbeat, it was slow, too slow.

What is happening to me?

He was soon distracted by a group of ladies who rushed towards him. Philipp scurried back to allow them past but not one of them looked up to see him there. They huddled close together; their conversation was loud and easy to eavesdrop on. They looked afraid. But why? Philipp edged forward to catch every word that they were saying.

'The doctor says we need more towels!'

'Who is supposed to be watching the little one?'

'She's been gone for too long.'

'Is Felix with her?'

Felix? Father!

Philipp stood directly in front of them.

'Felix is my father! Is he alright? Is he safe?' He called out, desperately searching each woman's face for an answer, but they continued to ignore him.

'Can you hear me?' Philipp asked, waving his hands in front of their faces.

'What are you all doing standing around?' A new, yet familiar harsh tone rang out. Philipp spun round. It was undeniably her. She was younger of course and just a few grey hairs adorned her head.

'Oma Angelica!' Philipp gasped.

Ever the commanding presence in the room, his grandmother set to work barking out orders.

'Anita, hot water. Gretchen, fresh towels. Liesl, Johann is by himself. Go!'

'Tante Anita. Tante Gretchen. Tante Liesl,' he whispered as his aunts rushed away to carry out their orders.

He followed Liesl, trying to keep up with her quick pace had always been a challenge. Her long legs carried her swiftly to wherever she needed to be. Philipp's breathing still troubled him as he tried to time his footsteps with his aunt's. But then Liesl passed through a layer of wispy, white smoke, out of sight. Philipp halted in front of the hovering smoke.

Surely not.

He raised a shaky hand towards the plumes and plunged it in. Feeling no obstacle on the other side, he extended the rest of his arm in. As he shuffled forward Philipp could hear muffled voices but, in the distance, someone was screaming. Philipp closed his eyes, unsure whether he wanted to see the scene, but he had to know what was going on and he walked through the smoke.

This room was different, the ceiling and windows were still bathed in the same bright light and smoke, but it was smaller, and there was a door at the far end. Bookcases adorned the right-hand side, and Philipp felt an electric thrill shoot down his spine. It had been so long since he had been able to immerse himself in books properly, and such a range of them. Tales of swashbuckling pirates, fantastical lands of magical creatures, detectives solving the most confounding of crimes.

He found himself lingering over the old binding of his father's catalogue of antiques that he had collected for the store. He was instantly filled with a warming nostalgia, but with it came an overwhelming feeling of homesickness, and regret over his lack of enthusiasm for the business in later years. Philipp longed to open it up, touch every single wrinkle of each page, curl up in the corner, and peruse every detail of his father's adventures, if only just to feel connected to him once again. He reached for the book, but his hand simply slipped through it. He tried again, and again, but each time he could not grasp it. Helpless tears filled his eyes as he continuously swiped at the book. There was a cry, but it wasn't his own. His aunt Liesl passed by the bookcase, crouched down low to the ground, and held out her arms, where a sweet-looking toddler clumsily tottered into her embrace. Dried tear marks lined his pudgy red cheeks, and a few small teeth lined his gums. His eyes were curious, constantly scanning the room despite his tantrum, his thick brown hair was messy as his fat hands kept scrambling it all up.

'Hush hush, Johann,' Liesl instructed as she carried him over to an armchair that had formed from the air, she sat him down and bounced him on her knee. But Johann would not quieten, his piercing screams rang out even louder. Philipp crossed over to the other side of the room, and he positioned himself behind the armchair where he could glance over his aunt's shoulder.

'Hopefully not too much longer now little Johann. Your mother wouldn't want you to be sad.'

Not too much longer until what? Liesl's soothing had done little to reassure Johann, who continued to wail at the top of his lungs. Philipp couldn't help but giggle.

'Always have to be the one to be heard the loudest, don't you?' He teased.

Suddenly Johann's face stilled, his eyes which had been squeezed tightly shut in his rage were now wide open and searching the room once again. Philipp gulped, could he sense him? Hear him?

'Hey, that's better Johann!' Liesl chimed as she wiggled him around.

Philipp backed off slightly, but as he did so, Johann's chin started to wobble, and he began to whine.

'No, no, no baby!' Liesl shushed.

'Johann?' Philipp said. Johann fell silent.

What to say to him? There was so much that needed to be said. But he was a child, how on earth would he understand? But it wasn't like any of this made sense. If this was the last time he would see his brother, he had to make it count.

'Johann. Brother. I am not sorry for leaving. I hate that I did, but I am not sorry for it. I gave myself a chance. It has been hell, but it has been an adventure I will never forget. I just wish you could have come with me. How I am still alive I do not know. But I promise, that one day, someday, I will find you again, and we will have the rest of our lives to embark on the adventures that have been ripped away from us.'

The pressure returned to his chest with vigour, he did his best to try and massage it away, but it persisted. But as he caught sight of the enormous grin that had broken out over Johann's face, he felt his spirit soar.

'It's a boy!' A bellowing voice yelled out, as a huge figure burst through the door at the end of the room.

Father!

Philipp hurried towards him, as his father turned around and ran back into the room. He dashed through the open door before it had any chance to lock him out. This room was bigger by comparison, stretching further back. Felix's thudding footsteps could be heard clattering across the floorboards towards an attending doctor who was swaddling a tiny, whimpering newborn.

'Congratulations Herr, und Frau Blau. A strong healthy son.'

'May I?' Felix asked delicately, and the doctor gently placed the baby into his arms. That glorious, huge smile of his lit up his face, Philipp had dreamed about that look so often.

'Philipp,' a tired voice called out, 'we should call him Philipp.'

Mother!

There were so many photographs of her all over the house. Philipp had always felt grateful to his father for keeping her image and memory alive in their household. In her photos, she was always looking so neat. Her long, sleek, golden hair would be pulled back into a tight bun that sat perfectly central between the top of her head and the start of her neck, but she kept it loose around the sides. Philipp always imagined it would bob playfully to the rhythm of her walk. Felix had often remarked about her magnificent hazel eyes, how they captivated him the first time he lay eyes on her and was immediately transfixed. She smiled so sweetly, with her heart-shaped lips and the one dimple that enhanced her beautiful complexion.

But now her hair was completely loose, Philipp suspected that it flowed far beyond her back, it was ragged from the toils of childbirth. Her cheeks were flustered, and she breathed heavily, yet she was still breathtaking. Her famous eyes were warm and exuded love as she stared longingly at her husband and child.

'Etta, my dearest, I think it is a fine name indeed,' Felix purred.

'My perfect family,' she whispered.

Philipp walked to the end of her bed. He could not believe it. This wonderful woman whom he had only ever been able to picture, was here, in front of him. He yearned with all his heart to speak to her, tell her he loved so much, and be held by her.

'Mütter…' he began.

But then his mother's face began to change, her smile dropped, and her eyes tried to grab someone's attention, something was wrong.

'Mütter, what's wrong?'

'Etta? My love? Doctor, my wife!'

The doctor who had been tidying away his instruments in the corner, suddenly snapped his head up, but his focus wasn't on Etta's eyes as they rolled back in her head, but rather on the rapidly growing, menacing red puddle emerging underneath her.

Severe postpartum haemorrhage.

'Oh, no, no, no!' Felix exclaimed. 'This happened to her with our firstborn as well doctor.'

'Felix. I remember. You need to stand back and let me do my work.'

It happened with Johann too!

Before he had any chance to process what was happening, the doctor pulled the modesty screen back around the bed, blocking Philipp's view of his mother. The last thing he caught sight of was the face of his father, stricken with terror, but never, not for a second, did he relinquish his protective grasp of Philipp.

Philipp knew what was coming, and it was too heartbreaking to witness. For his entire life, he had only had the memory of his mother to mourn, and he had shouldered the responsibility for her death. She had nearly died with Johann too. It should have lifted the burden from him, given him a right to be angry at his brother for inflicting that shame on him. But Johann didn't know, how could he? Felix would never have allowed either of his sons to accept blame for something tragic, unexpected, and uncontrollable.

The voices behind the screen were growing more frantic by the second, it wouldn't be long now, and all Philipp wanted to do was to get out, and far away. The door was mercifully still wide open, and through it he ran, only to collapse on the other side, the heaviness in his chest now so unbearable that he couldn't breathe at all. He started to panic, he needed someone to breathe air into him, and clear his airways, but no one was there. He felt a twinge in his side, internal initially, and then it was followed by another, but this was far stronger and this time it knocked him off balance. The room was edging away from him. He closed his eyes, resigning himself to his fate. If this was what dying felt like, then it sure felt bizarre.

What on earth is going on?

'Philipp,' a soft voice summoned him.

It was her! Her sweet voice.

'Philipp,' the voice spoke again, so gently.

People can see visions and hear strange voices just before they die. Just allow it to happen.

'Look at me, Philipp.'

He couldn't deny himself this opportunity, even if it was all in his imagination. He opened his eyes slowly so that he could believe what he was seeing.

'Mütter?' He wheezed, air slowly rising in his lungs again.

'My darling boy,' she said, 'I've so longed to see you again!'

'And I you,' Philipp gasped as he grappled with his breaths. 'I'm so sorry Mütter,' he cried, surprised at how fast the tears came.

'You have nothing to be sorry for my son!'

'It was my fault!'

'No, my love, never. And even if I knew that I would die, it would always have been worth it to lay eyes on your precious face.'

She stepped towards him and took him into her arms, and Philipp leaned into her, taking in every moment.

'I can feel your touch,' he said confused.

Etta chuckled warmly, Philipp could feel it resonate across her chest, it made her heart beat faster. She was so alive. But she was dead, Philipp knew that.

'Where are we, Mütter?'

'I've been sent to fetch you to bring you home my love.'

'Mütter, am I dead?'

She smiled at him. 'Not exactly. Your body is struggling, it's in between letting your soul go and clinging onto it.'

'Mütter. I can't!'

He was surprised to see her smile again at him.

'That's okay, my darling.'

'Mütter, I'm scared.'

'You are a fighter, Philipp. You always have been, and always will be. It's one of the things I love about you the most.'

'But how? We never…'

'I've always known you, my darling. You carry me with you wherever you go.'

'Who did you see Mütter?'

'My sister, Sophie,' she said quietly.

Felix had spoken little about Etta's extended family. It was painful enough to talk about her.

'If I go with you… will I meet her?'

'She's so looking forward to meeting you.'

A shadow grew behind her, Etta rose to her feet and began to walk towards it. Philipp felt himself trying to run towards her, to protect her, but he couldn't move.

'Mütter watch out! Behind you there's…'

But before he could finish his warning, a tall man emerged, he was proud, he was smiling, and he carried himself with an air of confidence. Despite his intimidating height, his presence was calming, a gentle… giant…

'Father?'

He returned Philipp's shocked stare with one of beaming

happiness, he placed his hand affectionately on his mother's shoulder and they looked at each other tenderly. But his father's presence alongside his mother could only mean one thing, and he could feel his heart shattering.

'Oh, Father no!' He gasped.

Felix's familiar yet disarming warm smile worked its magic.

'I'm so sorry, Father.' Philipp whimpered, his hands trembling.

'You need to choose son,' Felix said lowly, and gently.

'I left you and Johann. I'm so sorry.'

His chest was hurting, and the twinges were getting stronger and stronger.

'He will need you.'

'He's alive?'

Felix nodded.

'I cannot tell you how incredible it is to see you again my dear son. But you need to go back.'

'But I miss you!'

'As we do you. One day we will all be together again. But today is not that day.'

As the acceptance of his father's words grew in his heart, he felt the room drag back further, and he with it. The sight of his parents faded until they were both just shadows in his peripheral vision as he tried to catch one last glimpse of them.

***

'Come on, Philipp stay with me! We are not losing you too!' Etienne's strained voice echoed distantly. He could hear Marianne sobbing.

His chest was light, then heavy, then light again. And then, his heart, he felt it race, air rushed up his airways, cold and fresh. He choked himself awake, as the new breath reinvigorated him. He lay there for a few minutes, breathing, feeling the sensation return to his body, across his limbs, down to his fingertips.

'Philipp?' Marianne said quietly.

'W…wh…what?' Philipp stuttered.

'Philipp, take it easy, we found you collapsed. Your heart stopped beating. We thought you were dead!'

'He's dead! No, no, no! He's dead,' he cried.

'You're not dead, Philipp! You are alive!'

'I left him, and now he's dead!'

Etienne and Marianne looked at each other in disbelief.

'Pierre would have loved to have met you, Philipp,' Marianne said gently.

'Pierre? Pierre's dead?' Philipp exclaimed, trying to sit, up but immediately falling back as pain rushed up his chest.

'Yes? Who else?'

'My Father,' he wheezed.

They looked worriedly at each other.

'How do you know?'

He could never expect them to understand.

'I just know.'

His mind was as ragged as his breath as he tried to readjust to this reality. They had got to his father, but his beautiful soul did not belong to them, that was beyond even their grasp. But Johann hadn't been there. He was still alive.

ETIENNE

Avignon, May 1943

The sun had just sunk beyond the horizon by the time he left the house. Marianne had been reluctant to let him go, despite his reassurance.

'My parents will hear something if anything happens.'

'It's you I'm worried about, Etienne. The priest shows up out of the blue and asks you specifically to do this job and during the evening?'

'He's a man of the church Marianne, and he's been incredibly faithful to our family for as long as he has served here. We can trust him. Just stay here, you'll be safe.'

The air was surprisingly still as he slowly hobbled through the streets towards the house. Without sufficient food, his body struggled to support his lanky frame, and as a result, his pains were worse than ever. He had done this trip so many times, yet he took several wrong turns, hesitated, and stood silently against the wall for periods of time. He felt wretched, every step closer he got to the property felt like a clamp gradually squeezing tighter on his insides.

Forgive me. Forgive me. Forgive me.

At long last he finally rounded the familiar corner and stared up at the outline of the smallest house on the street, so unassuming, yet it stood out so clearly, even as darkness encroached. He paused again, inhaling deeply to still the torment that swirled around his empty stomach. Something in the air felt ominous, maybe Marianne had felt it, maybe it was why she was so jittery. But he couldn't change anything now, he had made a promise and he was always a man of his word. Etienne took another deep breath and teetered towards the house.

The doorway was smashed in, possibly still from the day that the Penauds were taken away. Etienne didn't doubt that it had been further damaged by thieves, most of whom were probably desperate citizens in search of food or valuables that would sell at a high price on the black markets. Etienne was angered by them but equally, he pitied them, and for a second, he wondered how what he was about to do was any different. This war seemed to justify the strangest of behaviours, good and evil.

Hold onto the items that bring honour to them.

No matter how many times he tried to justify the thought in his mind, he still felt unsettled with the responsibility. He waited outside the property for a few more minutes, he hadn't seen any official of the church on their way, however, it was dark, and it was possible he hadn't been able to pick them out. Time passed, and still, no one came. Maybe they were already inside the house? Etienne awkwardly clambered over the splintered pieces of wood into the pitch-black property.

'Father Joubert, are you here?' He called out. He was met with silence, tinged with the same unnerving ominous air that he had felt since he left.

A lump formed in his throat at the depleted state of the home. Chairs, tables, lamps, and the like were all gone, furnishings that his father had restored all those years ago, were gone. It struck him at how simple possessions that took little time to build turned a house into a home, and therefore how valuable his father's work was to the people he served. Cabinets and shelves lay empty but were littered with the smashed remains of photograph frames, which Etienne carefully gathered into his arms. He looked in the drawers, finding tattered papers, sheet music, letter correspondences, and war recruitment leaflets.

Gabriel. Please God keep him away from this mess.

He had not seen or heard from Gabriel's wife or children for a long time. Rumours had circulated concerning their absence. Some said they were caught trying to escape over the border into Spain, but Etienne doubted that they would have headed there, not into further trouble. He held hope in his heart that they were like Philipp, hiding somewhere, knowing that at any moment they could be caught, but taking the risk knowing it was their best shot at staying alive. If only Monsieur and Madame Penaud had gone with them when they had the opportunity. Etienne cleared his throat loudly to push the rising lump back down. As he did so, he heard a crunching sound, Etienne snapped his head around, and a dark figure moved in the doorway.

'Father Joubert? Is that you?'

A sliver of moonlight cast a fraction of light on the mysterious person's face, Etienne leaned forward to catch a better glimpse. There was no noticeable holy garment, and the figure was tall, broad, intimidatingly so.

'Etienne Touelle,' a gruff voice shattered the silence.

Etienne stumbled backwards.

The man chuckled a low, menacing chuckle.

'Marcel was right about you.'

Marcel? What did he have to do with this?

'Monsieur Chalamet?'

His foreboding figure stomped forward, he was older, but certainly not weak. Etienne noticed that he was wearing a uniform, unusual to see someone so well dressed with the lack of materials available these days. But then he saw the bowlike crest on the badge.

Milice.

'Monsieur? I…it's dangerous. You should return home.'

'I can't do that. I have orders.'

Etienne's heart began to pound.

'Monsieur, please don't.'

'I have to,' Monsieur Chalamet spat. 'I don't want to do this to a true French citizen. But they have Marcel, my son. They will kill him if I don't do this.'

'Monsieur, I'm sorry.'

Monsieur Chalamet shook his head as if to dismiss Etienne's sympathies.

'Your pity makes you weak. Your whole family too. We should have done a better job burning that place of yours down,' Monsieur Chalamet scoffed.

Etienne gawped. 'You were responsible for that? But why?'

'The same reason I am here now. You help vermin like the ones that lived here. France does not need that kind of filth infiltrating its society.'

He swung towards him; his fist collided hard into the side of Etienne's head. All the remaining light went out, leaving Etienne wishing for his end to come swiftly.

***

When he awoke, he was bleeding and there was a ringing in his ears. His vision was blurry as he tried to reacquaint himself with the world. To his horror, he could make out another figure in the doorway. Returning to finish him off? It moved fast, stooping down to him at a rapid pace. Etienne squeezed his eyes shut anticipating another blow, a shot, a knife, the final strike. But

350

instead, he felt himself being hauled to his feet and hurried out of the door.

'Walk?' The voice asked in clumsy French.

His cane was not in his hand, he must have dropped it during the assault. Etienne shook his head, as he tried to refocus his vision at the same time. He thudded into something rough and hard, and the grip of his rescuer relinquished from under his shoulder. The world spun around, he tried to remember where he was, his head felt light, and he thought he would pass out again.

Footsteps hurried up behind him, he spun around, but he had no idea in what direction.

'Wife. Danger. Go.' It was the same voice, but his words gave him little comfort.

'Where?' Etienne asked frantically.

The merciful stranger gripped Etienne's shoulders and gently turned him around.

'Go!' He ordered, pressing something into Etienne's hand as he spoke.

'Merci!' Etienne called out, but no voice replied, instead he found his hand clasped around a round, thin instrument. His cane.

He stumbled into the night, Marianne had been right, and now she was in danger. Every couple of metres, his vision began to clear slightly, but so many questions confounded him, making it almost impossible to concentrate. Why were the Milice carrying out orders to attack him? How had the church become involved in this? Where was Marianne? Why had she left the house? If this had happened to him, then who knows what has been intended for her?

He staggered around for what seemed like forever, he knew it was safer to roam in the shadows in silence, but by now he didn't care, he simply had to get to her, whatever it took. If there was someone else hiding down a dark alleyway, so be it. If bombs finally fell directly upon Avignon and he was caught in the crossfire, so be it. Or if his fate rested in the hands of another assailant, so be it.

'MARIANNE!' He yelled at the top of his lungs.

Etienne threw his arms out to feel around, striking the wall hard as he did so, he felt his knuckle crunch under the impact. He went to scream out but no sound escaped his mouth. He was stunned into shock at the sound of a gut-wrenching scream that emerged east from his position.

Marianne, please no!

He followed the horrifying sounds, as they kept coming. As he drew closer, his eyes focused, and he wished they hadn't. For there lay his beloved father, in a huge pool of blood, Marianne beside him, beaten, bloodied, and screaming.

'NO! NO! NO!' He finally screamed, his body giving up on him as he sank to his knees in defeat.

He couldn't tear his eyes away from Pierre's pale, still form, his open eyes full of anguish, frozen in his final frame, one of horror. He couldn't move, couldn't speak, couldn't comprehend what he was seeing, and there they all remained, frozen in time in a scene from a nightmare that would never be forgotten.

***

Avignon, June 1943

He worked at night by candlelight, in his solitude, and without his violin to hand. Death was everywhere, and it was unbearable. When they had thought they had lost enough, the war seemed to have one more morbid trick up its sleeve.

Within twenty-four hours of his beloved father's death, it seemed that every remaining citizen across the city had turned up outside of their front door, to offer condolences, giving what very little they had, or simply to cry with them. Sometimes it had been cathartic, other times it was too overwhelming. All the while Etienne was trying to make sense of a world without his father.

Familiar business contacts turned up at all hours, sometimes in the dead of night. Etienne knew that some of them were not local. Some were even living in occupation zones. How they had managed to sneak out under prying eyes was admirable, but terrifying knowing what fate could await them if they were caught.

'Pierre was the most honourable man we knew. It's the least we can do for him,' they had all said.

As well as coming to pay their respects, they had turned up with small pieces of wood, oak, ash, pine, cedar, birch, and elm. Each one standing individually in its own strength, power, and beauty. Etienne refused to let them work with him, meeting in secret was simply not an option, and he was going to bear no more responsibility for anyone's unnecessary death.

With resistance groups across the country gathering more momentum, the increase in executions of 'enemies of the regime' was also on a sharp rise. Cold, lifeless bodies hung motionless in the still warmth of the summer sun. Not many dared to venture outside at all nowadays.

He worked as quickly as possible to put the precious wood pieces together, keeping himself hidden away from everyone. Adrenaline kept him awake, as he frantically assembled, pouring his grief and anger into each motion, shaping, sanding, attaching. On a sweltering evening, Etienne leaned back in his chair and mopped the dripping sweat from his brow, he reached for his glass and tipped the last precious drop of water into his parched mouth. The timing couldn't have been worse for issues with the water supplies into the city when the temperatures had soared overnight, the people would suffer even more. With what happened to Philipp still fresh in his mind, Etienne shuddered. Philipp was still weak from his ordeal, any obstacle to his recovery could be fatal.

His head throbbed, dehydration and anxiety plagued him, but the lingering lump on the back of his head bothered him the most. He reached his hand around his neck and rubbed the sensitive area, wincing as a sharp twinge of pain shot down his neck. The lump although shrinking gradually, remained large and uncomfortable, a reminder of the immense pain that he endured that night.

In the evening dusk, Marianne would sit in the corner silently whilst he worked. She wouldn't speak, and she wouldn't sleep, but she didn't want to be away from him. But Etienne wanted to be alone. He knew perfectly well that the only one responsible for this was the one who killed his father. But his anger had to be directed somewhere. At Marianne, and himself. They were the ones out there that night, they had both sensed that something was wrong, but they had both chosen to ignore it, and Pierre had been the one to suffer, it simply wasn't fair.

He would play the violin until she would fall into a light slumber. But even then, he could find little to communicate with her. Before she had even had a chance to settle in her corner that evening, he had ordered her away.

'Marianne?' He asked quietly, but tartly. He glanced over towards her; her eyes were unblinking as she stared at the wall ahead of her.

'Marianne?' He repeated, louder. Still no response.

'Marianne!' He barked. Finally, she flinched.

'Please can you check on Philipp?'

Philipp was making progress despite the challenges. Yet Etienne wished that he would recover quicker so that he could be the one to take care of Marianne. He felt guilty for it, but he didn't know how to help her right now, Philipp just might, at least for her physical injuries which looked even more vicious than they did on that night. She gingerly pushed herself off the stool and limped towards the door, the hinge squeaking behind her.

He checked the final measurements, sanded, and assembled. The flickering dying of the candlelight rushed him along. In his pocket he pulled out a tiny bottle of olive oil, it wasn't much, but had cost him greatly. A burning sensation prickled the back of his neck as he sensed the void in the box where his mother's hairpin had once lain. He had kept his visits to rendezvous points to acquire such goods as secret as possible, but it had been essential to keep them alive up until this point. How did they think that Philipp got better? How did they think that they had managed to obtain any essential supplies?

He rested his head in his hands, puffing his sallow cheeks out. Nothing would relieve the crushing weight that he felt in his chest, not even looking at the completed product that he had worked so hard on over the last few days to complete. His final serenade to his father, and accreditation to who he was. It was a triumph to even make anything like this from scratch in these times, but he could see the flaws, its lack of perfection pushed him over the edge.

'*Merde!*' He cursed.

He hadn't cried. He hadn't given himself that luxury, whilst everyone else was falling to pieces around him. But now he sobbed and didn't try to stop the tears from flowing.

'Pierre?' Camille's soft voice drifted around the corner. Her gaunt frame barely took up any of the doorframe. Her eyes were glazed over, and she glanced airily around the room. She was sleepwalking again. It had happened every night since she had found out the news. Her zeal for life, her ferocity, her passion, and her love, all extinguished in a split second. She was merely a shell, living under a shadow that sucked all the life force from her. She talked as if she were in a completely different reality, in total denial. It had been almost impossible to convince her to accept that the funeral was taking place.

'Maman, the chapel has agreed to do the funeral on Monday.'

Camille had been sat at the kitchen table, her long hair loose around her shoulders, just like his father had liked it. She stared intently at the lavender placed centrally in the middle of the table.

'The lilies will be out soon,' she said, 'I think I will pick some and make an arrangement.'

'Maman?' Etienne asked. But she rose from her seat, touched Etienne's cheek, and quietly disappeared from the room.

She now swept towards Etienne quickly, still unable to quell his sobs, and cradled his head in her arms.

'It's okay Pierre. You are home. Lucien is not suffering. You are both at peace. Hush now.'

Just this once he wanted to be held, to not be the one to hold everything together.

'Who is Lucien, Maman?'

He felt her stiffen before she released him.

'Etienne? Ma pêche, what is wrong?' She asked, studying his face.

'I miss him too, Maman.'

***

Father Joubert stood at the altar, dishevelled. Rightly so. Etienne never broke his glare, clenching his good hand for the duration of the service. So many were dying it was rare that official funerals were happening for anyone, but somehow, they had made exceptions for them, it didn't take much to guess why.

'Pierre Touelle was an outstanding man in our community. His kindness, generosity, and incredible talents have touched us all and brought us so many blessings. There is a huge gap in our hearts, and in our community, and he will be sorely missed. But none more so by the devoted, God-fearing family he leaves behind. His wonderful wife Camille, his remarkable son Etienne, and his sweet daughter-in-law Marianne. May God bring peace to your troubled hearts at this most difficult of times and hold your hands to nurture you and guide you as you grieve.' He looked up from the parapet, caught Etienne's eye, and immediately cast his sights back down to his sermon.

You hypocrite. You bastard. You murderer.

He was distracted by Marianne's hand covering his, it was only then that he realised that he had been literally shaking with anger. He looked towards her; she had a pleading look in her eyes.

Not today. Please.

He ran his thumb across her paper-thin skin as a promise.

He should have been proud of his handiwork, but all he felt was emptiness as his father's handmade coffin was lowered into the ground. He picked out each error that he had made, lack of continuity in the wood pattern, poor match up of colours. Pierre would never have made such a mistake. In Etienne's mind, it was an embarrassment. Most of the men who had supplied him with the materials had stayed for the funeral, and Etienne was glad to have them there. Now and then he felt a supportive pat on his back, it was comforting but he felt it was ill-deserved.

He looked to the sky, as the first few raindrops started to fall. At least the weather had the decency to mourn with them. He felt the warm water trickle through his hair, over the prominent lump on his head, and down his neck, making him shudder in discomfort. When he lowered his head again, he saw many members of the crowd were dispersing. Camille and Marianne sat huddled together underneath the large yew tree in the grounds, neither said a word to the other, but their heads and hands were together.

Etienne remained rooted to the spot, peering around and watching the attendees pay their respects. He listed people's names in his mind as they passed by, everyone's face was etched with suffering, but it didn't honour them to remember them this way. Etienne concentrated hard to accredit their distinguished features. But one such man puzzled him, his ragged, long beard consumed most of his face, and he hobbled delicately on a frail looking stick. His trousers were torn almost to the knee, his pale blue shirt almost threadbare. Many looked similar in appearance, but as he limped closer, Etienne noticed strange looking scars scattered over his shins and forearms. He had never seen anyone like this in the local community before, perhaps he was from the central part of the city? Another contact of Pierre's that he hadn't met? Whoever he was, he was keen to make himself known to Etienne, as he made determined strides towards him. He looked too frail to be a member of the Milice or be any kind of watchman.

Only when he was a few metres away from him, Etienne could finally see him more clearly, and he nearly fell over in shock. His father stood before him.

'Etienne?' The man croaked.

All he could do was nod in agreement. The man held a shaky hand out.

'I have wanted to meet you for so long, dear boy.'

'W…wh…who are you?' Etienne stuttered, taking the man's hand cautiously.

'My name is Louis Touelle. Your Father is… was my brother.' He said sadly.

'I… I never knew he had a brother,' Etienne gasped.

'He parted with our family on bad terms. I was sad to see him go. But he loved your mother, and there was no stopping him from becoming a carpenter. But he would visit, secretly, of course, bringing products, you know. His work was nothing short of perfection.'

Etienne felt his stomach sink as it started to dawn on him the magnitude of the legacy that he would need to uphold. He nodded slowly, and his eyes drifted to the peculiar sharp-edged scars that painted his uncle's body.

'I was a lucky one,' Louis said, rubbing a particularly vicious looking scar that gnarled its way around his wrist.

'I don't mean to stare sir!' Etienne exclaimed.

'No worries, dear boy,' Louis assured. 'Pierre often talked about you in his letters. How proud he was of you.'

'My skills are nothing compared to his,' Etienne admitted.

'Oh, he would beg to differ,' Louis smiled, 'but he said that your violin playing was the most breathtaking experience a person could be a part of.'

He had heard him.

'I play the cello, probably nowhere near as well as you play. But one day, maybe we could play together?'

One day. That one day that they had all been yearning for since this whole torrid affair had begun. One day when the world would make sense again. But now with Pierre gone, that could never be. Etienne knew that, but his uncle's optimism moved him, he tried to smile at him, share his hope, and through taut lips he replied.

'One day.'

MARIANNE

Avignon, June 1943

It caught her eye as she swept the floor three weeks after the funeral. Attached to the lamppost adjacent to the house was something fluttering in the light summer breeze. At first, she ignored it. Sometimes papers were attached to accused traitors as an opportunity to shame or mock them long after their demise, now and then they became loose, floated away, and became attached to the next object they could find. But as she swept the dust out of the door onto the street, she noticed something peculiar about this note. Quickly glancing down the street she saw that no windows or other lampposts had documents attached to them, usually, there were at least a handful that would come their way, especially if the executions had been close by. Marianne shuddered and she started to think.

What if this is a target?

What if this is a signal for others to harm us?

Panicked, she peered out slowly and checked up and down the street ten times before scurrying across the mere metres to tear down the note and hurry back inside, locking the door firmly behind her and hastily pulling the curtain over the door.

A few days later another note appeared.

She tore as many down as she could. Desperate to catch them before Etienne noticed them. He was so preoccupied with taking care of Camille, she had barely left her bed since the funeral. The reality of what had happened finally hit her, and it hit her hard. Etienne would spend hours playing Madame Penaud's violin softly to her until she fell asleep. Marianne would only watch from a distance, convinced that somehow, she would cause more harm.

***

No one suspicious came to the house whilst she continued to tear down the papers. Every day that Otto didn't return to finish what he had started she counted as a miracle. But then the notes stopped appearing on the lamppost.

Maybe they have given up? But how would that make sense? Why bother in the first place?

She rose early one morning; crept out of bed, and opened the curtains a fraction to see the early morning sunlight showcasing the flowers in beautiful bloom as the flowerbeds were fit to bursting without Camille's regular tending to them. Marianne teetered down the stairs and grabbed the key to Camille's house from behind the violin. But something outside her front door made her hesitate in fright. It was blurred by the grubbiness of the window, but she could still see an ominous note plastered to the glass.

She took a deep breath before moving towards the door, careful not to wake anyone. She pried the door open just enough to push her hand through the gap and grab the note before hastily closing the door firmly shut. It took her a few minutes to catch her breath before she dared to look at it. Marianne's hands trembled as she turned the note over in her hands. It was a newspaper clipping, it warned of the 'barbaric Allied forces' increasing their bombing campaign over France. Rennes and Boulogne-Billancourt were the latest of the big losses, with more to come, and an endeavour from the strong and united Nazi front to combat this evil; Marianne scoffed at the hypocrisy.

Reassured that nothing was threatening about the note Marianne went to add it to the pile for burning when she noticed something different about some of the lettering in the article. Some letters had been marked subtly in a seemingly random pattern. Marianne took it over to Etienne's desk and on a scrap piece of paper started to record the letters in the order that they were marked until it revealed a short message.

```
Otto gone. New orders. Return unknown. Be
prepared.
```

Her mind began to race. Who would know of this? And who would know so much about their situation to warrant this watchfulness? The news was indeed very good, but it did little to ease her paranoia of who exactly was out there watching. But the following day fresh vegetables were left, and for the first time in so long, Marianne was able to make a nutritious meal that would feed everyone. The day after, a small amount of medicine arrived. On the third day, material scraps and yarn for mending clothes appeared. She was grateful, yet incredibly fearful, she knew that these kinds of items could only be found on the black markets. Her mind turned to Etienne, what if he had resorted to these means? It was dangerous. Many of the goods that were acquired were stolen or 'repossessed' as many liked to call it, from Nazi hands. Spies infiltrated this kind of business dealing, a simple report back to the Milice could mean shipment off to Germany, or worse. They all knew better not to get involved, especially them, keeping their heads down was the priority.

***

Avignon, December 1943

'Merry Christmas, Marianne,' Philipp smiled as he scooped the last of the broth out of his bowl. It had been a meagre amount, but to all of them, any food at all seemed like a feast. She saved the last of the latest delivery of vegetables for Christmas day, the first without Pierre, she knew it would be hard on everyone.

Etienne had risen before her to check on Camille. She was calmer whenever he was there, and Marianne was happy to let Etienne be with her, partly because she didn't know how to act around him anymore. They used to confide everything to each other, no secrets. Their arrangement was solely dependent on them being able to communicate with each other. She was resigned to try and show her goodwill through actions. She spent the latter part of the morning preparing a vegetable broth, chopping up parsnips, carrots, cabbage, mushrooms, and broccoli, relishing the moment of having a bountiful amount of food for the first time in what felt like forever. She softened the array of vegetables with a tiny drop of the precious oil that had been delivered, before transferring it all into a large pot, adding water, and leaving it to bubble on the side.

A short while later, Etienne gingerly hobbled through the front door. He looked drained and was frightfully thin. He had never been a brawny man, but his current state was incredibly concerning, and with the heavy burdens that he carried on his slender shoulders, it was a miracle that he was still standing.

'I've made broth,' Marianne announced.

He stopped and gave her a small, tired smile. 'Thank you, Marianne,' he replied.

'How is Camille this morning?'

She didn't need to ask; she had heard her muffled cries deep into the night.

'Not great,' Etienne replied curtly.

'Do you want to eat with her? I'm sure she would feel better for your company.'

'You don't mind?'

'Of course not. I'll eat with Philipp; it's been too long since he last ate.'

Usually, many questions would follow, how was Philipp's health? Was he comfortable? Is the medicine working? The topic of conversation that Marianne was hesitant to address. But instead, he simply said, 'Sure.' He winced as he tried to shuffle towards the kitchen.

'Go around next door to her. I will bring it to you.'

This time there was no smile, just a defeated retreat. Out of his eyeline, Marianne sighed.

Merry Christmas mon amour.

***

'I thought you didn't celebrate Christmas?' Marianne teased.

'We don't,' Philipp laughed, 'but Hannukah has been and gone already'.

'Is it a big celebration for your family? I am sorry, I confess to knowing very little about Jewish traditions.'

'Well, you were all led to believe that we were monsters, so how could you?'

She looked down ashamed. Listening to what Philipp had endured was awful. But it never dawned on her how far back it all stretched, how unforgivable history was, and the little they had done to learn from past horrors.

'It was always a big family event. Cramming everyone into one poor family member's house was always interesting, to say the least,' Philipp chuckled. 'Most of our cousins are younger than me and Johann, my brother. So, guess who was always on entertaining duty?'

'I'm sure you and Johann would have put on quite the show,' Marianne laughed.

'Oh, we did! Johann especially. He has such a wild imagination; he can remember stories off the top of his head.'

'He sounds like great fun'.

'Yes, he is,' Philipp smiled, his head bowed in what looked like a moment of reminiscence.

'I'm sure my son would have adored you entertaining him as a little one.'

'How old is Erich?'

'He would be nearly ten now.'

'Oh, I'm sure me and Johann would have enough tricks in the book to entertain a ten-year-old.'

Marianne chuckled, but inside her heart ached. Her precious son. Nearly ten years of age. Over five years since she had last seen him, held him, rocked him, told him how much she loved him. Half of his lifetime had been spent away from him; the guilt ate away at her every day.

'I don't suppose there's any more broth?' Philipp asked.

'Maybe a little. I'll go and get the rest,' she said rising to her feet so that Philipp couldn't see her heart pounding in her chest, quickly taking his bowl, she made for the door.

'Oh, and Marianne.'

Damn.

She turned slowly in anticipation of his next prying words.

'It's nice to finally see you smile.'

She flashed him a big smile before closing the door quietly behind her. Philipp was right to an extent, they enjoyed each other's company, but there was also further reason to smile amongst everything else. The latest note had arrived that morning, and it read: Progress.

Rumours were starting to circulate of increased Allied efforts. Whereabouts she couldn't guess, it certainly hadn't been tangible in France. But she had grown to trust the letters, all she could do was hope that they were right.

***

Avignon, January 1944

Her happiness and optimism ended up being short-lived. It always was. It had been months since the attack, and the pain would not cease. The physical side was healing gradually, but slowly, agonisingly so, but she knew it would heal, it had done in the past. The further repercussions ran much deeper. She couldn't close her eyes at night without seeing Otto's murderous look staring at her, the sensation of the cool of the knife against her neck, the feeling of her heart tearing in two at the sight of Pierre's life leaving his defenceless body.

All Marianne wanted was for someone to scream with her, cry with her, recognise and react to her trauma. For years she had internalised the pain. Etienne's tenderness had helped somewhat. But now he didn't dare touch her. She knew he did it out of consideration for the pain, but inadvertently he was treating her exactly how she believed herself to be, like a curse, bringing misfortune to everyone she got close to.

'How is the pain today?'

That depends on what kind of pain you're referring to. Knowing I could have prevented my father-in-law's death? Or the all-encompassing pain that I have been carrying for so long, ripped open once again?

'Pardon?'

'The muscle aches, and old fractures, Marianne? Are they still causing you discomfort?' Philipp asked so practically, so much so that it was infuriating. How could he be so measured about something like this? As a doctor it was his job, and maybe he believed he was helping by trying to be so balanced, treating this as if it were just another sickness. But rape isn't a sickness.

'They still feel… tender,' she sighed.

Philipp should have been trying to recover himself, but he insisted that putting his medical knowledge to good use was helping him feel better every day. There was no hiding the news from him, the house had been heavy with grief. There was no way that anyone close by could not hear Camille's haunting moans as she sleepwalked through the house each night trying to find her beloved lost husband. There was no way he could not sense the tension in Etienne as he tried to distract himself night and day because he refused to unleash his rage and distress. And there was no way he couldn't notice how Marianne's continued silence made her little more than a ghost merely inhabiting the space.

Even after his own ordeal, Philipp had done everything he could to help. He bandaged up Etienne's broken knuckles as best as he could, and he ordered them both to check in with him at least once a day to monitor the stages of healing in their head wounds. Even in the months after the attack, he was still trying to care for them. But what he didn't know was that Marianne didn't believe she was worth helping anymore.

Marianne stumbled to her feet and headed towards the door in a hasty exit, but Philipp's words made her pause.

'I know it's awful. But, with your permission, I want to make sure that your wounds are healing elsewhere.'

'W...wh...what do you mean?' She croaked.

'I know he didn't just beat you up, Marianne,' Philipp said gently. 'Pierre's murder will always cut the deepest,' Philipp continued. 'But other terrible things happened to both you and Etienne that night. Don't negate them or pretend they didn't happen.'

Marianne remained tight-lipped and unmoving, she hated how easy she was to read when all she was trying to do was to withhold her suffering so that no one else had to get hurt.

'It may be uncomfortable, but it would be wise to let me examine you.'

There was no fight in her anymore, Philipp would only insist, and she had no energy to argue.

'Very well,' she sighed.

Philipp politely looked away as she gingerly removed her underwear, wincing at the sharp stings that plagued her day and night. She lay out on her back and rolled up her skirt, and Philipp delicately began to inspect.

'How long have you been bleeding for, Marianne?'

'It's less now,' she insisted.

'I would have expected it to have stopped bleeding by now. Is the pain keeping you awake at night?'

She laughed out loud, but it felt hollow.

'Sleep? I haven't slept in years.'

'Have any of us?'

But you don't know what I went through.

Philipp was doing the best that he could, and deep down she was grateful, but for her, it didn't seem worth it. That night had marked her end, she felt herself die that night, and there was nothing more of her to take.

***

Avignon, February 1944

For a few weeks, the notes stopped appearing. Could this person have been caught delivering the packages to the door? Or were they watched as they prepared the notes? People would report others for a small reward, anything to keep them and their loved ones sustained. But always at the cost of another.

She knew that the delivered supplies were gone. Yet somehow some had lasted, as if there was extra. She knew now that Etienne was keeping something from her.

She found Etienne that evening trying to scoop up every last crumb of the measly portion of bread that had been their dinner that night.

'Can we talk?' Marianne asked quietly as she approached him slowly.

Etienne squirmed but nodded, pulled a seat out for her, and waited patiently for her to settle.

'These extra supplies…'

Etienne closed his eyes and sighed.

'Where are you getting them from?'

'Marianne…' he sighed, 'I had to do it. Philipp nearly died; we are all starving. The object that I traded… it was worth a lot, I have been making it stretch further, only when we absolutely need it.'

'I understand. Truly I do, and I'm grateful for you looking after us. But it's too dangerous.'

She expected him to at least apologise for his recklessness, but this time he seized up and glared at her.

'Marianne, I will not die over something that I can control. If I die by a bomb blowing up our house. So be it. If your murderous *other* husband wants to come and massacre me in my sleep. So be it. But they are out of my control.'

Marianne stepped back, turning her face away so that he would not see her cry.

'I thought we talked about everything. No secrets. I won't get in your way,' she whimpered, but she meant it, now she knew what she meant to him. Even more so when all she was met with was resigned silence.

***

Avignon, April 1944

Finally, a note came.

```
He is back.
```

Where he had been, or what he had been doing, she couldn't possibly know. But she knew that he was there to finish what he started. It was in his nature.

369

Etienne wouldn't talk to her, and there was no trying to talk to him. The very essence of what made their relationship survive was in tatters, and now they were more vulnerable than ever. She knew what had to be done. To keep her family safe once and for all. She waited until everyone was sound asleep, and then she crept downstairs, picked up the pen, and wrote.

Etienne,

I am writing these words down because I have no words to speak, and yet I still find myself with so much to tell you, but not enough time.

Otto is back. Do not ask me how I know. But he will not stop until he gets what he truly wants, which is me. Your life, Camille's life, and Philipp's life are in grave danger. After what happened to Pierre... I can barely bring myself to think about it. But remember it I do, in every awful detail. I cannot let the same fate befall you too.

I know you blame yourself, and it tears me apart to see you do this to yourself. You know there was nothing you could have done; it is me who should take full responsibility for what happened. Leaving is part of owning up to that responsibility. The safety of all of you is the most important.

I am sorry that I need to ask more of you, but this is the final time, I promise. Please do not come looking for me. By the time you find this, I will be long gone.

You married me to protect me, to give me an identity, and for that I am eternally grateful to you. But you also gave me a loving family and showed me what it was truly like to be loved, to be cared for. You showed me gentleness, kindness, and compassion in a way that I have never experienced before. I thank God every day that you came into my life. I will never forget you.

I love you.

Marianne

She pressed hard on the broken pen nib to get the last few precious drops of ink out onto the page. Mere words could never be enough, but it was the best she could do. Marianne skimmed over her words once more, one hand steady as her finger hovered over her farewell, convicted in her decision, as her other hand shook with vigour as she held the scrunched-up note which had sealed her fate. She took one final look around the small workshop and ran her hand along the desk where she had spent many an hour writing up order forms, invoicing clients, and reaching out to existing business links. She crept as quietly as she could towards the door leading upstairs, the floorboards moaned her plight as she leaned against the doorframe, and softly tapped it three times.

'Be well, Philipp,' she whispered against the long crack on the inside beam, hoping that it would swallow up the last of her secrets.

Turning around, she walked slowly towards the door. Her mind was made up, it was the most control she had had over anything in years, awful as it was. She was convinced, and she had to go through with it tonight. She opened the door, stepped out into the chilly spring air, and walked, refusing to turn back, just like the last time, only this time she knew exactly where she was going.

She didn't remember arriving at the lake. Her mind was clear, rid of everything, leaving only her body the responsibility of carrying it all out.

Marianne stared out at the undisturbed water as her hands searched for heavy pebbles and loaded them into her pockets. As the weight got heavier, she began to wade out into the water, breaking its stillness as her feet slipped under the surface, the shock of the cold instantly made her shiver. But she pressed on, slowly but surely descending beneath the black surface.

This is the only way they will be safe.

Camille. If it weren't for me, Pierre would still be alive. I'm sorry.

Philipp. I cannot provide enough for you to stay alive. I'm sorry.

Etienne. You tried everything you could. My existence puts you in danger. I'm sorry.

Erich. I love you. I tried to protect you. I failed. I'm sorry.

The silhouette of the trees, the embankment, the stillness of it all was captured beautifully in her final glimpse. She closed her eyes and let the water cover her, she extended her arms outwards and let gravity pull her down.

Her breath ran out quickly and she was met with a horrible burning sensation in her lungs, her limbs kicked frantically as her body willed her to survive. Even if she wanted to, the weight holding her down was insurmountable. She could feel herself losing consciousness. Above her, she heard a ripple, a force coming towards her, something holding her hand. Was this death?

Suddenly she was ascending, a small light gradually coming to the surface, and then she emerged spluttering and choking.

'No, no! Let me go!' She protested, but the hand would not let her go.

'Ada! No, I can't let you do this!'

Ada?

It wasn't Otto's voice. Her vision was blurred, but she could see the mole on the right side of his neck, the wonky canine prominent in his teeth as he gasped for breath himself.

Ernst

PHILIPP

Avignon, April 1944

No taps. No code words. Nothing. But there was one hell of a situation downstairs. Sleep eluded him at the best of times; whether it was worrying about a bomb being dropped, or a late-night raid. He had heard the faint cries of Camille wandering around her house as she sleepwalked. He had heard Etienne and Marianne arguing. He had jumped at every creak in the floorboard, every voice that travelled up from the street through the walls, every gust of wind that shook the house in varying degrees of ferocity. But these noises painted a different scenario entirely. He could pick out Etienne's voice, panicked, urgent, very unlike him.

'What happened?'

Trouble.

Another voice chimed in. Not one that he had heard before which made his hairs stand on end. He couldn't pick out any female voice. Was Marianne or Camille in trouble? What if he could help? All he had to do was leave the room. But that other voice! He couldn't risk it. But what if he meant harm to Etienne and Marianne? Without them he wouldn't survive he knew that.

Philipp tentatively approached the door, closed his eyes, and silently prayed. But before he could even turn the handle, the door flew open sending him flying backwards in fright. Before him stood what he had been dreading for so long. The Nazi officer had slicked-back dark brown hair, murky green eyes, and a hard-pressed lip. His cheekbones highlighted the look of sternness on his face. Philipp looked around frantically to find anything to defend himself, if he ran, he may give himself a fighting chance albeit rather slim. The tatty blanket that he had been sleeping under, some notes he had been keeping to refresh his medical knowledge, Marianne's French book, that would have to do. Scooping the book off his makeshift bed he threw it as hard as he could, striking the officer clean in the head. He stumbled backwards as Philipp darted towards the door, only to be grabbed and yanked back inside.

'No!' Philipp yelled.

'Be quiet! You'll alert them!' The officer hissed.

'Isn't that what you want?' Philipp cried, 'Make a public spectacle of us before you march us all off to God knows where!'

The officer released him, throwing Philipp to the floor. As he fought for breath, he tried to study his assailant. The officer knelt, picking up the book from the floor. He turned it over in his hands, chuckling to himself as he did so.

'Trying to wound me with my own brother's old French book,' he smiled, 'I never thought that day would come.'

Brother?

His words were curious, but Philipp didn't bite, his mind and heart were racing trying to comprehend that the game was up, and what horrors awaited him.

'You are a doctor, yes?'

Philipp couldn't move.

'Yes?' the officer repeated.

The officer sighed heavily. *This is it; this is where he kills me.* Philipp closed his eyes in anticipation.

'I know you are a doctor. I have seen your notes before.'

What? How?

'Look, there's no time to explain. You need to tend to my sister. You call her Marianne.'

Sister?

Now he started to recognise the resemblance. The officer held out his hand, gently pulling Philipp to his feet.

'Please, hurry to her.'

He still believed it was a trap. But if Marianne was genuinely in danger, then he had to do something, either way, their secret was out. Now it was just a question of how long they would all last.

The officer hurried him down the stairs across the landing and down more stairs to the workshop where he saw Etienne cradling Marianne's limp body in his arms, softly crying and muttering into her hair.

'Etienne?' Philipp asked, approaching him cautiously, when he was close enough, he lightly placed his hand on his shoulder, and Etienne flinched at his touch.

'I pushed her away Philipp. It's all my fault,' he wept.

He couldn't disagree with him, try as he might, he had overheard enough of their arguments to know that things weren't good, but he hadn't anticipated it to be this bad.

'Let me see her Etienne,' Philipp said gently but assertively.

Etienne's shoulders dropped in defeat; he shuffled as much as he could to let Philipp in closer. Philipp could feel the stares of both Etienne and the officer burning into the back of his head. Marianne was soaked all the way through, her already pale skin was almost translucent. The stray stones that spilled from her pockets told him everything he needed to know. He took her wrist in his hand, and he was immediately taken aback by the icy chill that the feel of her skin sent through his own.

Come on Marianne, give me a sign, anything!

Finally, he found it, incredibly faint but it was there. Immediately he rolled Marianne onto her front and moved her head to the side.

'Etienne, lift her arms.' Philipp ordered. Etienne obeyed, not caring for his own pain as he crouched down by Marianne and did as Philipp instructed. Trying his best to ignore the panic in Etienne's eyes, Philipp started to apply pressure to Marianne's back.

'She's not responding,' he heard the officer say, but it sounded distant, he was completely focused on Marianne. But he wasn't wrong, Marianne's body remained limp despite his best efforts. Philipp paused, took a deep breath, and pushed down with all his might onto Marianne's back.

'Philipp, is she dead?' Etienne asked nervously.

Philipp took Marianne's wrist in his hand again, he checked and checked but this time he could feel nothing. He hung his head. Behind him, Etienne let out a stifled sob. But Philipp felt far from sorrow, he felt rage. This was not how it was supposed to end. To everyone's surprise, even his own, he raised his fist in the air and pounded it as hard as he could onto Marianne's back. At the impact, Marianne finally choked and expelled water all over the floor. Sighs of relief flooded around the room, but Philipp was straight to Marianne's side.

'She needs warming up now! Etienne, fetch her some dry clothes.'

Etienne left as fast as he could, stumbling up the stairs as quickly as he was able to. Exhausted from the exertion, Philipp leaned back and took a deep breath in triumph, but hastily realised that he was once again alone with the Nazi.

Philipp couldn't bring himself to look him in the eye, surely now this was it, another officer would be outside the door ready to take him away. Luck, good fortune, if there was such a thing, had finally run out this time. But if this was his last act of goodwill before his own fate then so be it.

Marianne was weak, she could barely speak, and she was still freezing to the touch. Philipp knelt beside her, lifting her skinny arm over his shoulder. She weighed nearly nothing, but his strength had diminished drastically. He fumbled as he tried to seat her upright, desperately trying to prevent her crashing to the floor. He looked up at the officer, surprised by what he saw. He didn't know what he was expecting exactly, resentment? Anger? Malicious joy? But what he saw was relief in the relaxed muscles in his face, but his eyes, just like Marianne's, were swimming with tears, there was a brokenness there, a burden. He never suspected that the casualties of war could affect the evil ones too. That is of course if he was evil? He was Marianne's brother after all, someone who had driven her away in the first place according to her. But now he stood before him soaked and shivering, most likely from the cold.

'Please?' Philipp asked quietly.

The officer looked at him, snapping out of whatever emotions he was experiencing, and nodded, gently scooping Marianne into his arms and headed up the stairs with her. Of everything that he had endured thus far, Philipp never thought he would see the day that it would be him instructing a Nazi.

***

They all gathered around Marianne's bedside. She was dry, but still so cold.

'Will she be alright?' Etienne asked as he paced the room, not taking his eyes off Marianne.

'She is still cold, Etienne. Do you have any tea or coffee left over from the ration supplies?'

'No nothing. Will she die without it?'

'She needs something warm to ingest. I don't want hypothermia setting in. She's frail enough as it is.' Philipp stated.

'It will be soaked through. But there is a bag of coffee in my jacket,' the officer said. Etienne immediately galvanised into action, leaning heftily on his cane as he made his way back to the stairs.

'Etienne? Make two cups if you can.'

Etienne nodded and made his exit.

'Two?' The officer questioned. 'You need one too to watch over her?'

'Not for me. For you. You are still shivering; I need to prevent you from getting sick too,' Philipp replied.

'Why would you do that for someone like me?'

Philipp fiddled with Marianne's blankets whilst he collected his thoughts. Why was he doing this? Men like him were responsible for the deaths of Jews like him all over Europe. It didn't take much to read between the lines of the papers, and the rumours that circulated with them. He had expected to feel so much hatred, as he would have been entitled to, but instead, he saw a person. He couldn't escape the feeling that there was more to him than met the eye, after the lengths that he went through to rescue Marianne, to have followed his instructions, to have stayed here ensuring all was well. It didn't match the monstrous image he had in his mind.

'Because you need my help,' Philipp finally replied.

***

They sat in awkward silence whilst they waited for Marianne to fall asleep. Etienne sat protectively between Philipp and the Nazi officer, eyeing them carefully. Philipp could see Etienne's hand trembling, his body was tense, and the heavy outline of his cheekbones twitched.

The tension in the room was thick, but the officer seemed to pay no attention to Philipp, his concern seemed genuine for Marianne. Philipp allowed himself to lean back against the wall, as he did so his exhaustion finally caught up with him, he could feel the heaviness in his eyes compelling him to rest. He found a small crook in the wall and pinched his skin into the sharp edge to keep himself awake, wary of this stranger's motives. But suddenly, the officer spoke.

'How long has she been here?'

Etienne looked at Philipp, his eyes wide with a pleading fear that seemed to beg Philipp to stay by his side. Philipp nodded his encouragement towards him.

'I..I..I first met her in October 1938. My parents took her in.' Etienne stuttered, hesitating at the mention of both of his parents.

'Do you know who she really is?' The officer asked, but not in an accusatory way, he seemed curious.

'I do,' Etienne replied.

'You know who I am, yes?'

'I do,' Etienne repeated. 'Ernst, her last surviving brother.'

He was telling the truth.

'Yes,' Ernst said sadly as he glanced back towards Marianne, watching the consistent small rises in the bedsheet as she slept. 'She was alive this whole time' he whispered.

Etienne looked back to Philipp, bemused, and dumbfounded. But curiosity was niggling at Philipp, he knew that Marianne had a colourful past, but she had been reluctant with the full details. Philipp quietly cleared his throat, but not quiet enough to catch the attention of Ernst who looked at him sternly but inquisitively.

'W…Wh…Who was she?' Philipp stuttered.

'Her name is Ada. Ada Stein before she was married. Ada Neumann when she married… him.'

'What happened?' Philipp asked.

Ernst took a deep breath and began to explain.

***

Ernst

Stuttgart, September 1938

The cold water was instantly refreshing on his face. Their antics were getting worse as support for the Party increased. His notes on the latest meeting burned fiercely in his pocket and knowing it would have to remain there for another couple of hours until he could pass it onto his contact was deeply uncomfortable. Requesting the time away from Stuttgart this time round had been met with far more suspicion.

'Where could you possibly need to go this time, Stein?'

'Just to Frankfurt sir. I will only be gone for the day.'

'Third city travel in the last six weeks, Stein.'

'Distribution issues sir. A colleague has requested my help to sort it out.'

His superior officer drew up close enough to him that Ernst could smell the stale cigars on his breath. Beads of sweat started to run down his neck. If his loyalty was already starting to be questioned, how was he going to pull this off when the most significant motions were put in place, he knew they were brewing, and he had to bide his time, he couldn't lose this now.

'Very well Stein. But your stationing is here. This is the place where you carry out the necessary work. Do you understand?'

'Yes, sir.'

They saluted and then parted ways, and when he was confident that he was out of sight, Ernst shuddered, always disgusted with himself for the lengths he had to go to. His superior officer was right about one thing at least, he was carrying out very necessary work.

He was running late by the time his train pulled into Frankfurt station that evening, but thankfully the meeting point wasn't too far away, and he could shorten the twenty-minute walk by walking briskly. People hastily stepped aside for him as he exited the train carriage, dropping their eyes and shuffling away as they saw him striding through groups of people. He felt dirty parading around in his uniform, but it gave him manoeuvrability wherever he went. People cowered in fear as he approached them, but it meant that he would not be followed, nor would his actions be questioned, which is exactly what he needed.

The clock was chiming eleven when he eventually turned the street corner to behold the full scale of the cathedral. Panting, he found a darkened corner to the left-hand side of the clock tower looming above. He barely had a moment to catch his breath when a voice caught him off guard.

'Please, do you have any food to spare?'

Ernst turned towards the direction of his questioner. 'I do,' he replied.

A short, bedraggled man emerged from the darkness closer to Ernst so that he could finally pick out his facial features. A thick, shaggy beard, with equally messy auburn hair nearly covering his entire face. He wore flimsy sandals, long scratched trousers, and a thin stained white shirt that billowed around his torso. Ernst handed over his notes. The man scanned them, his brow furrowed in concern.

'Where the fuck have you been Ernst?' He asked gruffly.

'The train got delayed, Stefan,' Ernst replied, 'If I didn't know better, I'd say you were worried about me,' he teased.

But Stefan wasn't laughing, his expression remained stern and ominous.

'How easy was it for you to get away this time?'

'I managed it. But they are getting suspicious.'

'I thought as much,' he exhaled.

'What's happening, Stefan?'

Stefan looked warily around the side of Ernst's shoulder.

'Not here.'

The two men hurried down the street to the right of the cathedral, turning various corners in the now pitch black of the city for at least fifteen minutes before arriving at a small, dilapidated set of offices. Stefan plucked a key from his pocket, unlocking the squeaky lock and barged the stiff door open.

They ascended the rickety stairs to the top room of the building, opening the door to a dark, dingy room, thick with dust, mixed with a musty smell that tickled the back of Ernst's throat.

'Dietrich? Anna? Franz?' Stefan muttered into the darkness.

'By the bookcases, Stefan.' A female voice called out.

They waded through the maze of books that cluttered the floor over to the three individuals crowded closely together, their heads deep in discussion. At the sight of Ernst and his uniform, their eyes widened in fear.

'Relax!' Stefan exclaimed. 'He's one of our undercovers.'

'You couldn't get changed before you arrived? You scared the shit out of me!' Dietrich yelped.

'I don't think that will matter when you know that he's the advertiser.'

All three of them looked up in surprise at Ernst, who shifted his weight onto his left foot nervously, he wasn't aware of the notoriety that he had gained, it made him uncomfortable. Reputation came with investigation, he knew he had covered his tracks well, but he would have to do better.

'Why am I here, Stefan?'

'It's as we suspected. Ernst's notes refer to more emphasis on getting recruits for the army. It confirms the information provided by the others about Czechoslovakia. He's already there.'

'But there were rumours of a pact? I thought this would halt things for a while longer.' Ernst said.

'Have you been in that gang long enough to become as deluded as they all are?' Anna scoffed.

'They are gearing up for something huge. Our contacts around the continent believe so too. We must keep finding out as much as possible to report back, and when it all begins, which we are certain that it will, we will need informants everywhere.' Stefan interrupted, glaring at Anna.

Turning to face Ernst, Stefan continued. 'You've given us so much information on how they are recruiting, and what they are telling the people. We want you to try and get posted to the places that they invade.'

Ernst didn't question them; he had known for some time that this was what he both needed and wanted to do, despite the risks, despite the consequences if he was caught.

'How will I convince them?' He asked. They all smiled triumphantly at his dedication.

'Show your loyalty as much as you can. We will do our best to bring contacts to you to lower suspicion over your time away,' Franz assured.

'Unfortunately, you will need to team up with more of them. Is there someone believable that you could try and get posted with?' Anna asked, brighter this colour, seemingly reassured by his commitment.

Ernst sighed. In his mind, he knew that it would work, but it was incredibly risky. He had been careful up to that point. Now he would be walking on broken glass in everything that he did. He would be allowing *him* to re-direct his violence onto more innocent people, but it meant that he would be away from Ada and Erich.

'Yes,' He replied solemnly. 'My brother-in-law.'

They spent the rest of the night going over the details, but Ernst's attention drifted. The pretence was exhausting, worrying about what lay ahead was exhausting, worrying about his family was exhausting, worrying about the world they were shaping, it was exhausting.

He intended to leave at first light. But sleep had gotten the better of him. When he saw that it was nearly midday when he finally stirred, he leapt into action, bolted out of the office before he could even say goodbye to the group, and sprinted back towards the train station. He was grateful for the journey time to compose himself, walking in a measured and calm manner on the journey back to his parent's house. But when he arrived there was pandemonium, his mother hurried outside, she was shaking, and tear marks stained her face.

'Mütter? What is going on?' He asked, rushing to her side.

Gisela gasped as she tried to get her words out but failed.

'It's Ada,' a cool unmoving voice drifted from the doorway, accompanied by Otto's bulky, intimidating physique, 'she's gone and drowned herself.'

***

Philipp

Avignon, April 1944

'You were never one of them?' Philipp asked incredulously.

'Of course not,' Ernst smiled, looking as though a weight had been lifted from his shoulders.

'You certainly convinced us all!' Philipp laughed.

'If this was all for show, then why were you so cold to your family? To Marianne?' Etienne asked coolly.

'I had to be convincing, and playing the brute was the only way to stand out, to move up, to get where you wanted. My family bought into their nonsense, Ada married Otto, they were a good cover, and I had to make sure there were no cracks in this image.'

Etienne stared at him silently, but menacingly.

'I love my family Etienne. Truly I do. I left home young, I wanted to avoid getting caught up in the Great War. I wanted to work and earn money for the family, but I could barely make enough to look after myself. I found work in Munich as a clerk in a hotel, and as I'm sure you know that was where their awfulness was born.'

Philipp leaned forward eager to hear more, he glanced over at Etienne who had adjusted himself in his seat, he was going to hear him out at least.

'The family I worked for was concerned that their son had bought into their delusions and was attending meetings. They treated me well, and I knew I could be discreet. So, I followed him and lingered at the back to listen to them spout their nonsense. That's where I met Stefan, he had extensive knowledge about all the political factions all over Germany. He is actively opposed to any extreme forms of government, his investigations into them go back decades.'

'So how did he manage to procure contacts from all over the continent?' Philipp asked.

'Stefan's mother is British, she had government contacts, through what means I do not know. But they branded her a traitor when she married Stefan's German father. But she didn't lose contact with all of them, and they convinced her and Stefan to report to the embassy about what was happening in Germany.'

'So how did you end up here?' Etienne interrupted; the accusatory tone still resounded in his voice.

'Call it fate if you will. But I assure you it was a coincidence. I was actively looking to get posted to other countries to gather more information, but I never suspected what I would find when I got here.'

'The day that you first came here?' Etienne asked.

'I recognised her too; we look too similar to ignore,' Ernst chuckled. 'Otto was outside, he didn't get a good look at her, so I insisted that I would be the one to carry out a precautionary search.'

'There was never a search. There was always one of us in the house, I know that.' Etienne insisted.

'I had to coax her out. It didn't take me long to find you,' he looked straight at Philipp, but he was smiling warmly. 'Tucked in the corner asleep, you looked peaceful. Your medical drawings and notes are very impressive. One day you will be a fine doctor. And then I saw my brother's French book.'

'Your secret is safe with me, do not fret,' Ernst quickly added.

'If you want to take Philipp you will have to kill me first,' Etienne hissed.

'I'm a man of my word,' Ernst promised.

What about the ones you had to expose though? Why do I get to live, and they don't?

Philipp subtly clenched his fists to contain his rage. Mercifully, Etienne spoke and interrupted his thoughts.

'The night I was attacked at the Penaud house?'

'You were in a bad way; I was glad that you weren't dead when I arrived.'

'How did you know I was there?'

'We were on patrol. I noticed Otto speaking one-to-one with various people, I was suspicious, so I followed you, and sure enough…'

'So that he could get to her?'

'To you both. And if he ever found out that you were here then he would be after you too,' directing his attention to Philipp.

'Marianne… Ada said that Otto had told her that your mother is dead, Liselotte, Thomas…'

Ernst sighed heavily, burying his face in his hands to gain his composure.

'What he said about our mother is true, the same fate awaited our father. When my parents believed that Ada had died, they were torn apart. Some may not believe it, but I know it to be true. People can die of a broken heart.'

'She never believed her parents cared for her,' Etienne snapped.

'They did. In an unorthodox way,' Ernst sighed.

'Unorthodox is one way of putting it,' Etienne spat. 'What happened to her grandfather?'

'He couldn't live without their assistance, so he was put into a home, and the situation got taken out of my hands. Finally drank himself to death shortly after.'

'And Erich?' Both Etienne and Philipp asked in unison.

'Safe, and happy with Liselotte and Thomas,' Ernst replied, taking a relieved breath as he did so.

They talked until daybreak. Ernst promised to do what he could to keep bringing them goods and to see Marianne when he could. Over the next two weeks, he was true to his word, and Marianne seemed to recover quicker as a result. Knowing that Ernst was watching over them was both a relief and a concern, he had been careful, but every risk he took would inevitably come with more vulnerability.

***

Avignon, May 1944

'Philipp!'

Without code, without pre-warning. But without hesitation, Philipp hurried downstairs. He found Etienne white as a sheet, extending a long bony finger towards the front window of the house, his terror-filled eyes unmoving as Philipp followed the direction in which they stared. The sight that befell him was horrifying, he stumbled towards the glass, as if to hope that the image would fade from his mind, that what he was seeing wasn't real. But there he was, every inch of him was bloodied, his mouth agape, and his facial features twisted into a tortured look. As the body rotated in the winds, he saw the huge knife in his back, attached to which was a note. There was no code needed to decipher it, as all it read in big, bold letters was:

TRAITOR

ETIENNE

Avignon, May 1944

There was a strong metallic smell in the air that turned his stomach violently. The room was spinning when he finally opened his eyes. Eventually, he worked out that he was staring at the ceiling, he was lying flat on his back. The head rush was overwhelming as Etienne tried to turn onto his side, but what was more distracting was the strange sticky substance that his hand slipped in. He drew his hand close to his face and was hit once again by the strong smell of metal, but also by the realisation that this substance was red.

'Oh… oh, no, no, no!' Etienne croaked as the panic set in. Whose blood was it? Where had it come from? Why was there so much of it? Where was Philipp? Where was Marianne? Where was his mother? But also, where were those noises coming from? Whistles? Alarms? Terror-filled shouting of men barking orders. It took Etienne far too long to realise when the first explosion sent shockwaves throughout the house.

'MARIANNE! MAMAN! PHILIPP!' He screamed. Then the second explosion hit.

***

Ernst's body swayed lightly in the spring breeze, as Etienne and Philipp stood frozen in horror.

'Lord, have mercy!' Philipp gasped. 'Etienne, we can't leave him up there.' He insisted. 'After everything he's done for you, for me, for all of us!'

Etienne remained still and speechless, managing only to nod tightly as his mind tried to comprehend the situation.

'Nightfall. You should do it then, too many people could be watching during the day.' Philipp stated. 'I can't risk being spotted.'

Etienne gave him another stiff nod.

'Marianne...'

'Marianne cannot see this,' the words tumbled out of Etienne's mouth abruptly, he could see Philipp flinch in his periphery.

'She needs to know Etienne! She will wonder where he has gone!'

'She has endured more than enough. Her soul cannot take another loss.'

'Can any of us?' Philipp asked.

For the rest of the day, the two of them took turns keeping watch. Etienne would be equally worried and relieved when Philipp assumed his position, hidden in a blind spot behind the desk. All their best-laid plans were thrown out of the window now.

He couldn't bring himself to fully look at Ernst's lifeless form. He had been stripped of his uniform, dressed up in tattered civilian clothes, to be identified as no one outstanding, doing their best to tarnish his reputation.

Your true reputation will live on, Ernst. I promise.

Etienne tried to focus his attention on the wall behind Ernst, or on the spot next to his hand where the sunshine glinted off the cobbles. He tried to rub the exhaustion from his eyes, hoping it would also erase the knowledge that their last chance of security was gone. Their days were numbered.

As dusk began to fall, Etienne left Philipp to make sure that Camille was settled, locking all of the doors to prevent her from causing any harm to herself if she sleepwalked. It seemed almost meaningless when the threat was closer than ever, but he had to do everything in his power to keep her safe. He waited patiently for his mother to fall asleep before going back to his house. His hand shook as he tried to focus on putting the key in the lock. Etienne breathed a sigh of relief when it finally clicked, he eased the door open and tapped his cane three times in the darkness to assure Philipp of his presence.

Limping across the workshop floor, he reached the door to the stairs, opened it carefully, and ascended the stairs to check on Marianne. He could hear the crinkle of her departing note moving around in his pocket. It was a reminder of how close he had come to losing her, how lonely she felt, how desperate she was to protect her family, and that she loved him. The sight of her lifeless body on the workshop floor tortured him.

How could I have pushed her away so far? Why did I only realise then how much I love her?

He hesitated at the final step, choking back tears of remorse. It was hard to see her so weakened by her ordeal. She had remained almost entirely bedbound for the last two weeks. He would speak to her quietly, but still unable to find the right words to say to her. As he reached the top of the stairs, he took a deep breath and pushed lightly at the door which gave a bone-chilling creak. Marianne stirred; her eyes fluttered open as she met Etienne's apologetic look with one of grogginess.

'Sorry, I didn't mean to wake you,' he whispered.

'That's okay,' she croaked but smiled, patting the space next to her.

Etienne dutifully sat beside her, took her thin hand in his own, and kissed it tenderly. There was so much he wanted to say to her, about how grateful he was that she was alive, how amazed he was at her strength, how sorry he was for driving a wedge between them, how committed he was to his promise to keep her safe. For so long he had been searching for the perfect words to say to her and failing, but the words that found him at that moment were simply a return of what she had said to him in her letter.

'I love you too,' he whispered. Marianne let out a small sigh of relief before falling back into a deep slumber. The exact words she needed to hear.

He closed the door quietly but firmly behind him before jostling uncomfortably back down the stairs which were now engulfed in the latter stages of dusk light, making it difficult to see in front of him. In his mind he was planning it all out, when he reached the workshop he would grab his father's favourite wood carving knife and cut down Ernst's body from the lamppost. Ernst had had to become the threat to overcome it, and few would ever know that truth. But knowing that he couldn't give Ernst the decency that he deserved made Etienne feel awful. Once the body was down, the only way he could control Marianne not making the grim discovery was to hide it in the basement. As he neared the bottom of the staircase, Etienne took a deep breath and pushed the door open.

'Monsieur Touelle,' a sly but familiar voice filled the workshop.

There he was, enacting the vision from one of his worst nightmares. Ernst's body lay sprawled out on the floor in front of him, his glazed-over eyes met with his, their last experience of total horror etched into his expression. Otto stood at his full height, holding the knife that had been plunged deep into Ernst's back at the throat of Philipp.

'Otto Neumann,' Etienne replied.

Otto laughed his awful cackle, making Etienne's blood run cold.

'Been doing some family research have you?' He taunted. 'Unsurprising if it came from *him,*' he sneered looking down at Ernst, rolling his head to the side dismissively with his boot.

'Don't you dare touch him!' Etienne hissed.

'Or you will do what?' Otto chuckled, 'Stumble over to me and kill me? I'd like to see you try, you pathetic cripple. The Führer has places like that for people like you, and most definitely this one,' he jeered, as he squeezed tighter on Philipp's torso making him wheeze in pain.

The shelf that ran along the length of the room was just a few paces to the right, Etienne knew that the carving knife was there, and slowly edged towards it.

'Let him go,' Etienne said calmly.

'I don't think so. Tonight, I deal with all of you,' Otto said low and threateningly.

Etienne tripped, and crashed into the shelf, gasping as he hit it with force. Otto roared with laughter.

'As if I could ever consider you a threat!'

Etienne faced the floor for a moment longer. It wasn't his hip, or his leg that pained him for once. The blade sliced his palm.

'You care way too much about what people think.'

'Men need to be brave. Our country needs that. And because you are not, you bring shame.'

'Your pity makes you weak.'

In the face of danger here was his foe, this was his battlefield, and he knew he would willingly die to save the lives of the people he loved, now surely that made him brave.

'I think you misheard me,' Etienne said coolly. 'That wasn't a request. That was a command. So, I say again, let him go.'

The taunting sneer disappeared from Otto's face and was replaced with a thunderous glare.

'Do you get that arrogance from your mother, Touelle? Because your father was nothing but feeble, even as he lay there dying, choking on his blood,' Otto barked, thrusting the knife towards him.

Etienne could feel anger coursing through his veins, into his fists, but if there was anything he had become exceptionally skilled at during this war, it was controlling his emotions at the right moments. Now it was his turn to smile slyly at Otto.

'I wouldn't call it arrogance. Merely just a way to distract you,' he smiled as he slid the knife along the shelf into Philipp's ready hand, which he grabbed and thrust hard into Otto's abdomen. Otto screamed as he relinquished his grip on Philipp who ran to Etienne's side.

'You *dirty* Jew!' Otto howled. 'Your kind deserve exactly what they get!'

Etienne could see the dangerous look on Philipp's face, lip curled, breathing heavy, and his eyes squinted in focused fury. Before he had time to stop him, Philipp picked up the wooden chair by the desk and ran at Otto.

'Philipp don't!' Etienne shouted.

Philipp swung hard, but Otto even with his wound, was bigger and quicker than Philipp was and moved out of the way with ease. Before Philipp even had a chance to turn back, he was struck hard on the back of the head and crumpled to the floor.

'No!' Etienne cried. Otto paced to the side standing over Philipp and drew back his fist to deliver another blow. Etienne summoned all the strength he had and for the first time in many years, he ran. As he ran, he swung his cane back, concentrated hard to keep his balance, swayed forward with all his momentum, and struck Otto hard in the head. Finally, his balance gave way, and Etienne crashed to the floor, as he saw Otto hit the desk and fall to the floor.

Etienne tried to move, but he couldn't, his leg would not budge, and he couldn't find his cane, he must have dropped it in the struggle, panic started to set in as he scrambled around frantically.

He glanced to the side, a large pool of blood had formed where Otto had fallen, but to his horror, Otto was not there. Quick as a flash he was there again, fulfilling his nightmare. Even with one hand pressed to his side, he was stronger than he was. Otto held the cane tight against Etienne's throat pressing harder with each twitch in his determined, murderous face. Etienne thrashed around, he tried to push back against the force, he tried to reach out for something, anything to defend himself but to no avail.

You fought valiantly soldier. We commend you for your service.

***

'Etienne? Are you there?'

'Philipp?' Etienne groaned as the pain intensified in his lower body as he tried to scramble to his feet.

'Oh, thank God! We need to get out of here now!' Philipp yelled, finally coming into focus as he dragged himself to his feet.

'Where is everyone?' Etienne screamed.

'I don't know!' Philipp shouted, now at Etienne's side seating him upright and hauling him up with all his strength.

'Get to the basement now.' Etienne ordered.

More bombs were falling thick and fast, there was simply no time to waste.

'I need to find my mother and Marianne… you need to take Ernst with you.'

Philipp glanced down in horror at Ernst's contorted form; he shook his head quickly as if to block out the reality of what he had to do.

'Where's Otto?' He asked panicked.

Both men glanced around, Otto was nowhere to be seen but the door to the staircase was still open.

Marianne.

'Go and find her. I will take care of this,' Philipp instructed as he started to drag Ernst's body towards the door.

'Where's my cane?'

'I don't know. I didn't see it. Now come on we must hurry!'

Etienne clambered towards the stairs, nearly on all fours as he tried to ascend them. When he reached the bedroom, the bedsheets were thrown to the side and the pillows were in disarray. Marianne was gone.

'Marianne!' Etienne called out, as he did so, another explosion shook the entire street.

Maybe she had heard the alarm before they had and rushed down to safety already. He prayed over and over. He couldn't remember stumbling back towards the door, half falling down the stairs, pushing through every ounce of pain to get to Camille and somehow getting her back and into their basement.

None of them could see a thing in the pitch-black. Philipp made no sound. Camille curled up tightly in his arms, she cried as Etienne tried to calm her, she was as light as a feather. But there was still no sign of Marianne.

MARIANNE

Avignon, May 1944

There was a huge crash downstairs. Marianne sat bolt right up in bed, rubbing the bleariness from her eyes. She draped a thin shawl around her shoulders and tugged on her worn plimsolls, prepared to run down to the basement at any moment. She heard shouting, Etienne's voice resonated above them all, but it was strained with fear. More banging and clanging ensued before Etienne's voice fell silent. Her limbs were stiff from her lack of movement, and they cramped horribly as she moved, but it would not stop her from getting to her husband.

She hurried down the stairs, reaching the workshop to find Philipp lying unconscious by the desk. She ran to him, kneeling next to him she felt for his pulse, sighing with relief when she found it faintly beating. Before she could try to rouse him, the dreaded sensation from her night terrors returned as she felt a cold instrument pressing hard against her neck.

'Hello again dear.'

She closed her eyes as Otto dragged her up to her feet, turning her to face him. She gasped when she saw the state, he was in. Blood poured out of his head, and the hand that grasped his side was also completely soaked, yet he was still standing brandishing Etienne's cane.

Otto dragged her along the floor, and she saw two more bodies lying on the floor, neither moved.

'What have you done?' She shrieked.

'What I should have done long ago. Especially to this bastard,' Otto spat, as he kicked Etienne's body hard in the side.

'You are the bastard, Otto,' Marianne growled.

He moved quickly, lowering the knife from her throat and pinning her against the wall with his free hand, hoisting her off the floor as he did so.

'We've been here before, haven't we?' He taunted, tightening his grip as he spoke. 'I want to see the life go out of your eyes, Ada Neumann.'

She scratched, clawed, and tried to prise his hand away from her, but once again he was too strong. He couldn't be allowed to get away with what he had done tonight. She felt rage bring energy to her exhausted limbs, and she drew her knees to her chest.

'My...name... is not... Ada Neumann.' She choked. 'It's... Marianne... Touelle.'

She kicked out as hard as she could striking him exactly where it hurt the most. Otto keeled over, screaming in agony, as the blood from his wounds continued to seep out. Marianne pushed away from his grip, grasped Etienne's cane in her hand and ran towards the door.

'If you want me, you will have to get me,' she snarled and ran out into the night.

Marianne ran until her lungs hurt, she didn't think about the direction, making snap decisions only.

Right, right, left, right, straight ahead, cut off down the alleyway, left... halt.

398

She skidded to a stop on the shiny cobbles, still slippery after the light rain from earlier in the afternoon. The opera house was just ahead. The building stood deserted, the beauty it contained had been forgotten by many. Marianne hurried up the steps, easily pushing past the loose door that had been kicked in by gangs no doubt. As she entered the trashed foyer, she closed her eyes and breathed in the musty smell, and her fingers started to tingle. The magic of the place was still tangible, she finally understood what Etienne felt. Visions of his still body nearly made her collapse.

My brave husband.

She couldn't mourn for him now, she knew that she had to do this, and being in Etienne's favourite place was befitting of the end, however it may conclude. Marianne ran to the side door and hurried down the maze of stairs until she reached the seats at the front of the opera facing its glorious stage. She brushed her hands over the luxurious velvet chairs, closing her eyes as she took in every touch, every scent, every sound, just as Etienne would do. She settled into one of the beautiful chairs, immediately encompassed by its comfort, but all she could picture in her mind was the warmth of Etienne's hand in hers.

She glanced up and could see the underside of the balconies framing the magnificent ornate patterns on the ceiling, she traced the outlines her with her fingertips. The grand chandelier was shrouded in darkness, but she could still hear the light tinkle of the teardrop crystal pieces as they swayed in the low rumbles that were increasing in strength. Despite all the physical grandeur that had remained, she knew that this was not what impressed Etienne the most. Marianne sat upright in her seat, looked to the stage, and allowed herself to imagine. The flutes, clarinets, and oboes clustered together on the left. A cymbalist positioned at the back patiently anticipating their dramatic moment. The trumpeters, the tubas, the French horns, and the trombones, were all centrally seated, the splendid gleam bouncing off their instruments as they controlled the dynamics. Finally, the string section, the cellos, the violas, and the violins, with Etienne seated at the very front of the group, captivated and lost in his expression, whilst unveiling so much to everyone. Her heart beat strongly.

'Ada! Show yourself!'

Marianne smiled. Taking one final glance towards the stage, she whispered.

'Touelle always.'

She rotated Etienne's cane around meticulously in her hand before rising to her feet and walking towards the sound that had haunted her dreams for so long.

***

She would never remember how she got back to the foyer, but she could not forget the blood splatters that adorned her dress and painted a macabre picture on her hands. Debris was falling all around her, and the building was shaking violently. The raining rubble that trickled down her neck and over her arms felt like the blood that showered her as she drove Etienne's cane into the space where Otto's eye used to be.

As her knees buckled at the realisation of the horror scene she had left in the centre of the stage a huge explosion sent her flying into the front desk, the crack inaudible over the chaos outside but resonated through her chest. Grimacing in agony Marianne kicked the shards of the door away and darted out onto the streets. Smoke billowed from every street corner, piling high over the city, blanketing it in hazardous fumes. The piercing sound of babies screaming rang out in the darkness. Fires engulfed buildings, swallowing up everything in its path, Marianne moved as quickly as she could to avoid being its next victim. She could hear calls for help, but no one was coming, for a moment she paused but to immediate regret as another bomb fell behind her. She ducked behind a wall and covered her ears just in time to see the rubble fly over her head narrowly avoiding her.

In the distance, she could see smoke pluming from the opera house, a section of it had been hit. Her heart skipped a beat.

Could this erase what I've done?

She shook her head to clear the ringing in her ears and refocus her thoughts, she still had a way to go. She had no idea who was watching, no idea what was happening, or which step could be her last, all she could do was run. Covering her ears, and ducking her head, she took off once again into the night from hell with no clue where she was going, and she didn't stop until she found herself hurtling over Camille's garden wall, her chest burning in pain. A fire explosion illuminated the night sky as she wrenched open the outside hatch doors to the basement, leapt inside, and yanked the doors tightly shut, slipped on the stairs and plummeted to the cold floor below.

When she came around it was morning, and she could hear the shuffling of feet. Her head felt fuzzy, and the basement was still dark.

'Etienne! Come quickly, she's in your parent's basement!'

'Who's there?' She croaked as she tried to lift her head.

'Marianne, it's Philipp! Are you okay?'

She could feel his hands searching for her shoulders, she held out her shaky hand to him, and he grasped it and helped her to her feet. She swayed unsteadily, she could feel Philipp buckle under the weight, but then another person was by her side propping her up, even if it felt uneven.

'I thought I lost you,' Etienne gasped; a tremble caught the edge of his voice.

'Oh, Etienne!' Marianne breathed in relief. 'I thought I lost *you*!'

Together they worked their way out of the darkness of the basement into the blooming garden where they relished the cool morning breeze and watched the sun dawn on the horizon.

***

525 DEAD IN ONE NIGHT.

AVIGNON CRUMBLES UNDER HUGE BOMBARDMENT.

CONCERNS GROW FOR CIVILIANS STILL MISSING AS PEOPLE SEARCH FOR THEIR LOVED ONES UNDER THE MOUNTAINS OF RUBBLE.

SEVERAL MILITARY OFFICERS ARE IN THE NUMBER OF MISSING PEOPLE THAT HAS BEEN STEADILY RISING OVER THE LAST FEW DAYS SINCE THE ATTACK. FEARS THAT THEY WILL NEVER BE FOUND BECOME STRONGER AS MORE BOMBINGS ARE EXPECTED TO COME.

For three days no one was mentioned specifically. Marianne guessed it was a case of people collecting data and reporting initial findings. They busied themselves along with the rest of the city in clearing up the mess. Etienne instructed Philipp to remain in their basement for safety, but Marianne could not ignore the uneasy glance that was shared between them each time the basement was mentioned.

They figured it was safe for Philipp to look after Camille, she didn't question anything, and Philipp's French was vastly improved. He kept her company which allowed Marianne and Etienne to re-arrange the house. Much had been damaged during the bombing. They set to work clearing away broken pieces of furniture and glass that was scattered all over the floor. The next task was to bring the thin mattresses and blankets downstairs so that they could be near the basement in the event of further emergencies. Marianne brought down everything from the attic that Philipp would need and when she came back, she saw Etienne seated at the edge of their mattress, staring straight ahead.

'What's wrong, Etienne?' She asked gently, setting the blankets beside him. Etienne looked up at her pensively, patting the space next to him for her to sit down, she did so taking his hands in hers. She looked at him earnestly, trying to get him to meet her eye, but his head was hung low.

'I let you down again,' Etienne murmured.

'How can you possibly believe that?'

'He… overcame me. Again. I allowed him to go straight to you. I had no idea where you were. I couldn't find you; I was so worried.'

She pulled him into her arms, cradling his head against her chest, making sure that his ear was over her heart so that he could hear it beating strongly.

'You were protecting me, which is all you have ever done, and you succeeded,' she whispered.

'Succeeded? How can *you* possibly believe that?'

Marianne smiled at him, tilted his face to look at her, and softly kissed his lips.

'Because I am here Etienne, and I am not going anywhere. I promise.'

They looked at each other deeply, with a look of connection that Marianne thought they had lost long ago. Etienne sat up and slowly began to unbutton his shirt. Her heart began to beat faster.

'Etienne, we don't have to, I know you don't like it,' she assured him, but she felt the passion burning inside of her, stronger than the pain that stabbed at her ribs, the yearning to find each other again was all-consuming.

'All I want is to be close to you Marianne. I can't bear to lose you.'

Then his mouth was on hers, and then all over her, exploring every part of her as if this was all brand new to them. They quickly pulled off their clothes, almost in a frenzy, desperate to be close to each other. As they lay next to each other, their hands remained firmly clasped together, heads bowed together as they caught their breath.

'You know we used to confess the information that we both needed to know?' Etienne whispered.

'Mmmm hmmm', Marianne replied.

'Otto attacked us here... I think me and Philipp might have killed him.'

'The same way he killed Ernst?'

'How did you know?'

'I saw him, Etienne. But Ernst warned me. You didn't think his visits to me were just to keep me company? He gave me papers that I could hand in at the embassy to get Otto transferred away if necessary.'

'He was putting measures in place?'

Marianne nodded. 'After Otto's return, and when I tried to…' Etienne pulled her close, as she nuzzled into his neck. 'Ernst believed it was only a matter of time, that his time was running out too, and he was right.' She murmured.

'He was a brave man, Marianne.'

'Yes, he was,' she agreed. 'Where is Ernst now, Etienne?'

Etienne took a shuddered breath. 'In a peaceful place, I promise.'

'Thank you,' Marianne replied holding onto Etienne tightly.

They lay in silence for a short while.

'You and Philipp didn't kill Otto,' she admitted.

'He was bleeding so much from what we did Marianne, I was sure he was going to die.'

'Perhaps. But you see this…' She rolled over enough the expose the emerging bruises on her side extending across her torso. Etienne's eyes widened in shock.

'I fell into the reception desk at the opera house.'

'Why on earth were you there?'

'I had to lure him away from the house, from all of you, and then… I finished it.' She admitted, swallowing hard as she recalled how Otto had tried to grab her and stumbled; her hand grasping the cane as she seized the moment, and squeezed her eyes shut to spare herself the haunting image. But she would never forget the feeling of the cane sliding through the gaping wound,

Otto's final howl and then the silent abyss, the ending of the show once and for all.

Confessing to Etienne helped ease her conscience, once again there were no secrets between them. But it didn't stop her heart from pounding when the newspaper arrived the next morning.

```
CONFIRMED    VICTIM    OF   AVIGNON   BOMBINGS:
SCATTERED    REMAINS    FOUND    AT    THE    OPERA
D'AVIGNON  CONFIRMED  TO  BE  THAT  OF  OFFICER
OTTO NEUMANN. HE IS BELIEVED TO HAVE DIED IN
THE  LINE  OF  DUTY  WHILST  OUT  ON  PATROL  WHEN
THE ATTACK TOOK PLACE.
```

***

Avignon, August 1944

Their immediate threat was gone, but they still had to wait. They had survived so much, yet the war continued to demand more from them. They eagerly awaited the day and expected the worst. Violent skirmishes on the streets, enemy sides in a fierce standoff to fight for territory. But that was far from what took place.

Liberation. The word felt funny in her mouth. They were gone, they were actually gone. Many didn't believe the announcements that Franco-American troops had taken control of the city. The streets remained deserted, out of fear and for their own safety. Huge areas lay in ruins after the relentless bombings leading up to the day they had been wanting for so long. It had been a terrifying couple of months, but they still paled in comparison to the events of *that* night.

When the realisation finally dawned, people took to the streets for huge celebrations. Rapturous cheers erupted when allied vehicles drove past bearing the American and French flags. Neighbours hugged each other for the first time in years, tears turned to those of joy instead of mourning, the restoration of hope to a city, to a nation that had been torn apart in every way.

The Touelle household was one that could not believe what was happening. Their joy was locked up in a state of shock. Endurance, survival, trauma, and loss were all that they had known for too long. But the day that Philipp took his first steps outside into the warm summer sunshine was overwhelming for all of them.

'How does it feel?' Marianne asked as she choked back tears of jubilation.

'Bright!' Philipp laughed as he squinted in the morning sun that was rapidly ascending in the sky. 'It's been dark for a long time.'

'Agreed,' Etienne sighed, but he too couldn't hold back the huge grin on his face.

'So, this is Avignon,' Philipp remarked as he pranced around on the uneven cobbles. 'Will you show me?'

Marianne looked up at her husband. The lines on his face had dramatically aged his forty years, a prominent silver streak lined his hair. His body was frail and almost hunched over, his makeshift cane made from debris they had collected was starting to fail him, but it would have to suffice for now.

Etienne smiled warmly at her; she couldn't love him more if she tried. They looked back towards the house where Camille was happily re-arranging the kitchen after the latest bombings had left it in disarray, completely unaware of what had caused it. She lived in her own world where she was content. It was sad to lose her this way, but her positivity was infectious, as it always had been.

'Let's give him the tour,' Etienne chuckled.

Marianne looped her arm around his slim waist, and together they walked. As they did so, Etienne pointed out all the sights with pride. Even though so much had been damaged, he would never see it as anything other than magnificent.

Finally, they reached the Opera d'Avignon, which stood tall and proud, defiant the entire time. As they crossed the small courtyard, they saw Milice officers being marched away, to the cheers and jeers of onlookers. One such man with a huge frame was being led away, his head hung low, but as he crossed their path he looked sternly at Etienne, not breaking his stare until they were loaded into a vehicle and driven away.

'What's his problem?' Philipp asked.

'I have no idea,' Etienne said nonchalantly.

She knew that he was lying. Etienne never gave anyone that much attention if he did not have at least some connection with them. She rubbed her hand delicately on his back, he looked back at her tenderly.

We will talk about this later.

They all looked back towards the opera house, and Etienne burst into his passionate speech about his love for the building, reminiscing about the orchestra that had moved him so deeply from such a young age, and how he had finally understood how to express himself. As Etienne talked Marianne smiled as Philipp nodded along, smiling, discovering. After all this time he was fully understanding how Etienne worked and receiving further insight into the greatness of his character. These two remarkable men who were both so important to her stood in front of her, in a liberated city. Their plights shared and overcome.

Marianne's gaze returned to the opera house. She looked it up and down knowingly and shuddered.

'Are you okay?' Etienne asked, halting his speech.

'I'm fine,' she said smiling reassuringly, 'keep going.' He squeezed her hand lightly and continued.

News of what had happened at the opera house had remained quiet even when it first broke. That night had claimed 525 lives in the heavy bombardment, and the scattered remains of an officer had only been a fraction of the chaos that had ensued.

PHILIPP

Avignon, January 1945

'Good as new' Philipp chimed as he watched Etienne pace down the street, challenging his new cane to perform on the cobbled obstacles.

'It feels great Philipp, Merci,' Etienne beamed.

'Sorry that we had to destroy a cabinet to make it.'

'We will rebuild another someday.'

It had been an honour to help Etienne and Marianne rebuild. The community came together to help repair, doing their best to put losses behind them and look ahead to a future that now held so much more promise.

Not only was the house becoming more stable, but so was Etienne and Marianne's relationship. Philipp also felt renewed, his heart beat stronger than ever, and his muscles got bigger and firmer the more he moved.

Time running out was finally something to be embraced, not feared. The evil that had pervaded Avignon for so long was gone.

Although the war was not officially over yet, there was an unwavering optimism that the Nazis' time was running out, and they were all ready for that day to come.

'Philipp?' Marianne said quietly as she floated into the room. She was pale, her hands trembled making the papers in her hands rustle, and he could see that she had been crying. Etienne hobbled back inside, concerned for his wife, he drew close to her.

'What's wrong, Marianne?' Philipp asked, crossing the room towards her.

She could barely look him in the eye as she slowly handed the newspaper over to him, when he saw the picture and read the headline he could understand why. He stumbled backwards, nearly falling with shock before Etienne quickly pushed a chair underneath him.

'What's going on?' Etienne asked.

Philipp's heart felt like it dropped straight to his stomach, he didn't know whether to cry, scream, or throw up.

27TH JANUARY 1945

HITLER'S HORROR UNMASKED AS FORCES STORM NAZI CAMP IN POLAND WHERE IT IS ESTIMATED THAT OVER 700,000 JEWS HAVE BEEN SLAUGHTERED IN A MASSACRE BY THE GERMANS, THE SCALE OF WHICH IS UNPRECEDENTED IN WORLD HISTORY, WITH FEARS THAT THERE ARE MANY MORE VICTIMS TO BE DISCOVERED.

'Oh…'

'Philipp?'

'Oh my…'

'Philipp?'

His fists clenched, he balled up the paper in his hands and began to shake.

409

'No!' He screamed, 'Oh God please no!' Marianne tried to put her arms around him, but he threw them away.

'Philipp, we had no idea' Etienne said apologetically.

'*They all knew*!' Philipp roared.

'Philipp…' Marianne pleaded, tears welling in her eyes.

'No, Marianne!' Philipp spat, 'They *all* knew, and did *nothing!*'

'How do you know?' Etienne asked.

'You saw it before you left, Marianne,' Philipp said coolly. She looked away in shame. 'People like Ernst.' He continued, 'They reported on these animals' activities long before they had any kind of *power*! They knew.'

Names burned through his mind- Max, Georg, Marta, Eva, Kurt, Tante Anita, Tante Gretchen, Tante Liesl, Johann, Father, hell even Professor Bergmann and Elias could have suffered these unfathomable fates. He knew that there would be many more victims, from many walks of life, too many.

If we go down, we go down together.

He had chosen to be protected and to protect himself.

'I should have been there with them,' Philipp asserted as his anger turned to grieving sobs, this time he let Marianne hold him.

'You survived Philipp. That is the ultimate victory,' she ordered, forcing him to look at her.

'I wish I could believe you,' he cried.

'One day you will,' Etienne assured; his hand rested firmly on Philipp's shoulder.

'One day? Etienne, I need to go now! If survivors are returning home, I need to know if any are my family!'

'And one day you will,' Etienne said sternly. It was strange to hear an edge of aggression in his voice, yet it was still full of care.

'The war is still going on. Until Germany officially surrenders there is no way that you will be able to move around safely,' Marianne added, as she scooped up the scrunched-up newspaper, opening the page back up and showing him the other headline.

ALLIES MAKE THEIR MOVE IN THEIR BOMBING OF GERMANY

Philipp ran his hand over his chin, sighing deeply. He saw the damage in Avignon, and he dreaded to think of the fury being unleashed on Berlin. Despite the horrors, Berlin would always be his home, and he worried that they would not be able to rebuild the same way. He couldn't help but imagine what returning home on the losing side would look like.

'How long?' He groaned.

'That I don't know,' Marianne sighed.

***

His answer would come, albeit nearly three and a half months later. No newspaper was needed for that day. The ecstatic cheers that took to the streets that day told the story.

'They have surrendered!'

'The war is finished!'

'It is all over!'

Perhaps. But for many, this is just the beginning.

***

Avignon, May 1945

'Philipp, wait!'

Philipp threw his papers into his bag, some clothes, and shoes he had picked up from one of the aid charities sweeping through the

411

war-torn cities and clasped the bag shut.

'Philipp, please!' Marianne continued to protest.

'Marianne, I have to go!'

'I know you do but how are you going to get there?'

'I'll walk.'

'Are you insane?' She scoffed. 'The landscape is completely destroyed, there could be unexploded bombs everywhere! People are still desperate; they will attack you without a moment's notice! Do I need to go on?' She persisted, testing Philipp's patience.

'I'll take my chances,' Philipp asserted.

'Marianne's right Philipp, this is madness!' Etienne chimed in, blocking the doorway as he spoke. Philipp took a deep breath to try and calm himself down.

'I love you both, I will never forget you, but you have to let me do this!' He insisted.

'It's because we love you that we can't let you walk out into the unknown like this!' Marianne exclaimed. He hated it when she used his rhetoric against him, more so because he knew that she was right.

'So, what do you propose I do?' His patience wore thin as the volume raised in his voice. 'Sit around and wait for longer? Like I haven't done that enough for the last few years!'

His words clearly stung as Marianne took a tentative step back.

'Marianne, I'm sorry, I didn't mean it like that. I'm truly grateful to both of you for everything you sacrificed for me.'

She looked up at him sorrowfully, his heart ached to hurt her this way, but he had to leave, and they knew it deep down too.

'Etienne has an idea. Hear him out before you do anything, please?'

He paused, knowing just how much he owed them, it was the least he could do. He nodded in agreement.

'Come with me,' Etienne ordered calmly, ushering Philipp towards the door. They walked together slowly down the winding streets in silence whilst celebrations continued to go on all around them. They carried on past the midday drunken partygoers up towards the direction of the military units set up for monitoring and carrying out aid missions. They saw several American trucks stationed as they drew closer.

'Why are we here, Etienne?' Philipp asked confused. Etienne said nothing and walked determinedly towards the soldiers.

'Can we help you, gentlemen?' A tall broad American soldier with a strong southern accent addressed them.

'Excuse moi, sir?' Etienne began.

'Nicolas!' The soldier called out, and a young bespectacled private ran over.

'Oui, monsieur!' He called. The soldier gestured for Etienne to speak.

'Philipp Blau...' he started as he pushed Philipp forward.

'Woah, woah, woah!' the American soldier intervened, hushing Etienne immediately, a couple of troops stepped forward with intrigue.

'You are Philipp Blau?' the American soldier said pointing at Philipp.

'Ja... sir,' Philipp stuttered.

'Ernst Stein spoke highly of you, sir.'

Philipp looked down at his feet. Poor Ernst, he didn't deserve what happened to him. He hoped that he was at peace surrounded by the flowers. He and Etienne exchanged a subtle but uneasy look.

'Ernst Stein… hero,' Philipp replied in broken English.

'Yes, he was. We owe him a lot. The man planned for every eventuality, even after his murder.'

Finally, someone said it for how it was.

'We are indebted to him, and according to his notes, he was indebted to you. What can we do for you, Mr Blau?'

Philipp was too dumbstruck to speak, he couldn't believe what he was hearing.

'Can you get him home to Berlin?' Etienne asked, clearly unsure of everything that had just been said, Nicolas translated Etienne's message and the American smiled.

'Sir, it would be our pleasure.'

***

Five days later at the crack of dawn, Philipp assembled the last of his belongings, and a few extra food items courtesy of his group accompanying him back home. *Home.*

He swung his backpack over his shoulder, and instead of heading towards the door, he found himself ascending the stairs until he reached the attic. He pushed the door open quietly and glanced around the tiny space that he had occupied for so long. The room that had nearly killed him, hidden him, nursed him back to health, been his prison, been his safety, been the place where he had met the two of the most incredible people.

'I'm sorry you had to be up here for so long,' Marianne's voice broke through the morning dusk.

'It kept me alive. You and Etienne kept me alive,' Philipp said, smiling broadly.

She smiled back but she couldn't stop the tears from overflowing. Philipp pulled her into a tight embrace.

'You know I have to go.'

'I know.'

'I will never forget you.'

'I know.'

They stayed locked in their embrace, neither of them wanted to let the other go.

'Do you want to come with me?' Philipp asked. Marianne drew back from him.

'You could see Erich, Liselotte, and Thomas again?' Philipp continued.

A look of both confusion and contemplation troubled Marianne's face, she hesitated for a moment.

'I can't,' she finally concluded.

'Of course, you can, I'm sure they can make space for you! Haven't you always wanted to see Erich again?'

'More than anything,' she sighed, 'but it's not as simple as that. Etienne is my husband, my life is here, I owe him everything.'

'I'm not saying leave for good, just… he would understand. You would come back, of course, you will.'

'Knowing that Erich is being raised by Liselotte gives me peace, Philipp,' Marianne interrupted. 'Besides, Etienne needs me… Camille died last night.'

'Wait… what?' Philipp gasped.

'She slipped away peacefully in her sleep. Etienne and I were with her, there was no pain.'

'Why didn't you wake me up?' Philipp asked.

'We didn't want to give you any more obligation to stay. Plus, Etienne needs to be alone right now to say goodbye to her.'

'As if he hasn't lost enough. Is he?…'

'He wishes you nothing but the best and urges you to stay safe.'

'He has my promise and my deepest condolences,' Philipp said softly. Marianne nodded and took his hand; she didn't let go until she had walked him to the end of the street. When she finally released him, Philipp pulled her into another tight embrace.

'You are always loved, and the bravest woman I have ever met,' he whispered into her ear. She pulled away from him gently, resting her hand on his cheek.

'Be remarkable Philipp, always, and write to us!'

'Always. Marianne Touelle.'

Their moment abruptly ended with the familiar friendly sound of an American accent drifting around the corner.

'Mr Blau. Are you ready to go?'

'Yes, sir,' Philipp replied.

They walked at pace, but he made sure to turn around once more to see Marianne waving in the distance, he waved back. But there was something in her hand, he squinted to make it out, a blue ribbon?

***

Berlin, June 1945

'God have mercy!' Philipp gasped.

'Yeah, it sure ain't pretty. This is where we leave you now Mr Blau.'

'Thank you, Private Harmon.'

'Hey, it's Clyde, come on man!' The Texan teased.

'Philipp. *Man.*' Philipp teased in return, 'where will you go

416

now?'

'Back to policing duties. The fallout of this is gonna be ugly. Oh, and Philipp? Stay away from the Russians. Hell, the whole world hates your nation right now, but their hatred runs deep to the point of psychotic rampaging murder.'

'Got it,' Philipp replied uneasily, shifting awkwardly on his feet.

'Good luck to you, sir.'

'And to you, sir,' Philipp said, shaking Clyde's hand firmly.

As they parted ways Philipp finally beheld the horror scene that lay in front of him. Entire rows of houses, offices, and shops had been obliterated, all their contained memories, successes, and failures left to roam around aimlessly in the lifeless air. The rest of the scene had deep holes punched into its features. Overkill came to mind. Beaten into submission. Not that it wasn't warranted, but to see his nation, his city, his *home* in this state of deplorability was tough to comprehend.

As Philipp took his first cautious steps forward, he winced at every sight he saw, each seemed to get worse than the last. Wisps of smoke continuously drifted into the air in endless surrender. A flurry of bedraggled people pushed past him, most of whom were children. *Families.* A look of despair etched on their faces, carrying not just the few belongings that they had been able to salvage, but also the knowledge that not only had they lost everything, but no help was coming to them. All the world would see was that they were German, that association alone was unshakeable and condemnable.

He was no longer being watched, yet he still felt like he was being judged. He had returned, when everyone's expressions seemed to accuse him, if he had any common sense he would have stayed well away. But *they* were gone, fled, hiding. It was funny how the hunters so quickly became the prey. But there was no sense of vindication, just sheer incredulity at what had happened, why it had happened, what had been left behind, and the abyss that somehow needed to be fixed.

A solitary bench stood in the middle of the street where two elderly gentlemen sat surrounded by mountains of rubble piled high to the sides of the road. They were silent, solemn, one shifted a tired-looking eye to look at Philipp directly, catching him staring. Philipp diverted his gaze, jumping at the sound of a crash behind him, he spun around to witness the free-standing wall that had been swaying finally give way, crumbling into dust. The two men on the bench didn't even flinch.

It didn't take long to find the house, but it lay in complete ruin. Philipp had expected the worst, but it didn't make the loss any less devastating. He fell to his knees, scrunching pieces of rubble in his hands as he wept.

'Oh Father, I'm sorry!' He moaned into the last of the day's light.

He lost track of time, not knowing how long he had been kneeling there. Hauling himself to his feet he scoured the rest of the deserted street until his eyes fell upon the shop and he staggered towards it. The windows were smashed, the door was busted, and some of the interior had been knocked around, but it was still standing, structurally sound. Philipp carefully eased his way in through the flimsy door.

All the furnishings were gone, most likely ransacked, and used as fuel. Philipp closed his eyes, spread his hands out, and began to map out the cabinets, the displays, and the reception desk, and for the first time in so long, he allowed himself to remember, and remember fondly.

***

Johann charged around with boxes, which lightly tinkled as he hurried towards the back of the shop floor.

'Be careful with those Johann! They are fragile!' Felix boomed.

'I know Father!' Johann replied, almost annoyed.

Philipp remained sat at the reception desk reading a medical journal, staying out of the way.

'What's in the boxes, Father?'

'Crystal glasses Philipp, nearly one hundred years old.'

'And you found them in perfect condition?'

'I can hardly believe it myself!' Felix laughed. 'How is the studying going my boy?' He asked peering over Philipp's shoulder.

'It's great. Fascinating. We have a test on the lungs coming up this week, so I need to prepare,' Philipp replied.

'Prepare to succeed, and I know you will Philipp.' Felix smiled, clapping him on the shoulder.

'What is it?' Johann asked, swaying into the room.

'We were just saying what a good find you got there Johann,' Philipp smiled.

'Oh, and this one is all on your brother too. Researched it, found it, bought it, start to finish,' Felix gleamed.

'Nice going, Johann,' Philipp said.

'There's no need to be sarcastic, Philipp,' Johann grumbled.

'I'm not!' Philipp protested. 'You have done a really good job!'

'Oh... well... thank you. And you too,' Johann replied glancing down at the book in Philipp's hand.

'I've got your back brother! Always,' Philipp chortled; Johann chuckled.

***

'Ph...Ph...Philipp? Is that you?' A faint voice stuttered.

Philipp's eyes flew open. Before him stood a tall, scarily skeletal man, his brown hair shaven, but a small stubble had begun to grow back. His skin was sheet white and covered in bruises, blotches, welts, and burns. His eyes were hollow and sunken, haunted by dark rings that nearly swallowed up his entire face. And the lopsided jaw that had never quite gone back into shape…

'Johann?'

Philipp rushed towards his brother as he collapsed.

'I knew you would come here!' Johann cried.

'I've got your back brother, always,' Philipp replied sobbing just as hard as his beloved brother.

They reclaimed the shop as their own, no one questioned them, it was rightfully theirs after all. The brothers barely left each other's side for two weeks. Philipp gave Johann the extra clothes and shoes that he had acquired, and they hung off him like curtains. Johann's bones looked like they were nearly poking out of his skin. Philipp's outrage and curiosity was overwhelming, but Johann couldn't talk about it. He got clues from Johann's screaming during his night terrors as he tried to piece together what he had been through.

The days were gradually getting warmer; poor Johann could barely get any peaceful sleep as it was, let alone in the sweltering night air. Even though there was hardly any glass left in the windows, the sun still beat down on the shop during the day.

'I forgot how hot it got working here in the summer,' Johann reminisced.

'I need to take a walk Johann; do you want to come?' Philipp asked.

The smile on Johann's face dropped, panic set into his eyes and he began to tremble.

'No! No walks, no!' He screamed.

'Woah, woah! Okay! It's okay!' Philipp assured holding Johann close to him.

What did those monsters do to you my brave, brave big brother?

'Please don't leave me again,' Johann begged.

'Hey, I came back, didn't I?' Philipp teased, trying to mask his guilt as best as he could. It seemed to work as Johann's shoulders relaxed.

'Where the hell did you go, Philipp?'

'Oh, where do I begin?' Philipp smiled.

Johann listened attentively to Philipp talk for hours about Professor Bergmann and Elias, how they had personally acted on his plight and forged his papers for him. He spoke of Max, Marta, Kurt, Georg, and Eva, how they had taken him in as a stranger and equipped him with the means to travel and hide effectively. He spoke of his long hikes across countries, his imprisonment in Gurs, about Alejandro and his friends and their daring escape. He spoke about his arrival in Avignon and everything that happened with Otto, Ernst, Pierre, and Camille, and especially about the two bravest people he had ever met, Etienne and Marianne.

'Shit!' Johann guffawed, 'You went on quite the adventure little brother!'

'I wished you could have come with me. Like when we were kids.'

Johann sighed. 'You were always the braver one, Philipp.'

'After what you have been through. I think I may have to relinquish that title.'

Johann's face fell. 'Our Father is dead, Philipp.'

'I know,' Philipp said sadly.

'You do? How?' Johann asked, confused.

'It's complicated.'

'They came for the both of us in the night. When we arrived… there… Father was so weak, he could barely stand. They separated us. I tried to get to him Philipp I swear to you!' Johann spluttered; large teardrops lined his already gaunt eyes. 'But one of them hit me, I blacked out… and then he was gone.'

It was the most simplistic way he would ever retell it. It would always be too painful a memory for him to re-live.

'I wanted to be there for you both. I truly did,' Philipp muttered between his tears.

'No. Knowing that you had managed to get out gave us both hope. We were proud of you. I'm always proud of you,' Johann said solemnly, as Philipp pulled him in close.

'You are a miracle, Johann. But are you too proud to let me examine your feet now?'

Johann looked at Philipp coyly. Tired of being stubborn he stretched his feet towards Philipp who began examining them carefully, gently rotating them, but it didn't stop Johann roaring in pain.

'Okay breathe Johann, I'm sorry!'

Johann closed his eyes, trying to steady his breath.

'Your ankles are broken, and these sores are deep and infected. It's a miracle that the tissue hasn't died, and you haven't lost them!'

'Enough of the science Philipp! Please. Can you treat them?'

'I can but I will need the right tools and medications… Johann, I will be back in half an hour maximum!'

'Where are you going?'

'I'll be back soon, I promise!' Philipp exclaimed, jumping to his feet, and taking off out the door. He raced down the street, taking shortcuts down the alleyways.

Please be there! Please be there!

Philipp rushed up to the door, the door that he used to call on nearly every day. Taking a deep breath, he knocked, and a chain rattled on the inside and a small gap appeared, the light glinted off her large unflattering glasses.

'Ja?' She asked irritated.

'Hello Celine,' Philipp breathed a huge sigh of relief.

***

He was grateful for her predictability, hoarding her medical supplies, trying to maintain her own practice as much as he had done. It warmed Philipp's heart to see Celine and Johann reunited. Nothing had changed between them after they were over the initial shock at seeing each other again. The way they talked, softly brushed against each other, the affectionate glances they exchanged that they thought Philipp wouldn't see. They used Celine's supplies to the best of their ability, washing and dressing Johann's feet and strapping them up to set the bones correctly to heal properly.

'They need to be accurate,' Philipp warned.

'I know that,' Celine insisted.

'If they're not he'll be in pain for the rest of his life.'

'Hey, I know that too, don't worry,' Celine assured.

'Sorry, it's just, I know someone who suffers from something similar.'

'Poor soul,' Celine said sympathetically.

'He doesn't let it hold him back,' Philipp said, smiling fondly.

Celine came by daily to check on Johann. Together they nursed Johann's physical wounds. There was little they could do for his psychological scars, but they refused to let him suffer alone.

'You left. I understand why of course. But you came back, why?' Celine asked one evening as Johann slept fitfully in her arms.

'I can't give up on him, Celine.'

'No, you can't,' she smiled, 'you never do on the ones you love,' she said looking down at Johann. 'I can't tell you how happy I am to see you both alive.'

'And us with you! I missed you so much! And he definitely did,' Philipp winked. Celine kicked him playfully.

'I never stopped believing. But not seeing you made me think the worst. And now you're both here!' Celine laughed through her happy tears.

Philipp grasped her hand, kissing it lightly. But what she said got him thinking. You could never truly give up on the ones you love, but seeing them, and being with them, brings fulfilment to a person's life that couldn't be surpassed or fully described.

'Celine. I need to take a trip ...'

***

Stuttgart, August 1945

He asked every person who would speak to him and tried to remember the landmarks they had discussed, but eventually, he found it. A faint smell of bread lingered in the air and made his stomach growl.

A tall, stick-thin woman rose from the doorstep that she was fixing as he slowly approached. Her long, glossy, blonde hair was loose, cascading past her waist, in it she wore a blue ribbon.

'Can I help you, sir?' She asked wearily. Fine wrinkles lined her face with an exhausted look that he had seen in too many faces, yet it did not take away from just how stunningly beautiful she was.

'Are you Liselotte Huber?'

'I am. Who's asking?' She stepped towards him with a suspicious look in her eye.

'Forgive me, my name is Philipp Blau.'

'I have never heard of you, and I can't help you. My family is struggling to get by as it is, we have nothing to spare I'm sorry,' she said, turning back.

'I don't need charity, Frau Huber!' Philipp called after her, 'I bring news of Ada Neumann.'

Liselotte froze, her hand hovered over the door handle, and she slowly turned to face Philipp again.

'Ada?' She gasped. 'She's alive?'

'May I come in, Liselotte?' Philipp asked, 'There is much to tell you.'

ETIENNE

Avignon, May 1945

'Etienne, come quickly,' Marianne said urgently.

'What's wrong?'

'It's Camille. Her breathing is very laboured.'

They hurried downstairs to Camille's bedside; Marianne was correct about her condition, but neither of them was surprised. Camille's state of mind had deteriorated rapidly over the last few days, she often had no idea where she was or who she was; but somehow, she could recall who Etienne and Marianne were, and mercifully, trusted them to help her. Her condition had also led her to struggle physically, she was knocking into more things and so had remained in bed for most of the time.

'E…E…Etienne…M…Ma…Marianne?' She rasped.

'We're here Camille,' Marianne reassured her.

'I am going to see Pierre soon,' Camille said smiling weakly.

Etienne and Marianne shared a look. Was she having some clarity of thought? Camille rested her hands to her sides, stretching out her fingertips towards them, they dutifully took one of her hands in theirs.

'We love you both… so much,' Camille wheezed as she fought for each breath.

'Shhh Maman don't speak if you don't need to,' Etienne cooed as he stroked her beautiful, long soft hair from her face.

'Water… please,' she gasped.

'I've got it,' Marianne whispered, gently releasing Camille's hand, and kissing her forehead before heading into the kitchen.

'Etienne?'

'Oui, Maman?'

'The peaches.'

Etienne stiffened, 'What about the peaches, Maman?'

'Three…this year…three.'

'Is that so?'

'That…young man,' Camille spluttered.

He was amazed that she could remember her brief time spent with Philipp.

'Oui, Maman,' Etienne confessed. A fresh rush of guilt hit him for the years that he had endangered her life through his actions. He felt her hand squeeze his, he looked up at her and the big smile on her face made him relax, releasing him from the weight of the secrets he had been carrying for so long.

'They always needed you,' she whispered. 'I am so proud of you, ma pêche.'

'Always?' Etienne asked. Camille looked at him knowingly. 'How long have you known?'

427

'A Mother always knows,' she smiled. Then she closed her eyes and fell asleep for the last time.

***

Avignon, June 1945

There was so much that he wanted to say to her. It seemed so cruel for her life to have ended at the dawn of a new era. But he had thought deeply on the matter; whilst the population was eager to start again, without Pierre by her side there was no fresh start for his mother. Perhaps this was the final chapter that she wanted to conclude.

But now the day of her funeral had arrived, and the weather that day was stunning. The light rainfall from the previous night gave way to the shimmering dew on the greenery surrounding the churchyard. The fresh smell of the grass and flowers delighted the senses, something that Camille had taken such joy in, and therefore could only be a reminder that today her life was to be a celebration.

The entirety of the old town and citizens from all over the city turned up, filling the chapel to its maximum capacity. Etienne knew how many lives his mother had blessed, but the huge numbers affirmed this in a way that touched his heart deeply. He watched alone quietly in a secluded corner of the churchyard as people filed into the church. Marianne had been amazing in the organisation of it all. She requested a different priest to officiate much to Etienne's relief, but she also asked all attendees to bring along a single flower of their choice which she collected at the door as she greeted people, gradually adding them to the bouquet she had put together. Etienne smiled gratefully towards her as he watched her busily working, grateful for the space she had given him to process it all, time that was taken away from him when his father had died.

Etienne leaned heavily on his cane, combatting the fierce pain that was plaguing him. He was captivated by the natural beauty of the day; it allowed him to pause and reflect. He glanced at the yew tree next to him and ran his fingers up and down the knots of the bark, piecing a melody together in his mind just as he did as a child. He didn't know how to feel, he wondered how a heart could feel so full, yet so broken at the same time. A light brush against the skin of his hands distracted him from his contemplation. Marianne sat next to him, watching him closely.

'It's okay if it's not perfect you know. No one else will know.' She said, smiling at him affectionately, a small tear glistening in her eye dropped onto her hand. Etienne rubbed it away with his thumb delicately.

'Thank you,' he smiled.

Marianne kissed him softly on the cheek. 'I'll be waiting for you inside. Take your time.'

Etienne sat in his spot and watched until his wife had disappeared behind the door before tucking the wooden box under his arm and walking towards the chapel.

As he entered the building, all eyes turned to him, he felt the heat rush up his neck. He searched the sea of faces until his gaze fell upon Marianne smiling her encouragement at him. His cane clunked loudly on the stone floor as he hobbled towards her, but he didn't care about who was staring. As he took his seat next to Marianne the young priest began:

'Dearly beloved…'

Etienne knew he would be sensitive in his summary of his mother's life, but that was all it could ever be, a summary. It would not even scratch the surface of showcasing exactly who Camille was, which was why he had decided to tell her life story in his own way.

'I would like to invite Camille's son Etienne up here to play a special piece for us.'

Marianne kissed his hand tenderly, which he squeezed gently in return, and approached the altar. He caught a glimpse of his aunt Georgette and Uncle François sitting in the front row, heads bowed together and crying quietly. News from Paris had been far worse than they had expected, the loss of family had been extensive. The only family present were the survivors.

Etienne dutifully removed Madame Penaud's violin from the box and did what he had done so many times before, raised the rest to his chin, and hovered the bow over the strings, but then he froze. How could he possibly represent the fullness of his mother's life? Where should he begin? He closed his eyes to collect his thoughts and kept them closed as he drew out the first minor, mournful notes.

The piece started startlingly sad, lonely, and isolated, the strings cried out with longing, and for a time they sang solo the sorrows of their heart. But soon there was a slight hope, a responder to the lonely plea, and the strings began to dance. Etienne pictured his parents approaching each other cautiously, but before they knew it, they were swaying together in a graceful waltz, spinning around, and staring adoringly into each other's eyes. The melody lifted, bursting with joy and life, but was slow and beautiful. Life between Pierre and Camille was never rushed, despite the peppering of sharp notes representing Camille's fierce loyalty and defensiveness. The melody continued to be warm and vibrant, but at the end, there was a stark return to the isolated, devastating minor notes, the lasting note forte, gradually fading into nothing. Etienne could feel himself crying, this wasn't how Camille's life should be concluded, he recalled what she had said.

'I am going to see Pierre soon.'

Together their lives were brighter, and now they were reunited. In death, they continued to live, and it needed to be part of their story. Etienne converted back to the height of the waltz, and he could hear the audience collectively hum in relief. When he finally concluded he opened his eyes, unable to see much through his tears, but enough to see Marianne weeping quietly, her hands outstretched to him. He stepped straight into her arms, and at that moment, they were the only two people in the room, realising that so much of his parent's story sang their story. The cautious approach, their gentle waltz, although theirs was tinged with chaos and secrecy. But one thing he knew for certain, his life was brighter with Marianne.

'It's okay,' she whispered, 'that was perfect.'

Following the service, they stood together outside of the chapel thanking guests for coming, The day's exhaustion caught up with them.

'How is the pain?' Marianne asked.

'Bad,' Etienne replied honestly.

Marianne looked at him. She knew when he wasn't referring to his physical pain, which was raging all over his body, yet it only remained fractional compared to the pain he felt in his heart.

'That was a beautiful service,' a familiar gentle voice called out.

'Oncle Louis, thank you for coming!' Etienne chimed, taking his uncle's hand in a firm handshake.

'Anything for family my dear boy. I'm sorry that we keep meeting under such circumstances. Can we take a walk?'

Etienne looked to Marianne who was smiling at him.

'Go ahead. I'll finish up here,' she said softly.

Etienne and Louis walked gingerly to the other side of the churchyard; both of their heads bowed in deep contemplation.

'I received your letter, and I have considered your offer Etienne. Have you filed for the business to become official again?'

'I have. I am hopeful that I will receive confirmation soon.'

Louis nodded, processing the news.

'I want nothing more than to continue my brother's craft. Me and my son, your cousin, will need extensive training…'

'I can do that,' Etienne assured, 'are you sure that you want to leave Paris?'

Louis didn't hesitate in his response. 'Most definitely. Nothing will be the same there ever again. We have all lost far too much, we just need…'

'A fresh start?' Etienne interjected.

'Exactly,' Louis smiled.

'How soon can you be moved in?'

'Whenever you are ready, my boy.'

***

Avignon, July 1945

'Where shall I put my things, Etienne?'

'Upstairs, in the room on the right.'

'Merci.'

It felt strange moving Louis and Andre into his parent's home. But there was peace in knowing that it would remain a family home.

Touelle always.

Andre was a good man, thirty-five, steady, and measured. He had broken both of his legs during his initial military training ruling him out of fighting in the war. He had had to sit back and watch the horror unfold like the rest of them. Only he lived in an occupied zone, Etienne couldn't begin to imagine how tough it had been on his uncle and cousin. Andre was tall, stocky, and strong, his sweeping red hair covered up a nasty scar on his face. Louis warned Etienne not to talk about it to him.

'He got caught up in the resistance movement,' Louis reminisced solemnly when they were sat in private. 'One night he and his comrades attempted to sabotage a power grid and take down their communications when they were ambushed. The reason the whole group survived was because Andre stepped in, bearing the assault on his own. The animals damn near killed him.' Louis' lip began to quiver.

'But they didn't. He is a brave man,' Etienne stated.

Louis laughed slightly, 'A stupid boy! But yes… a brave man indeed.'

'We are grateful for this Etienne, truly,' Louis beamed as he placed his small suitcase at the foot of the stairs.

'It is I who should be grateful to both of you. I need the help. I have ideas, but I can't do it alone.'

'I have one,' Andre announced, taking Etienne and Louis by surprise.

'Andre, not now, we haven't even unpacked and I'm sure…'

'No, no, go ahead,' Etienne encouraged.

'Have you thought about knocking the walls through? Expand the building and with that the workshop?'

'Andre! This is the family home, we can't just…'

'We need a fresh start, all of us?' Etienne interjected. His uncle and cousin nodded in agreement.

'I say we do it. I just have one request?'

'Anything,' Louis and Andre said in unison.

'Did you bring your cello, Oncle Louis?'

'Oui,' Louis beamed.

***

Avignon, September 1945

Etienne knew that reaching out to the old business contacts would yield so much productivity, but he never expected the lengths they would go to. Once again, they had rushed to their aid, providing materials and labour, speeding up renovation time dramatically. Andre had been right, and now with his extra workers, they would need the space. It was all completed with no time to spare, people needed new furnishings, and items repaired.

'Their plight, they have endured far too much. I know it will seem small, but we will relieve some of their struggles, and finally bring some normality back to their fresh start. This is the level of care that we will put into our work.'

'Understood.'

'Agreed.'

'Okay,' Etienne smiled, taking up the chisel and mallet in his hands, 'let's get to work, watch and listen carefully.'

***

It was a balmy night for September when they finally re-opened. Marianne and Andre placed chairs onto the street just outside of the house and stood back to their vantage spots. Louis took his seat, shifting his magnificent, gleaming, chestnut-coloured cello in front of him.

'Ready?' Louis asked.

'Oui,' Etienne replied, taking his seat next to his uncle. He took a longing glance down the twilight street, lit delicately by the streetlamps creating the perfect ambience. He caressed Madame Penaud's violin in his hands, it would never feel like his own, but that was perfectly fine. It had got him through his darkest moments; Madame Penaud had taught him how to express himself, helping him help others and change the lives of people around him.

Merci Madame, he thought as he looked to the heavens.

'Un, deux, trois.'

Haydn. Austrian composer. A controversial choice for the day. But Etienne was tired of fighting, tired of judging others for associations that they couldn't choose, he wanted to appreciate people for who they were. With the cello as support, the music was beautifully enchanting and charmed its way through the streets. They had meant for the performance to be low-key, private even. But before they knew it people flocked to the streets, and neighbours stood outside their homes, music unifying what once was a deeply fragmented city. The looks on their faces were of glee and contentment, the numbers affirming Etienne's feeling, *people finally feel safe in their city.*

The scene was perfect, almost as perfect as the night he attended the opera house with his mother. The regret of not telling her still ate away at him, but as he and Louis concluded the piece to a huge round of applause, Etienne was overwhelmed by a sense of peace.

A mother always knows.

But there was one thing missing, or rather a person, he could feel it in the space in his heart.

I wish you were here Philipp.

MARIANNE

Avignon, November 1945

'Be careful with those Andre, they have just been varnished. Could you place them on Etienne's workstation? He should be along soon to show you how to attach them.'

It had been a busy morning, and with Etienne out on business calls the structure of the day had been more chaotic.

'Of course, Marianne!' Andre called out, hurrying around, as usual, the man never stayed still for a second. 'Do you have any idea as to when he is coming back?'

'Soon I would have thought? He is doing an assessment for Madame Corbin, and you know how talkative she is,' Marianne chuckled.

'That I do,' Andre rolled his eyes playfully before busying himself carefully arranging the varnished door handles on the table surface.

Marianne turned back to her pile of invoices. It was going to be a long morning, but it felt so good to be working again, and the joy they were bringing back to their customers made her heart feel full.

The business had only been officially re-opened for two months but Louis and Andre were learning quickly under Etienne's close supervision. The work that they were producing was as exquisite as the work that Etienne and his father produced.

'You could say it runs in the family,' she had joked to Etienne multiple times. Every time he had smiled sweetly at her.

They worked all through the morning and into the early afternoon, Marianne lost count of the amount of people coming through the door. The sign on the door performed its duty perfectly once again, squeaking its greetings to long-lost friends. Commissions for rocking chairs, cabinets, bookcases, chest drawers, bed frames, and even highchairs were all coming through.

Keeping busy hadn't stopped her from thinking about Philipp's offer to take her with him. Deep down she knew that it was the right decision to stay, Etienne needed her, and she needed him. On her own she wouldn't be able to take care of Erich, it would be difficult enough to start over in Germany as an individual, let alone as a single mother. Knowing that Liselotte and Thomas were caring for him was enough… right?

Erich's beautiful face still flooded her dreams, but now they were a comfort, he was safe and that was most important. She tried to imagine what he would look like now as a nearly teenage boy. Did he still have his glossy blonde curls? Would he be tall like his father? Did he speak harshly or softly? Was he curious? Studious? Was he creative? Logical? Emotional? There was so much that she had missed out on and knowing that it *could* be possible to see him, however slim the chance may be, gnawed away at her.

'Marianne?' Etienne's voice drifted through the door shaking her from her thoughts.

'There you are!' She grinned, walking towards him, 'Andre and I were worried that Madame Corbin had captured you for the rest of the day! Her cakes are good I will admit,' Marianne chortled.

But Etienne wasn't smiling along with the teasing this time, he looked serious and there was an alarm in his wide eyes.

'What's happened? Is something wrong?'

'Come outside,' Etienne urged, but now he was smiling.

Normally he would have brought the project inside the shop if he was particularly excited about it. But he wasn't supposed to be bringing anything back to the shop for repair today. Marianne tentatively approached him, he took her hand gently and led her towards the middle of the street.

'Etienne, what is it?'

'Look…' he breathed, pointing his finger south of the street, Marianne followed the direction with her eyes. Two figures walked side by side towards them, one was tall, wearing a flat cap and a long coat, and there was something familiar looking about the bag draped over their shoulder. The other figure was smaller, coming up to the other person's chest. The closer they got the smaller figure retreated behind the other. At one point they both stopped. Marianne could see them talking, she and Etienne were the only two standing in the street, they must have been talking about them, and she suddenly felt uneasy. The smaller figure's face looked at the ground, glancing up now and then. The taller had their hand placed reassuringly on their shoulder. But soon they walked slowly towards them again, Marianne felt the same urge to stand behind Etienne, but there was something about the way that he seemed so enthused about what he had seen. Their features started to come into light as they stepped out of the shade into the midday sun.

'Oh my!' Marianne gasped.

'Couldn't keep away for long,' Etienne teased.

'Monsieur, Madame Touelle,' Philipp laughed.

The boy was tucked behind Philipp, face cast to the ground. Marianne's heart was pounding so hard in her chest that she could hear it ringing in her ears.

'Marianne. Ada. This is Erich.'

She took a tentative small step towards him, to which Erich shuffled back further.

'Hallo Erich. Ich heiβe Marianne... Ada,' she quickly corrected.

She couldn't believe that the day had finally come. The day that she had only dreamed of, but now she could barely get any words out. What could she possibly say to him that would express everything that she had wanted to say to him for so long? I love you. I have always loved you. You have grown so much! I'm sorry. I'm so so sorry. I'm so sorry that I wasn't there for you. I did my best to try and protect you.

Instead, she found herself cautiously reaching out for him, Erich stayed perfectly still as she delicately brushed his cheek with her hand.

'Mein Sohn,' she whispered as she tried to hold back tears.

Erich glanced up slowly and shyly to meet her gaze, and Marianne was shocked to see every feature of herself in her son's face. His hair was still mostly blonde, the curls had become wavier over time, but it was still lusciously thick and tinged with her dark brown hair to give it an almost golden shimmer. His eyes were the characteristic Stein murky green; his cheekbones were hidden underneath his remaining childhood chubbiness. Erich looked just as taken aback, Marianne started to worry that this was almost becoming frightening for him. But Erich extended his hand towards hers, placing a small blue ribbon in her palm.

'Tante Liselotte says the specialist loaf has arrived,' Erich muttered.

Marianne threw her head back in laughter, tears flowed down her cheeks.

'I accept it with all my heart,' she giggled.

It must have been the response he was anticipating because a huge grin spread across Erich's face revealing big gaps in his teeth, he took Marianne's breath away, he was so beautiful!

'Mütter!' Erich exclaimed before throwing his arms around her waist and holding her tightly. She returned his embrace with the same vigour.

'I have missed you so much,' she whispered over and over into his ear, running her hands over his hair, undoubtedly soaking him with her tears. She felt a dampness on the sleeve of her dress, Erich was crying too.

'Are you sad my darling?' Marianne asked suddenly panicked.

'No Mütter, I am very happy,' Erich hiccupped.

***

The next two weeks they all spent together were blissful but rushed by far too quickly. She knew that Erich would have many questions about everything that had happened, but for now, Marianne was adoring every moment that they spent together.

Erich was fascinated watching Etienne, Louis, and Andre at work. Etienne had let him work on some of the smaller projects, their contemplative and tentative quietness worked to their favour as they slowly became better acquainted. Erich's French wasn't bad, enough to convey what he was trying to say, and Etienne understood. He was friendly, curious, polite, and a keen learner, Liselotte, and Thomas had done more than she could ever ask for.

'Can we make Bauernbrot today, Mütter?' Erich asked.

'Better than the ones the farmers would sell at the market?' Marianne winked.

'Ja!' Erich beamed.

'Well then, we had better get started!' Marianne smiled.

They crumbled the yeast, added water, and a bit of sugar, and mixed in the flour.

'It needs time to rise now Mütter. It will be better that way.'

'Thomas taught you well I see.'

'All of us,' Erich giggled.

'Us?'

'Me, and my five cousins. Lina, Ingrid, Rudi, Joachim, and Ada.'

Ada.

'Wow.' Marianne gasped. 'That sounds like a busy household!'

'They can be annoying,' Erich said.

'But you love them and that is what matters,' Marianne reminded him.

She was grateful for Etienne's resourcefulness, a few practice bed frames remained from some of Louis and Andre's earlier attempts. Etienne immediately fixed one up to be functional and Philipp and Marianne had moved it into the attic for Erich to sleep in.

'I wouldn't have minded sleeping in here again if you wanted him closer in the spare room?' Philipp offered.

'I couldn't let you sleep in here again, Philipp.'

'It wasn't that bad…'

Marianne looked at him coyly.

'Okay yes, it wasn't that comfortable, but Erich will be perfectly fine up here!' He chuckled.

'How on earth did you find him Philipp?' She had barely had a chance to even ask how this had all come to be.

'I tried to remember everything you told me of where you are from in Stuttgart. Your friend Liselotte is a remarkable woman by the way! Johann helped me put a visual map together, he's good at that…'

'*Johann!*' Marianne exclaimed. 'Your brother is alive!'

441

'I thank God every day,' Philipp gave a half smile, but he hesitated, choking a little on his words. 'He's endured the unspeakable. But he is strong,' he concluded.

'It's a miracle he survived?' Marianne asked warily.

'Most definitely,' Philipp sighed.

'I'm so sorry,' Marianne said, pulling him into her arms. 'We are not limited to one miracle in our lifetime though, remember that' she added.

***

Every night she helped Erich up the stairs when he was slowly nodding off to sleep after full days of taking in people's conversations, helping around the workshop, and touring around the city with herself, Etienne, and Philipp.

She couldn't help but think back to the times when she would scoop him into her arms, inhaling that sweet baby smell on his head and watching as he slept peacefully. So much had been missed out on, and for that, she would never forgive herself, but she knew how precious these moments were.

She tucked him into bed, smoothed his hair out of his eyes, and sat, prayed, and read him one of the books that he brought with him until his eyelids would flutter and he would drift off to sleep. She kissed his brow before quietly making her exit, but not before taking a last glance at him. *Her son.* But as she looked back at him that night, Erich had stirred himself awake.

'Mütter?' He asked groggily.

'Ja, mein Liebling?'

'Is Vater coming back?'

Marianne gulped. She had been dreading this question, but she knew that she had to be honest with him, refusing to have the foundation of their relationship built on lies.

'Nein mein Liebling. I'm sorry.'

She awaited his response, whether he would be sad, angry, or confused, she braced herself. But what he said made her take a step back.

'Gut. He was mean.'

'I'm so sorry Erich,' Marianne apologised, quickly at his side, holding him close to her.

'Was he mean to you too, Mütter?'

There were some horrors that she could spare him from, maybe that he would understand when he was older should he ask. But for now, he needed to be a child, live in the fullness of that precious time of his life, and never question that he was always loved.

'Yes, he was,' Marianne answered. She could feel Erich nod slightly against her chest as if to process it all.

'Tante Liselotte said the same. She said that was why you had to leave.'

'I never wanted to leave you, Erich,' Marianne sniffled.

'She said that too.'

***

When she got back downstairs, she found Etienne and Philipp sitting together in the kitchen drinking slowly and thoughtfully from their coffee mugs.

'Where are Louis and Andre?' She asked.

'I gave them an early night,' Etienne smiled, 'They have worked so hard lately, they must be exhausted. Is Erich okay?'

'That was good of you Etienne. Yes, he's comfortable and asleep,' she assured, as best as she could. Etienne gave her a funny look.

'I'm glad that both of you are here now,' Philipp interjected. 'I have some news. Or rather, I received a letter to tell me the news.'

'Who is it from, Philipp?' Marianne asked.

'My good friend Celine, the one I attended medical classes with. She says that our old professor has heard that we are both back in Berlin. He is now in charge of teaching and training medical professionals at Leipzig University. He wants to personally oversee the rest of our training.'

'Philipp, that's wonderful news! This is your destiny; you have to go!' Marianne exclaimed.

'But that means…' Etienne said slowly.

'I need to be back in Berlin by the end of the month. I need to leave very soon.'

Marianne looked to Etienne, who was in deep thought.

'I will leave you to talk it through,' Philipp smiled, taking his leave.

Marianne slumped back in her chair in disbelief. It was all coming to an end so soon, her heart that was so full felt like it was breaking all over again.

'We knew he wouldn't be able to stay for long,' Etienne stated.

'I know. I've just missed him so much.'

'As have I.'

They held hands for a time in silence, both quietly thinking, knowing the next issue that would need to be confronted, Marianne was nervous to ask.

'Etienne…'

'Did he ask about his father?'

His ability to read her was uncanny, but it was never intrusive, and only when it mattered the most.

'Yes,' Marianne admitted. 'He wondered if he was coming back.'

'What did you say?'

'I told him the truth, but spared the details…'

Etienne nodded. 'It's for the best,' he agreed. 'Erich will need to decide where he wants to go,' he added.

'You mean… he can stay with us if he wants to?' Marianne stuttered; her heart fluttered.

'That was never in question Marianne,' Etienne smiled. 'Erich is family.'

She threw her arms around Etienne's neck, he grunted as she collided with him, but she could hear him laughing.

'But it has to be his decision where he goes, Marianne.'

'Yes,' she sadly agreed.

She was already losing Philipp, the thought of losing her son all over again was unthinkable. She didn't sleep a wink that night with worry, she waited for Etienne to start snoring softly before plodding slowly back down the stairs. Whilst she waited for her coffee to brew, she peeked at the dough she and Erich had prepared. It had risen gloriously and emanated a characteristic sour, yet pleasant aroma; her mouth watered with anticipation at the finished product. That was if Erich would stay long enough to finish it. Marianne pulled out a chair and sat and thought.

The sun was just breaking through the windows when she heard the floorboards creak in the workshop, she got up to inspect.

'Mütter?' Erich called out, his voice still heavy with sleep.

'Erich, are you okay? Can't you sleep?'

'Philipp said he needs to go home.'

'When did he tell you mein Liebling?'

445

'He's packing up now. Is it true? He's leaving?' Erich looked up sadly.

'It is my love. But Philipp needs to go home to see his brother, and he is going to become an amazing doctor.'

'That makes sense now,' Erich laughed.

'What does my darling?' Marianne asked.

'He talked about science nonstop on the way to France. That, and all the adventures he had been on. Are they all true?'

'Ja, all of it!' Marianne giggled.

'It sounds exciting!'

'Not exactly, my love.'

'What do you mean?'

'I will tell you when you are older. I promise. You will understand more then.'

'About that, Mütter…'

Realising immediately what she had said, expecting him to stay, the anxiety crept in again, knowing the rejection would be crushing if he decided to go.

'How long can I stay with you and Etienne?'

'Forever!' She burst out without thinking. 'As long as you want!' She quickly added.

'Forever sounds good, Mütter,' Erich beamed. 'We will need to make the rest of the bauernbrot today.'

Marianne couldn't help but chuckle at his childlike impulsiveness.

'I was thinking exactly the same. Lead the way, chef,' she smiled.

PHILIPP

Berlin, May 1952

'So, what do we need to look for before we set the bone into its cast? Yes, Fräulein Brandt?'

'The bone needs to be in line and held in place until the cast goes on.'

'That is correct. Why is it necessary to do this? Yes, Herr Ziegler?'

'It can become infected, or the patient could suffer from a deformity.'

'Leaving them in a lot of pain most likely for the rest of their life, indeed. That concludes our class for the day, a reminder that Dr. Celine Blau is expecting your papers on typhoid on Tuesday.'

As his students filed out of the room, Philipp was left to pack up his lecture notes into his briefcase and roll up the skeleton diagram that he had spent so long detailing, giving him a precious moment to enjoy what he had. Professor Bergmann's retirement announcement had taken them by surprise, but neither he nor Celine had fully believed that he would step back entirely. They

447

were right but taking over some of his classes had been a real honour, it was a glimpse back into some of the happiest times of their lives.

'So, *you* are the reason that my students are so late to my class?' Celine teased, standing in the doorway.

'You do realise it is impossible for you to hide around the side in your condition?' Philipp smirked, as his eyes drifted towards Celine's enormous bump.

'I'll make sure you get all the babysitting duties for that comment, Dr. Blau!'

'My apologies Dr Blau. I just thought that covering all your classes for the next couple of months counted for something.' Philipp chuckled.

'I am grateful Dr Blau, truly,' Celine smiled, gently caressing her stomach.

How she had managed to work nearly up to her due date was truly remarkable. Even though they worked together, they were kept so busy between classes and patients that their paths barely crossed.

'How are you feeling?' Philipp asked.

'Fine,' Celine answered quickly, too quickly, Philipp gave her a knowing look.

'I do feel fine, genuinely. But… I'm scared Philipp.'

'Of the birth?'

'To an extent, it could be tricky, but my midwives are wonderful, I trust them.'

'Then what can possibly be troubling the indomitable Dr. Celine Blau?' Philipp reassured. Celine already had quite the reputation for being strict, but for the ones who understood her, it was what made her a focused and diligent doctor.

She finally allowed herself to take a seat, exhaling heavily as she did so. *She is human after all.*

'It's just… Johann will be an incredible father; he showers people with love.'

'And that would make you a bad mother?'

'You know what I mean, Philipp. And my mother was never around.'

'We show love in different ways. You and I are more introspective, but that doesn't mean that we love any less than the ones who are more expressive.'

Celine shrugged.

'You are one of the most determined people I have ever met Celine. When you set your mind to anything you achieve it, and you achieve it well.'

'But having children isn't something to achieve, Philipp.'

'Yes, but you always do your best. And there is no doubt in my mind that you will always do your best when it comes to your family.'

'Danke Philipp. I mean that. We appreciate everything that you do for us.'

'You are family. I have no choice,' Philipp winked.

Celine threw an abandoned pencil at him, giving him a teasing look before heading to her next class.

***

His office was a short walk across the city away from the school which on a regular day he took his time to enjoy. The division of the city caused him unease, but he was glad to see the infrastructure returning, he prayed for good things to come. But today he had to rush, as well as patient appointments to keep he knew that there was a mountain of outstanding paperwork and assignments to grade. It was going to be a late finish today.

'Good afternoon, Dr. Blau,' his cheerful receptionist called out.

'Good afternoon, Gretl!' Philipp called back to her hurriedly, as he rushed into his office.

Settling into his chair, he noticed some familiar handwriting on a letter. Philipp looked at the clock, relieved to find that he was running slightly ahead of schedule. He sat back and eagerly opened the letter devouring each word.

Dearest Philipp,

Or should we be calling you Oncle Philipp?

We cannot begin to tell you how thrilled we were to hear of you and Celine being appointed as teachers in Professor Bergmann's program. We both agree that he could not have appointed anyone better, but then again, we are biased!

I am in awe of Celine, still being able to work whilst expecting twins! I struggled to move seven months into my pregnancy let alone be carrying out the workload that she has! She and Johann will both be in our prayers. It is the most incredible honour; I do not doubt that she will discover this for herself.

Etienne is keeping busy, ensuring that Louis and Andre are ready to take over when we leave for our extended trip back to Germany. Erich cannot wait to see Liselotte, Thomas, and his cousins again. But I can guarantee that nobody is more excited than me! We will be staying with them for a time before travelling to Berlin for the wedding. We are so eager to see you and to finally meet Magda, Brigitta, and Annelise, and to share in your happiness.

At the mention of his wonderful fiancée Philipp couldn't help but let his eyes drift over to the photograph on his desk, a memento from their seaside trip the previous summer. Even though they were both teenagers, Brigitta and Annelise stood beaming with their ice creams in hand, Philipp and Magda's eyes locked on each other's, in love, in bliss. They had endured similar struggles, Magda's husband had sent her and their young daughters away to stay with his family in Switzerland before the war had started, another one who had anticipated how bad things were to become. But sadly, he was not so lucky.

Magda and her daughters returned to Germany in 1949, a year after the nation split, hoping to make a fresh start in their home country. They too had been questioned as to why they would want to return to a nation that was so despised by the rest of the world, and now deeply divided. It was home, pure and simple, and they couldn't turn their backs on it, wanting to be part of rebuilding for the better.

Brigitta and Annelise had been amazing from the start, they adored Philipp and he adored them. He had known immediately that he wanted to marry Magda, but he also knew that their family dynamic was a unique one and had to be nurtured. They were engaged eighteen months later, but the wedding was now fast approaching, and Philipp couldn't wait to see Etienne, Marianne, and Erich there. Of course, it brought him so much joy knowing that they would be there, but it was more than that, he *needed* them to be there. Without them, none of it would be possible, and in his heart, he knew that he would always need them. He turned his attention back to Marianne's writings.

You will not believe how much Erich has grown. Not only is he tall but he is smart, kind, gentle, and loyal, he reminds me a lot of Etienne. He gives so much love to the community and they love him in return, he feels so accepted in Avignon and I couldn't be prouder of him.

We procured new papers for him this year, Etienne is now officially named as his father, but Erich has called him father for years. My heart is full. But there is more, which I hope will bring you joy. Not only is Erich now 'Erich Touelle', but at his request, he wished to change his name, so consider this correspondence as emphatic confirmation of the three of us attending the wedding under the following names; Etienne Touelle, Marianne Touelle, Philippe Touelle.

With all our love forever and always,

Marianne, Etienne, Philippe

Philipp wiped the tears from his eyes just in time before Gretl knocked on the door.

'Dr. Blau? Your first patient is ready.'

'Send him in please Gretl.'

As she left momentarily, Philipp exhaled emphatically and contentedly. A small old man hobbled delicately into the room.

'Herr Schubert,' Philipp called brightly, pulling a chair out for his patient, 'tell me about your plight sir, and how can I help?'

***

The End

ABOUT THE AUTHOR

Rachel has lived in Shakespeare's Stratford upon Avon for most of her life so she's never short of her next literary inspiration! She's dreamed of writing novels for as long as she can remember and combines her fascination with history with her passion for writing. During her university studies and subsequent research in the years that have followed, Rachel has continued to be shocked, moved, and inspired by the magnitude of historical events and remarkable people. She aims to create stories that reflect reality, turmoil, and jubilation that readers can strongly resonate with.

Thank you so much for reading *The Plight of Others*. As an independent author, reviews mean everything, and it would mean so much to me if you could take a moment to leave a review on Amazon and/or Goodreads!

 Rachel Welland Writes

 @rachelwellandwrites

 @RWellandWrites

Vels. 3.45 Riley